The Patterson Chronicles

VOLUME 1

GRACIE'S GHOST

The Haunting

Frederick Loeb

Copyright © 2007, 2009 by
FREDERICK LOEB

All rights reserved.

SFC Publishing Division

SFC Publishing, Write Right Ink
1210 Lillian Street
Jordan, MN 55352
1.952.492.2122

All rights reserved. No part of this publication may be reproduced, stored in a retrieval system, or transmitted, in any form or by any means, electronic, mechanical, photocopying, recording, or otherwise, without the written prior permission of the author.

ISBN 13: 978-1-442-14828-4
ISBN 10: 1-442-14828-4

Cover Design Write Right Ink
Interior Set in Garamond, Berlin Sans FB, Calisto MT
and Lynn fonts by Write Right Ink

Printed in the United States of America

THE PATTERSON CHRONICLES

VOLUME 1

GRACIE'S GHOST
THE HAUNTING

FREDERICK LOEB

ACKNOWLEDGEMENTS

Topping the list of contributors is Lee W. Merideth and his remarkably detailed book, *Grey Ghost – The Story of the Aircraft Carrier Hornet CV-12, CVA-12, CVS-12*. Virtually every nugget of known technical information concerning the Hornet, its origins, heritage, and nomenclature, came from Merideth's work. Anyone interested in U.S. Navy aircraft carriers should read this book (Rocklin Press at ***www.rocklinpress.com***).

A large amount of motivational support came from the U.S.S. Hornet Museum in Alameda, California (***www.uss-hornet.org***). In September of 2006, I visited the old ship, now converted to a museum under the auspices of the U.S.S. Hornet Association. My visit proved to be a startling reawakening for me. As a much younger man, I had served aboard the *Hornet*, and was still aboard at the time of its decommissioning in June of 1970.

A decommissioned Navy warship is not a pretty sight; *Hornet* looked like it had been wrapped in a pale, washed out gray cocoon and with all her service markings and armament removed, *Hornet* was just plain ugly. In preparation for scrapping her we had spent months scraping paint, stripping out equipment, sealing compartments and voids never to be opened again. Apparently, an Australian, or Japanese, or some other foreign salvage operation had agreed to pay $250,000 dollars for her, and the Navy just could not resist the opportunity. Nevertheless, here she was, thirty-six years later, moored to her own pier in Alameda, dressed in fresh paint and lovingly restored by the U.S.S. Hornet Association! All the information the museum provided was invaluable to the writing of *Gracie's Ghost*. See this great warship up close. It is worth the trip.

The National Aeronautic and Space Administration (NASA) also provided invaluable detailed information and photographs concerning all aspects of the Apollo 11 mission. See ***http://nssdc.gsfc.nasa.gov*** for more information.

Additional documents were pulled from the omnibus reference book covering the common history of NASA and the U.S. Navy, *Splashdown! – NASA and the Navy,* by Don Blair. Blair's book is a marvelous compilation of every NASA mission recovery operation from the unmanned Mercury-Atlas 1 on July 29, 1960 all the way to July 1975 and the Apollo-Soyuz Test Project (ASTP) splashdowns. Many extraordinary photographs taken aboard *Hornet* during the Apollo 11 recovery operations were enjoyable for an "Old Salt" who was on board during that exciting time. Purchase Don's book at the U.S.S. Hornet Museum in Alameda (***www.uss-hornet.org***).

Photographic credit for old *Hornet* photos goes to the web site ***www.history.navy.mil/photos*** and the exceptional collection of materials there on all types of naval ships:

    The Department of the Navy
    Naval Historical Center
    805 Kidder Breese SE
    Washington Navy Yard, Washington DC 20374-5060

I also acknowledge the valuable contributions of Max Hellmueller, Bill Stiene, and John Gallagher. The conversations and written correspondence I've shared with these old shipmates helped correct my poor and often inaccurate recollection of many of the events we experienced together. Special photography credit goes to Max for his photographs providing a visual context to this story.

Thanks go to Ms. Judi Schulte, Paul Bliss, and especially Ms. Nancy Weiss for their diligent editing, careful review, additions, corrections, and valuable input. This work is so much better than it would have been without their help.

Finally, I thank my wife, Lynn, whose support made the writing of this story possible.

F.L.

***

Forward

The United States Navy aircraft carrier USS *Hornet* CVS-12 was known as the "Grey Ghost." How it earned the nickname was somewhat of an enigma. In October 1942, Japanese naval and air forces sank the warship's predecessor, USS *Hornet* CV-8 at the first battle of the Santa Cruz Islands. However, less than fourteen months later, *Hornet* reappeared in the Pacific theater and the moniker "Grey Ghost" just seemed to happen.

Some believed the Japanese first called *Hornet* the "Grey Ghost." Others surmised the nickname came from her unique camouflage paint job effectively hiding her in plain sight while at sea. The word "grey" itself, the British form of "gray," was the most frequently overlooked clue to the origin of the label "Grey Ghost."

New paint job, avenging resurrection, or an ally's homage, the great Essex class aircraft carrier added to its own mystique when she emerged unscathed and unscarred from the largest, most destructive military conflict in human history.

It was on the "Grey Ghost" where Gracie's ghost first appeared...

Chapter 1

Over the Side

**0130 HOURS
07 DECEMBER 1968
NIGHT AIR OPERATIONS
USS HORNET CVS-12
YANKEE STATION VIETNAM PATROL DUTY
GULF OF TONKIN**

Turned into the wind, *Hornet's* twenty-knot speed combined with nature's gusts of over 35 knots. This delivered a pounding 45 to 55 knot near gale that raked across the flight deck. The rolling seas of the Tonkin Gulf undulated into beefy rows visible only by their pale foamy crests. It was a completely black night. Thick clouds blotted out the moon, the stars, and every source of light the heavens normally offered. The air was a heavy, thick soup of tropical heat. A storm was looming.

Making its way through the dark veil, the twenty-five year-old aircraft carrier sliced through the writhing seas effortlessly. Wave after wave fell before the aged warship, almost bowing in homage. *Hornet,* an older lady now, was regally dressed in the updated fashions of the latest in anti-submarine warfare technologies. She was almost an entirely different ship from the straight-decked USS *Hornet* CV-12[1] of 1944. In 1956, under the Navy's SCB-125[2] modernization program, *Hornet* was reconfigured with an angled flight deck that ended at the curled forward edge of the number two elevator. The open bow with its twin gun tubs had been replaced by a modern enclosed hurricane bow. The island was stripped of gun emplacements, and then virtually rebuilt to accommodate the relocated Primary Flight Control Center and improvements to the navigation bridge. Enhanced radar arrays were added on top of the island superstructure, above and forward of the stack. On the flight deck, the old center deck number three elevator had been removed, sealed over with deck planking, and replaced with a larger starboard side elevator mounted behind the rebuilt island structure. These changes were followed in 1957 with a change in the carrier's primary function to that of anti-submarine warfare (ASW) and the re-designation to CVS-12. In 1965, under the FRAM II[3] conversion program, *Hornet* was fitted with the new SQS-23 sonar in the bow dome for improved ASW self-defense, the Combat Information Center (CIC) was redesigned, air conditioning was installed into critical electronic areas, radar was upgraded, and close-circuit television was added.

More powerful and with greater lethality, *Hornet's* nickname "Grey Ghost" remained from its previous iteration. The name still fit both her heritage and her redefined mission.

On this night, darkness draped the ship. *Hornet's* hurricane bow sliced through the growing swells displacing tons of sea water to produce a natural illumination fully revealed in her wake — an eerie glow of trailing phosphorous foam caused by the colossal collision of millions of microorganisms. The pale glow thinly trailed along both sides of the ship at the waterline; the luminescence, joining at the stern, boiled up by the churning force of the ship's four massive 15-foot diameter 27,000-pound propellers. The broad trail of luminous froth fell far behind in the ship's wake and disappeared into the darkness.

The only other visible lights were the scattering of faint yellow wands moving about on the most dangerous workplace on the planet — the flight deck of a U.S. Navy aircraft carrier.

Air operations to recover aircraft had begun more than an hour earlier when the gathering storm started to strengthen. All aircraft were now back on board. A single SH-3A Sikorsky helicopter remained topside being prepared for towing and sending below to the hanger deck. As a safety precaution with this last aircraft, Blue Shirts temporarily chocked and chained each wheel to the deck before hooking up the tail wheel tow bar to a low-slung, extremely heavy, black-tired tow tractor. The tractor looked as if it had been carved from a solid block of steel and painted a deep yellow. The tow tractor driver, just approaching his eighteenth birthday, expertly backed the tractor into position at the rear of the helicopter, the dim yellow glow of the Yellow Shirt's wand guiding his way. With the easy calm of a seasoned veteran, the young Blue Shirt eased the tractor's rear tow hook slowly back against the tow bar's loop until it loudly clicked into place.

Below on the hanger deck, all three bays were hidden in a dark, blood-red dim glow that did little for illumination. Compared to the pitch black of the flight deck, however, it was positively brilliant. Virtually everything and everyone was in silhouette, eerily backlit by the reddish hue bouncing off the white painted bulkheads of the hanger deck. It was like looking at everything through a glass of red wine.

It was night air operations, so one could not see much past his arm on the hanger deck. The few black-red lamps from the bulkheads provided only faint help. The open areas of the port and starboard sides were closed by gray-painted overhead steel roller curtains now made muddy red by the dark lamping. The roller curtains extended all the way to the deck, effectively making the ship invisible at night. Except for the ramps of the number two and three elevator openings, the hanger deck was sealed.

Above on the flight deck, the young tractor driver waited behind the steering wheel of his vehicle as the Yellow Shirt surveyed the rest of the plane handling crew for readiness to move the final helicopter to below deck.

At the same moment below in Hanger Bay Two, Steeg Patterson waited patiently with his fellow Yellow Shirt, Karl Klinger. Karl, a 6' 2" blonde-haired, blue-eyed ex-high school jock from Kentucky, was a take-charge guy with a ready smile. Karl was probably the best friend Steeg had in the division, although neither Karl nor Steeg probably realized it. The two worked well together, yet infrequently fraternized when in port. Four inches shorter and not nearly as athletically lean as Karl, the twenty year-old Steeg preferred solitary sojourns into the various ports of call *Hornet* visited while on overseas duty (commonly referred to as WestPac in the South Pacific). He rarely ventured beyond the familiar haunts of the surrounding local business district of any particular port. When ships were in port, especially aircraft carriers, local businesses were flooded with Navy enlisted personnel. A sad mix of bars, strip joints, stores selling all manner of merchandise, along with the occasional church mission offering free food to servicemen were the standard offerings while on liberty in overseas ports.

There were two exceptions to Steeg's solitude while ashore: one was *Hornet's* home port of Long Beach, California, the other, Olongapo in the Philippines, outside the base gates of Subic Bay. Carved out of the jungle, surrounded by mountains that dropped into the sea, the local population held intense 'love-hate' emotions for the U.S. Navy. The town feasted on the Navy economically, but the locals resented the servicemen. The first time he and his small cadre of four shipmates walked across the short bridge spanning the town's mud-brown main sewer also known as the Olongapo River, more than a dozen shirtless Philippine boys treaded the filthy water below clamoring for the pocket change servicemen would throw into the river. The kids would dive after the coins and somehow manage to retrieve every thrown coin without fail. None of them wore goggles. To Steeg, it was both amazing and tragic.

As for Long Beach, it was home-away-from-home as long as Steeg couldn't go back to Minnesota. During an 8-month long stay, Steeg and two other friends on KP (Kitchen Patrol) duty rented a small house on the near side of town. The house offered a sense of freedom for the three young men. Unfortunately, word spread that Steeg, Collin, and Mark had a "pad" and soon it seemed as if half the ship's company was using every square foot of the place to sack out. Rarely finding an open spot in the house to lay down, he spent more time at the Silver Dollar bar on Long Beach Boulevard, or one of the several all-night movie theaters in town. Wherever he found himself, there was never a shortage of familiar faces dressed in civilian clothes. Steeg was rarely alone in Long Beach, and truly appreciated the camaraderie that at least temporarily masked the struggles with the isolation of military life and the complications of being a single guy. Sometimes, when he congregated with some of those appreciated comrades, a too familiar darker side of his character would surface. He did not always appreciate that.

Karl, on the other hand, liked to sightsee. Every port was a new adventure for him. He planned it all out ahead of time, knowing exactly where he would go and who would accompany him. Karl also took many pictures. On ship, or on shore, he always seemed to have a camera within easy reach. To Karl, it was all good. Only the occasional sour attitude from Steeg kept Karl from more frequently teaming up with him when liberty rolled around. They both respected each other, trusted the other to know the right thing to do when at sea. However, Karl often found his friend too moody. Besides, for Karl, liberty time was always too valuable to risk not having fun.

Waiting in the darkness of Hanger Bay Two, the two third-class petty officers leaned up against the front grill of a tow tractor the twin of the one on the flight deck. Blue Shirt John McIlhenny was behind the steering wheel.

Karl relaxed with arms crossed over his chest. "You ever hear about the ship being haunted?"

Steeg twirled the lanyard of his whistle around his index finger, first to the left, then to the right. "Yeah, I've heard that. This First Class Petty Officer in my first division told me the boat was haunted. He said sometimes you could hear, and actually see, ghosts walking around from time to time, especially when you were on watch somewhere alone late at night."

"Yeah, Bonia told me the same thing. You believe it's true?"

"No way, it's just something the First Class P.O.'s tell you to spook you, that's all."

Karl nodded, somewhat relieved. "Yeah, I don't believe it either. Still, when things are quiet, at night, you know? You can hear sounds you don't normally hear."

Steeg shook his head. "You hear the sounds because it is quiet. When it's noisy, when things are moving around, lots of stuff being done, that kind of thing, the sounds are still there, they're just not loud enough to be heard. Don't worry about it."

"Still, all those sounds, it's kinda creepy, don't you think?"

"I said, 'don't worry about it.'" Steeg kept twirling his whistle lanyard. "Look, all that creaking noise you hear at night, all that is, is temperature changes in the metal."

"Temperature changes?"

"Sure. Look at it this way. The ship is nothing but a 900 foot long piece of steel floating in the middle of the ocean, right?"

"Right."

"Right. So, this big piece of steel is under the sun, baking, getting hotter all day long. Then, night comes, and what does the big hunk of hot steel do?"

"Cools down?"

"It cools down. That means the ship actually shrinks at night with the loss of heat. The ship creaks and makes funny noises because of temperature changes. That's why some people think it's haunted. But, it isn't."

"Okay."

On the flight deck, the Yellow Shirt had confirmed everything was ready for his crew to move the chopper safely to the number two elevator platform. The roar of the wind pushing across the deck drowned out the sharp whistle blast as the Yellow Shirt, with two yellow wands, one in each hand, twirled them then sharply pulled them apart in a "release tie-downs and pull chocks" signal to the Blue Shirts. The Yellow Shirt then directed his attention to the plane captain sitting at the controls in the cockpit. He crossed his glowing wands overhead and pulled them away in a "release brakes" signal and slowly waved the tow tractor driver down the center of the deck toward the elevator.

On the hanger deck, Steeg continued to fill the waiting time. "Change of subject for you, Karl. You know Yokosuka, right?"

Karl lit up enthusiastically. "Oh, yeah! Yokosuka, Japan. Kinsey and me, we took a train from there to Tokyo. Man, what a city!"

"Do you pronounce it 'Yo-**Koo**-Ska' or 'Yo-ko-S**oo**-ka?'?"

"'Yo-**Koo**-Ska' I think."

"Yeah, but its spelt 'Yo-ko-S**oo**-ka" isn't it?"

"That's in English. In Japanese, it's 'Yo-**Koo**-Ska.'" Karl's abrupt, purposeful sneeze-like rush of air on the middle syllable mimicked poorly what he believed to be a Japanese dialect.

"Okay," Steeg accepted. "So, you didn't see Yo-**Koo**-Ska? You went to Tokyo on a train instead?"

"Sure did, with Tom," Karl smiled broadly. "That place lights up like Las Vegas every night, only much, much bigger. You can buy anything there. I got pictures!"

"I bet you do," Steeg nodded with a chuckle. Karl with his camera was a common sight for the V3 Division crew.

Karl took a lot of pictures, many with the guys in various stages of undress. At first, Steeg had felt a little uneasy around the guy, especially after he had seen the first pack of photos Karl had processed. It didn't cause a full-fledged attack of homosexual panic, but Karl sure seemed to have a lot of pictures of division guys in their underwear, including several of Steeg. Over time, after he got to know Karl a little better, Steeg's initial concerns and apprehensions fell away, and the two young men developed a strong respect for each other.

"I stayed in port – Yo-**Koo**-Ska." Steeg used the now accepted Japanese pronunciation. "I visited one of those mission places one night."

"Missions? You mean one of those holy-roller places?"

"Well, they're not really holy-rollers. They just want to help."

"Okay. What did you do there?"

"I had a hot beef sandwich with mash potatoes and gravy, along with a side of green peas. It was pretty good, real honest to goodness American food. Not very big, but good."

Karl sniffed as he flicked a non-existent piece of lint from the sleeve of his yellow plane director's shirt. "I don't like those places. They're always trying to recruit you for something."

"Convert – they're trying to convert you," Steeg corrected his friend, struck by the irony in Karl's recruiting comment. Steeg glanced quickly around the confines of the hanger bay. "Heaven forbid we'd ever allow ourselves to be recruited for anything…"

Karl looked around the hanger bay, too, sharing Steeg's wry observation. "Yeah. I guess your right about that."

Above on the flight deck, the tow tractor driver made an effortless turn onto the port side number two elevator platform and completed the curl back inboard. The towed helicopter pivoted on its two main wheels and came to rest at a slight angle and a perfect nose-inboard position. The Yellow Shirt blew his whistle. Both the tractor driver and the Brown Shirt plane captain seated in the cockpit applied their brakes simultaneously, bringing all movement to an immediate bouncy halt. Loud clatter and thuds quickly followed as Blue Shirts threw wheel chocks into place and secured heavy steel chain tie-downs into the deck's padeyes. Within moments, the aircraft was anchored to the deck.

Below on the hanger deck, Steeg and Karl easily heard thudding clatter coming from the flight deck crew above them.

Karl rubbed at his nose to relieve a sudden itch. "It's just that places like that make me feel uncomfortable."

Steeg nodded with understanding. "Yeah, well, they just want to help where they can. We can all use some help now and then."

Karl arched an eyebrow in concern. "Look, I gotta ask you something, and I'm not criticizing, okay? I mean, I believe in 'The Man Upstairs' just as much as the next guy, okay?"

"Okay."

"I don't know why you go to those places, but if you're telling me you're a holy-roller, that's gonna put a real damper on our relationship."

Steeg grinned. "I'm no 'Holy Roller,' Karl, but I've been a lot worse things than that. I go to 'those places,' because…"

He looked away for just a second. This was new territory for him. His family upbringing was Christian in the accepted sense of the term, but in actual practice, not very church going.

He was in ninth grade in 1962 when the U.S. Supreme Court decision came down that effectively banned prayer from public schools. The uproar from every adult with whom he came in contact and, he supposed, across the whole nation as well, surprised him. Steeg didn't understand all the hubbub. He could not remember one teacher ever leading a class in prayer. Now, years later, he was in the middle of the Gulf of Tonkin, almost evangelizing to a friend who might not want anything to do with him if he were to say too much, or say the wrong thing. He didn't know what to say, so he said the truth as he knew it for himself.

"... I go to 'those places' because, as long as I'm out here, I figure I haven't got anything to lose by having Jesus look out for me. He's made some promises, and I'm just trying to give Him a chance to work some stuff out for me. The mission places give me somewhere to go to help me do that. That's all there is to it. No offense intended."

Steeg didn't say his relationship with the Son of God was a new one. He didn't tell Karl he had prayerfully accepted Christ little more than a year earlier, shortly after reporting to *Hornet*. He didn't tell his friend he accepted Christ primarily because he was scared of getting himself killed, and his even greater fear of losing the only thing truly important to him – losing Gracie. He didn't mention any of that because of another fear – fear of offending his friend.

"No offense taken," Karl shook his head. "It's just that those people drive me nuts. They practically camp out on the street corners in Long Beach, passing out their pamphlets, singing those goofy songs, trying to get you to go on their bus to take you to their church – right in the middle of the week, for Christ's sake! It's creepy."

The chopper was secured and the flight deck crew and tow tractor withdrew to make their way toward the ship's Island on the starboard side of the flight deck. Inside the helicopter's cockpit, the plane captain relaxed, letting up on the brake. He shouldn't have.

On the hanger deck, Steeg was agreeing with Karl's sentiments. "Yeah, I guess evangelists can be a little creepy. But I'm sure their hearts are in the right place."

"I'm not too sure about that," replied Karl. "If it's okay with you, I think I'll just stick with the rest of the tourists when in port."

"Sounds like a plan."

Flight Deck Control was located in the Island superstructure. The yellow vested Duty Flight Deck Officer came in from outside and took off his radio helmet. He turned to the young Blue Shirt manning the sound powered phones, "Tell Hanger Deck we secure from flight ops as soon as that bird is parked."

"Aye, sir," the sailor responded crisply.

The officer then stepped to the squawk box and pressed down on the first of six black switches. "Pri-Fly, Flight Deck."

The metallic reply was perfunctory. "Go ahead, Flight Deck."

The officer toggled the switch again. "Last bird going down now. We can secure from flight ops when it's put to bed."

"Roger that, Flight Deck."

Below, the loud blare of the number two elevator alarm "bah-ooo-gawed" across the hanger bay. Steeg, Karl, and the rest of the small crew shifted into readiness. V3 Division elevator operator Paul Muggins, a brown-haired Minnesotan, short in stature but large of heart whom everyone called "Teddy Bear" let out a loud "Stand clear!" He threw the control lever that sent the elevator into motion.

The massive platform lowered easily to a stop at hanger deck level as the wire cabled guardrail receded into the deck ramp. The tractor and crew made their way onto the elevator. Suddenly, the entire ship dipped heavily to port and the sea below rushed up to lick at the elevator's undercarriage.

"Whoa!" Steeg steadied himself against the front grill of the tractor. "We're rolling out here!"

Karl blew his whistle long and hard to make sure he had everyone's attention. He walked to the cockpit and rapped on the side window. "Plane Captain! You keep braked hard, okay?"

Inside the chopper, the Brown Shirt gave a nod and a thumbs-up signal as sea spray splattered across the windshield. Karl rapped the window again in confirmation, and then moved cautiously toward the tail wheel of the aircraft. Steeg and Frank Santini, a 19 year-old Blue Shirt from Brooklyn, were already latching the tow bar onto a tail wheel that had somehow worked its way under the fuselage. Fastened securely, the tow bar pointed tail-to-nose and would not budge. In that position, the bar's tow loop could not be latched onto the tractor's rear tow hook.

"Can you get it out?" The sea rushing beneath them almost drowned out Karl's question as he walked up to the men. Steeg unfolded himself from under the aircraft.

"Only if she absolutely insists!" Steeg joked.

The ship took another deep dip and upward roll. Karl steadied himself against the rear of the tow tractor, which the driver, McIlhenny had expertly spun around to point toward the chopper. "That's funny, but not from a Jesus freak."

Steeg placed a friendly hand on the other man's shoulder and, over the wind and the rushing sea, loudly apologized. "You're right. I've a reputation to think about, don't I?"

Steeg and Karl both grabbed the rear of the tow tractor to catch themselves as the ship took another stiff downward roll, throwing up a blast of spray that came across the elevator platform.

"I don't know how that wheel got under there," Steeg wiped the spray from his face. "The chopper must have rolled after they unhooked it topside."

"Well, the weather isn't getting any better out here," Karl yelled back. "Let's get some guys to force it around and get this thing off the elevator before the whole ship capsizes!"

"Not a good idea," Steeg shook his head. "If the tire sticks to the deck when the wheel pivots, it'll lose air pressure and go flat on us. Then, we've got a real mess."

Steeg glanced about the tri-wheeled aircraft and how it was anchored to the deck. "Santini took the tail wheel tie-downs off. Maybe we could ease up on the brake a bit to pivot the tail wheel and hook the bar up to the tractor, but with this rocking, I'm not crazy about pulling the chocks or other tie-downs before we get the tractor hooked up."

Karl nodded. "Right, it stays tied down and chocked while the plane captain releases the brake. That should keep things safe as the wheel is turned around."

Steeg nodded in agreement and Karl headed back toward the cockpit.

"What do you want me to do?" Santini stood on the opposite side of the tow tractor, a heavy chain-linked tie down draped over each shoulder.

Steeg bent down to eyeball the aircraft undercarriage, the tail wheel, and tow bar pointing toward the nose of the chopper. He looked back at the young Blue Shirt.

"I'll take this one. There's not a whole lot of room under there, and if things go wrong, one guy getting out of the way fast will be easier than two." Steeg waived the crewman back. "Stay off to spot the tail, will you? Go to the tractor's front bumper, and follow that. We're too close to the guardrail to suit me. Watch your step, Frank. I don't want to lose anyone tonight."

"No sweat." The young sailor, tie-down chains rattling as he moved, back-stepped to where McIlhenny sat behind the tractor steering wheel. "I don't wanna get under there anyway."

Santini laid the pair of tie-downs on the front hood of the tractor, and continued in casual conversation with McIlhenny as Steeg disappeared under the aircraft to straddle the tow bar.

Karl instructed to Blue Shirts near the cockpit to leave the aircraft's two forward side-wheel chocks and tie-downs in place. This way the only wheel unsecured would be the tail wheel Steeg was about to pivot out from under the fuselage. The short yellow tow bar provided enough leverage to get the job done.

From under the chopper's nose, Karl peered into the darkness toward the tail wheel. "You back there, Steeg?"

"I'm ready!" Steeg yelled back. "I'll give you three whistles. Let up on the brake on the third whistle and I'll push the tow bar clear."

Karl yelled just audible over the noise, "Okay, let me tell the plane captain, first." He rose up to share the news with the Brown Shirt in the cockpit. A couple of seconds later he was back under the nose, yelling loudly for all the crew to hear. "All Blue Shirts leave all tie-downs and chocks in place! Stand clear! Steeg – ready when you are!"

Steeg slid from the top of the tow bar, positioning himself toward the aft side to get his whole body behind the push. His near-prone position gave him about six inches of head clearance below the aircraft. The whistle clenched tightly in his teeth, Steeg set his feet and made a quick visual check around the tail wheel, the tow bar and the deck to make sure nothing would impede the turning of the tail wheel.

Another spray of salt water hit Steeg across his face as the ship dipped again to port and then rolled back up. His precarious position compelled him into something for which he had no training – a simple, silent prayer.

Jesus, I can't see crap out here. You think You could smooth this out a bit, sort of, like You did before. How'd that go? 'Peace. Be still'? I mean, not to be disrespectful, or anything, but I have it on good authority calming raging seas is right up Your alley. Any help would be really appreciated.

He waited several seconds just to see if his silent prayer was having any effect on the seas that continued to roll the great ship slowly port to starboard and back again. Nothing changed.

Yeah... Sure. One of these days, You're going to have to fill me in on why You're so non-responsive to my little requests. It makes for poor public relations, if You ask me. But, You did think the 'only if she absolutely insists' joke was funny, right?

He was running out of excuses to delay any longer. Steeg blew the first whistle hard; a pause, followed by a second whistle blast; another pause as he braced himself more firmly against the tow bar, bringing it tight into his chest. He blew his whistle a third time and leaned his body into the tow bar.

With the third whistle, Karl banged on the cockpit window with his hands wide open in a "release brakes" signal and the plane captain let go. It was at that exact moment the ship took an unexpected dip to starboard, and the helicopter rolled forward.

Steeg's grip on the bar slipped. Without warning, the tow bar was under him, jerking him up from the deck giving him a ride as it swung hard aft and then around to the port side, passing over the elevator's low guardrail.

Steeg's whistle soundlessly flew from his lips by the centrifugal force of the spinning tow bar. His grabs at the slick painted tubular steel tow bar were desperate and completely ineffective. In a blink, his body spun free from the bar. He failed to grab the bar's thick tow loop, his last desperate attempt to save himself from the unceremonious dump over the port side of the elevator. Steeg silently disappeared over the side, saved only by the wet darkness of the steel-cabled safety nets.

A whistle blew and the aircraft halted as brakes jammed back on. Still secured to the deck by front wheel chocks and tie-down chains, the helicopter had definitely shifted toward starboard. Karl hurried to the back of the chopper. At the tail wheel, the tow bar lay in perfect alignment with the rear tow hook of the tractor. He reached down, lifted the bar into position.

"McIlhenny, back it up!" Without looking at the tractor driver, Karl signaled him with a hand roll barely visible in the darkness. Santini trailed the front bumper as McIlhenny backed the tractor slowly until the hook latched with a loud metallic click.

"All right," Karl yelled, backing clear to the inboard side of the chopper. "Off chains and chocks! Off brakes! Get it outta here! Santini, spot that rotor!"

The crew efficiently pivoted the aircraft tail-first into the hanger bay. Once completely clear of the ramp, Teddy Bear returned the elevator to flight deck level and the crew slowly moved the chopper into the last remaining spot of clear deck space. It wasn't until they began to maneuver the helicopter into final position Karl realized he was missing his trusty pair of spare eyes on the opposite side of the aircraft. He blew his whistle to stop the procession.

"Where's Steeg?!"

Consciousness returned to him in waves as the blackness slowly cleared. His forehead throbbed with a strong, dull pain. Groggy, he could see the sea froth below being split by the prow of the ship. A murky figure emerged from the phosphorous glow rushing beneath him. The apparition took shape below him, rose from the water to float just above the wisps of pale blue-green neon trailing toward the stern. The figure turned to flesh and the woman who appeared looked right through him. A recognizable warm, dull ache filled him. Her deep brown eyes pulled him closer. She had the same familiar impish smile he remembered, the one that always preceded mischief or passion. He felt the familiar agony of unrecoverable loss.

Are you dead? Steeg thought. Her lips parted as if to say something, but he only heard the sea. *You don't feel dead to me... Maybe I'm the one who's dead.*

The thought of his death strangely comforted him. He was face down in the wire cable safety net below the outboard edge of the elevator platform. Even with a warm wetness trickling from his palms, Steeg gripped the netting hard as he felt himself rising, and the sea fell away below him. The dull glow of luminescent foam sped past far below him now as the elevator eased to a stop at flight deck level. Still pressing his face against the meshing of the safety net cables, Steeg peered back down to the sea now almost fifty feet below searching for her. She was gone. He felt the ache for her grow along with regret as he realized he was not dead.

Loudspeakers crackled over the angled flight deck, "Now hear this. All hands secure from air operations. All hands secure from air operations."

With more effort than he knew he had in him, he reached with his inboard arm, pulled himself up and snaked over the low 4-inch guardrail he could feel but not see in the darkness. Steeg rolled his sweat soaked body onto the flight deck. For several minutes, he lay on his back trying to force air into his lungs. His body's demand for oxygen outpaced his lungs' ability to supply it. He remained on his back for a long time, recovering. Finally, he rolled to a half-kneeling position. Then, first with one foot followed by the other, he stood. Painfully stooped over, hands on knees, he willed his heart to return to normal.

Slowly he stood erect. Wiping the sea spray and perspiration from his wet face, he looked up into the starless black sky and wondered if Christ was anywhere at all.

"I guess You didn't find my little joke about 'only if she insists' all that funny." The stiff wind rushing across his face swallowed his words. "Thanks for the net, but what about her? I asked you to take care of that, remember? Now, I see her when she's not even there? Hallucinations?"

The wind rushing across the vacated open deck drowned him out as his anger burst forth. "Are You kidding me, Jesus?! What is that?! I ask for help, and you give me visions!? Me? Is that the way it's supposed to be? I accept You just like I'm supposed to, and things just keep falling apart, one thing after another. Nothing goes right. Nothing is working. And, now You give me mirages?! What do You want from me? She's back home. I'm here – in a war, for God's sake! What do You want me to do about it? Is all this part of the deal, or what?!"

The wind gusts pulled roughly at his body as he grabbed the sides of his head with both hands. His forehead throbbed so hard it sent him back down to his knees. Staggering back to his feet fighting the roll of the ship, Steeg turned toward the Island superstructure on the starboard side of the flight deck. Leaning into the wind to make his way across the deck, his anger slowly ebbed.

"Remembering isn't doing me any favors, Lord. I certainly don't need her to drop in for any ethereal visits, if You know what I mean. So, I'm counting on You to do what's right on this one, okay? Please? Just take it away. Please, take it all away."

Compared to the black-red shroud covering the hanger bay, the light from the V3 Division crew's lounge was a painful blinding white. The small room tucked behind Hanger Deck Control on the 01 level was strewn with steel framed vinyl-padded chairs, a couple of card tables and two old, dark blue vinyl-covered sofas, each one against its own bulkhead. Nearly every seat was taken by the night shift crew of the division's total roster of 36 men.

Steeg shielded his eyes from the bright, overhead lights as he walked through the door.

"Oh, man! What happened to you?" Karl jumped up running to him. "You're covered in blood!"

Steeg pulled his hand down from his face and looked at it. Blood dripped from both his palms, ran down his arms, and smeared the upper thighs of his pants to the knees. His face was streaked in red where he had moments before wiped away what he had thought was sweat. He hadn't seen any of it in the dark red lamping of the hanger deck.

"I cut myself," Steeg weakly replied. "What does it look like?"

Karl grabbed him by the shoulders and sat him down on the nearest sofa. "I knew it! I knew when I couldn't find you something was really wrong!" Karl jerked a thumb toward Airmen 3rd John Tyner. "John, get a corpsman up here right now!"

"Right, Karl." Tyner disappeared out the door, made a U-turn into Hanger Deck Control, a glorified closet with a Plexiglas bay window overlooking Hanger Bay Two. Small, flat aircraft-shaped pieces of plastic were laid out on a stainless steel status board showing where each aircraft by type and number was parked across all three bays of the Hanger Deck. There was also a squawk box. Tyner toggled the second switch.

"Flight Deck, Hanger Deck."

"Go, Hanger Deck."

"Is the corpsman still up there?"

"That's affirmative – having coffee."

"Send him down to our lounge, will you? We got an injured man here."

"Roger. He's on his way."

Back in the crew's lounge, Karl and the V3 Division night crew gathered around Steeg slumped on the sofa. Someone had pulled the first aid kit from the wall bracket, and Karl was hurriedly rifling through it to find something he could use to dress the wounds on Steeg's hands.

"Where'd you go?" Karl asked, frustrated by the inadequate contents of the box. "I practically had that bird parked before I realized you weren't even there!"

"You wouldn't believe me if I told you."

"How'd you get so cut up?"

"I think it's only my hands," Steeg said, looking himself over as best he could. "I guess I'm okay. Probably got cut when the tow bar slipped."

"Slipped?" Karl looked at Steeg square in the eye. "I don't get it. You had that bar lined up perfectly when I got back there. I thought you were on the other side."

For only a moment, Steeg wondered if he should level with his friend. The Kentuckian might appreciate his second profoundly ironic statement of the night. Steeg decided against it. "I guess you could say that."

Two corpsmen rushed into the room. The lead man wore his white reflective flight deck vest, and the second corpsman carried a large red case with a white cross on it. The crew made way as the medics went to work on Steeg. The medic in the vest took charge, checked Steeg's visible wounds, and immediately began cleaning away the blood from the young airman's hands and face.

"How'd this happen, sailor?" the corpsman asked.

His answer stuck in his throat. Two years earlier, Steeg had learned within minutes of entering Boot Camp that it was rarely in his best interests to volunteer information unless it personally affected someone else, and then only if the affect on the other person was nothing but positive. He knew it would definitely not be a positive for Karl if Steeg admitted his accidental episode of safety net diving happened right under his friend's nose. He decided there was little reason to go against the 'never volunteer' edict just because of a few nicks and cuts. "Well, I was trying to push a tow bar and it must have slipped."

"Uh, huh, I see," replied the corpsman as he busily attended to the wounds. He saw the raised knot in the center of Steeg's forehead, just below the hairline. "Nice egg. How'd you get that, and all this blood all over you?"

"No big deal," Steeg lied. "I lost my balance and hit my head. I didn't know about the blood, I thought it was sea water and I tried to wipe it off, or something."

"Uh huh, I see." The corpsman continued working. With his partner handing him materials from the big red case, the corpsman sanitized and wrapped the hand wounds neatly, and then cleaned but otherwise ignored the bump on the head. Several minutes went by as the corpsman quietly worked on the petty officer.

"They look worse than they are," the corpsman commented. "But I want you below now to see if you'll need stitches. Doc needs to look at these cuts and the bump on your head."

"Okay," Steeg agreed calmly, needing only a little help to get to his feet.

The two corpsmen led Steeg out of the lounge, down the ladder and to the hanger deck. Karl, Teddy Bear, and John Tyner followed, watching from the ladder's landing outside Hanger Deck Control.

"That was weird, man," Tyner said as he watched the two corpsmen and Steeg below cautiously work their way down the main deck hatch to disappear below decks.

"Did you see those cuts and scratches on the side of his face?" Karl asked.

Bear shrugged. "Well, sort of. He was kinda bloody. What about them?"

"They were tiny, and in different directions, criss-crossed like some kind of pattern or something. That's odd, doncha think?"

The other two men nodded in agreement.

Everyone onboard called Lieutenant Commander Peter Franke 'Doc.' Thirty-nine years old, a disaffected victim of male pattern baldness since he had been twenty-eight, Franke had made the Navy his life's work. He was married, with two kids, one in college already, but his real home was the U.S.S. *Hornet*. The way he saw it, his most important work was what he was doing at that moment – rendering aid as a ship's doctor.

Steeg sat upright on the examination table as Doc carefully removed the bandages to examine the damage. Doc dabbed an antiseptic swab across the wounds. It didn't sting, but felt actually cooling.

"Interesting."

"How's that?" Steeg asked.

Doc pointed first to Steeg's right palm, then the left. "They're not cuts so much as tears. More like a series of little tears in rows, like you were holding onto a rope that pulled your skin really hard."

Steeg looked down at his hands. He could see what Doc meant. "Yes, that is interesting. I thought I cut them on the tow bar when it slipped."

Doc shook his head. "Not cuts, a lot of little tears in a row. They bled a lot, but they aren't deep, and they don't require stitches. You're lucky."

Steeg didn't feel lucky. "Yes, Sir."

As Doc applied fresh dressings to Steeg's hands, the white-vested medic who had accompanied him to sickbay pointed to the golf-ball sized whelp at the hairline on Steeg's forehead.

Finishing with the bandages, Doc pulled a pen light from his white coat pocket, and leaned in to get a closer look. "Ah, yes. You bumped your head a good one, didn't you?"

"I guess I did."

The pen light flashed in Steeg's eyes as Doc checked for dilation response. This was repeated several times in each eye.

"How are you feeling now?"

A snorted chuckle came from Steeg. "Like I'm being interrogated."

Doc smiled easy. "I mean physically. Any pain from the knot on your head? Any nausea, dizziness, jumbled thinking that you're aware of?"

Steeg shook his head.

"You're sure about that?"

"Yeah, I think so," Steeg was growing more uncomfortable with the questioning.

Doc returned the pen light to his coat pocket, turned to a small cabinet behind him and opened it. From the middle shelf, he removed a bottle of aspirin, opened it, dropped two tablets into a small paper cup, and handed the cup to Steeg. "Take these now."

Steeg took the paper cup with a mild protest. "I think I'm okay, Doc."

"Maybe, maybe not. You may have a slight concussion. It'll be easier for you to take the aspirin now than in a moment or two when the nausea comes."

Just the suggestion of it made Steeg's stomach queasy. He slid the tablets into his mouth, chewed them up, and then rinsed them down with a paper cone of water handed to him by the flight deck corpsman. Doc instructed Steeg to lie down on the table and relax for a few minutes, and then he and the corpsman left the room to walk down the passageway.

Left alone in the quiet of the overly lit examination room, Steeg mouthed his barely audible complaint. "This is a little embarrassing. Look, Lord, I know there's a lot of stuff I don't understand, a lot of rules I don't follow, a lot of mistakes I keep making. But, You're not doing so great, either. I thought if I 'sought Your Kingdom first,' everything else would fall into place for me. That's what You promise, right? I must've gotten that wrong, because it seems to me everything that's happened since I handed everything over to You has been anything but 'in place.' In fact, Jesus, it seems like I'm on some kind of divine 'IT-List,' if You know what I mean.

"If that's the way You want it, if that's the way it has to be, then, I guess I have to go along with it. Would you answer me this, though — why me? Why is everything I do wrong? Why did this thing tonight have to happen? I don't get it. And, I don't get You. I thought I got You before, but let's face it; nothing in my life is working out! I almost got killed tonight! Is that what You want, for me to get killed out here?! Because if that's true, I hope you don't mind if I don't go along with it."

Raising his arm to shield his eyes from the bright overhead lamp above the table, Steeg fell silent as a slight pang of nausea rose in his stomach. Doc had been right. He didn't feel all that great after all. Several minutes passed.

"Okay, Jesus," he quietly breathed the words. "I'm sorry. You're in charge. Whatever happens, happens. I'm along for the ride and that's good enough. I won't worry…. that is, I'll try not to worry…. on second thought, just don't ask me not to worry about stuff, okay?"

Doc strode in from the passageway. "Worry about what stuff?"

Steeg quickly pulled himself up to a seated position, purposely trying to hide his slight dizziness. "Nothing, Doc. I was just talkin' to myself."

Doc produced the pen light and checked Steeg's eyes again. "How you feeling now?"

"A little uncertain in the gut, Doc."

Doc nodded. "Figures. Okay, here's what I got for you. I can hold you here in Sickbay for observation, or I can put you on bed rest for twenty-four hours in your crews' quarters. Which would you prefer?"

Steeg didn't like Sickbay. "I think the crews' quarters idea would be better."

"Fair enough. I'm sure you'll be okay. I just want you to stay in bed for a while and take it easy. Go to chow as normal, but no work. That's an order, understand?"

"Yes, Sir."

"Good." Doc handed him a small bottle of aspirin. "Just in case you get headaches. I'll notify your division. The corpsman is going to accompany you up to your bunk, okay?"

"Yes, Sir."

"He's waiting down the hall. Get out of here, and be careful from now on." With one hand on Steeg's elbow, Doc helped the young man from the table.

"Yes, Sir." He acknowledged. Mildly surprised by the noticeable weakness in his knees Steeg proceeded toward the door as he added, "Thank you, Sir."

Chapter 2

Home from "The Devil's Brigade"

**Sunset
18 Dec 1966
Minneapolis/St. Paul International Airport**

Almost two years before he was thrown over the side of *Hornet's* number two elevator by a helicopter, eighteen-year-old Steeg Patterson began his adventure in the Navy the evening of November 11, 1966. Leaving on a Northwest Orient Airline Boeing 707 bound for San Diego, California, Steeg began 9 weeks of boot camp not quite two months after he helped Gracie move into her new dormitory room in Mankato, Minnesota. He emerged a month and a week later, a little thinner in some spots, thicker in others, dressed in a regulation wool "Pea Coat," immaculate dress blues, spit-shined shoes and the traditional white cotton sailor hat that poorly hid a still too-short Navy crew cut. Steeg was home again in Richfield, Minnesota on a two-week Christmas leave.

There was only one person he wanted to see, and it wasn't his mother.

Walking from the airport concourse toward the baggage claim area, Steeg's recalled his graduation from Richfield High School the previous June. It was a time when Gracie and he were practically inseparable. They had first briefly met as Juniors, and the two young people dated each other through their Senior year. Willingly spurning other opportunities for a more varied high school social life, Steeg developed a need for Gracie's near-constant physical closeness almost as vital as his need for air to breathe. Gracie genuinely cherished being with Steeg as well and, in return, Steeg accepted early in their relationship her obvious hesitancies concerning the risk involved with personal relationships.

Within two months after graduation, Grace was already preparing to leave for Mankato State College. Steeg, accepted by the same college, didn't have the money to cover tuition and fees for the first quarter, so he decided not to register. His dad was a good plumber, but with three sisters and a little brother, money was always in short supply for the family. Steeg had decided early on he would not be a financial burden to his family. For him, college would have to wait.

That summer after graduation, they took advantage of the extra time to be together. One of their favorite places was the east beach of Lake Nokomis in south Minneapolis. In their swimsuits, they relaxed on an old blanket spread smooth on a grassy knoll overlooking the east side of the lake. Sometimes they stayed on the blanket, sometimes they played in the warm waters of the lake, and sometimes they simply walked along the lakeshore, damp sand sticking to their feet. Later in the afternoon, they were back on the blanket, enjoying the remains of the day's hot sun.

Fingers entwined and bare skin lightly touching, Steeg inhaled Gracie's intoxicating fragrance.

"So, this college thing, this is going to be tough."

Gracie's deep brown eyes looked deeply into his. "I know. Do you think you'll be able to be there by winter quarter?"

Steeg felt a sudden twinge of something really uncomfortable and unwanted swell up inside him. He let go of her hand, slowly coming to his feet in frustration. "I don't know, Gracie. It depends on how much money I make and when."

She followed standing next to him as he looked across the lake.

"Working with your dad, you mean?"

"Yeah, I guess so." Steeg's father had insisted he join him on the job site right after graduation, but Steeg had resisted. Instead, he kept the part time job he had worked for the past two years at Dayton's Department Store. He told his father he'd start full-time on the construction job site in September. "I don't know what he wants from me."

"Your dad?"

"Yeah. He keeps trying to push me into digging ditches for him. Every summer since I was twelve, I've been digging ditches for him. Gees, Gracie, he had me on job sites playing in sand piles when I was in elementary school! I really don't like it, and I really don't like the thought of doing it for a career either."

She took his hand and held it tightly. "You don't have to do it for a career. You only need to save up enough money to cover expenses at Mankato. You could start at the beginning of the second semester."

"That's true," he said with a little more hope, but not as confident as he would have liked. Instead, his confidence was in her, and what he felt for her. In a couple of months, she was moving far away, too far away. He wrapped his arms around her and held her close. "Grace, I need you… "

"I need you, too."

"No, I mean more than that. I mean, sure, I 'want' you in the way we've always wanted each other, but I mean more than that… more than, you know, the sex thing."

She smiled just a little and a faint pink came to her face.

"I'm so much more when you're with me. When we're not together, it's like a big part of me is just plain gone."

"Steeg, what am I supposed to do? My parents have planned for me to go to college. I've planned on it…"

He stopped her. "You should go. Gracie, you're smart. It's one of the things I love about you."

"Oh, that's it?" She smiled. "So you don't always have your mind on only one thing?"

"You're doing what's right," he ignored her not too subtle put-down. "You have so much on the ball, it only makes sense to get your degree and grab for everything you can. I want to be there to help make all that happen. That way we could be together, helping each other. You know, you charge me up. It's true. Somehow, with you, I feel like there's nothing I can't do!"

She held him closer as he added, "That's a worry sometimes. The opposite could be true, too. Without you, I might not be able to do anything."

"That's not true! You can do anything you want."

Steeg smiled down at her, sharing a relaxed little laugh as he led her back down to lay on the blanket.

He appreciated her confidence in him, but inwardly he was not convinced. "Thanks. I'm sure you're absolutely correct in every possible way."

"Thank you," her warm smile returned his. "I am."

"You are what?"

"Correct."

"Oh, yes. Then you'll understand why I have to ask you something very important right now."

"And what would that be, Mr. Patterson?"

He searched her eyes for any sign of promise as he asked, "Will you be my Mrs. Patterson?"

He should have known her response would be nothing he would have expected. She blinked a couple of times and asked, "What?"

He took a deep breath and tried again. "Grace Ofterdahl, will you marry me?"

The few seconds turned into something feeling painfully like an eternity for him as she said nothing. She pulled away, sat up on the blanket, bringing her knees up close to her, and stared across Lake Nokomis. The water glistened in the warm early evening sunlight. He sat off to her side, looking at her as she continued looking away from him.

After forever, she asked, "Are you serious?"

"Absolutely," He said without hesitation.

"But, what about the mystery?"

"What mystery?"

Her gaze seemed glued to the far shore. "The mystery I've maintained over all the time we've been together. You know – the mystery you need to stay interested."

He shook his head with growing concern. "I know you think, for some reason, you have to be mysterious, but I always figured it was some kind of joke. I'm not joking about this."

She hugged her knees closer. "I've always figured the only reason you were with me was because of the mystery – I've worked hard to keep that mystery going."

"I'm with you because I love you more than I love anything else."

Her face creased with a frown. "So, I'm a 'thing' now?"

"No, that's not what I meant." He felt as if she was trying to put him on the defensive now, and he had to protect himself. "Gracie, I don't want to pressure you, or push you, or make you do anything you don't want to do. I only want the very best for you, for as long as you live and for as long as you let me help give it to you."

Turning fully to him, legs crossed, she took both of his hands into hers.

"Look, Steeg, we love each other, I know. At least, I know I love you. I'm sure you feel the same. I know this, Steeg, and I don't doubt the sincerity of your proposal. But, Steeg, it's marriage…"

"Yeah, I know…"

"Yeah, so, it's really serious, right?"

"Of course."

"Right. So, we have to think about this. I mean really *think* about this."

Steeg was confused. "I thought I had?"

"Sure, you did in one way. But, there are other things."

"Like what?"

Her lips tightened as she tried to think of the best way to proceed.

"There's a bunch of things, Steeg. What about my mother?"

"I don't want to marry your mother."

"In a way, you just might. You know, she really doesn't like you, Steeg. She never has."

"Yeah, I kinda knew that."

"I'm Catholic…"

"And I'm not," Steeg acknowledged.

"Well, that's important. If we get married outside the Church, it's not a real marriage."

"So? If that's the big thing, I'll convert. I'll do whatever I have to…"

"I know. I know." She interrupted, turning away again to look across the lake. After a long pause she repeated, "I know."

Together, they stayed on the blanket talking until the sun fell behind the treetops on the west side of the lake and the sky began to turn a cloud-streaked azure blue, purple, and gold.

Later, comfortable inside his old '48 Buick DynaGlide sedan Steeg and Gracie put street clothes on over their now completely dry swimsuits. More than a year earlier, Steeg had bought the huge old car from a neighbor down the street for the grand total of fifty dollars. The odometer read a paltry 63,349 miles and certainly had turned over at least once if not more. The car, with a monstrous "Straight-Eight" engine badly in need of an overhaul, had a top highway speed of about 40 miles per hour, an embarrassingly poor a level of performance for a young man of his age. Steeg, however, took comfort in his sincere appreciation for the car's high sides, narrow windows, and the soft, gray-brown cloth upholstery on the high-back bench seats. Together, they made a great make-out car. They continued to discuss Grace's concerns as he drove for a long time up and down Minnehaha Parkway. Steeg delayed returning to Richfield as long as he could.

By the time he pulled up to the curb across from her parent's home, they had talked themselves to near exhaustion. Steeg had tried to share all of his aspirations for the two of them, while Grace had countered with a sequence of reluctances, including her mother; his non-Catholicism; her college; his delay in going to college, and a few others that mattered not at all to Steeg. Parked in the shadows, Grace noticed the shadow of her mother peeking out from behind the closed curtains that covered the front window of her house.

"She knows we're out here," Grace said, nodding across to her parent's house. Steeg turned to see a shadowy figure withdraw from the curtains.

"Eyes like a hawk," Steeg said soberly.

"Well," Grace looked up to him. "I guess I'll go in."

"You still haven't actually answered me, you know."

"I know."

"Then know this — I really love you. I don't want to push you into anything you don't want, but I feel so certain that you want to be with me, too."

"I do."

"Then, I don't understand what's holding you back on this?"

She cupped the side of his face with her hand. Almost reluctantly, she said, "I'm not holding back because I don't want to marry you. It's because it might not be the best thing for you… to marry me."

Steeg was lost in utter confusion. For several long silent moments, he looked at her in the pale light that fell from the corner street lamp. Finally, he softly replied.

"You fill my thoughts all day and all night. You thrill me more than you know. You're in my soul. I need you in every way possible right down to my toes. How can that be bad?"

She fell into him and wrapped her arms around his neck. "It's probably not. But, Steeg, this scares me. Marriage is so final. You love me now, but later you might grow tired of me…"

"Not possible," he objected.

"It is possible. It happens. I couldn't stand it happening to us. And, marriage will put you into a big corner…"

"I don't think so."

"I know you. Don't argue. You'd feel like you had to be the big 'provider,' build a house, work for your dad even though you don't want to just to bring in money to provide for me. You'd never go to college. Never. I would, but you wouldn't. You'd carry me every way you could, sacrificing all the way, and that wouldn't be fair. Not for you."

"It would be worth it, Gracie. It would be a great…" He searched for the one word that could adequately describe what he needed to say. Then it was there. "It would be a great adventure."

Their eyes met, and her soft lips pressed against his with a passion that surprised him. Then, she left the car, quickly walking toward her front door. He watched through his open window as she stopped half way up the walk, turned on her heels and ran back to him. Leaning through the window she kiss him again, her arms held him tightly about the neck as she whispered in his ear.

"Yes," she breathed. "I'll marry you!"

As she slowly pulled away, Steeg was now completely confused. Her voice was a whisper. "But let's keep this quiet for a while until we have a plan to make it work for both of us, okay?"

Steeg both nodded in agreement and shrugged his shoulders in the same movement. *She's driving me crazy, this girl,* he thought.

"Call me tomorrow," she said, turning to scurry back up the front walk and into the house.

"Always," Steeg said to the closing front door.

Her acceptance of his proposal brought a brief moment of elation quickly replaced by something else: a hollow apprehension he had never before felt. It was as if he had suddenly lost something so very dear to him. That didn't make any sense. Gracie was more dear to him than anything or anyone else ever could be.

He continued to ponder this new foreign emotion as he put the car into gear and drove away.

"You sure took your sweet time getting home tonight." The complaint bit into Grace as she closed the door behind her. Her mother sat heavily in the old wooden rocking chair in the corner of the too small front living room. A cigarette hung from the woman's mouth, a half-inch of ash falling into the lap of the baggy smock she wore. "You spend too much time with that boy."

Grace had heard that before, too many times. She tried to change the subject. "Anyone call for me?" She asked, almost making it across the room and into the kitchen. Her mother grabbed her daughter's arm and stopped her.

"I know what you do with him," she sneered. "I wasn't born yesterday. You can't spend as much time as you do with that hoodlum without something happening."

Grace firmly but slowly pulled her arm from her mother's grasp. The older woman stood in the archway, blocking her.

"He's not a hoodlum," defended Grace. "He treats me nice. He makes me feel good."

"I bet he does," she sneered, her fists balling in growing rage. "My God, Grace, when are you going to wake up?! He just wants your body. Sex. That's it. That's all. Find someone else, for God's sake!"

Grace refused to allow the tears to come, choosing anger instead. "What difference would it make?" she stiffened in resistance. "No matter who it was, you'd hate him!"

The slap that cracked across her face was more than a surprise. Grace stood her ground, feeling the stinging heat rise from her face. She willed herself not to shed a tear. Haltingly, her mother withdrew, returning to the rocking chair. It was not an unfamiliar encounter for either of them.

"What about that other boy?" her mother asked in a low, barely audible voice. "Last month. You seemed to like him."

Grace resented the older woman's interference. Shortly after graduation, Steeg and his family had left for Washington State on a two-week vacation. He had asked her to come, but knowing her mother would never allow it, she declined. One night, while attending a party with her friend Cyndi she met Raymond. He asked her out for the next night. Flattered, she said yes. It wasn't much of a date, really, but she seemed to need him there. As he caressed her, she returned his affection as warmly as she could. It felt good to her.

"He was nice," Grace agreed reluctantly.

"So why hasn't he called back?"

"He did."

Her mother looked at her, sarcastically staring back at Grace, holding her hands opened in an unasked question.

Grace resigned. "I turned him down."

"He must have been Catholic," her mother took another drag on her cigarette.

"I don't know," Grace crossed her arms across her chest wanting to end this all too familiar line of conversation. "Maybe he was. I think he might have been. We didn't really talk about that."

"Of course not," her mother scowled as she came to her feet, turned and walked down the short hallway to her bedroom where her father was already sleeping.

Grace quietly took the steps leading upstairs before her mother made it through her own bedroom door. In her sparsely furnished makeshift bedroom in a poorly converted upper half level, sleep would be welcomed escape.

Things quickly changed for both of them. The pre-induction physical notice from Selective Service arrived shortly after Labor Day and told him that he was guaranteed to be drafted. Steeg had no qualms about serving his country, but he had real problems being drafted. The Army or, heaven forbid, the Marines, held absolutely no appeal. His uncle had been a Major in the Army, and as a young boy, Steeg had visited his uncle's base in Texas while on a family vacation. He hadn't cared for it, especially when his uncle took him up to the top of the parachute jump practice tower, strapped him into a parachute harness, and pushed him off! Steeg was only ten years old and from the tower the ground looked a thousand miles down. He screamed without stopping as he dropped all the way down the guide cable, landing face-down in a sand pit. He pretty much knew, even at that tender age, the Army was not for him.

He chewed on his alternatives and came to an easy decision. After the compulsory physical at the Federal Building in downtown Minneapolis, Steeg climbed into his old Buick sedan and drove to the Navy Recruiter's office on 65th and Lyndale Avenue in Richfield. There he learned about the marvelous opportunities available to "See the World."

"On top of all that, you pick your field of Navy training before you sign up," the First Class Petty Officer boasted. "And you get the G.I. Bill to finance your college education after your hitch is over."

It all sounded good to Steeg. He sat across from the Navy man, paging through the few pamphlets that were handed him.

"College," Steeg nodded to himself. "Paid for."

"That's right, just as soon as you complete your hitch," the Petty Officer confirmed. "Of course, to get the full G.I. Bill, you'll have to sign up for four years active duty, but you'll only have two years inactive reserves after that."

"Inactive reserves?"

"Just a technicality. It's when you're in the service but in name only. They're never called up and reactivated, so don't worry about it." The recruiter checked his paperwork. "Let's see, you want to go to Photographer's Mate 'A' School, is that right?"

Steeg had been a yearbook student photographer for each year of his high school career. "Yep. That's right."

The recruiter made a check on the sheet and turned the page. "How does San Diego sound for basic training?"

"Sounds great," Steeg agreed. "Where else can you go?"

The recruiter's face turned sour as he explained about Great Lakes Naval Training Center outside Chicago. "You don't want to be on Lake Michigan in the winter."

The recruiter made a few more marks on the sheets of paper.

"In a couple of weeks, you'll get the official notice. In it you'll have all you need – tickets, scheduled airline departure, instructions on what and what not to bring with you. You'll have 30 days from the date of the notice to get your affairs in order. Then, you're off to San Diego."

The petty officer turned the papers around and handed him a pen.

"Sign on each 'X' sailor," he instructed. Smiling, he joked, "You are eighteen, right?"

Steeg signed and things were set in motion for his new career in the U.S. Navy. Less than two weeks later, he was helping Grace move into her dormitory room at Mankato State College's Gage Center dormitory.

His seabag came up the conveyor ramp and dumped onto the luggage carousel at the Minneapolis/St. Paul International Airport.[4] The carousel slowly carried the seabag to where Steeg stood. He grabbed the seabag by its thick woven strap and slung it over his shoulder, remembering the recruiter who had enlisted him. He knew if he ever saw the guy again, he'd probably beat the crap out of him. From the day he had first signed up, until that very moment as he adjusted the position of the strap and the extra weight of the seabag hanging from his shoulder, the only solace available to him was what Grace had said after he told her he was joining the Navy.

"Oh, I love sailor uniforms!" She gushed. "You'll look so sexy in bell bottoms!" Steeg fell for it, hook, line and "Anchors a'weigh."

He had told no one at home he had the time off at basic training. Approval for the two whole weeks of Christmas leave had come late, and besides, Steeg wanted to surprise the people back home. Grace was still at Mankato State College, he was sure. But he knew she would be back for Christmas. He couldn't wait to see her again.

It was well past dark when the taxi pulled up to his parent's modest 1947 Richfield bungalow too small to house his parents, three sisters and brother. The driver took the heavy green canvas seabag from the rear trunk. Paying the man, Steeg slung the bag easily over his shoulder, turned and walked up the drive. The house was fully lit as any Minnesota family home would have been in December. Frozen snow crunched beneath his feet as he walked to the back door.

"STEEEEEG!" His thirty-nine year-old mother screamed as he walked through the back door. "You're home!"

His mother was a born and raised Minnesotan who had met her Georgia born husband-to-be on the corner of Washington and Oak on the University of Minnesota campus in 1943. At that time, Steeg's father-to-be was in the Navy attending service training classes at the university and Steeg's mother-to-be who dropped out of Marshall High School her sophomore year, liked hanging around the campus. They fell in love and then he left for duty aboard a coastal patrol boat in the South Pacific. The two of them were only sixteen years old.

Steeg was overwhelmed as he placed his heavy seabag against the wall. The whole house smelled of freshly baked Christmas cookies. His mother ran up and wrapped him in a big hug. She wore her usual flowery housedress with a blue kitchen apron tied across her waist. Then, she pushed him in his chest a little too hard.

"You didn't even say anything!" She scolded.

Steeg grinned back at her. "Surprise!"

"How you doing, son?" The heavy voice came from behind as Steeg's father walked in from the front room. Steeg turned and looked his father in the eye with a level of respect that surprised both men, and then extended his hand. His dad, a full head shorter than Steeg but with shoulders nearly twice as broad, took the offered hand firmly and wrapped his other hand around his son's solid upper arm. "What do you think, Ma? He doesn't look all that bad. Maybe this Navy thing is doing him some good after all."

Trevor Patterson, Steeg's father, was a man hardened by hard life. The son of an abusive father, Trevor's mother drowned in a boating accident when he was only six years old. Trevor's father had no time to look after Trevor or his little sister, Steeg's aunt Alice. So, the senior Patterson remarried. The marriage didn't last long. There was another marriage. Then, there was another marriage followed that. By the time Trevor reached the age of fifteen, Steeg's grandfather was on wife number three. Steeg's aunt Alice had told him of his father's early rebellious nature too difficult for the third wife to handle. The fifteen-year-old had no desire to stay at home. It was the summer of 1942, the world was at war, and the war presented a beneficial solution for Steeg's father, his grandfather, and his grandfather's third wife, as well. The parents signed papers falsely claiming the fifteen year-old boy was really seventeen and eligible to join the Armed Services. And, so he did.

After the war, Steeg's parents married. As Trevor became a father himself, his early treatment of his firstborn son often patterned how he, himself, had been treated. It wasn't always pleasant, but whenever his father punished him, Steeg held onto two beliefs. First, his dad still loved him and second, he probably deserved what he was getting. Steeg was only half-right.

"STEEEEG!" Another yell and a cacophony of footfalls came down from upstairs as his three younger sisters stampeded into the kitchen. Seventeen year-old Mary, the oldest sister, got to him first and wrapped her arms around him.

Steeg smiled in response. "Hey, Mare – How's my goofy little sister doing?"

Fourteen year-old Edith, and Hilde, the youngest sister at ten, greeted their big brother with an open admiration for the uniform he was wearing.

"That is cool," Edith swooned as she ran her hand down his arm caressing the wool fabric.

"Really cool," Hilde repeated. "Can I wear your hat?"

Steeg removed his cover and placed it on the little girl's head. She ran to find a mirror.

"Where's Daniel?" He asked.

"I'm in the living room watching TV!" Came the voice of his seven-year-old little brother.

"You come in here and greet your brother!" His mother ordered loudly.

Steeg could hear Danny's mumblings as the youngest of the Patterson brood pulled himself up from the floor and peeked around the corner into the kitchen.

"Hi," Daniel waved, then did an about-face and returned to the living room to resume his TV watching.

"Different priorities," Steeg apologized, and his mother immediately asked him if he was hungry. Before Steeg could say, "No, I ate on the plane" she quickly went to the bread drawer, pulled out a loaf, moved to the refrigerator, retrieved the remains of the evening beef roast and went to work making two large sandwiches.

For the next three hours, Steeg shared the details of his new Navy life with his family as his mother made sure he had plenty of food to eat, milk to drink, and to top things off, cookies; lots of cookies.

The evening grew very late. His sisters and brother had already gone to bed, and his mother was upstairs preparing his old room for him.

His father looked at him, a shadow of concern on his face.

"Any clue about your duty station after basic?"

"No, not yet, Dad." Steeg sat down in the stuffed chair opposite his father was. "I'm still waiting for word on the Photographer's Mate 'A' School."

"Hope you get that, son. You're a good photographer."

"Thanks, Dad."

"You could end up in this Viet Nam thing, though."

"Oh, I suppose," Steeg shrugged. "But, I'm an 'air-dale' so that's going to keep me to either land bases or maybe a carrier. That wouldn't be too bad."

"Carriers are big ships," his father responded soberly. "Big ships make big targets."

"I don't think Viet Nam is going to get all that big, Dad."

His father looked at his son with a wary eye. "Johnson keeps sending in more ground forces. More ground forces means more Navy ships to keep them supplied and more Navy aircraft to keep enemy heads down. Navy aircraft need aircraft carriers. Each carrier has its own cruisers, destroyers, escorts, and submarines. This thing in Indochina could get a whole lot bigger, a whole lot faster than you think."

Steeg could see his father's logic. Since September when he had signed his enlistment papers, the 'policing action' in Viet Nam had grown significantly.

"Well, maybe," Steeg agreed. "But I'll be careful. Besides, I'll be going to 'A' School anyway. After that, who knows? Maybe the Mediterranean!"

"Maybe," his father's smile did little to hide his concern.

They watched the flickering television screen for a few moments, not really paying attention to the old black and white movie playing on the Late Show. After a bit, Steeg's mother rejoined them, sitting next to her husband on the sofa.

"Steeg, what are you going to do tomorrow?" she asked.

"I thought I'd give Gracie's Mom a call to find out when she's going to be back from school, then maybe call the gang and see if we can get together for some pool at Wedge's, or something. Just take it easy, I guess. If that's okay with you guys?"

Both parents agreed.

"How are things going with you and Gracie?" His father asked.

"Fine!" Steeg answered a little too enthusiastically. "I write her every day, and every day I get mail from her," Steeg lied just a little. "Sounds like college is really keeping her busy."

"I just mean," his father continued. "You know, you're away and she's away. You both have to handle different demands, different pressures." He paused, then added, "You, uh, still pretty serious about her, son?"

Steeg had not told anyone about the secret 'engagement' with Grace. That was the number one topic he needed to cover with her on this trip.

"Well, sure, Dad. She's great. You guys like her, don't you?"

Both parents assured their son they loved Grace dearly.

"She's a very attractive girl," said his father.

"I can tell you care deeply for her," his mother said.

Steeg was suddenly uncomfortably warm in his dress blues. "Yeah, well, of course. I can't imagine being with anyone else. It's just that, well, you know, you need to take things slow. There's a whole lot of stuff going on…"

"Stuff?"

"Sure. Stuff. Like you said, Dad, she's got demands on her, I've got demands on me…" Steeg's voice trailed off when he felt his anger begin to swell. He clenched his jaw as he brought the unwanted emotion under control, but he didn't hide it well. Both parents could see he was bothered by something.

He slowly rose to his feet and walked to the front window to look out onto a front yard darkened by the lateness of the hour. It was beginning to snow. His face flushed with the anger he could not will away.

More to himself than to his parents, Steeg said, "I might've screwed this up."

Chapter 3

Changes in the Wind

The Gang was made up of five, sometimes six guys: Steeg Patterson, Horace "Ace" Johansson, Butch "Wedge" Widger, Matt Cummings, Mark "Jockstrap" Wilson, and on occasion Dave Brunswick. Wedge and Brunswick were the 'outlaws' in the group, both owning Honda 250 Scrambler motorcycles and drinking beer since they had been sophomores in high school. Horace and "Jockstrap" had joined the Navy together a full month before Steeg, and had already completed basic training. Both were assigned to the USS *Tripoli*, one of the Navy's new helicopter carriers. Cummings worked with a team of cooks staffing the Valley View Room restaurant at the Dayton's Southdale Department Store. Cummings and Johansson knew each other since Catholic grade school. All of them graduated from Richfield Senior High School the previous June. All of them, throughout high school years of near constant camaraderie, spent most of their time hanging out at Wedge's house.

It was a roomy four-bedroom rambler on the near west side of town. It had a completely finished basement done in knotty pine paneling from ceiling to floor, a real wood-burning fireplace, a stocked bar, a big TV, and the most important feature of all — a regulation-sized green felt covered billiard table with genuine leather basket-weave pockets.

Wedge's old man, who was a marvel at completely ignoring the gang whenever they populated his basement, was an executive at a major construction equipment manufacturing company. Unlike every other parent of the gang, Wedge's dad had money.

On this evening, Wedge and Matt played a bad game of 'Eight Ball' while Steeg sat on a bar stool watching the extraordinary bad play.

"You guys are crap at this." Both friends ignored Steeg's opinion. Matt's carefully planned shot bounced the four-ball off the right corner then the left corner of the same pocket and rolled to a stop at the center of the table. The cue ball rolled slowly into the opposite corner pocket: scratch.

"I'm just carrying him." Matt poked the butt of his pool cue painfully against the bridge of his foot. Matt avoided pain at every opportunity. The pool cue to the top of his instep was a just reward for a really bad shot.

Wedge pulled the cue ball from the leather netted pouch. "Right."

Steeg finished his can of soda in two gulps. "Wedge, how is it you've had this beautiful, old pool table down here for as long as I've known you, and you play this bad? Matt only sinks shots by accident and he's ahead of you!"

Wedge scowled as he counted the balls on the table. He had stripes and there were two more stripes than solids on the table.

"Just dumb luck," Wedge dismissed with a quick wave of his hand. He positioned the cue ball behind the second diamond, lined up his shot and promptly sank the next three stripes before missing an impossible fourth shot.

"Wish you hadn't said anything," Matt directed his complaint toward Steeg as he surveyed the table for his turn. Sarcastically he added, "By the way, nice haircut."

Steeg self-consciously ran his hand across his short-cropped bristles.

"It looks okay. Kinda looks like me now," Wedge chimed in cheerfully. For as long as Steeg had known him, Wedge had always worn a flattop style haircut. Matt, in contrast, always seemed to need a trim, a shave, and a bath.

Matt sank the shot and lined up for the next. "Heard anything from Ace and Jockstrap?"

"Nope. They don't write to me anyway." Steeg answered.

Wedge leaned against the far wall, tipping what was left in his beer bottle into his mouth. "You write to them?"

"Nope."

"Well, there you go." Wedge carefully placed the empty bottle on the wall mounted ball rack.

"I suppose you do?" Steeg countered.

"Nope." Wedge didn't care.

Matt missed his shot and Wedge walked over to take his turn.

Matt went behind the bar to the one feature that testified to the magnificence of the basement recreation room's design: an actual miniature refrigerator. "I need a soda."

"I need a beer!" Wedge requested, surveying his options on the table.

Steeg asked for a Coke, and each man quickly had his beverage of choice.

The game slowly and poorly progressed. Conversation turned to Viet Nam and the increasing number of high school friends already drafted into the military.

"You guys are going to be next. You'll be wading through rice paddies before this time next year."

Wedge shrugged as he lined up his next shot carefully. "That's okay with me. I'll go wherever they want me, and I'll be done with it in two years. Not four years like some people I know."

Matt wasn't comfortable. He didn't like the war, and he didn't like talking about it either. It made him angry. "I'm either getting a student deferment or I'm moving to Canada."

Steeg frowned. "Canada?"

Matt left his pool cue leaning against the wall. "I'm not going over there, and I'm not killing anyone." Wedge tossed out a short laugh as he teasingly flapped his elbows.

"Chicken, chicken, chicken!"

"Call it what you want," Matt shot back, irritated. "I suppose you'd look forward to blowing someone away?!"

Wedge leaned on his pool cue and smiled. "Well, I'll tell you what. If the time came where it was either me or the other guy, I gotta believe I'd do what I'd have to do."

Matt waved his hand in disgust and sat down on the barstool next to Steeg. "Don't you worry about stuff?"

"What stuff?" Steeg looked at his friend with a smile.

"Just stuff. You know, killing, getting killed. It's gotta scare you a little, doesn't it?"

Steeg hadn't thought about it all that much. "I don't know, maybe a little. That's probably why I joined the Navy – less of a chance to get shot at. I do know you can't let fear stop you from doing what's right. I do know that."

"You think the war is right?"

Steeg shrugged. "The Navy is just a way to pay for college, Matt. That's what I'm doing. If I'm afraid of anything, it's probably the idea of being separated from my friends and family for so long. I'm not real crazy about being alone like that. But, what the heck, you know what they say – the Navy isn't a job, it's an adventure!"

Light laughter followed, but the tone had changed. Several moments of silence passed before any of them spoke.

Steeg looked at his watch. "I guess I should get going. It's getting late."

Wedge complained. "Why? What else you gotta do?"

"Well, nothing much, really. I called Grace's Mom this morning and she told me she wouldn't be up from Mankato until Thursday – something about late final exams. I called her dorm room three times this afternoon, but there was no answer. Kinda think I should borrow Dad's car and go down there to surprise her."

Wedge nodded, thinking that sounded like a good idea. "Sure, why not?"

"NO!" Matt jumped up. "DON'T!"

Steeg leaned back, surprised by the sudden burst from his friend. "Why not?"

"Man that would NOT be a good idea."

"Why not?" Steeg repeated.

"Do you know what you're saying?" Matt grabbed Steeg by the front of his shirt. "Just think about this, will you? She's a college freshman. She's pretty. She's riper than a Georgia Peach in September…"

"She's what?" Steeg felt vaguely insulted.

"You know what I mean. And, here you are, home from the Navy showing up without warning on her dormitory doorstep? Are you nuts?!" Matt let go of Steeg's shirt and Steeg smoothed the more obvious wrinkles away.

"I think it would be a nice surprise," countered Steeg.

Matt grabbed him again, this time by the shoulders. "Look, you're not listening. She's at Mankato State College – the number one party school in the nation…"

"A 'party' school? – Mankato?!"

"My God, man, don't you read 'Playboy Magazine'?! Look, she's there, right?"

"Right."

"Guys are there, too. Lots of 'em. Football jocks. Basketball jocks. Tall, good looking, and over-sexed – thousands of them. They're all partying all the time…"

"Not all the time," Steeg protested.

"Every night, a million great looking, hunky guys…"

"There aren't a million people between here and the Iowa border," Steeg objected.

"A million of them, I tell you, all on the make for every little thing in skirts. It's frickin' Sin City down there. And, you're just going to drive down and say 'Hi' to her?"

"Maybe," Steeg was suddenly concerned, but after a second or two of self-imposed doubt, he waved Matt off. "Nah, you're exaggerating this. Gracie and I have an understanding. We know each other. She's not like that at all."

"You may be right, and I hope you are. But buddy, ol' pal, you don't know what it's like down there. Any girl would fall for any of those studs. Their muscles have muscles, and their dicks are as long as your arm."

Steeg grimaced. "Nice. That's a little crude, don't you think?"

"I'm just telling it like it is. Not all men are created equal in that department, you know."

"I think it's okay," Wedge observed more quietly from the far side of the pool table. "You wanna go down there and surprise her, go ahead. I'm not telling you something you don't already know, but she loves you. Remember Matt's uncle's cabin on Lake Minnetonka last summer?"

A warm memory returned of the private group outing and the few moments he and Grace were able to share alone in a secluded loft in the cabin. It was like yesterday to him, and he smiled. "Yeah, that's right. She does love me. She trusts me, too. And I trust her. And you should apologize for saying what you just did about her."

Matt held up his hands in surrender. "I didn't say she didn't. I didn't mean to say anything bad about her. I mean, I'd like to date her myself, for God's sake!"

Steeg's eyes narrowed to slits, and Matt took a step back.

"I'm sorry – didn't mean that, either. Look, Steeg, do what you want. You only got a couple of weeks, so make the most of it."

Steeg nodded in agreement, resolved in his new decision. "Thanks. I think I will."

He grabbed the Pea Coat he had thrown on the sofa near the stairs. "I'll let you guys know how it goes."

He slid the coat on and bound up the stairs to the kitchen, out the back door, around the snow-covered walk, and to the borrowed family car parked on the cul-de-sac. His father's loan of the vehicle was a necessary accommodation since Steeg's old Buick, still out of commission after throwing a rod the previous September, was still resting on blocks in his dad's garage.

When Steeg got home, everyone was in bed and all the lights were dark, save the one over the kitchen table. Under the light, Steeg saw the handwritten note his mother had left for him:

> *Grace called at 8:47. She wants you to*
> *call her as soon as you get in.—Love, Mom*

The phone receiver almost flew into his hand as he quickly dialed the long distance Mankato number. He looked at his watch. It was almost 1:30 in the morning. Very late, he knew, maybe too late. Her phone rang four times before she picked up.

"Hello?" She sounded tired, but her voice washed over him with a startling joy.

"Gracie, it's me."

"Oh, Steeg! You're home?"

"Yeah. I wanted to surprise you."

"You did."

He felt the unfulfilled longing for her rising up from deep within him. "I miss you so much. You're Mom told me you're not coming up until Thursday, is that right?"

"Yes. That was the plan, I…"

"I want to come down tomorrow."

"Oh, well, I guess you could, but things are pretty busy right now…"

"Exams still going on?"

"Yes, well, that is, no. I'm done with those now. I was going to get some last minute things done before I went home for Christmas. You know, shopping and stuff."

"Well, you could do that up here couldn't you? I can come down to pick you up!"

Her short, quiet chuckle touched him deeply. "Yes. That would be nice. We'll catch up on the drive back."

They talked for another twenty minutes before Grace pleaded exhaustion, and they said "Good night" to each other.

Later, lying on his old bed upstairs in his old room, Steeg could see her face looking down on him. He barely closed his eyes at all that night.

Chapter 4
The Reunion

When Steeg Patterson walked through the twin glass doors of Gage Hall on the upper campus of Mankato State College, Grace Ofterdahl was in the lobby waiting for him. She was dressed in flared jeans, a form fitting pull over sweater with a high roll collar that did everything good for her figure, her tan artificial suede winter coat with the fake fur trim hanging loose and open. She was lovelier than Steeg had remembered, and he started to tell her so but stopped as she fell into his arms. Their lips met in a long, soft kiss and the reality of how much he needed her slashed across his consciousness. The few remaining students coming, going or sitting in the lounge ignored them as they embraced. She tasted the same to him. She felt the same to him. The one thing about which he was absolutely certain was that he would always want to be with Gracie. It was a short prelude to a week when their passion for each other would build beyond anything either one of them would want to control.

Gracie pulled away, ran her hand across the short brush-like bristles covering the top of his head and smiled. "Nice haircut!"

Steeg rolled his eyes and made a face. "Glad you like it. I was going to wear my uniform for you – knowing how sexy you find Navy bell bottoms

– but I didn't want you to lose control of yourself right here in front of all these impressionable kids."

Gracie's light laugh sprinkled real joy over his entire being as they turned to leave. She traveled light with only a small suitcase and a shopping bag partially filled with packages wrapped and ready for the Christmas tree. He carried her bag and suitcase with one hand while she hugged his other arm close as they walked to the parking lot and his Dad's Oldsmobile Delta 88. He held the passenger side door open for her first before storing her stuff in the back seat. When he eased in behind the steering wheel, she immediately closed the distance between them to sit at his side. She laid her head on his shoulder; the smell of her hair was intoxicating to him. The power of his unexpected deeply pleasurable emotions almost frightened him.

Driving from the parking lot, they both said at the same moment, "I missed you."

They laughed after they both replied, "Me, too."

The long drive north on U.S. Highway 169 wasn't long enough for Steeg. He wanted to drive away with her to some place, any place, where they could be alone together. She talked about school with a nonchalance Steeg found curious. She mildly complained about one of her professors whom she described as a complete male chauvinist pig. Not surprising to him she more vigorously complained about the too long hours spent studying. Grace was remarkably bright, academically capable and very intelligent. During all the time they had been together, more than once he had failed to answer a particularly annoying question in the back of his mind — how was it that this extraordinary person ever wanted to be with him?

He shoved his doubt deep down inside as he drove. He had no time for it now. It was December 20, and his leave was melting away. Somehow he had to figure out a way to slow everything down, and the only thing he could think of was to spend every minute with Grace. Maybe that was why his foot seemed unable to maintain steady pressure on the accelerator. Every few minutes he noticed the speedometer needle had slipped well below the posted 75 mph speed limit. He'd slowly bring the speed back up where it should be, only to begin another slow down cycle within a few minutes. Except for the brief 30 mile per hour limit through St. Peter, this continued for the entire 80-mile trip. Long moments of silence did not bother them. They were comfortable just being with each other, and she remained close at his side the entire ride back to the Twin Cities.

However, by the time they had reached Shakopee, another problem bothered him – his lack of power over his circumstances. Having her there, feeling her easy breathing as she rested against him, he bridled against the realization that his enlistment had violated him in some way he didn't fully understand. Motivated by the threat of being drafted into some other branch of military service he didn't want, Steeg had signed his life over to the military, four years of it anyway. It was the military that gave, and the military would take away. The Navy had given him two weeks. The Navy would deny him four years of being with the one person he loved and needed more than he could say.

He knew he needed Grace, but other than to say he loved her, he couldn't explain why he needed this one person so desperately. He only knew he did. He had obligated himself to the United States Navy – volunteered, of all things! The draft justified that decision, but the lack of viable alternatives more than riled him. Steeg tried to push those thoughts down deep. Now was not the time for anything that would take away from the joy he felt being near her.

They turned onto the road east of Shakopee that led to the old single lane Bloomington Ferry Bridge to cross the Minnesota River. Slowing to 20 miles per hour, Steeg cautiously made his way across the rickety wood-planked structure as more bothersome thoughts came to his mind. Like Wedge, he had no problem honoring his obligations to his country, but like Matt, he had no desire to 'blow away' a fellow human being. The Navy had seemed both a safe alternative and the most effective way to pay for a college education he could not expect his parents to cover. He hadn't fully considered the reality of four years, however. Four years without Grace now was all he could see. No matter how he tried to shape it in his mind, it was a future of separation and isolation. He hated it.

Safely on the Bloomington side of the river, he followed the winding Old Shakopee Road past the Minnesota Country Club and the old Masonic Home. More driving, slower now, and they reached the France Avenue intersection. Steeg turned north.

"You're quiet," She said not moving from his shoulder.

"Sorry."

"Something's on your mind?"

"You."

"Oh," She warmly caressed his right hand draped over her shoulder. After a bit, she said, "I think I know why."

A short chortle as he said, "I get it. It's that 'Psych. 101' class you took. You're a mind-reader now."

"Sort of, maybe."

A brief flash of real fear crossed his mind as he wondered if she hadn't had ESP all along. He dismissed the idea with a quick "Yeah, right."

As the car crossed over the northern Bloomington city limit into Edina, Grace sat up for a quick look around.

"I have an idea," she said. "Let's not go home right away. Let's go to Southdale, have some lunch and do some shopping."

Steeg needed her to stay with him more than he could say. Her need to shop was a readymade excuse to delay their eventual parting.

Opened in 1956, Southdale was not only Minnesota's first great shopping center, it was the very first fully enclosed shopping center in the nation. The marvels of unsurpassed, climate-controlled merchandizing awaited them. They parked in the overflow lot next to the blue painted Southdale water tower. Working their way through the heavy crowds, they were soon seated in the too busy, but colorful holiday-decorated Garden Court Restaurant where they ordered and slowly enjoyed their lunch together. Despite the noise of the constant hustle and bustle all around them, neither one was in a hurry.

After lunch, they took the center escalator to the second level, and turned right to survey the storefronts. At J.B. Hudson Jewelry, the wedding ring displays grabbed them as if they were shackled to the floor.

"I haven't given you a ring yet," he said softly as his eyes came to rest on a perfectly matched combination with a blinding solitary round diamond at least a full carat large.

"We should pick it out together," she replied, giving his fingers a slight squeeze.

They stood looking at the sizeable selection. After a long time, he said:

"We should set a date."

She nodded without saying anything.

"What date should we set?" he asked, his impotence over everything in his life inhibiting him in even this simple task. "Things seem so different now."

She turned to him. "In what ways are they different?"

"Not in how I feel about you," he quietly told her. "Everything else, though. It's all changed."

She said nothing as he led her away from the jewelry store to continue around the corner. They took the staircase leading down to the Garden Court. Once there, they walked into the B. Dalton Bookstore, Grace's eyes often returning to him when he looked elsewhere. She knew he was bothered by something.

The aisles were jammed almost shoulder to shoulder with holiday shoppers and the bookstore had tables covered with all manner of books. More tables had displays of calendars, or pre-boxed gifts of one sort or another. Steeg spied a table with neatly folded stacks of heavy sweatshirts, each pile sorted by their own color. He walked over to get a closer look at a pile that had a silk-screened Snoopy dog on the front.

"Hey, look at this," he called back to Grace. "A 'Peanuts' sweatshirt!"

As he held the shirt up so she could see, he saw the familiar mischievous smile cross her face. She quickly moved close to his side and whispered, "Did you say 'penis sweatshirt?!'"

His brow wrinkled as she began to giggle.

"No, I didn't say 'penis.' I said 'Peanuts,' like in the comic strip. Penis is something entirely different!" He almost laughed himself as she muffled her giggles in the padded shoulder of his pea coat. He felt the eyes of several people on the two of them. He slipped his arm into hers. "Come on, let's get out of here."

They left the bookstore to resume their tour of the huge shopping center. She simply held his hand with both of hers as they walked. After a long time, they had come full circle and found themselves standing in front of the same J.B. Hudson display window as before. They both had their eyes on the same, round stone ring set.

The dazzling sparkles from the diamond jewelry behind the glass bounced up into his eyes. "What style do you like? Square, oval, or round?"

"Round, I think."

"Me, too."

They stood there quietly for a long while. He knew he didn't have anywhere near the money to cover the cost of the rings. He'd have to finance it. He also knew that, once she had the ring on her finger, the secret would be out. There'd be no hiding it. He didn't want to hide it anymore. It should be announced to the world – an announcement that would be like a slap in the face for her mother, the one person he absolutely knew hated him. How he was going to handle that, he had no clue.

Then there was the other thing. How would he support her on an Airman 2C pay of what – seventy-five bucks a month?! Just thinking about it seemed crazy to him. Where would they live? Where could they live on so little money? Money, money everywhere, but none in his pocket. He tried to see it happening but too many doubts and questions clouded his thinking. Steeg knew it was possible somehow if only he could figure it all out. He had to find a way to make it happen. Then, the doubts and questions began to fall away as an entirely workable solution appeared before him perched on a white satin covered stand in the radiant light of the display window.

A ring on her finger could be the perfect answer to everything. A ring could keep her safe while he was away. Yes, that was it. It was a near perfect 'NO TRESPASSING' sign. He could deal with their economic challenges, as well as her mother, later. At that moment, it all made perfect sense to him.

He set his jaw firmly. "Let me buy it for you. Right now."

She looked at him with surprise. "Are you sure?"

"Absolutely," he nodded.

She kept her hands on his. "That's important for me to know – that you're absolutely sure. But, you can't afford this, Steeg. It's over a thousand dollars."

"I can finance it."

"No."

"Why not?"

"Because, we need to talk about it some more."

"I thought that was what we were doing."

"Not here," she turned away from the display. "Later."

She was right, he knew. They needed to talk about all the things they needed to talk about, many of which neither of them was fully aware. Beyond finances, circumstances, or potential in-laws, what should be a simple matter was very complex, indeed. They both sensed this and they both resisted the risk of talking about it.

As the afternoon turned to early evening, they had purchased surprisingly very little: a few small items for her, nothing for him. It was already dark by time they found their way back to his father's parked car where Steeg had left it – in the overflow parking lot near the big blue water tower. He joked when they finally reached the car how he was certain it had been daylight when they had left the mall. Grace smiled. Surprising to him, she didn't seem to be too anxious to get home. Instead, she suggested they go to his parent's house. Not wanting to give her up, Steeg readily agreed.

At the Patterson household, things couldn't have been more calamitous. The energy of all the sisters and little brother Daniel were reaching peak levels. The pile of presents under the tree had been growing daily as each person added his or her own offerings. There were more to come. Grace relaxed, warmed by the colorful confusion of brightly wrapped packages under the tree, the blare from the constantly running television in the corner, and the noises coming from the kitchen where Steeg was supervising his mother's progress in putting dinner on the table.

Steeg's sister Mary, only a year younger than Grace, plopped down next to the young woman on the couch and asked boldly, "Grace, is my brother a good kisser?"

An eyebrow shot up as a smiled curled the corner of her mouth. "Well, as a matter of fact, yes. He is."

"You really like him?"

"Why do you ask?"

Mary smiled, shaking her head and teasing. "I just find it kind of curious, that's all. I can't imagine liking him so much you'd want to kiss him – gross!"

A mischievous grin came to Grace's face. "Well, yes, I guess you're right about that. It's something you get used to."

"Are you going to marry him?"

Caught unaware, thin tears suddenly moistened Grace's eyes. She quickly blinked them away. Mary saw it and, concerned, reached for Grace's arm.

"I'm sorry. I didn't mean… It's my big mouth and I'm always saying things without thinking first."

Grace patted the younger girl's hand. "Oh, that's okay. Nothing, really. It's just kind of a sensitive subject right now."

Mary saw something in Grace's face that surprised her. To her it looked like sadness.

"You love him," she said with certainty.

Grace nodded slowly. "Yes. I do."

The moment was interrupted as Steeg yelled from the kitchen, "It's time to eat!" and everyone, except Steeg's father, herded into the next room. Sitting in his big, stuffed recliner-rocker opposite from the couch, his dad hadn't heard the exchange between Mary and Grace, but he had seen the tears, and he wondered what was behind them.

The evening was fun for all. The kitchen dinner table too small to seat the entire Patterson family, was now even smaller with Grace squeezed in next to Steeg. She genuinely appreciated the closeness of the gathering. More than a little attention was paid to Steeg, his haircut, his experiences as a Navy recruit in basic training, his questionable taste in friends, especially that Wedge character and his motorcycle. His mother asked a question or two about Grace's major and minor at college. His sister Edith made a crack about not knowing why Grace hung around with Steeg, or what she saw in him. Steeg mildly protested, irked only a little when Grace quickly shrugged and came back with "Oh, he'll do for now." Everyone but Steeg laughed. The simple, yet plentiful dinner progressed with the same easy tone.

After dinner, Grace helped Mrs. Patterson with the dishes. Leftovers were wrapped and stored in the refrigerator. Dishes, glasses and cups were stacked and marshaled in organized rows next to the sink now full of hot, sudsy water. Steeg's mother dug elbow deep into the sink, and Grace used a second dishcloth on the table. They didn't say much to each other, but Mrs. Patterson appreciated the help.

In the living room, the younger kids divided their attention between the TV and the wide spread of Christmas presents under the tree. Daniel and Hilde were having a particularly difficult time keeping their hands off the packages. Comfortable in his recliner-rocker, Steeg's father encouraged the two to relax and watch television. Steeg sat in the corner stuffed chair, looking at but not watching TV. Something was eating at him. *Why didn't she want the ring?*

The only answer that came to him was the obvious one. She didn't want the ring because she didn't want to get married. If she wanted to marry him, she would have accepted the ring. It was that simple. It was also that deflating. He shoved the unwanted answer to his self-doubting question down deep until it was as if it had never existed.

Later, Grace and Mrs. Patterson joined the family in the living room. Grace chose to snuggle in between Steeg and the arm of his chair. He leaned toward her ear.

"Should we go, soon?" He asked quietly so only she could hear.

Grace shook her head. "In a bit."

Steeg nodded, wanting to add in a whisper that he'd like to talk with her privately.

Before he could whisper anything, Grace turned and asked him, "Would you like to go to Christmas Eve Mass with me Saturday night?"

Mom and Dad looked over to Steeg. Steeg looked at them. They looked at each other as Steeg looked back at Grace. "Christmas Eve Mass?"

Grace nodded.

"That's, uh, kind of a busy night for us." Steeg stumbled. "We do a lot of family gift exchange stuff on Christmas Eve – special dinner, gifts, things like that."

"It's a midnight mass," Grace offered quietly. "It's a very beautiful service."

Steeg wasn't about to admit that going to a Catholic Mass made him feel strangely uncomfortable. However, he had no easy excuse not to accept Grace's surprise offer. In near panic, Steeg turned to his parents with an unspoken plea to save him. What he got was betrayal.

"You could go, Steeg," His mother offered with a smile. "We're done with everything else long before midnight."

Abandoned by his own mother, Steeg's mind raced to find a way out. He wasn't a big 'church' person and especially not a big 'Catholic Church' person. One thought he couldn't avoid blocked his way out of this sudden predicament: it would be another opportunity to be with her. Once more, he looked to his parents who returned little more than pleasant smiles and nodding heads. There was no rescue coming from the folks.

Steeg gave in with a thin smile and a shallow nod of his own. "Sure, Grace, that would be nice."

Grace gave him a quick hug, adding a quiet "Thank you."

Chapter 5

On "Fairness" and Other Impossible Goals

The next morning, Steeg was at her front door at 7:30. They had made the breakfast date on the same doorstep just eight hours earlier. Grace's mother opened the door and without looking at him, offered a cool "Good morning, Steeg," as she turned back toward the kitchen. She was anxious to return to a burning cigarette in the ashtray next to the sink. She yelled "Steeg's here!" as she passed the open doorway leading upstairs. Her mother spent a lot of time in the kitchen whenever Steeg visited.

Light footfalls preceded Grace's appearance at the base of the stairs. Her smile was radiant as she rushed up to him. Knowing her mother was looking around the corner at that very moment, Grace wrapped one arm around his neck, pulled him close, and kissed him warmly full on the lips. He, too, knew her mother saw it. He was embarrassed. They usually tried to keep their all too brief but frequent affectionate displays private.

"I'm not sure when we'll be back," Grace said loudly over her shoulder as she donned her winter coat with the artificial fur collar, grabbed her purse and led the way out the door. Steeg followed closely behind, anxious to leave before her mother's condemning scowl burned holes through the back of his Pea Coat.

The morning was crisp and the sun turned the newly fallen snow so white it hurt their eyes. They climbed into his father's Oldsmobile, the chill of its cold, pale green vinyl upholstery penetrating their clothing.

"I miss your old car," Grace remarked as the icy vinyl shot its chill to her skin.

Steeg turned the key in the ignition. "Me too."

The engine sprang to life, Steeg slipped the automatic into gear and the big car rolled away from the curb, crunching loudly on the snow covering the street.

Their early arrival at the Perkins Restaurant near Southdale assured them of their choice of seating; as usual, they picked a booth in a quiet corner away from as many patrons as possible. Service was efficient, the food was what was expected, and they didn't have to say all that much to each other to enjoy their time together.

After he had finished with his breakfast, Steeg looked out the window at the Burger King Drive-in a couple of blocks down 66th Street. "Remember that Edina-Richfield football game in '65?"

Grace nodded, finishing her plate of scrambled eggs and ham.

Steeg nodded toward the store down the street. "After the game, everyone knew there was going to be a big rumble at that Burger King. Gees, they almost leveled the place. Pulled out stools at the counter, ripped up seats in the booths, did they break windows? I don't remember. For Pete's sake, I don't even remember who won the football game!"

"They did," Grace offered. "They always won. That's why we hated them so much."

"No. We hated them because they're from the rich side of town, and we're not."

She nodded in agreement. "True."

"The Lake Conference wasn't big enough for both of us. Sooner or later, it had to come to blows. It sure did that night."

Several minutes went by without either one of them saying much. Grace finished her breakfast, and, as if on cue, the waitress came over to clear away the dishes and ask if they wanted anything else. They both declined. With a polite 'thank you', the server left the check on the table.

They looked out the window at the traffic passing by as Steeg reached across the table and took her hand.

"What would you like to do today, Gracie?"

"Oh, I suppose I should get my shopping done. I don't know. What would you like to do?"

He looked straight at her and, with just a second of hesitation, said, "I would like to get a cozy motel room somewhere, and make love to you all day long."

She held his eyes with hers as she digested the suggestion, only to break away to the safety of the traffic passing by.

"Bad idea?" He asked.

She shook her head, but said nothing.

"Good idea?"

One eyebrow raised as her head bobbed briefly in an unspoken question.

It seemed to him that he had been with her hundreds of times at almost every possible level of passion. At every opportunity, she was warm, always inviting, up to a point. It was frustrating for him, but he had learned to manage the physical consequence of their prolonged petting sessions after the fact. Lifting heavy objects in the garage helped more than the coldest shower. It was a simple fact that whenever they reached the 'point of no return,' they had never crossed it.

Steeg truly believed the unconsummated element of their relationship was mostly his doing. He wanted her, of that he was certain. He also knew she had to want him more. He would not take her by force. At the critical moment, he always acquiesced for her to take the lead. She never did.

Sitting in the restaurant at that moment, he felt like a fool. Maybe he was a fool – a fool for her.

After a while, she said, "This is all we talk about, isn't it?"

"It seems so. When we're alone together – it's not easy for me..."

He could see her bristle defensively. "Me, either. It just makes me wonder sometimes, are we together because we haven't gone all the way yet? Or are we together because we want to go all the way?"

He felt the conversation turn down an all too familiar path. It was a path he didn't want to revisit. "I'm with you because I love you."

She ignored him. "It doesn't matter. Either way, after we 'do it,' the reason for staying together goes away, right?"

A bolt of anger shot through him. "Wrong!"

"Oh, I think so. Guys are like that."

He would have preferred a slap across his face – it would have hurt less. Where was she getting this stuff? Was he causing it in some way he didn't understand? Had he said something or done something that made her doubt his loyalty and affection for her? He just didn't know.

"When, in the nearly two years we've been together, have I ever treated you with lack of respect or concern for your happiness?"

"I'm not saying you have," she deflected. "I'm just saying that when guys get what they want, it's over."

Truly angry now, he grabbed the bill from the table, pulled money from his wallet, made sure the tip was adequate, and secured it in a stack on the table under the peppershaker. He got up to leave and she slid from the booth to follow him to the door.

Outside, he opened the car door for her, slowly yet firmly pushing it closed behind her until he heard a click. He joined her inside, sliding in behind the steering wheel. Both of them sat quietly, Steeg choosing not to start the car. For some reason he did not understand, this young woman had no real trust in his feelings for her. More than anything else, he needed her to trust him. After a long silence, he had to say something. He began poorly.

"Sometimes, I hear your mother in things you say to me. They may be true for other guys, but they don't apply to me or how I feel about you. You don't know when I first fell in love with you, do you? I do. It was the very moment I first looked into your eyes. Do you remember when that was?"

She turned away, looking out her quickly fogging window.

His fingers lightly touched her turned shoulder. "It was after school on a Friday in late February of our Junior year. I was in the gym blocking out my photo positions for that night's basketball game. A girl I sort of had a crush on, Marilyn Mason came into the gym with another girl I hadn't seen before. Seeing me there, Marilyn started joking too loudly about the nerdy student photographer. I was used to it by then. My friends called me worse names. Anyway, the two girls came over to where I was standing. Marilyn asked me if I was going to be at the game that night. I told her I was at every game, and she should know that. She wanted to know that if I was going to take a few shots of people in the stands for the yearbook, would I make sure I included her. I assured her I would, and that I'd include the person standing next to her, too if she was going to be at the game. I looked at this beautiful brown-haired girl, and fell into the deepest brown eyes I had ever seen. The girl was you. I've been captured by those brown eyes ever since."

Grace mildly complained. "You didn't ask me out until the next fall."

"Gimme a break – I was shy," Steeg pinched the bridge of his nose, feeling a little embarrassed. "It took me a while to get up the nerve."

She fell into his arms, small rivulets of tears falling from her eyes. She did love him, he was certain.

Steeg buried his face into her soft brown hair. "The Church may say it would be wrong for us to go all the way before we are married. I guess it would be, but that's not the whole of it with me. When the time is right, we'll know. Until then, I want you to know this — if we do, my love for you goes on. If we don't, my love for you goes on. I will love you always, no matter what."

Chapter 6
Almost Love in the Broken Car

The next few days of Steeg's valuable Christmas leave went by quickly. He and Grace were together as much as possible, foregoing his earlier motel room suggestion in favor of holiday opportunities with her family and his. Friday was cut short. Before he could offer to take her to dinner, Grace reluctantly told him she and her folks were going to visit a family friend that evening. No, she didn't know how long it would be, or when she would be home. She asked Steeg to call her around noon the next day. That would be Christmas Eve, and she reminded him of his promise to attend Midnight Mass with her. He assured her he was looking forward to it, gave her a warm kiss on her doorstep, and returned to his father's car.

When he wasn't with her, Steeg felt a peculiar mixture of aloneness and comfort at the same time. The familiar combination of emotions wrapped around him as he drove back to his parent's house. He needed to be with her more than he could really understand. What was it about this one person who could fill him up with so much joy, and yet, in the same moment, cause him such profound insecurity and unbearable self-doubt? He had no answer, but whatever it was, it held deep and extraordinary meaning for him.

Steeg wasn't sure when it happened that Grace had stopped being just a 'girlfriend.' It had occurred early in their relationship. Then, with his enlistment the previous November, she had become his constant frame of reference for everything right in his world, a world where less and less was staying right for him. She was now even more his reason for being. In some way he couldn't understand, Grace legitimized him, even validated him. The thought of being without her was too much of a threat so he immediately forced it from his mind.

All around, everything had changed; everything was now beyond his control. It was as if he were on some kind of horrible amusement park ride that kept pitching, dipping and lurching too much to be fun.

His "fun" had abruptly ended shortly after November 11 of that year – probably around 0330 the morning of November 12 in boot camp, when the drill instructors came into the barracks throwing large metal garbage cans and slamming against lockers to wake up the new recruits on two maybe three hours of sleep. Before breakfast that morning, Steeg realized the colossal error he had made. He was in Foxtrot Division, Company #666. By the time morning chow was over, and Steeg was dumping the mostly untouched tray of inedible reconstituted scrambled eggs and pale gray gravy into one of a line of garbage cans near the chow hall exit, he and his fellow new recruits had already come to the same conclusion — they were all in the 'Devil's Brigade.' The company's number 666 only confirmed it.

Now, seven weeks later he was home on Christmas leave sitting in his dad's Oldsmobile parked in the garage. His out-of-control situation was unfair, not to him but to Gracie. He blamed himself for rushing to join the Navy, along with the draft board and its eminent threat. He could see now how his hasty decision had been a mistake.

Looking through the windshield at nothing at all, his spirit felt weighed by the heaviness of his complete impotence over what was quickly becoming the colossal mess that was his life.

Next to his Dad's car rested his old Buick, its front end elevated on blocks. The car had thrown a rod early the previous September and its front end had remained up in the air since. Trying to find parts for a '48

DynaGlide straight-eight engine was almost impossible and Steeg knew the car would never run again.

"Too bad," he said to no one as left his parents' car, walked up to his old Buick, and looked inside the large passenger compartment to the back seat.

He remembered the last time he and Grace had been in that back seat. In this very garage, after he and his dad had jacked up and blocked the Buick's front end to more easily pull the oil pan and the remains of the thrown rod, he and Gracie had one last chance for the seclusion of their private sanctuary.

On that September evening, their longing for the broken car, combined with her pending departure for college, compelled them to seek out the back seat within minutes after his parents had left to visit family friends across town. With the garage door closed, the solitude of the back seat was dark, safe and warm. They were both surprised by how much they missed the car. Their hurried embraces were filled with nervous and nearly uncontrollable passion.

Control was in short supply that night. Once they were safely hidden inside the darkened garage, they removed each other's clothing in near record time. Quickly naked, they clung to each other in the darkness. Once again, he silently cursed his own cowardice. Earlier that day at the drug store, the assuredness he felt of his pending sexual conquest with Gracie was shaken by the more mature woman behind the counter. His inexperience and embarrassment had forced him to return the box of condoms to the shelf twice, retreating to the magazine rack both times where he pretended to read something while he re-summoned his nerve. After the third try, Steeg left the store empty handed. Now, in the back seat with the only woman he has ever loved, he was completely unprepared to go much further in the heavy necking session.

Grace was not concerned with his lack of preparedness. She was content to 'play' with him, almost teasingly so, to an unbearably pleasurable point of peak arousal. It also caused a familiar uncomfortable heaviness in his groin.

Inexperienced, fumbling, and just plain scared, he nevertheless had to have her. He moved to position her under him. Her sudden gasp of surprise was premature, and he immediately braced himself for another bout of her fending him off as he pressed closer to her.

However, Steeg sensed something was not right, too. The darkened interior of the garage began to lose its depth, and without warning, the glare from the back porch light flooded into the car as the garage door began to rise up!

Grace panicked, sliding out from under him and diving for the floor. She desperately flattened herself to the rough fibers of the carpet, groping for clothing strewn everywhere, trying to avoid the drive shaft hump painfully digging into her bare hip. Steeg stayed on the bench seat, flat on his back with his head jammed against one door, his feet pushed hard against the other. The once dark garage filled with the glare of headlights as his father slowly moved the Oldsmobile into its regular parking spot. In a second or two that seemed to last fifteen times longer, the headlights went out and the old garage was again dimly lit by only the back porch light from the house.

"Steeeeg!" Grace hissed loudly.

"Sssssshh!" Steeg cautioned her as quietly as he could.

He could hear his parents emerge from their car as Grace raised her face to his ear. "You're showing!"

Steeg looked down. Because the old car's front axel was raised on blocks, the rear passenger window was angled lower in a way that directed the pale illumination from the house's porch light downward across the rear bench seat. His erection, although average in all respects, stood at rigid attention, perfectly visible against the dim but adequate glow of the rear porch light.

"Oh, gees!" he moaned as he saw his parents coming around to the side windows of the Buick. If either one of them turned to look in, it was over.

It was then he felt Grace's hand on him, pushing him down into the darkness below the illuminating stream tumbling through the rear window. She held him there as his parents walked passed.

He could hear them talking to each other, but not clear enough to make out what they were saying. He could see them from their shoulders up as, too slowly, both parents walked from the garage. He did not take a breath until he heard the back door of the house close behind them. Then, as quietly as possible, he and Grace scrambled to get their clothes back on. After dressing, they sat side by side in the back seat trying to figure out what they should do next.

"We can't just go in and say 'Hi!' to them," Steeg said. "They just got home. We come waltzing in all flushed and warm, it isn't going to fly two feet."

"We can't stay out here all night," Grace countered.

"No, but we can't just go in. Look, this is what we'll do — we went for a walk…"

"A walk?"

"Yep. That's it. We went for a walk and we just got back."

"I don't know. I don't feel like I went for a walk," she shook her head, not comfortable with the idea of pulling off the deception.

"You don't look like you went for a walk, either," he said, smoothing her tussled hair with his hand. Steeg added, "So, let's very quietly leave the car, not make any noise, get to the street, around the corner, we'll quickly circle the block and go inside. By then, we'll be, you know, normal, and we can honestly say that we 'went for a walk.'"

With her familiar, inviting impish grin she asked, "How's 'Little Steeg' doing?"

"About the same as usual," he complained mildly, adding, "'Little Steeg' will be fine after I lift something heavy."

Steeg smiled as he remembered it all. The 'look-like-we-had-gone-for-a-walk' ploy apparently worked. No questions from the folks, and he had his father's car to return Grace home that evening. And, returning home, Steeg got to haul five 40-pound bags of salt downstairs to the water softener, which helped 'Little Steeg', too.

He stood there, looking at his broken car while trying to think of a way to make his relationship with Grace work after he returned to basic training and the 'Devil's Brigade.' After basic, he assumed he'd get orders to Photographers' Mate 'A' School. She'd be at Mankato. He'd probably be in Pensacola if it was 'A' School or, worse, a ship if 'A' School didn't happen.

If it was a ship, it would be an aircraft carrier of some sort, and if it were a carrier, chances were more than good he'd go to Viet Nam.

"How does anybody make a mess like this work for two people?" he asked no one.

It was a question for which he had no answer. It was a question that dogged him through the night and into the next day. Throughout a quick breakfast of corn flakes, the question kept turning over in his mind. His mother noticed his silence and blank stare. She figured when he was ready to talk about whatever it was, he would, but she had to get laundry done early before things got too far along. She left him alone in the kitchen where he finished his breakfast in silence.

Later, helping his father clear the driveway from freshly fallen pre-dawn snow so shallow his help wasn't really needed, in a sudden burst of anger he swung his snow shovel at the pavement, severely bending the shovel's corner edge to a sharp angle.

Trevor Patterson looked over his shoulder at his oldest son, and then returned to clearing his side of driveway. "Yep, that'll happen sometimes."

"What's that?" Steeg asked irritated, still gripping the handle too firmly, seriously considering giving it another swing.

"Snow sticks, so you gotta knock it off once in awhile."

The shovel was absolutely clean, and the snow wasn't sticky. In fact, it was loose-powder dry. He could have blown the snow off the driveway with a good sneeze. Feeling the beginnings of a headache Steeg pulled a glove from a hand and rubbed between his eyes.

The elder Patterson draped one arm over the shovel handle and stopped his work. "You know, son, sometimes you have to let things just run their course. I don't know what's on your mind, but something sure is. Whatever it is, my advice, for what it's worth, is if you can't change it, try to sit back and watch for a while. It might change on its own."

Steeg didn't want to look at his dad. He didn't want to be seen like this. He shoveled a few more feet worth of his half of the driveway to catch up with his father.

"That might be a good idea, Dad, but I don't know if there's time to wait for things to change on their own. I sure don't know what to do about it right now."

"That's understandable." Dad resumed his shoveling and together they worked to the street in just a minute or two. "Too bad every snow fall can't be this easy."

Steeg agreed as they turned toward the garage to return the shovels to their places on nails that served as hooks on the inside wall. After they had stowed the tools, they passed the old Buick still sitting on blocks.

His father swung a thumb at the old car and asked, "What do you want me to do with that thing, anyway? Are we going to fix it, or do I junk it, or what? I could use the space."

"Yeah, I know, Dad. I'd kinda like to keep it if I could..."

"Sentimental value?"

"What?" Steeg looked at his father with only a bit of uncertainty.

"Well, it's just that, you know, I can see where you might have some fond memories of the car, and things you might have done in it."

"What?" Steeg grew more uncomfortable.

"But then, again, it is winter. It's too frickin' cold to be sitting in the thing now, right?"

Steeg felt as if there were suddenly no more secrets. "Right."

"Right," his father confirmed. Turning to go into the house, he added over his shoulder, "Besides, if you ever needed some real privacy, you're old enough to get a room somewhere, don't you think?"

Oh, my God! He saw us! The truth of it hit him like a brick in the face. He blurted out a little too loudly, "I guess... we could junk it then, right, Dad?"

His father turned back to him with a nod.

"Dad!" Steeg took two desperate steps forward, lowering his voice. "Did... did Mom see us?!"

With his lips pursed and eyebrows arched, his father nodded again. "She's the one who told me." And, with that, Trevor Patterson knocked his boots clean of snow on the side of the stoop, and walked back into the house.

Steeg stood in the middle of the freshly cleared driveway, not knowing what to do, or even how to move. The one unsettling question he couldn't answer for sure was if he would ever be able to look his mother in the eye again.

Chapter 7

Christmas Eve and Midnight Mass

Grace's mother answered the phone.

"No, she's not here right now."

"Oh, okay. Do you know when she'll be back?"

"No."

"Oh, okay. Well, just tell her I called, okay?"

"Sure."

The rude click was followed by the irritating hum of dial tone. He looked at the stove clock. It read 11:30. She had asked him to call before noon, didn't she? He was sure she had.

He would try again after lunch, if she hadn't called back by then.

It was well past mid-afternoon before she had returned his calls. She had been out with her friend Cyndi, and it just went way over the time she had thought it would. Steeg knew Grace and Cyndi were best friends, with a history that stretched back to elementary school, so he didn't protest too much. Unfortunately, now it was too late to really do anything, except meet after Christmas Eve dinner and go to the midnight mass. He invited her over to his house, but she declined explaining that it would be better for her to stay home that evening, especially since the two of them were going to mass together. They agreed that he would be there around 10:30 and they would leave from there.

With the revelations of that morning's driveway shoveling still fresh in his mind, Christmas Eve at the Patterson's was, for Steeg, an excited, loud family gathering sprinkled liberally with frequent internal bursts of embarrassment every time he saw his mother looking at him. As far as Steeg was concerned, the whole matter had gone far enough with just his parents knowing. There was absolutely no reason for his younger siblings to know the truth – that he was a hedonistic sex maniac. Technically, he was still as virginal as a guy could be, but a hedonistic sex maniac just the same.

Their traditional Christmas Eve casual supper included homemade Christmas cookies, Yule Kaka, rolled lefse with butter and powdered sugar, a tray of fancy multi-colored hard candies, too-rich fudge, and some sliced fruitcake. Afterward, they settled in the living room around the tree and passed around the presents they had for each other (the really good stuff was to come the next morning). Steeg helped sort the packages, and the littler kids could barely contain themselves with the too slow sorting. Finally, everyone had their own pile of colorfully wrapped gifts as Steeg announced, "That's the last of them."

In seconds, the front room was an eruption of wrapping paper scraps and ribbon as everyone tore into their private hoard of goodies. It was a warm scene Steeg had known and look forward to every year of his life. It would be more than fours years before he would experience another.

And, it would never be the same again.

The size of the church surprised him. Inside, the ceiling had to be 40 feet high. Row after row of stiff wooden pews about half-full of parishioners stretched toward the center altar where the priest and attendants conducted the mass in Latin. Steeg didn't understand a word of it, but he could see that it was, indeed, a beautiful service. Grace sat next to him, a white laced cloth covering her head. Earlier she had instructed him to just do what she did after he had voiced his concern about not knowing exactly what to do or how to do it. As each prayer ended, she crossed herself before rising from their kneeling position, and Steeg did a poor imitation of the same.

He hadn't known what to expect from the service, but it struck him that it seemed like a ballet of sorts, neatly choreographed, with each movement and gesture purposeful and well scripted. The building itself was large with many truly beautiful statues. To Steeg, this would be the type of building God probably would like to live in – if He needed a building to live in.

The service was shorter than he expected. Toward the end, Grace excused herself to approach the altar and take Communion. Steeg stayed in the pew watching. *She's so beautiful,* he thought watching her as the priest administered the sacrament to her and others kneeling side-by-side at the altar. *I love her so much, Lord. Please help me know what to do.*

He had lost his heart to her completely. The only thing that mattered to him was her happiness. Sitting in the pew watching her as she walked back to him, out of nowhere came the thought that her happiness may not include him. The pain stabbed deep. The sorrow swelled up inside and he reached for the sudden heavy pressure in his chest. As she sat down next to him, he looked away to hide anything his face might reveal.

She leaned close to his ear and whispered, "It will be over soon, now."

"I liked the service," Steeg concentrated on the road as he drove.

"That's okay. You don't have to say that."

"I mean it. Really. It was different, but I liked it."

"I'm glad you came with me."

"Any time," he reassured her. After a bit, he asked, "I guess you go to confession regularly, then?"

"I went today..." Grace caught herself too late.

"Today?" Steeg glanced at her quickly then returned to the road ahead. "I thought you were with Cyndi today."

"I was. She went with me, actually. We had lunch together and talked about a lot of different things. I felt the need to go to confession, and she asked if I wanted company. I said yes and she and I went together. That's it."

They didn't say much more for most of the drive home. As he pulled the car to a stop in front of her house, Steeg leaned over and kissed her as softly as he could. Then he said, "It's important to you, isn't it, this Catholic business?"

She nodded.

Steeg left the car, walked around the front and opened her door. After he led her to the stoop, he asked her if it would be better for her if he were Catholic.

"That's not it," she replied. "It's me, not you. I need to figure some things out first."

"But, if I were Catholic, that wouldn't hurt, would it?"

She smiled at him. "No, I guess it wouldn't hurt."

He wanted to ask her what she had to confess to a priest that she couldn't tell him, but he said nothing. Instead, he gave her another soft kiss. "You have a happy Christmas morning, okay? I'll be over around noon."

"Okay," she said. She watched him walk back to the car, get in and wave as he drove away.

Chapter 8

Wedge Revisited

Steeg's stroke on the cue ball was flawless, and the neatly racked solid and striped orbs scattered across Wedge's pool table, sinking the five-, nine-, and two-balls.

"I've got solids," he smiled in satisfaction as Wedge grunted from the bar stool with a shake of his head. Steeg surveyed the table to carefully plot out his next shot. "Where's Cummings?"

Wedge shrugged. "Don't know, probably with 'Putts.'"

'Putts,' a very cute blond-haired young woman with a ready smile and the type of demeanor that silently reaffirmed her fragility, was Matt's steady girl from high school. Steeg wasn't sure why everyone called her 'Putts,' but everyone did.

"I thought they broke up?"

"At least twice since graduation. I guess her old man wants Matt to work for him in his shop."

"Sounds a bit too intimidating for Matt," Steeg offered, lining up an easy shot on the six-ball and sinking it with ease into the side pocket. "Although, I'd say it would be a good way to get him out of the kitchen and into a real job with a future."

Wedge nodded in agreement, draining his second bottle of Pabst since his friend had arrived. He left the stool, walked behind the bar to retrieve another bottle. "What about you? How's your Christmas?"

"Pretty good, I guess."

"I haven't seen you since last week, so you must have been busy doing something."

"Yeah, '...or something,'" Steeg repeated. He missed the next shot and he and Wedge traded places. He had left the cue ball in perfect alignment for an easy shot that Wedge immediately slapped sharply into the far corner pocket.

"You gettin' any from Grace?" His friend asked crudely.

"Come on, Wedge, don't talk like that." Steeg defended his girlfriend's honor.

"Hey, I just want to make sure she's treating one of our country's finest the way she should, that's all."

"Knock it off," he said more firmly.

"Okay, okay, I'll be good." He lined up his next shot, sunk it and the cue ball came to rest in another perfect alignment for his next shot, which he successfully handled with easy effort. The game was suddenly too close, and Steeg was one ball down.

Wedge searched the table for his next shot. "What did you get her for Christmas?"

"A necklace. It's one of those artisan jobs with hand crafted multi-colored beads, shiny metal things. Kind of 'hippie' like, you know?"

Wedge jabbed the tip of his cue in Steeg's direction. "No ring?! How can you two be together as long as you have and not taken it to the next level?!"

"Well, I also got her a big bunch of roses, too. How's that?"

Wedge shook his head in disgust. "Pretty poor, my good man, pretty poor."

Steeg threw up his hands. "What is it to you, anyway?"

"When are you two getting 'hitched?'"

The blunt question was something for which Steeg wasn't prepared. He had no immediate answer, and his silence was telling.

"You're not getting hitched, are you?" It was more of a direct statement than a question.

Steeg still said nothing, although he felt he should say something, anything.

Wedge lined up his next shot and it darted into the chosen pocket. Two balls ahead, he calmly added, "You two haven't done 'it' yet, have you?"

Steeg felt the hairs on the back of his neck bristle. His ego threatened, he had to counter with something. Wedge was bigger, stronger, and could probably beat him bloody if he wanted to, so Steeg used the one advantage he had as defense. "By 'It' you're referring to sex?"

"I'm referring to gettin' it on, that's what I'm referring to."

"That's private, Wedge. It's none of your business."

"That answers it. You ain't gettin' none."

Steeg's glare drilled directly into his friend's eyes. "I think 'ain't gettin' none' is something called an oxymoron."

"A oxie-what?!"

"Oxymoron. It's when you say something stupid and self-contradictory. They call it 'oxymoron' because it's usually a moron that says things like that."

Wedge didn't know how, but he was sure he had just been insulted. After a moment of deliberate thinking about it, he knew what he had to do. Surveying the table once more, he found his next position and proceeded to sink the remaining striped balls one at a time. He ended nicely with a nifty banked shot on the eight-ball into the called corner pocket.

Game over.

Disappointed, Steeg inspected the table now devoid of all things striped. "Nice game."

Wedge put his cue stick back on the wall rack, walked to the bar and took the stool next to his friend.

"Look, either you want to be with her, or you don't."

Steeg shook his head. "I do, but it's not that simple."

"Sure it is."

"No, it's not. There's nothing I'd like better than to take her with me to my next duty station. We'd set up housekeeping either on base or off, and just be together. For me, I can't imagine anything better."

"So, do it."

"I can't. It's not fair to her."

"That's crap."

"It's not, man. She's in college, working for a degree in social work. She's going to be really great at it. It's important for her. I should be helping her get that, not take her away from it."

"More crap."

Steeg impatiently sighed. "You don't know what you're talking about, Wedge. This is a really complicated deal."

Wedge nodded, agreeing. "Okay, but I'll tell you what – I know enough to know that two people can help each other get to where they need to get easier than one or the other doing it alone."

Steeg was overly harsh. "Where'd you get that, watching 'As the World Turns'? You know, when two people really care about each other, they really try to do what's best for the other. It's not all grabbing for what you can get. It's not just 'you' all the time. It's putting the other person first and you second. It's making sure you do nothing to hurt them and everything you can to help them."

Wedge nodded again. "Okay, let's say all that is true…"

"It is true!"

"Okay. It's true. Then tell me this — If you're not going to marry her, or, if you're not going to marry her in the foreseeable future, how are you helping her now?"

Leaning forward with elbows on the bar, Steeg rubbed both hands across his face in frustration. "I don't know. Maybe by not getting in her way so she can get done what she needs to get done. Maybe I'm helping that way."

Wedge shook his head. "And, in the meantime, you expect her to just wait for you to complete your tour of duty, fill in your time, forsake all others as she completes her studies and you complete your hitch in the Navy. Then, four years from now you two are back together, everything peachy-keen and you just pick up where the two of you left off?"

Steeg grimaced. "If you say Mankato is a 'party school' this conversation is over."

"I don't know if Mankato's a 'party school' or not. That's not the point. My point is simple. If you're not going to be together because it's not fair to her, then it certainly isn't fair to keep her dangling on some leash for four years and think she's going to like it, because she won't."

This stung. Steeg couldn't deny it. No, it wouldn't be fair to Grace either way, would it?

"So, what should I do?"

"Marry her," his friend said firmly. "Or, let her go."

Chapter 9

Leave 'Afoot'

Steeg had two questions, but he would deal with only one of them. The most obvious question concerned Grace and the real depth of her feelings for him. He knew Grace loved him, but he needed to know more. He needed to know the true extent of her personal commitment to what they shared and what they would build for their future together.

For Steeg, Grace always controlled what happened, what was done, what was not done, and ultimately, how anything turned out for either of them. He was more close to Grace than any other person he had ever known, family members included. Yet, with Grace, he had always felt she was the one keeping him at a predetermined distance, preventing their relationship from going to the next level, whatever that meant.

For Steeg, the 'next level' transcended sexual intimacy, which for him was an expression of personal commitment he was willing to wait for until they were both fully ready. That notwithstanding, Steeg needed Grace to consider something much deeper, something that would bond them closer as they grew old together; a richer, more rewarding spiritual intimacy the two of them could share.

This was dangerous territory for Steeg if only because to explore it with the love of his life, the two of them would need to discuss something they had never openly and honestly discussed before — God, and how their particular beliefs in Him were held in common, or, how they differed. If they were in agreement, it would be an exciting arena they could develop together. If, on the other hand, they shared little in common spiritually, it could be very difficult to grow to a level Steeg considered essential. It was an important issue. He just did not know how to discuss it with her.

Whether it was his changing circumstances, or simply a matter of growing maturity, Steeg found himself considering the truth of what God was in his life more frequently, and more seriously. He had come to believe God had taken a hand in bringing Grace and him together. If God somehow ordained their love, Steeg intuitively knew the spiritual aspect of their relationship had to become a two-way reality for them to grow. For Steeg, it simply made sense. He accepted it as a natural development in what he shared with Grace.

The second, more important question he needed to answer Steeg could not consciously acknowledge. That was because it simply didn't occur to him. He knew what was true for him — he needed Grace. He loved her, and he needed her. Period, end of statement. It was fact, and that was good enough for him. He accepted Gracie as God's blessing, a person Steeg believed to be extraordinary because he knew God intended her to be with him. God was like that, Steeg was certain: always doing things for him for His greater purposes. Grace was the best example of His grace. What Steeg didn't know was why he needed Grace so desperately. What was it that compelled him so completely to be with only this one person?

If he could have grasped the true answer to this second question, he would have understood everything, including Grace and all that had happened, or was about to happen, in an entirely new and different light. But, the second question would stay in his subconscious and not occur to him for a very long time.

All that mattered to Steeg was his love for Grace. What he didn't realize was his ability to answer both the obvious and the subconscious question suffered from a fundamental lack of understanding on his part — his lack of understanding God.

His deeper understanding of God was limited by the simple fact that he didn't even know what he didn't know. When it came to God, Steeg barely knew what he did know! Steeg was a product of a Christian-oriented upbringing lacking direction. After his resurrection, Jesus had promised his followers a comforter, the Holy Spirit. However, Steeg had not experienced that blessing, at least not in any way he could confidently acknowledge. His faith in God and in Christ's promises was simple and untested.

This lack of divine direction wasn't going to stop him from finding out whether or not Grace would forego college to be with him. If she said 'yes,' it would be elation beyond words followed in a microsecond by the fearful reality of having to deal with her parents' reaction, especially the reaction of her mother. Assuming that colossal hurtle was overcome, there would be the setting of the date, arrangements for the Catholic ceremony, the premarital Catholic instructions and the dealing with the Catholic expectations of his pending in-laws. It occurred to him that before any of this was done, it would be best for him to convert to the Catholic Church. That meant Catechism classes, and he had no idea how to do that in the Navy. Perhaps the base chaplain at his first duty station could advise him on that one.

What if she said she couldn't leave college? What if she said, 'no' to him? It would mean they'd have to let each other go, just as Wedge had said. Steeg didn't know if he could do that. No matter where he was going or what he was going to do in the Navy, he knew keeping her was the only way any of this made sense. Even if she said 'no' to his question, he'd hang onto her as long as he could, not for her sake, but for his.

The Tuesday following Christmas, his father had woken early to return to the daily grind of his job. Steeg, not having to return to anything, stayed in bed enjoying the aromas and sounds of his mother preparing his father's breakfast. He could hear the two of them talking in the kitchen below.

At the counter, his mother prepared sandwiches for her husband's lunch as his father ate breakfast at the kitchen table. "Well, at least you're working. There have been times in winter when there was no work."

From the kitchen table, his father paused between bites of 'eggs over easy'. "True enough. It's not cold enough yet. It will be, though."

"Steeg seems to have changed, don't you think?"

His dad made a noise, agreeing.

"He isn't as easy going as he used to be."

"He's still hung up on that girl." He shook his head as he scraped the edge of a half-eaten slice of toast across the remains of egg yoke on his plate, and then shoved it into his mouth.

"Gracie's a nice girl," Steeg heard his mother reply. She wrapped the two sandwiches in waxed paper, folding the edges clean and sharp, and then stacked the neatly enclosed pair into the well-used black metal lunch bucket his father always carried to work. She turned to the apple and banana she had placed on the counter earlier and placed them into the lunch pail next to the sandwiches.

His father washed down the last mouthful of his breakfast with a healthy swallow of black coffee. Returning the cup to the table, he said, "Sure, she's a nice girl. She's also Catholic. I don't know about that. That could be trouble."

Steam clouded up around her as Mrs. Patterson poured the hot water she had used for pre-heating the large Thermos down the sink drain. She then filled the Thermos with fresh, black coffee from the pot on the stove.

"She might be just what he needs right now," she said. "The Navy is changing him. I can see it. Besides, Catholic isn't much different from the Episcopalian Church at St. John's in Puerto Rico. Steeg's not all that unfamiliar with a lot of that kind of church stuff."

He watched his wife put the stopper in the Thermos, followed by the screw-on cup-lid. "Well, maybe. But, when we lived in Puerto Rico, I didn't have a whole lot of choice where to send the kid, or the other two, either. St. John's was the only English-speaking school in San Juan, next to the American school at the Army base, and we couldn't get him into that. Religious instruction every day, Mass twice a week, and who knows what else went on there besides the three 'R's' I don't know. It probably scarred him for life."

She walked over and placed the Thermos and full lunch bucket on the table. "I worry about that, scarring him for life. It wasn't an easy time for him back then, twelve years old, living in a foreign country, not speaking the language."

He left his chair to take his dishes to the sink. "That's probably why he was such a handful back then. The kid almost made me crazy with some of the stuff he pulled."

Her eyes saddened. "You were too hard on him."

He shot her a quick warning glance. "I did what I had to do. You weren't going to keep him in line, so I had to."

"All I'm saying is he changed in Puerto Rico. We lost our little boy in Puerto Rico. He hasn't been the same since then."

Walking back past the table, he took his jacket from the back of the chair and pulled it on. "He's not a little kid anymore. He's learning to be his own man. That's a good thing, all right?"

With his left hand, he picked up the Thermos and lunch pail by their handles, gave his wife a quick peck on the lips, and then turned to leave. At the door, he turned back to her.

"Look, I admit I made mistakes. I probably made too many when Steeg was growing up. But it's too late to do anything about any of that now. It just seems to me that you do the best you can with what you got. Sooner or later, you reach a point where you can't do anything else. Steeg's on his own now. I did the best I could to get him where he's at. For good or bad, whatever happens from here on out, it's his call."

She nodded sadly as her husband shrugged and reluctantly left for the Olds waiting in the garage.

Steeg heard the outside storm door swing closed. The clock on his dresser read ten minutes past seven o'clock. He turned his back to the clock, wrapping the blankets closer around him. He didn't like remembering Puerto Rico. He'd stay in bed for a while, and not get up for an hour or more after his father had left.

His father returning to work meant the car was not available during the day. Steeg was on foot in the daylight hours, and he didn't like it. But, it didn't stop him, either. Each morning without a car, he would call Grace first, and then walk the mile and one-half to her house. Her mother stayed in the kitchen while Grace and he sat on the front room couch or they went for a walk outside to nowhere in particular, talking about anything and everything as they enjoyed each other's company. The hours went by too quickly and more than once Steeg had the opening he was looking for to ask the question that wouldn't go away. But, he didn't ask it.

A couple of days would go by before he'd have his first best chance.

Thursday morning was met with the same sequence of events as the past two days. He called. He walked. He stayed with Grace in her parent's house.

As noon approached, Steeg asked her if she'd like to walk over to the Fireside Pizza Restaurant for lunch. She quickly agreed, and the two took an easy two-block stroll to Penn Avenue. The conversation was effortless and fun for both of them as they split a pepperoni pizza, the bustling rush of the few wait staff whirling around them in the busy compression of the lunch hour.

"You know, you're really easy on me," he offered.

"I know. It's my biggest fault," she joked.

"Seriously, it is so nice to be with you, every time."

"Of course," she was still being funny.

"Okay. I'm changing the subject now…"

"Not on my account, I hope."

"Always. Let's see… When do you have to return to classes?"

"The third, I think, although my schedule for next quarter doesn't have any classes on Tuesdays, so I don't think I have to be there until the fourth."

"You have a whole day without classes?"

She nodded taking another bite of pizza.

"I didn't know you could do that. I thought you had classes every day."

She shook her head, gently dabbing the greasy residue from her fingers onto a napkin as she explained between chews that sometimes the class scheduling just worked out differently. At least that's the way it was going to be for the coming quarter.

He reflected on that bit of information for a moment, realizing he had a logical opening for 'the question.' He decided to ease into it gracefully.

"So, how do you think it's all going with college?"

She shrugged. "About what I expected. Good grades. A lot of studying. More expensive than I'd like."

"Do you like it?"

She shrugged again. "It's about what I expected."

A waitress came to their table to offer refills on the drinks, and they both agreed. A moment later fresh sodas were placed in front of them.

Steeg leaned forward. "Gracie, if I, that is, if you were..." He grappled for the words that suddenly weren't as gracefully available as he had hoped.

"If I were, what?"

An exasperated sigh preceded a deep breath and another try. "What I'm wondering is, if I asked you to, you know, sort of leave, you know, college..."

Her eyebrows arched in surprise. He continued with gathering difficulty.

"Not forever, but temporarily, just for a while, so I could, that is, we, we could, you know, be together..." He searched her face for some indication that anything he was mumbling was connecting with her on any level. What gracefulness he thought he started with began to melt away along with his resolve. This was not the way he wanted this to go. "Wait a minute. Let me start over on this..."

Only, he couldn't start over. He was stumbling all over himself with doubt and uncertainty. And, with fear. *She had turned down the engagement ring, hadn't she? She's certain to turn me down on this, as well.* A short, clipped chortle escaped as he cleared his throat. She sat across from him waiting for him to continue, but he didn't know what to say next.

So, pointing a single finger in the air, he bought time for himself by shoving an entire slice of pizza into his mouth all at once. His mouth was so full, he could barely close it. She observed it all in disturbed silence as he slowly chewed the mass of dough and cheese down to a more manageable wad. As Grace continued to watch, she realized the remaining pizza slice resting in the round serving pan no longer held any interest for her.

Prior to swallowing, Steeg took a couple of preparatory sips of his soda to aid things along a bit. The liquid helped lubricate matters for him, and, finally, he finished with an uncomfortable cleansing gulp.

She followed her disappointed sigh with, "You were saying?"

He cleared his throat, mildly chuckling in response. "Yes, I was. I'm sorry about all that. I didn't think it was that big before I ate it! Funny how wanting to eat pizza before it cools off can blind you to how big the piece really is."

Grace wrinkled her nose in response.

Steeg's gastrological effort to buy time was wasted. He had lost his way in how he was going to ask her if she'd leave school to marry him, and he needed time to regroup. He needed a lot of time to regroup. So, he sat there, a vapid smile on his face, looking at her and saying nothing.

After several moments of sitting there waiting for him to pick up where he had left off, Grace broke the silence.

"Do you want to leave?"

"Good idea." He quickly paid the check.

They said little on the short walk back to her house, but the silence communicated a lot.

Steeg left her at her door, promising to return that evening to take her out for dinner and a movie. He could feel her eyes on his back as he hurriedly walked away, and the sensation didn't let up until he rounded the corner on 69th Street.

Halfway to his parents' home, he was still verbally abusing himself for his juvenile stupidity. He mouthed every thought as he kicked at the snow under his feet. *You're still a little kid, for the love of… !* He was angry with himself. He wanted to hit something. *There's no way you even come close to the maturity she sees every day on that campus. All those jocks with all those big… It doesn't matter! You're such an idiot! Why she stays with you… You idiot! Idiot!*

For the duration of the afternoon, he stayed in his father's special chair, rocking slowly, completely lost in his thoughts. His mother took notice without much comment. She could see in the way he avoided making eye contact that something was bothering her son. She wanted to help him, but beyond the terse "nothing" response when she asked him what he was thinking about, she knew of no way to force him to talk. So, hoping he'd open up to her when he was ready, she decided to get caught up on the house cleaning and laundry.

It was dark by the time Steeg saw his father turn into the driveway and pull up to the back door. Trevor Patterson walked into the house, saw his eldest son sitting in his favorite chair and swung a pointed finger at him.

"I'm going to want that chair in a minute," he warned with a smile, placing his empty lunch box and Thermos on the kitchen table. Steeg hurried into the kitchen to see his father and mother embrace as she stood at the stove stirring something good in a large pot.

"Dad, I'll trade you the chair for the car keys," Steeg offered expectantly. His father gave him a suspicious glance as he pulled his car keys from his jacket pocket and tossed them to his son.

"It's a deal," his father agreed. "Just make sure the tank's full when you get back."

Steeg promised it would be as he rushed to the phone on the wall to call Grace. He confirmed that he was coming over right away, ended the call with a brisk "See ya," and begged off dinner as he rushed to the bathroom for a hurried personal grooming check. In seconds he was back, grabbing his Pea Coat from the hook on the basement staircase wall, and leaving out the door.

His father shook his head as he peeled off his winter jacket and headed toward the bathroom to clean up for dinner. "Hormones," he sighed.

"Fantastic Voyage" with Raquel Welch in scuba gear. It was the perfect movie choice for the evening, destined to become a Holiday Season masterpiece, Steeg was sure. Showing at the Southtown Mann Theater, Steeg bought the tickets an hour before the show so he and Grace could grab a quick dinner at the Lemon Tree Restaurant just across the parking lot.

In the restaurant, after they ordered, Steeg jumped in with both feet.

"I really screwed up in the pizza place this afternoon, didn't I?" he asked, hoping she would say "No."

"Yes, you did," she agreed, and then quickly added, "But, I've been eating a whole lot better since you came home, so it's not all bad."

"I'm really sorry…"

"Don't be. I'm not. You take me to lunch, I eat. You take me to dinner, I eat. You take me to your house, your mom cooks, and I eat some more. It's been pretty nice, actually. You know, we don't have cook tops or anything like that in the dorm rooms…"

"I mean about how I screwed things up earlier today. I'm sorry about that."

Her grin gave way to a giggle. "I know what you mean. I'm just trying to help you not take things so seriously all the time. You've been a little less than the free wheeling camera stud I fell for in high school, you know."

"Well, we've talked about a lot of serious stuff since I've been back. It has been kind of a serious time what with you in school, me in the Navy, time running out with this leave – it's all pretty serious. Through it all, I guess I have been pretty boring."

"That is one thing you will never be." She reached across the table and took his hand into hers. "So, let's just get some things out of the way so we can enjoy the evening."

"Okay, what things are those?"

"First, yes, I still love you. Second, I still want to marry you. Third, we can't get married now, and we probably won't get married for a while yet. I could leave school to be with you, but we don't even know where you will be stationed yet, so we can't really set any plans in motion until all that settles down. And, finally, the best thing for both of us to do until then is to just continue doing what we are doing."

She batted her beautiful brown eyes at him several times. She had nailed it with such ease he was stunned. *How can she do that?* He wondered in amazement. Then, it hit him. *Did she just say she'd leave school to be with me?*

She squeezed his hand. "Okay?"

"Okay," he nodded, completely impressed and totally taken by this young woman's calmness under pressure. *She did say that about leaving school, didn't she?* He wondered again.

After dinner, in the darkened theater, they missed most of the film. Sitting in the back corner of the huge auditorium with no one within rows of where they were, most of the movie was spent with the two of them locked in deep kisses and tender embraces. The only time they really looked up at the screen was during the scene where Raquel Welch had been attacked by human anti-bodies. Stephen Boyd and Donald Pleasence had to peel the life-threatening organisms from her scuba suit, especially from around her chest area. It was a film destined to become a holiday classic, of that Steeg was certain.

Chapter 10

Keeping Busy

He woke up the next morning poorly after a night of shallow sleep. The edge of his bed in his old room provided the best place to look out from the narrow upstairs window across a small, heavily wooded backyard with eighty-year-old oaks now devoid of their leaves and color. Winter in Minnesota was usually a slate of grays and white. Through the single pane window glass outlined with iced frost, he could clearly see the snow on the ground and the covered roofs of the houses in the surrounding neighborhood. It was a quiet, cold morning.

With an uncomfortable tightness in his chest, his breathing required a little more effort than usual. The return flight to San Diego was coming Sunday evening, less than 60 hours away, and his anxiety level was increasing. Sitting on the edge of his bed looking out the window he could actually feel his time running out, slipping from his grasp. The anticipated loss pressed down on him especially heavy. It was a feeling he didn't like.

Grace's skillful summation of their situation at the Lemon Tree Restaurant the night before had comforted him. But, with dawn mercifully ending a less than satisfactory cold night of restless sleep, little of that comfort remained. The 'fairness' issue was still there, a whispering voice that wouldn't go away. Fundamentally, he agreed with her that, given all that was or was not within their control, they should just 'continue doing what we're doing.' Her intelligent and logical evaluation notwithstanding, Steeg wasn't convinced that it was the fairest thing for Grace.

He accepted that his fate was not his own. The Navy controlled it. Chances were good that he'd be going to war within the next year, and he had multiple years remaining on his enlistment. Who knew what would happen? Grace didn't know, and neither did Steeg.

Grace's fate, however, was completely in her hands. She had the power and freedom to plot her own course through college and beyond. She could do what she wanted with her life, when she wanted to do it. That was the way it should be, or so Steeg believed.

The gray of winter outside his window reflected the gray of his own gathering depression. He thought of Grace shackled to an anchor that prevented her from making changes she should make when she needed to make them. The anchor kept her from getting what she wanted, doing with her life what she wanted, and barred her from the rewards of her own accomplishment. He was her anchor. It was not a good thing for him to be.

In the downstairs bathroom, a hot morning shower did little to soak away the concern. He leaned under the steady steamy spray, letting the water pour over his head, across his shoulders and down his body, mentally trying to will the confusion all away. It did no good. Later, at the bathroom sink where Steeg slowly lathered his day old growth, he even more slowly scraped the razor across his face, pulling skin and pressing down so firmly the blade drew small dots of blood in many places. It took him more than twice the time as normal to shave that morning. With time running out, slowing everything down made an odd kind of sense to him at that moment. He cupped his hands under the running faucet and dowsed his face with cold water until all the blood trickles had disappeared. The Old Spice aftershave stung with a vengeance. He punished himself by splashing it on twice. A bath towel still wrapped around his waist, he leaned in close to the reflection in the mirror, searching for some acceptable answer he couldn't find. *Maybe there is no answer,* he thought more melodramatically than he realized, falling even deeper into his own self-pity. *Maybe there's only doubt, confusion and uncertainty every day for the rest of my life.*

Beyond self-pity, Steeg was angry. He was angry with the Navy, with the government, the Selective Service, himself and with God. He needed to hold onto Grace with everything he had, and he was angry at how everything in his life had not only stopped working for him, it now seemed to be working against him! The Navy was the easy target for blame, but he raged against more than the Navy. It was an assemblage of circumstances covering a list of conflicting factors: his age; his inability to support himself; his lack of education; his lack of finances; the Selective Service Board; a distant war growing larger and more desperate every day; a sense of duty and obligation to his country. He was even beginning to resent his devotion to someone he loved with all his heart. Now, more than ever, he wanted to put that someone ahead of himself. All of it was too overwhelming. Certainly, God should be helping him out here, clearing the way to make things happen the way they should happen. Yet, the obstacles remained. They even seemed to be increasing in number.

Trying to find in his mirrored reflection some kind of answer to all this, Steeg reluctantly accepted responsibility for the consequences of the poor decisions he had already made in his young life. The external forces working against him and Grace made her his lifeline. Hanging onto Grace would somehow see him through it all, save him and keep him whole. But, what was the price to her? He replayed what she had told him at the restaurant. She did say she'd leave school to be with him, didn't she?

He shook his head and groaned in frustration. Even if they were to marry, live together near his duty station, he could easily be shipped out, and then killed in a war zone somewhere. If that happened, what would happen to her? If they were married and it happened, if they had gone that far and he was killed, it would be terrible for her. He knew if the situation was reversed and he lost her, it would devastate him. That could not happen. He wouldn't set her up for that.

Returning upstairs to his old room, he dressed in clean jeans, a long-sleeved knit shirt that hung loose on his frame, and his old sneakers. Everything felt good on him, civilian clothes; civilian life. The dresser mirror showed a person older than he remembered. He was proud to serve his country, anxious to fulfill what he considered to be his responsibilities in that regard. But, standing alone in the room, looking at a man in the mirror he almost didn't recognize, Steeg wondered again if joining the Navy hadn't been the biggest mistake of his life.

It didn't occur to him that, in the greater scheme of things, he hadn't been given very many alternatives from which to choose.

In the kitchen, with his mother at the sink cleaning up the morning dishes, he sat at the table with a bowl of corn flakes and a cup of coffee. His father had left for work almost two hours earlier. His little brother Daniel was in the living room watching morning cartoons on the television. Mary was still in bed, while the two younger sisters had long since finished breakfast and were now playing together with their dolls in the cluttered basement family room.

"You know, Mom, what you need is your own car," Steeg offered between two quick spoonfuls.

His mother rinsed another plate and placed it in the strainer. "Can't afford it, Steeg. Cars are too expensive."

"Yeah, but, if you had your own car, then I could borrow it when Dad was at work," he explained with a smile. "I'd chip in for gas and maintenance. That would make the car cheaper, right?"

She was not convinced. "Well, maybe, but maybe not. I have an example of your car maintenance skills still sitting on blocks in the garage, you know?"

The embarrassing reminder of her seeing him and Gracie in the back seat of the old Buick brought a flush to his face. He quickly returned to his corn flakes without comment. Finishing his breakfast and bringing the bowl to the kitchen sink, he meekly offered, "I told Dad we should just junk the car."

His mother nodded. "That would be nice. It will free up the space in the garage."

Steeg agreed and quickly left for the basement and the safe solitude of the small photography darkroom he and his father had built early in his sophomore year in high school. The tiny room, essentially ignored since his graduation, was in need of a good cleaning. For the duration of the morning, that was exactly what Steeg did. Starting with the sink, then moving to the counters,

Steeg progressed to the chemical trays, utensils, film developer tanks, reels, drying cabinet, racks, the small, two-sided print drier, and finished with detailed work on the Beseller Enlarger and the two Minolta 35mm cameras he had stored in the bottom cabinet. When the room was finally at its best, it was past noon.

As he stepped from the darkroom door, he looked across the small utility room to see Grace standing there.

"Gracie!" he said in surprise.

"Hi!" she smiled as he kissed her. "I thought I'd surprise you."

"You've succeeded. I am surprised." He took her hand and led her from the utility room into the family room his sisters had vacated some time earlier. "You walk all the way over here?"

"Yes, I did," she proudly said.

"Why?!"

"To be with you, silly!" Her answer told him he had just asked a very stupid question.

He hugged her closely as they went back upstairs to the kitchen. They joined his mother at the kitchen table.

"Gee, Mom, thanks for telling me Grace was here," Steeg criticized, adding, "Darkroom is all cleaned up."

"She didn't want me to tell you," his mother parried with a smile. "As for the darkroom, big deal. How about cleaning up the bathroom, wash the walls, vacuum the carpets…"

"Wait a minute. I was just saying…"

His mother continued. "Laundry! There's a good one you could help out with."

The ribbing Steeg was suddenly getting warmed Grace. "I wanted to spy on you," she admitted.

"Spy? That's interesting," he wondered aloud. "There's something you don't know about me? I thought I had been completely open and honest with you about everything, but, noooooo! You need to spy on me."

"There's always something more a girl can learn," Grace rebuffed.

"I have always been truthful."

GRACIE'S GHOST – THE HAUNTING 97

"How do I know that?"

"Because I say so."

His mother draped the dishcloth over the faucet spout. "You two gonna fight now? You want me to leave the room?"

"No, Mrs. Patterson, I need you here to help me keep him honest."

Steeg wasn't sure where this was going, but he wanted to keep it light. "I'm as honest as the day is long!"

His mother walked over and patted Grace's hand. "Well, pretty honest, most of the time, I'd say. But, without question, he is completely loyal to every friend he has ever had."

Grace cast a knowing nod in his direction and Steeg smiled, satisfied with what he perceived to be his mother's defense of him.

"Loyal," Grace repeated. "I can see that. Like a little puppy. Yes, like a cuddly little golden retriever who licks your face every time you give him a hug."

His face fell. "Not exactly."

"Yes," she replied with a self-assured smile. "Exactly."

It was time to change the subject. "I'm hungry. What do we have for lunch, anyway?"

He came to his feet and walked toward the refrigerator. His mother quickly headed him off, offering to fix both of them something to eat as she directed her son back to his seat next to Grace.

Grace leaned over and reminded him in a whisper how well she had been eating since he returned from the Navy. Steeg nodded in somber agreement.

After a light but satisfying lunch of cold cut sandwiches on white bread and chicken noodle soup, the two of them did next to nothing for the rest of the afternoon. They simply stayed with each other, comfortable just being together. They watched an afternoon movie on the TV. Later, they listened to Johnny Canton's afternoon rock and roll radio program on WDGY AM 1130. Briefly, they paged through Steeg's high school yearbook, with him pointing out every photograph he had taken. It was a quiet day with little reason to do anything more.

Chapter 11

New Year's Eve

"You're invited over here tonight, if you'd like," Steeg said into the telephone receiver. "It isn't going to be much, just a few family friends, the next door neighbors I think, of course my dorky brother and sisters, but it's usually fun. There'll probably be some games and eggnog and punch. Count down to the New Year, that sort of thing."

She hesitated because she promised to attend her friend Cyndi's party and she had hoped he'd go with her to that.

"Yeah, but I don't think Cyndi likes me all that much." It was a lame excuse that didn't fly with her at all. "Yeah, I know you have, and you've been great letting me drag you all over town since I've been back...

"No, I'm not embarrassed to be seen with you...

"You want me to wear what? Oh, gees, no. I'd really rather not do that... Yeah, I know you think I look sexy in it, but I like regular clothes, especially when everyone else is wearing regular clothes... Please? Thank you... Okay, how are we going to work this? When does her party start? Then, when do we leave for my folk's place? No later than that? Okay, that's workable. I'll clear it with Dad." He told her he loved her, waited to hear her hang up on her end, and then returned the receiver to its cradle.

His father sat at the table the entire time, listening.

"Dad, about tonight," he began, but his father stopped him.

"I need the car until dinner time tonight. I've got a toilet install for a friend that I promised I'd do this afternoon. When I'm back from that, you can have the car as long as you promise you're not going to drink and drive."

Steeg smiled assuredly. "I promise."

"And, you promise to bring it back with a full tank."

"I promise."

"And, you don't do anything in it that I wouldn't do."

"Come on, Dad, that thing in the garage just kind of happened..."

"I meant driving safely, no doing 'donuts' in the snow, or trying to impress people with your big car. I wasn't thinking of the 'back seat' thing at all. I kind of figured you learned your lesson on that one."

"Oh. Yeah. I promise."

Cyndi's party surprised him. It was not what he had expected. Her parents were nowhere to be found, and the total number of attendees equaled only seven people, including him and Grace. The small West Richfield house was dimly lit with candles in the main rooms, only the kitchen was well lit by a lone ceiling fixture encased in a plain white globe. The kitchen table was a staging area for hard and soft beverages, an assortment of packaged snack foods, and a large pot of miniature meatballs in a sweet red sauce of some sort that Steeg found tasty, but unfamiliar. Too loud music from a too small hi-fi stereo console blared over the conversations of the scattered puddled groups in the two small common rooms of the house. At that moment, it was "The Isley Brothers" with their hit *"Shout"* drowning out all but only the closest mouths straining to be heard over the song. The racket was out of proportion with the small crowd.

As usual, the three girls had congregated among themselves, finding their space in the dining area adjacent to the main room. This left the four guys to mostly lounge around in the living room, drink beer, rum and cokes, or something softer and look at each other. Seated on the sofa, Steeg had struck up a casual conversation with a sandy-haired, broad shouldered young man named Michael who sat one vacated cushion away. Michael attended Mankato State and was dating Cyndi.

"At a party?" Steeg verified.

"Yep, and we've been dating ever since," Michael completed his wordy narrative on how he and Cyndi had met, and took another swig from his beer can.

"The party was at school?" Steeg continued.

"Yep, and we've been dating ever since," the young man repeated, apparently unaware that he had just said that.

"I hear there are a lot of parties at Mankato."

"Oh, yeah, that's true," Michael agreed. "You know, if you wanted to, you could find parties and girls every night down there."

"You don't say," Steeg glanced over to Grace seated at the dining table on the other side of the room in deep discussion with Cyndi. The other young woman he didn't know sat across the table from them.

"I do say!" Michael boasted.

"So, you and Cyndi are pretty serious, then?"

"Serious?" the college student took another swig. "What do you mean?"

Steeg shrugged. "You know, serious: like a meaningful relationship, growing closer, building a future. You know, serious."

"Oh, hell no!" Michael denied, laughing. "Why the hell would I do that with a whole college loaded with more pussy than any one guy could possibly handle?!"

Steeg was suddenly disappointed in the man. "Ah. Yes. I see."

"So, Cyndi tells me you're a high school year book photographer?" Michael changed the subject.

"Well, I was when I was in high school."

"What are you doing now?"

"I'm in the Navy, actually. Home on leave."

"The Navy?!" Michael leaned back and looked him over with a leery eye. "Why?!"

Suddenly, Steeg was very thirsty. He politely came to his feet. "Well, it seemed like a good idea at the time. I'll be back, Mike. I need something to drink."

He headed into the kitchen to find a beverage, any beverage. Remembering his promise to his father about not drinking and driving, he picked a Coke from a Styrofoam cooler and popped the top. His quick downing of about half the can was followed shortly by a satisfying belch. That was when the music fell away, filling the house with sudden silence as the overworked stereo changed LP's. Within seconds, a rocking Beach Boys' guitar riff filled the house, and the familiar lyrics felt good to hear.

> *Well, she took her Daddy's car*
> *and she cruised to the hamburger stand, now.*
> *Seems she forgot all about the library*
> *that she told her Old Man, now...*

He hummed the bouncy melody to himself and turned to look for Grace, whom he nearly crashed into entering the kitchen he was just leaving. She grabbed his arm and pulled him to the corner of the small room.

"You're not going to believe this," She said excitedly.

"Probably not," Steeg agreed.

"Guess who thinks she's pregnant?" she leaned in close to him.

Steeg felt a chill run down his back as he looked into her eyes, searching. "Gracie, we've come real close sometimes, maybe too close sometimes, but I don't think we could have possibly gone that far..."

She socked him hard into his shoulder. "Not me, you dummy!"

"Oh, yeah, I know that," Steeg quickly agreed again.

She leaned in close and whispered strongly into his ear. "Cyndi!"

Steeg looked around her to the archway leading into the living room. He couldn't see Cyndi from where he stood.

Grace pulled him back to face her. "Cyndi thinks she's pregnant!"

"How did that happen?" Steeg was a little confused.

Her look told him she suddenly realized how stupid he really was. "How do you think it happens?"

The best he could do was stutter. "I don't mean, 'how did it happen?' I mean what happened, that made this happen. That is, caused this sad thing, unfortunate, uh, event to happen?"

"I was there when it happened," Grace gushed, keeping her voice down. It was Steeg's turn to give her an accusatory look. She shook her head. "I don't mean I was actually with them when they did 'it.' I mean I was at the party where they did 'it.'"

"They did 'it' at a party?"

She nodded as she hurriedly explained. "They just met before Thanksgiving. It was at a party at a frat house, and he started hitting on her right there, at the party, you know. Anyway, after awhile, she disappeared with him – she just tonight told me they went up to a room on the second floor and, you know, did 'it' right there. Well, she's late. Really late."

"Late? For what?"

She socked his shoulder again, only harder. "You got three sisters, and you don't know what I mean when I say she's 'late?'"

"Oh. That." Steeg nodded. Still rubbing his shoulder, he leaned in closer to her. "This is that Michael guy?"

She nodded, and Steeg felt unexpected compassion for Grace's friend. Even though he knew Cyndi didn't like him, it was no reason not to feel a little sympathy for the situation she was facing. This was especially true if only because of the kind of person Michael seemed to be.

"That's too bad. What's she going to do about it?"

"She doesn't know," answered Gracie. "She wants to tell Michael, but she doesn't know exactly how to bring it up."

Steeg shrugged and raised an eyebrow. "Well, she could say nothing at all, let enough time go by and maybe he'd get the message after a few more months."

She hit him really hard in the shoulder, hard enough to elicit an audible "Oow!" from Steeg.

"This is serious!" she scolded. "Why I even bother to tell you anything, I don't know." And, with that, she turned and left him standing alone in the kitchen.

It had not been a playful punch, nor was it an unfamiliar one. Cyndi was her best friend and Gracie's protective response was understandable. Still, his patient, kind, and polite understanding didn't ease the lingering pain in his shoulder.

"She's so physical sometimes," Steeg said to himself returning to the front room as he rubbed away the stinging reminder of her too-violent rebuke.

The party progressed slowly, giving Steeg ample opportunity to introduce himself to the two other young men, Richard and Walter. Both were students at Mankato State, as well. Both were business administration majors. Walter had come to the party with a date. Richard had come stag. They were friends from Wayzata High School before registering at Mankato. Walter's date was an attractive freshman named Jessica. Like Michael and Cyndi, Walter and Jessica had met at a campus party. Both Walter and his friend Richard were a little drunk.

"So, this Navy thing," Walter slurred over his freshly mixed rum and coke. "How do you think that's going to work out with you and Grace?"

Steeg could see Grace still huddled in conversation with Cyndi at the dining room table. Jessica still sat in the chair opposite from the two friends. He looked back to Walter. "Well, that is problematic."

Richard rolled his eyes as he gestured toward Grace and said a little too loudly, "I can see where it would be, Swabbie!"

Steeg blushed slightly, noticing a head or two turning toward his direction.

"It's not that it can't work out – it can," Steeg defended. "She's got a good thing going at college…"

"Going on the side, you mean?" Richard asked, too loudly again, and obviously too drunk. Steeg was quickly becoming irritated, but he let it pass.

"She's got a lot on the ball…"

"I'll say!" Richard laughed.

"By that, I mean," Steeg poked his finger firmly into Richard's chest to make the point and to encourage the young man to gain self control. "The girl is the smartest person I've ever met. Whatever she ends up doing, she's going to be excellent at it."

Walter could see his friend was having a little bit too much 'fun', so he stepped in to help Steeg out. "I think Dickie could use a little break, right now."

As Walter led Richard down the hall toward the bathroom, it was Steeg who felt relieved. He could see Grace still engrossed with her friend at the dining room table. He wished he could leave with her right then, but he stayed where he was. In a few moments, Walter came back offering Steeg one of two rum & cokes he was carrying.

"Sorry about that, Steeg," Walter offered, slightly slurring his words again. "He gets that way sometimes."

"It's okay," Steeg pretended to sip from the drink Walter had handed to him.

"Still, he has a point," Walter continued. "I don't know how the two of you are going to handle the separation. It's gotta be tough on you. I mean, always being away, not being with your girl, wondering who's hitting on her when you're not around. Man, it would drive me crazy if that were me and Jessica."

The way Walter had said it bothered Steeg. At first, he actually thought Grace would have too much self-respect to let someone 'hit' on her. But, within an instant he knew how 'Pollyanna' that thought was. Of course she was 'hit' on down in Mankato, probably daily; indeed, probably in every class, and every break between classes. How could he expect her to be immune to that? How could he expect her to resist that kind of pressure, every day, day after day? He looked over to her. She was turned away from him, so he could only see her back.

It was then that he realized if she left him for someone else while he was away, it would destroy him. The complete, open and honest realization of his own vulnerability came crashing down around him in that single, crowded blip in time. He was almost frozen in numbing shock as it hit him all at once.

"You okay, man?" Walter asked. Steeg, mouth hanging slightly open, staring at nothing, didn't reply. Walter tugged at his elbow. "Hey, Steeg, you okay?"

A slight nod of his head put Walter at ease.

"Well, that's good. For a moment there I thought you might have mixed your stimulants with your depressants."

Another slight nod as Steeg's mind flew into gear. *If she dumps me for some other guy, and I'm on the other side of the world, what will I be able to do? Nothing, absolutely nothing. Why would she dump me? Would she dump me?*

Outta sight, outta mind...Absence makes the heart grow fonder...A bird in the hand...Marry this girl, now...Continue doing what we are doing...It isn't fair... It isn't fair... Not for her... Not for me...

"You sure you're all right?" Walter asked again.

"Sure," Steeg replied, taking the drink firmly to his mouth and tossing it down in a couple of heavy gulps.

Throughout the rest of Cyndi's party, Steeg stayed within sight with Grace, but gave her the time and space she seemed to need to be with her friend. It was strange to him, this consoling aspect of her character. It was a side she did not display to him, but a side he had seen her share with others. Their all-night graduation party came to mind. For many students, the party had begun as a booze-smuggling exercise to challenge the small army of chaperones. More often than not, the adults spotted the culprits at the door. Efficient frisking had produced enough confiscated liquid refreshment to cover a large table with more bottles than Steeg had ever seen in one place. It was Steeg's first 'All Night' party, and he wanted to try all the planned activities. Grace, on the other hand, spent almost the entire night in the converted dance hall where the bands played loud music, and where she could find the largest concentration of students and just sit talking. He would stay with her for a while, and then excuse himself as he left for the game rooms, or the movie room, or the food area, each time returning to the dance floor and finding her talking to someone else about who knew what. It made him feel only slightly jealous, so he ignored it back then. He ignored it now, too.

Nevertheless, throughout Cyndi's party, Steeg's mind worked overtime. Although Grace had said that continuing doing what they were doing was okay with her, it was becoming obvious that it was not okay with him. For Steeg the solution was marriage. He wanted her. He wanted her with him. He didn't dispute the facts that his current enlistment status and the complications he would most certainly face with her family – specifically her mother – made for a difficult challenge. But, it was a challenge he was willing to accept. Nor did he argue that his situation was most probably solvable only farther down a timeline that obviously extended beyond his present two-week leave from Boot Camp.

That meant he was stuck with the 'continue doing what we are doing' scenario whether he liked it or not. He didn't like it. Knowing what would happen if she left him – if she 'Dear John-ed' him while he was stationed on a boat in the middle of some ocean somewhere, unable to reach her, unable to hold onto her – was more than upsetting him. It hadn't even happened, and it hurt too much already.

It was still eating at him after they had arrived at his parents' house. Nearer to midnight, in the kitchen his mother and Grace made ready the beverages – punch for the kids and champagne for the adults. Steeg walked in from the front room with an empty cookie tray.

"They need more cookies?" his mother asked.

"I think they've O.D.'d on the cookies, Mom." Steeg put the cookie tray on the counter. "But they might go for more of your spiked eggnog."

His mother explained that they were going to pass out the punch and champagne in a few minutes, and the eggnog was running low anyway.

"That's because it's spiked," Steeg replied.

His mother opened the cookie tins, arranged a variety of gaily decorated holiday cookies on the tray and handed it to Steeg to take back into the living room. As he exited the kitchen, Grace turned to her boyfriend's mother.

"He's bothered about something, isn't he?"

Steeg's mom shrugged as she returned to her careful filling of the plastic champagne flutes. "He's not looking forward to going back tomorrow."

Grace looked toward the living room, unable to see Steeg. "I guess not."

Just short of 1:00 a.m., Steeg and Grace once again shared space on her parents' living room sofa. The house was quiet and her parents were in their bedroom asleep. She held his hand in hers. He looked at her, not really knowing how to say what he felt he had to say.

"I'd like to go with you to the airport tomorrow," Grace said.

"That would be nice," he smiled back at her. "It would mean a lot to me to have you there."

She nodded.

They sat there for several minutes, not saying anything, not really looking at each other, just holding hands and sitting on the sofa. Finally, after a long while, Steeg took her left hand into both of his and held it up to lightly kiss her ring finger.

"More than anything, I wanted that engagement ring to be on your finger before I left," he started. She smiled a little as she looked away. He continued. "But, then, I had to be honest with myself about why I wanted you to have the ring, and it wasn't for the right reasons."

Concerned, perhaps confused, she looked at him. "What do you mean?"

"I mean my reason for it wasn't pure. It was driven by lack of trust in you, or lack of trust in me, or because I was afraid that without it, I'd lose you some how."

She kept looking at him, but said nothing.

"And, that meant the ring wasn't as pure a symbol of my love and devotion for you as it should be. It was a kind of 'Hands Off' sign to keep guys away when I'm not around; it helped me protect my interests. It should honor you and what we hold for each other, our promises to each other, the future we hope to build together, but it wasn't that at all was it? If we're not ready for marriage, Gracie, we aren't ready to be engaged, either. Not until or unless my trust in you is stronger than my own pettiness, jealousy and self-doubt."

She touched his arm gently as she said, "That's okay. That's good, really…"

"Maybe," he interrupted. "Maybe not. There's more, and you may not like it."

Steeg turned to face her on the sofa, taking both her hands into his.

"Grace, if you love me, you will be here when I come back. If I love you, I'll come back for you. If, for some reason, you find someone else who makes you happier, or fills you with more joy than what you do for me, you should be free to be with that person. Your happiness is what should really matter."

At first, it didn't register with her. Then, her eyes filled with tears that soon overflowed and fell down her face. "Are you breaking up with me?"

The words she sobbed sliced into his heart. *Oh, God! This is so hard.* His own pain increased beyond what he felt he could endure.

"No, I can't. I love you too much to just walk away." He tried to hold her eyes with his, but she wouldn't look at him. "At the same time, I love you too much to keep you a prisoner for four years until I'm done with all this."

Tears continued to fall. She pulled away to the end of the sofa and sobbed again, "You are breaking up with me."

"I don't want to."

She wrapped her arms in close to her chest, covered her mouth with her hand to muffle her quiet weeping. He sat there, not reaching for her even though he wanted to with everything that was in him. He felt like his guts were kicked in. How he could say these things to her, he didn't know. He wanted to take it all back. It was too late.

"Grace, I'm so sorry. But, it just seems to be the right thing to do. You said it yourself — we're not in a good position to take things to the next level right now. We'd have to wait for years, anyway. This way, if something happens to me, you won't have to carry it with you. You'll be free to be with who you want to be, without guilt, or anything like that."

She sat for a long while, her face wet with tears, resigning to what was happening. She searched his face for some thing something he wasn't saying. When she couldn't find it, she said, "Steeg, I want you to know you're a very special person to me. No matter what happens, you'll always be in my heart. I thank you for loving me as much as you have. It has meant more to me than I can say."

She sagged back into the sofa, tired, and defeated. He reached over and put his hand on top of hers. For a long time he sat there with her. They said nothing. Only her quiet sobs, now fewer, could be heard.

It was a while longer before he slowly came to his feet.

"I'm sorry I've hurt you," he offered meekly. "I didn't want that."

"I know," she said as she followed him to the door. "I'm all right."

It had been snowing heavily since their arrival at her house. Large gloppidy flakes had quickly coated everything in sight. He turned back and took her face into his hands. She returned his soft kiss, her lips still damp from her tears. She held him close for a long embrace, then let go. She watched him go down the walk to his father's car parked at the curb. He looked back and held up an open hand to her as she stood in the doorway. He climbed in behind the wheel, started the car and drove off down the street. She slowly closed and latched the front door.

Less than two blocks away, feeling like he was going to throw up at any minute, he repeatedly pounded the steering wheel with his fist.

"You idiot! You idiot! You idiot!" he screamed at himself with every blow of his hand. He broke hard, throwing snow up around the car, and slid to a halt in the middle of the street, slamming his hands into the steering wheel several more times in the process. He couldn't let this stand. Taking the next left, he drove down the block, took another left, and drove to the street that led back toward her house. At the corner before her block, he pulled to the curb and turned off the car. The heavy falling snow had already deposited more than three inches on the ground. From his new position, her house looked completely dark. The lacy shroud of falling snow turned eerie in the glow of the corner street lamp as he sat in the car, wondering what he should do next. He didn't know. He didn't have a clue as to what to say to her that would fix the mess he had made only a few short minutes before. He sat alone in the car, the quiet snow falling all around him.

After several more minutes, he saw a lone figure half a block ahead and barely visible through the shower of snowflakes. Whoever it was, they were walking toward the intersection where he was parked. Steeg turned the wiper switch to clear the gathered snow from the windshield for a better view. From the size and the way the person was moving, he recognized it was Cyndi.

The interior light streamed from the open front door of her house, and Steeg saw a jacketless Grace run down the front yard and across the street, only to slide out of control and fall on her backside, kicking up a cloud of snow at Cyndi's feet. Steeg sprang from the car and ran across the intersection to gently pick her up and make sure she was okay.

"Steeg?" Grace said as his strong arms slid under her and helped her to her feet. "I thought you left?"

Steeg looked at her, then at Cyndi, then back to Grace. "Well, I did. I just wanted to, well, to… are you okay?" He tried to change the subject. "That was a nasty fall."

"I'm fine," she said, brushing herself off.

"Yeah, she's fine," Cyndi added harshly, taking her friend by the arm and walking past him toward the house.

"Look, Grace," he began before she was too far away. "About tonight, we should talk more tomorrow, don't you think?"

"Sure, Steeg," she said over her shoulder as the two girls walked up to the front door of the house. "Call me tomorrow."

And, then she was gone.

Chapter 12

The Return to 'The Devil's Brigade'

He couldn't sleep, so at 2:30 in the morning he crawled out of bed, slipped his clothes back on, tied on his sneakers, bundled up in the Pea Coat, his father's woolen hardhat liner skull cap and went out to retrieve a snow shovel from the garage. The snow was still falling, and the accumulation on the driveway was above his ankles and growing. It took him nearly a full hour to clear his way to the street. With the snow falling as heavily as it was, when he reached the street and turned around, the farthest part of the driveway looked as if it had hardly been touched. That suited him fine. He wasn't tired, and it felt good to do some heavy lifting. So, he trudged back to the top of the drive and started over.

When the driveway was done a second time, he cleared the front walk that wrapped around from the driveway to the front door. Then, he cleared the steps leading to the back door. Then, he cleared the back yard patio, along with about four inches of packed ice that had been collecting on the patio concrete since the start of the season. It was hard work. He needed it. After the patio was cleared to the edge, Steeg returned to the driveway. The rate of snowfall had slowed to almost nothing as he started to clear the pavement to the street a third time. Now, when he finished, the driveway was cleaned to the edges, barely a flake remaining on the entire length of asphalt. As he looked it over with satisfaction, he felt the ground tremble before he saw the flashing yellow lights. A city snow plow made the turn and moved down his street, leaving a two-foot tall by eight foot wide uniform barrier of snow in its wake, completely blocking the foot of the driveway entrance as the plow passed by. The plow driver looked straight ahead, never acknowledging Steeg's presence or his effort. The wall of snow that now blocked his father's driveway was tall, wide, and packed heavy – a great deal heavier than the snow he had just finished clearing. Down the street, the lights of the snow plow were shrinking away. Steeg took up his shovel one more time to clear the freshly dumped obstruction.

It was past 5:00 a.m. by time Steeg returned to the house, pulled off his sweat soaked clothes and collapsed into bed. He was asleep in less than a minute.

When he awoke, he cursed at the side table clock that read 11:37. Less than 4-1/2 hours remained before he had to be at the airport. He immediately headed for the downstairs shower to clean up. In record time he was done, and with a towel wrapped around his waist, he called Grace from the kitchen phone, made a lunch date with her, and sprang upstairs to get dressed.

He expertly guided the Olds Delta 88 down the once snow covered side streets, now virtually dry in the midday sunlight. The drive was short and quick. He pulled to a stop at the curb in front of Grace's house. She had been waiting at the window, so she stepped from her front door before he was half way up her snow covered walk. They kissed and embraced warmly as he whispered "I missed you."

"Me, too," she smiled at him, and with her hand in his, walked to his father's car.

They had lunch at the Perkin's Restaurant on 66th Street, sitting in the same booth as before. They ordered, and when the food came, he barely touched his cheeseburger and fries as he desperately tried to explain the night before and apologized for everything. It had all been a mistake, he told her. He only wanted to do what was right for her, but he knew what he had done the night before was all wrong as soon as he had left her at the door. That was why he had come back, but he didn't know how to make it right, so he sat in the car and did nothing. Then she had run out into the snow and fallen. He thought she had hit the ground too hard and he was worried she had hurt herself. He apologized again.

Throughout his soliloquy, Grace would thoughtfully nod her head and not miss a bite of her chicken salad sandwich. He marveled at how she could always eat even under the most difficult of circumstances. He told her he loved her more than ever. He wanted to ask her if she still loved him, to reassure him that he hadn't blown it totally away, but he knew that wouldn't do at all. Instead, he asked her if she still wanted to see him off at the airport. She nodded, eyebrows raised as she vigorously chewed her final bite of sandwich.

He felt better.

It was approaching 2:00 p.m. by the time they were ready to leave for his parents' house. Steeg still had some packing to do, and she asked if she could help. He genuinely appreciated the offer, telling her "Absolutely," as he led her to the car for the drive home.

Somewhere high over the Western Plain States, he could still feel the warmth of her lips on his. At the terminal gate, as he said a final 'good bye' to everyone, Grace had flung her arms around his neck and, in front of his parents, little brother, and sisters, she kissed him deeply. As she pulled away the familiar mischievous smile accompanied a pink blush to her cheeks. He pointed his finger at her and said, "You write. Every day. I need your letters."

Steeg exited through the gate toward the waiting aircraft without looking back. With everything that was in him, he didn't want to go. If he looked back, he wasn't sure he would have the strength to keep walking down the ramp to the airplane.

Now, seated next to the window, still feeling her kiss, he resolved to make this thing right for both of them. How that was going to happen, he didn't know, but he committed himself totally to making it work somehow. He completed his first letter to her before the plane crossed the Rockies. A second letter was written before touchdown in San Diego.

Chapter 13

Change in the weather

0530 HOURS
14 APRIL 1969
USS HORNET CVS-12
YANKEE STATION VIETNAM PATROL DUTY
GULF OF TONKIN

"I don't know, John," Tom Kinsey cupped his hands behind a head thick with flaming red hair, leaned back into the ugly blue vinyl sofa, and propped his feet up on a gray metal vinyl padded chair in front of him. The freckle-faced young sailor knew Second Class Petty Officer John Dickenson to be a straight shooter, a born-again Christian and not the type to broker gossip. Still, Tom couldn't see much profit in talking about a fellow shipmate behind his back.

"It's just that he's kind of dropped out of our little study group," John explained. "I thought you might have some idea as to what might be bothering him, that's all."

Tom shrugged again, squirming just a bit to avoid the lumps in the sofa, and maybe to relieve the uncomfortable feeling he was getting from John.

John apologized. "I'm sorry, Tom. I didn't mean anything by it, really."

Tom quickly countered to put the other man at ease. "No. That's all right. Maybe he just needs a break from the routine. It's been a long cruise. We all get tired."

"True enough," John agreed with a humorous chuckle. "'Twelve on-twelve off' gets a little old after a half year or so, doesn't it?"

Tom nodded in agreement. "You know, John, officially you're his superior. You're a second class P.O., and he's just a third. You could order him back into the group if only to talk about what's buggin' him."

John smiled as he shook his head. "Bible study allows you opportunity to talk about a whole lot of things, Tom, but there's an unwritten rule against pulling rank." The lanky, blonde-haired Nebraskan rose to his feet. "Look, when you see him, ask him if I can buy him a milk shake at the gedunk sometime, will you?"

"Sure," Tom nodded. "His shift starts at 0600. I'll see him then."

John warmly smiled his thanks, and turned to leave the hanger deck crew's lounge. Teddy Bear left his chair at the far side of the lounge and joined Tom on the sofa.

"What was that about?" Bear asked.

"He's concerned about Steeg."

"What's wrong with Steeg?"

"Probably nothin', but, maybe somethin'. Who knows?" Tom lowered his ball cap over his eyes to either try to nap or try to end the conversation before it got much deeper. Bear wouldn't let his friend off that easily.

"In Subic, I barely saw the guy," Bear offered. "We used to hit the beach all the time in Subic, if only for survival purposes."

"Yeah, me, too," Tom replied from under the cap brim. "Had a great time in Sasebo over Christmas."

"But, not lately."

"No," Tom agreed. "Not lately."

After several moments of silence, Tom thumbed his ball cap back on his head, and pushed up to a more erect sitting position.

"We went into Singapore together, Bear," he said. "Things happened there I didn't like."

Bear laughed, "Yeah, like the entire bar district just about got leveled in a race riot!"

Tom shook his head. "No. Steeg and I weren't in that mess. We went into town. Bright and early, we got a bus to the Thai Gardens – you know the place with all those fancy oriental sculptures, statues and stuff. That was really something. Unusual artwork, unusual plants. Very oriental-ish. It was kinda neat. Later that afternoon, back in town, we actually went to a movie. 'Romeo & Juliet' playing at a big old movie house. Really a great film. That Olivia Hussey, she played Juliet, she's gotta set on her..."

"I thought you said you didn't like what happened in Singapore?"

"Yeah, I was getting to that," Tom regrouped. "After the movie, Steeg seemed different. I didn't think much of it at the time. I don't know, Bear, maybe he was upset about something. Anyway, I figured we'd catch a cab to go get something to eat. We didn't. We caught a cab and Steeg slipped the driver some Singapore cash and told him to find us some hookers."

"Hookers?!" Bear blinked. "Steeg?! Our Steeg?!"

"Yeah, of all things to do, that was one thing I didn't want to spend my meager pay on. But he insisted. So, the driver took us to a place where a pimp had two girls for hire. We sat in this dingy little room and Steeg bartered with the guy for a while. They reached some kinda agreement. Then this pimp turns to me and asks me if I liked either one of his girls. I couldn't believe what I was hearin'. I took Steeg into the hallway and told him I didn't want no girls or what he was planning, and that we should chuck all this and head back to the ship."

"What did Steeg say about that idea?"

"He said, and this is a quote, Bear, he said, 'Look, Tom, you don't want to have some fun, that's okay by me, but I gotta get laid before I go back to that ship!' So, he went back into the room with the hookers and the pimp, and I took the cab back to the ship."

"That was it?"

"That was it. I didn't see him again until we left port. I don't know where he was, or what he was doing, but I have a pretty good idea."

"Yeah, really," Bear agreed, now concerned. "It doesn't seem to fit the nice, clean cut Minnesota guy we both know, does it?"

"Not really."

"What's going on with him?"

"That's what John wanted to know. Steeg doesn't go to their Bible study meetings anymore."

"Any wonder? A guy who picks up hookers in Singapore going to 'Meetin'' on a regular basis? Doesn't make sense," Bear shook his head. Just then Steeg walked into the lounge, a freshly filled coffee mug in hand. Santini and Tyner followed right behind him.

"What doesn't make sense?" Steeg asked, taking a healthy, yet cautious, sip of the steaming black stuff.

"Just about everything around here," Bear volunteered, covering the conversation he and Kinsey had been sharing. "How you doin', Steeg?"

"4-0 and squared away," came the crisp reply as the petty officer placed the mug on the table, pulled his leather gloves from his back hip pocket, and took a chair, slipping the gloves on as he sat down. "Where's the rest of your crew?

"On deck policing the bays," Tom offered.

"That's good," Steeg said, lifting the cup to his lips. "Quiet night?"

"Like the dead," Tom continued. "No flight ops. Nothing really going on right now. Beats me. We're in a frickin' war zone and we don't even have birds in the air on RECON."

Steeg nodded with understanding. "It's Nixon. It's his 'no bombing' policy as long as the North Vietnamese stay at the peace talks in Paris."

Tom spat, his anger showing. "Dumbest thing I ever heard of. It was the bombing that got them to the peace talks in the first place. They take the better part of a year just to decide on the shape of the table, for gawdsake. Now, we stop bombing Hanoi because of what? You keep the pressure on, you get what you want. You don't keep the pressure on you get what the other side wants. Gees, it's driving me nuts!"

The other sailors in the lounge nodded, mumbling their agreement. The war was not going well. It had not been going well since before their return from the previous WestPac cruise in October of '67. In '68, Nixon won the Presidential election partially because his opposition, Humphrey, was a democrat and the Democrats carried the blame for getting the country into the war, and partially on his promise to implement his 'secret' plan to end the war. Apparently, this current bombing halt was part of that plan.

The previous year had been rough, and things had changed dramatically on the home front. When Steeg was on liberty in Long Beach in 1967, it was common to see dress uniforms walking down every street. There had never been any love lost between the citizens of Long Beach and the U.S. Navy base on Terminal Island. Every sailor had heard stories about lawn signs reading "No Dogs or Sailors Allowed." But, the downtown areas were always flooded with sailors in uniform. As 1967 gave way to 1968, servicemen in civilian clothes dominated the downtown scene. Navy regulations required uniforms when leaving the ship, so some sailors changed in restrooms before leaving the base, others changed in locker facilities just inside the town limits. By mid-1968, uniformed servicemen in Long Beach virtually disappeared. The war was not going well. The citizenry knew it. The servicemen knew it. Civilian clothing helped keep things in town civil.

"I don't like Nixon," Tom concluded with a scowl.

"Me, too!" Santini offered from the far corner.

Between sips of coffee, Steeg nodded in silent agreement.

Bear chimed in. "Steeg, John Dickenson was up here."

"That's nice," was Steeg's nonplused reply.

"Yeah," Tom picked up on Bear's lead. "He says he wants to buy you a milk shake at the gedunk later on."

"Really? That is nice, isn't it? I just might take him up on that. It's getting pretty warm on the day shift now."

They had agreed to meet at 1430 hours at the gedunk. The gedunk was amidships on second deck, aft of the Ward Room, forward of Sickbay, and right next to the ship's store. A small walk-through area serving as a link to the port side passageway, it was where ship's company could buy candy, snacks, soft drinks, milk shakes, and other goodies. Opposite from the service counter, a tight grouping of tables surrounded by overused blue plastic stacking chairs helped keep candy wrappers and drink cups confined to the immediate area. By 1445 hours, Steeg's break time was practically over.

"So, it's nothing I said, or anyone else did?" John confirmed.

Steeg shook his head. "I'm sorry, John. I didn't realize my absence was such a problem for you."

"It's not, really. It's a small group, so it's easy to think someone might have done or said something that might have rubbed someone else in the group the wrong way. It's good to hear that wasn't the case. But, I do wonder about one thing, though."

"What's that?" Steeg sucked down the last of his drink until the straw drew air.

"We've been in the study since before we left Long Beach. Remember all those months in dry dock when we all lived on that barracks boat? The group started there. That's a long time."

Steeg nodded. "Yes, I guess it is. Doesn't seem that long."

"Well, it's like you just lost interest. What was it? That Shellback initiation too much for you, or what?"

A short laugh from the younger sailor was followed with a light hearted comment about the equator crossing "Shellback" initiation tradition, and both men shared another short laugh. Then John asked more seriously, "Something bothering you, Steeg? Something I can help you with?"

Steeg's eyes darkened and he averted his gaze. After a moment, he looked back to his friend. "Things can change, John."

"What kind of things?"

Steeg never was one to spend a lot of energy talking about himself, and he certainly preferred not talking about his own imperfections.

"Sometimes, when things aren't working out the way you thought they would, or the way you think they should, you can change your mind on stuff, that's all."

"Change your mind on what stuff, Steeg?"

He lowered his head to gather his thoughts, wondering if it was a good idea to continue with this. Still, John had proven to be a good friend, someone he knew he could trust. "Stuff like going through the motions. It's like saying one thing, but doing the other, the opposite, if you know what I mean."

John nodded with a slight shrug. "Okay, I think I get it, a little. You were in the group, and now you're out of it because you felt you weren't living the way the group's study urges you to?"

"Something like that."

"And, that made you uncomfortable?"

"More than that, John. I got to the point where I couldn't handle the hypocrisy of it anymore. I didn't like lying to myself. I didn't like lying to you or the rest of the guys. It was better for me to leave."

John Dickenson understood better than Steeg realized. He wondered if it would be wise to relate a personal experience. Steeg continued.

"John, do you remember when you accepted Christ?"

Relieved for a moment, the Second Class Petty Officer smiled. "Yes, I think so. I was in sixth grade. Just a kid. My folks were church-going people. I was raised in a praising home. I knew then, as I know now, I am Christ's." Steeg nodded slowly and John asked, "How about you?"

Steeg's voice was calm, but his tone hardened. "I know exactly when and where. It was on Broadway and 4th in downtown San Diego, on a corner bus bench across from the USO building, just after dawn on 27 March 1967."

"Wow. Not too long ago. You're just a babe."

Steeg's face turned harder. "I guess, but I don't use that as an excuse. I was a month and a half out of boot camp. Up until the time I reported onboard to *Hornet*, I had temporary billet at NTC San Diego. I was expecting orders to Photographer's Mate 'A' School. The orders never came," Steeg's voice fell a touch lower. "Instead, I got orders to report to *Hornet* in Long Beach on 14 March. That was the first thing to go wrong. On the 26th, we steamed down to San Diego to pick up stores and the air groups for my first WestPac tour. I had a 24 hour pass, so I spent the time in town. Visited the zoo, went to the Enlisted Men's Club, USO, a couple of movies, all of it by myself."

"Where were the rest of the hanger deck guys?"

"I wasn't assigned to V3 Division then. I was first in OC Division, CATCC."

"Oh, yeah, that's right – Carrier Air Traffic Control Center."

"Yep. That didn't last long, but that's another story." The episode flashed briefly in his mind, but Steeg dismissed it. "Anyway, after bumming around San Diego all night, I found myself on a bus bench on Broadway and 4th watching the sun come up over the hills. For the first time in my life, I was completely alone, and absolutely powerless over anything in my life. It hit me like the proverbial ton of bricks. I was 19, scared, going to war, and half a continent away from anyone, or anything, that made sense or held any meaning for me."

John returned a silent nod.

"You see, John, I realized then my whole life had been taken over by something I had no control over, something that had no real concern for me or whatever I was to make of my life. I was there, on that bench, because I had allowed myself to hand over my life to, of all things, the United States government and the U.S. Navy. And, in the process, I had given up everything that mattered to me."

John wanted to comfort his friend, but he remained silent.

"I was angry with that, and with myself, angry and scared at the same time, and completely alone. I needed someone to help me; someone a whole lot stronger than I was to protect me, keep those I loved safe, and get me through whatever was going to happen as a result of this really stupid decision I had made.

"So, I turned to the one person whose promises I believed I could trust. Right there on the bus bench, I handed my whole life over to Christ. And, then I waited for the fear and anger to leave me."

"Praise the Lord," John said breathlessly.

"Yes," Steeg agreed as he slowly rose to his feet, needing to return to the Hanger Deck. John stayed seated. "It helped. It helped get me through the day. It helped me get through a bunch of trouble on that first WestPac. You see, John, I believe Christ and his promises. However, I also know I surrendered to Him because I was a coward. It's easy to come to Christ when you're desperate, or dying, or just so plain scared you worry you're going to wet yourself. I didn't accept Christ because of some deep sense of spiritual devotion or love for Him. I accepted Christ because I was afraid of losing everything important to me. My acceptance of Christ had a big profit motive behind it. That's a little unfair to Him, don't you think? Making a commitment based on such shallow faith? To pin Him down to His own promises just because you accept Him? And, of course, my life and all those in it would be protected as well. What better way to cover your backside than to have Christ?

"But, I was wrong. I had no idea of the string of mistakes and missteps that would follow. No matter how much I try to avoid them, something always trips me up. I keep failing. And, the mistakes continue. I seem powerless to stop making them. That's the hypocrisy. That's why I left the group."

He looked at his wristwatch. "My break time is over. I have to head back up."

John didn't know what to say, so he was surprised as the words fell from his lips. "We're funny creatures, Steeg. Sometimes we do things to hurt ourselves because somehow we believe deep down we deserve punishment for something we did, or didn't do. But that's all wrong. Christ's victory was complete on the cross. Because of that singular truth, we are all reconciled to the Father through His shed blood. He has forgiven us for it all, and we have no right to deny His victory by punishing ourselves for something He has already washed away. He loves us, and His complete salvation is available to all of us. He only asks us to love Him back."

Steeg nodded quietly as his friend's words sunk in. "Thanks, John. You're a good friend. We should pick this up later. But, not in the group. The group is better off without me. Trust me on that one."

A real feeling of helplessness came over John as he watched Steeg turn and disappear down the port passageway.

Two nights later, at 0130 hours, Steeg lay in the top of a stack of three bunks in the V3 crew's barracks room on the 02 level. His bunk was located just below the number 3 arresting wire on the Flight Deck. It was hot, stifling, and the air venting into the space just above his feet pushed out even hotter air making it difficult to breathe. Not able to stay asleep was unusual for most of the hanger deck crew. They had all long since become used to the incredibly loud cracking that exploded across the crowded sleeping quarters with every landing of a fixed wing aircraft. Hooking the number 3 arresting wire was considered a perfect carrier landing, and *Hornet's* air groups had excellent Navy pilots. But every hit of an arresting hook pounded the sleeping quarters like the firing of a five-inch gun, and Steeg was certain the number three wire was directly above his head. It certainly sounded as if it was.

That night, air operations continued at a somewhat heavier than normal pace. Activity had been picking up all the previous day, prolonging air operations beyond the standard intervals, even for the Gulf of Tonkin — lots of take-offs, and lots of aircraft recovery. Night operations were only slightly less busy, but it never seemed to bother the 'day' crew's sleep. Sailors could sleep anywhere.

But, this night Steeg couldn't sleep. For hours he had lain in his sweat-soaked bunk staring at the dimly lit overhead barely two feet above his head. When his eyes became heavy, bringing the relief of sleep closer, the unwelcome vision of Grace would fill his mind and he was quickly awake again. Since Singapore, the visitations had become more frequent. It had been a month and a half of nearly nightly reminders from a specter of someone once more dear to him than any other living person. When visitations from Grace occurred, sleep came only when his body could no longer deny its exhaustion. This night, exhaustion wasn't enough to keep his eyes closed.

Suddenly, the landings stopped, and everything was quiet.

The silence was louder than the racket it had replaced. He was awake and awake he would stay. He rolled out of the rack, landing with both feet on the dark green vinyl tiled deck. On the aft bulkhead, he opened his locker, pulled out his shaving kit, walked past the rows of racks and sleeping crewmembers, and into the head. He quickly washed away stale sweat that was quickly replaced with fresh sweat. After shaving and brushing his teeth, he returned to his locker to pull on crisp denim bell bottoms, a clean yellow shirt and his navy blue baseball cap with the gold third class petty officer emblem center-pinned below the yellow embroidered "U.S.S. HORNET CVS-12." The steel-toed flight deck boots completed his work ensemble, and he left the crew's quarters to make his way to Hanger Deck Control.

"You should be sleeping," said Joe Bonia, V3 Division First Class Petty Officer, sitting in cramped overlook surveying from the command chair the parking and securing of aircraft taking place in all three bays.

"You're right," Steeg agreed as he entered the tiny room with the Plexiglas bay window that overlooked Hanger Bay Two. As normal, the dark red lamping of night air operations shrouded the three hanger bays. He pulled his coffee mug from the hook rack mounted on the rear bulkhead. "I'll be back."

Bonia watched the young man exit the room, move easily down the steep ladder to the hanger deck, and make his way in the shadows to the hatch that led to second deck and the mess hall. Steeg's nocturnal visits were becoming more frequent. They were also becoming more of a concern, and he said as much several minutes later when Steeg returned from below decks with a full mug of hot, black coffee.

"You know, if you need to, the Doc can get you some sleeping pills," Bonia said as he kept his eyes on the activity below.

Steeg shook his head. "No thanks."

"A lot rides on you being alert out there, on your toes, for your safety as well as your men."

"I know, Joe."

"Have you taken a good look at yourself lately?"

Steeg looked up and saw his pale reflection in the plastic window pane. Even in the subdued lighting, he could see the dark circles under his eyes and the drawn lines in his face. He had looked better.

Bonia continued. "Steeg, there's a reason why you're not sleeping so good. You sick?"

Steeg shook his head. "I feel fine."

"You don't look fine," Bonia said frankly. "How are things at home?"

"Fine, I guess," he shrugged. "I don't hear too much from the folks, not like I used to. My sister writes more and she doesn't say anything is really wrong. It's not that, anyway. Whatever is keeping me up, it isn't home."

"We all need rest, Steeg."

"I get rest, Joe. I just don't sleep very well, that's all."

"You should find out why."

"What do you want, Joe? You want to be my chaplain or something?"

"Maybe a talk with the Chaplain is a good idea."

Steeg's chin fell to his chest. He had had his talks with the Chaplain, and Bonia's simple suggestion to see the Chaplain again reminded him of the first time he had done so.

It was early during the ship's 1967 WestPac tour to Viet Nam. At the time, he considered his sessions with the Chaplain part of a long string of fortuitous circumstances resulting from a very serious heat rash infection he had contracted while serving KP duty on the mess decks. The pain and suffering the heat rash inflicted was severe. That was the down side. The up side was the fact that the rash had put him on medical orders for light duty, got him off the mess decks and back into one of the few air conditioned spaces onboard the ship – CATCC (Carrier Air Traffic Control) – to help heal the condition. Steeg decided his light duty respite was the ideal opportunity for him to pursue his conversion to Catholicism. That was when he sought out the ship's Chaplain for help.

In 1967, Chaplain Gerald Regenfuss was new to *Hornet*, just like Steeg. He was an inch or two shorter than Steeg, a little stockier, wore thin, turtle shell framed glasses on a rosy-cheeked face, and he had light red hair with streaks of blond that made him look older than his twenty-eight years. The Chaplain was a lieutenant, and he had transferred from Pensacola earlier that January. *Hornet* was his second sea duty assignment as a Navy Chaplain. Seminary educated with a divinity degree, Chaplain Regenfuss was a Catholic who conducted religious services while providing religious counseling to men of all faiths. In that regard, Chaplain Regenfuss took pride in his ability as a general theologian. But, he was first and foremost a Catholic.

The first talk was in the Chaplain's office, a room so small it lacked a fourth bulkhead, had no door, and yet was hardly large enough to hold two people. Chaplain Regenfuss turned in his chair to face Steeg who sat so close to him their knees almost touched. He finger pushed his glasses to the top of his nose as he responded to the petty officer's request with his first question.

"Why?"

As simple as it was, the one word question caught the young recruit off balance. For a few seconds he fumbled for a response, trying not to scratch at the calamine-coated rash under his dungaree shirt.

"Why what?"

"Why do you want to become a Catholic?"

Steeg took a deep breath. "Well, actually, it's because I need to."

That raised a questioning eyebrow followed by a repetitive response.

"Why?"

Steeg's left knee started a nervous, shallow bounce. "That's a little involved, Chaplain. It would take a while to explain…"

The Chaplain patiently smiled. "I've got time."

Under his shirt, his flesh felt as if it was crawling as the rash grew more irritating. His knee bouncing increased in frequency, too.

"Yeah, of course you do. Well, okay, here it is, the Catholic Church is the true church, right?"

Steeg waited for an agreeing response from the Chaplain. It didn't come. The Chaplain's eyes calmly held his as he waited for Steeg to continue.

"So, seeing how I accepted Christ before this tour started, I figured I should join up." The end of the statement was punctuated with Steeg's hearty exhale of relief.

Chaplain Regenfuss nodded as he digested what Steeg had just told him. "Join up? Interesting. You accepted Christ before the tour?"

Steeg nodded.

"Were you a church member before then?"

Steeg nodded again.

"What church was that?"

He hesitated, but only for a moment. "Church of Christ. My parents go there. It's a non-denominational thing, I think."

"Yes," the Chaplain replied contemplatively. "So, let's see. You were raised a Christian by your parents, grew up in a Protestant church environment, accepted Christ before shipping out for Viet Nam, and now you want to 'join' the TRUE church – the Catholic Church. Does that pretty much sum it up?"

Again, Steeg nodded, beginning to feel they were starting to get somewhere. The feeling of progress would not last long.

"Why?" the Chaplain repeated.

Steeg's knee started to bounce a little faster. The seconds ticked slowly by as his mind searched for an answer different from the one he didn't want to say. Nothing different came to his mind, so, he sheepishly shrugged without saying anything. Chaplain Regenfuss smiled for comfort sake, and then sheepishly shrugged back. Steeg wasn't going to be let go on this one, not by the Chaplain, and not by Christ. He had to explain things first.

"You have to understand, Chaplain, certain things have to happen before certain other things can happen."

"Interesting. And, one thing that has to happen first is to become a Catholic?"

"Yes. That's it." Steeg was again prematurely relieved.

"Why?"

"Oh, gees," Steeg moaned. "I'm sorry. I didn't know it was going to be this hard."

Chaplain Regenfuss chuckled, patting Steeg's nervous knee to a more quiet state. "Relax, Steeg. It's not confession. It's just important that you have a good understanding of why you do what you do with your life – your career choices; your friends; your relationship with Christ and how best to live your life through it. You want to, as you say, 'join' the TRUE Church. I can help you do that. That's part of my job, a job I chose for my own reasons. It's important for you to know what your real reasons are for following through on a very important decision you've apparently made. So, tell me, why have you made this decision?"

It was at that moment Steeg realized the man sitting in front of him was a friend, not an adversary. His apprehension gave way to relief.

"So I can marry my girl and have it be a real marriage. If I'm not a Catholic, our marriage won't be a real marriage."

The Chaplain leaned back. "You mean your marriage won't be recognized as legitimate in the eyes of the Church."

Steeg nodded.

"You know, other people get married all the time outside the Church. They are legal unions, with the same rights, privileges, and responsibilities."

Steeg shook his head. "That's not it. She's Catholic. I need to be Catholic."

He stroked his chin thoughtfully. "I see. Well, you should know you don't 'join' the Catholic Church in the same way you might join a club, or a bowling team. It's not like that. In Catechism you will study the structure of the Church, the meaning and importance of the rituals, the liturgy, the sacraments, the saints, the Holy Mother, and the vital role of the Papacy, all that stuff and more. There's quite a bit to it. It will take awhile."

Steeg nodded in acceptance as the Chaplain reached over to a small wall shelf heavily burdened by all manner of books. His finger followed the bottom row, coming to rest on one small volume. He extracted it and handed the book to Steeg.

"We'll start with the basics. Try and read at least the first half of that book before our next session. How about the same time a week from now? Would that work for you?"

Steeg remembered agreeing with the Chaplain to start the instruction that would ultimately make him acceptable to Grace's mother, and his marriage to Grace recognized by the Church. Now, two years later, sitting in Hanger Deck Control with Bonia, his first talk with Chaplain Regenfuss seemed almost too long ago to be remembered. It would have been conveniently ignored but for Bonia's snoopy suggestion.

"No thanks," Steeg replied with finality. "I had my Chaplain talks a couple of years back."

"Oh, really? How's that?"

Steeg rolled his eyes as he pinched the bridge of his nose to relieve a pressure he felt growing behind his eyes. "Gees, Joe, you're really something."

Bonia held up a single hand in surrender. "Okay, Steeg, forget it. It's dropped."

With that, both men sat quiet for several minutes. During the uncomfortable silence, Steeg finished his coffee. That's when he filled in some of the blanks with Joe.

"The Chaplain was helping me with my Catechism. It was over a month of oral instruction, questions and answers. I was going to convert, become a Catholic. It didn't work out."

Bonia was surprised. "Really? I'm Catholic! What happened?"

Steeg didn't know if he wanted to answer that question. It wasn't Joe's business. But, then, he was the one who had brought it up, wasn't he?

"The Chaplain couldn't answer my questions about Papal infallibility, the sufficiency of Christ versus certain dictates of the Church, among other things. After awhile, it became clear that there was no real reason to continue. I ended it. He agreed."

Bonia nodded again. "Well, that's interesting. I grew up Catholic, so questions like that just never came up. You were taught to go to Mass regularly, go to confession, believe and behave. That was it. But converting to it from another religion has to be different. I can understand having real questions about real stuff you're just not familiar with."

"Well, that was pretty much it," Steeg acknowledged, hoping to end the line of conversation gracefully. "When you don't get the answers that make sense, it doesn't make sense to make them up on your own."

"Amen," Bonia's reflection in the bay window smiled back at Steeg. "So, what religion are you?"

"Methodist, I guess." Steeg couldn't say 'Church of Christ.' It didn't sound right to him.

"Still a Christian, not a Muslim or anything. What was it that made you want to become a Catholic in the first place?"

For Steeg, the conversation had gone far enough, maybe too far. He bluntly answered Joe's reflection in the bay window. "It seemed like a good idea at the time."

"Oh," Bonia could sense Steeg's sudden defensiveness. "Too bad it didn't work out for you."

Steeg rose to his feet to leave.

"I need more coffee," he said walking to the door. "I'll be back at shift change."

"Sure thing," Bonia said, and Steeg left Hanger Deck Control to return below decks to the mess hall.

The clock on the bulkhead in the mess hall read 0347 hours when the port side began a swift, steady rise. Within seconds, the few sailors sitting in the chow hall were grabbing onto anything to keep from falling over. The deck continued its rise and began to vibrate with the strain of the ship's sudden maneuver. An abandoned coffee cup and one metal tray slid from separate tabletops and crashed to the floor.

Steeg had better balance on his feet. His chair slid away from him as he held his coffee mug in one hand and extended the other to help center himself. The ship continued its severe turn to port. He felt the shaking of the deck through his steel-toed boots, and he could see the coffee urns and milk dispenser in the center of the mess hall strain against the constraints of their bolted stands. He knew the ship was turning, but this severe change in course for a ship as large as *Hornet* was chewing up literally miles of ocean in the process. Something was going on.

As the aircraft carrier came out of the 180 degree turn, Steeg made his way from the mess hall, down the port passageway, up the ladder to the main deck, and then again up the ladder to Hanger Deck Control. No one was there. He turned to the short passageway that led to the crew's lounge where the entire night shift crew was relaxing either playing cards, or reading, or just snoozing. Bonia was at the Yeoman's desk in the back. Muggins was there, Kinsey, Denoso, Karl, McIlhenny, and all the blue shirts brought the total to 15 men.

Karl and Bear saw Steeg come in and waved him over to their side of the room.

"What's going on?" Steeg asked, taking the offered chair.

"Change of course," Karl shrugged.

"Ya think?!" Steeg smirked. "The ship is still shaking. The screws are full out. We have to be kicking up a rooster tail off the fantail, for Pete's sake."

Karl agreed. "Wherever we're going, we're going to get there in a hurry."

Karl was right.

Chapter 14

The return of Raquel Welch

1330 HOURS
17 APRIL 1969
USS HORNET CVS-12
SOMEWHERE NEAR THE STRAITS OF TAIWAN

It had been 33 hours of hard steaming for *Hornet*. The heavy vibration was constant as all engines ran full out, the carrier's speed pushed to the unofficial limit of 33 knots[5]. Many of the crew suspected the ship was moving a bit faster than that. The weather had changed. It was getting colder. Orders had come down to break out winter gear, a relief for the flight deck crews working out in the open servicing and arming the aircraft crowded in neatly grouped rows across the deck. Skies were heavy with overcast. Sheets of driving rain swept over the ship as *Hornet* pounded through the choppy, gray-black seas. On the Main Deck all three hanger bays were loaded with aircraft.

Just forward of Hanger Deck Control, Steeg and Teddy Bear stood near the cable guardrail of the number two elevator, wind whipping into the bay. Both men wore their insulted navy blue wind breakers and division ball caps.

"Some of the guys are so cold they want to break out the parkas," Bear said, shoving his hands deeper into his jacket pockets.

"Wimps," Steeg scowled, a popping noise followed as he fastened the top snap on his windbreaker. "Too bad they're not from Minnesota, like us."

"That's affirmative," Bear agreed, his teeth only mildly chattering. "You see anything out there?"

"No," Steeg shook his head as he pulled his jacket collar up and closer to his neck. "But we're not alone."

"Scuttlebutt is something big happened off North Korea."

"Wouldn't surprise me," Steeg peered outboard, catching a faint hint of what he thought was a ship far off on the horizon. "What is that? Can you see that? Out there, about ten o'clock."

Bear squinted but couldn't see anything. It was either too far, or the scattered rain was hiding whatever it was from view. "Beats me. I haven't seen a DE, or any other ship since we made that dipsy-doodle move yesterday. Captain's gonna have to tell us something soon, don't you think?"

"Ours is not to reason why..." Steeg mumbled, shoving his ungloved hands into his jacket pockets.

"Ours is but to do or die," Bear finished.

Steeg took a half step toward the rear, leaned back and looked up at Hanger Deck Control. Three men framed by the shallow protrusion of the bay window looked down at him. Two of the three were blue shirts, and one of the blue shirts, Santini, had his thumbs in his ears wiggling fingers and sticking his tongue out at Steeg. The petty officer's face hardened just enough to make Santini knock it off.

"I think it's about time to get all the Blue Shirts on deck," Steeg mused. "We could use a good hanger deck FOD[6] patrol right about now."

Bear followed Steeg's turn toward the ladder to Hanger Deck Control. At the top of the landing, Steeg opened the door and leaned into the small room.

"All Blue Shirts assemble on deck. Now." Steeg ordered. He turned to Bear. "Get 'em out here."

Bear nodded, turning around the corner into the crew's lounge to add six blue shirted airmen to the party. Moans, mumbles and complaints as all eight slowly shuffled their way down the ladder to Hanger Bay Two.

Steeg stood at the top of the ladder's landing to address the loosely assembled squad.

"Gentlemen, you all know how hard I try to look out for your better interests. At every opportunity, I try to do whatever I can to make your tour of duty as pleasant as possible. You all know that."

The small crowd of blue shirts below continued their mumbling.

Steeg ignored the complaints. "Well, I can see you all at least have an opinion about that. Unfortunately, your opinions don't count. So keep them to yourselves. In the meantime, start in Hanger Bay One and work aft. FOD patrol! Collect it all. I want to see every bit of it when you are done. If there's not enough, we'll just have to do it again. Get to it."

The cadre of eight moaned louder, some waving Steeg off in disgust, as they turned in mass to head forward into Hanger Bay One.

Steeg hollered as the pack of airmen kept walking without looking back. "Unless you want Captain's Mast, that better not be a middle finger, Johnson!"

Steeg turned to join Bear in the crew's lounge and passed Bonia coming through the door.

"Good idea, Steeg," Joe said as they squeezed by each other. "They were getting on my nerves."

At 5' 10" and 200 pounds, dark-haired Bill Denoso was something rare. Denoso was a college graduate, in his mid-twenty's, a Third Class Petty Officer, and a Blue, not Yellow, Shirt. Not only did he have a Bachelor's degree from San Jose State, he was also the only reservist in the division. Reporting aboard *Hornet* just prior to leaving Long Beach for the tour, Denoso had two additional distinctions unique to the V3 Division. First, his entire active duty hitch would be over before the end of 1969. No other regular Navy swab jockey in the division had an active duty obligation less than three years long, and some, like Steeg, had signed up for four years. Denoso had eighteen total months of active duty.

Denoso's second distinction was that, unlike every other Blue Shirt in the division, he hadn't so much as lifted a wheel chock since reporting on board. He wore his college sheepskin like a shroud. So, as soon as he had reported on board, the division Senior Chief made Denoso the division yeoman responsible for supply and procurement.

All things being normal, every man in the division would have hated Denoso's guts, plotting to make sure his abbreviated stay on *Hornet* was as unbearable as possible, or at least as unbearable permissible limits would allow. But, as with his other exceptions, Denoso also possessed a remarkably disarming personality. Boisterous with a relaxed humor, he had a talent for colorful story telling and jokes that never seemed to be in short supply. Instead of hating him, the men tolerated him, justifying their more affable attitude toward the reservist with their appreciation of the comic relief Denoso often produced whenever the opportunity presented itself. For the rank and file, Denoso was free entertainment.

By 1930 hours, the day shift was over, and most everyone had finished evening chow to return to the cramped V3 Division sleeping quarters on the 02 level. On the far port side of the crew's quarters was an open conversation pit, the borders of which were three large vinyl covered sofas, and a scattering of steel-framed chairs. Many of the crew now relaxed in the makeshift lounge area, a few of the guys read, a few talked amongst themselves, some watched the wall-mounted black & white television set tuned to the ship's single closed circuit channel. A second class petty officer was on the TV screen, a plain gray curtain as a backdrop behind him, reading Armed Forces Network wire service news copy. It was not all that informative of a program, nor was the production quality up to 'back home' standards, but it was better than nothing. It was also only a half hour before the evening movie, a nightly event everyone looked forward to if only for the diversion it supplied.

Denoso made his way from the head and plopped down heavily between Santini and McIlhenny sitting on the couch against the port bulkhead.

"Another tough day plane pushing, right guys?" Denoso exclaimed, too loudly as usual.

"Another tough day pushing a pencil, Denoso?" Santini chided. Laughter came from most of the others in the room, including those in the bank of racks fronting the lounge area. Denoso noticed but shrugged off the obvious derision with a humorous retort.

"True enough!" he acknowledged with a big grin. "It's tough, but somebody's gotta do it!"

"Somebody give me something to throw at that guy," Bear half-joked from his place on the sofa against the aft bulkhead. A pillow flew across the room from behind a second-level blanket draped rack, landing at Bear's feet. Reaching down to pick it up, Bear said "Thanks" as he directed his squinted intensions at Denoso sitting across from him.

Denoso held up his hands in mock surrender. "Bear, that's government property and you've all taken an oath to protect government property."

Steeg tilted back in his stiff steel-framed chair to make sure Bear had a clear field of fire. "I think the oath was to defend the country against all enemies foreign and domestic."

"Yeah," Bear agreed. "I think reservists fall under those categories somewhere."

Denoso's grin widened. "No, now, that's not exactly fair. I'm government property, too…"

That struck a sensitive chord with McIlhenny who disgustedly turned toward the reservist. "Maybe, but not as long as I gotta be."

"Okay, point taken. I give," Denoso brought his hands over his head in anticipation of the pending attack.

Nothing happened. Bear tossed the pillow back to the man leaning out from the rack behind the blanket. After several seconds, Denoso looked up from under his arms. Satisfied that he was safe, he quickly fell deep into a story about his 1968 Big Sur experience. As usual, it was a too long tale with a quick climax of disappointing proportions.

"…and there were women, hundreds of them, and you wouldn't believe what they were doing!" He boasted.

"Listening to music?" Hugh Bauer asked.

"No, man, not even close," Denoso responded with a slyly raised eyebrow. "Thousands of them…"

Third Class Petty Officer Jerry Terry strode into the lounge area, taking a seat next to Bear on the sofa. "I thought you said it was hundreds?"

"It's growing by the second," Bear mused.

"Look, I'm just telling you the way it was."

A corporate "yeah, right" rose from the small group.

"No, really, I am. And, I'll tell you what – I wasn't lonely there, that's for sure."

"I bet you bagged at least one, maybe two hundred of them that weekend, didn't you?" Terry queried.

"Jerr, you go where the girls are, you're going to get some action, that's all I'm saying."

"Is this any way for a college graduate to behave?" McIlhenny kidded.

"It's the only way!" Denoso roared with a laugh.

"So, how'd you do it?" Bear was only somewhat interested.

"Whadda ya mean?" Denoso came back.

"How'd you do it? You know, was it in a motel room, or out on a hill top overlooking the bay? Did you get all of them at one time, or did they take turns? How'd you do it?"

Denoso nodded with understanding as his eyes narrowed. "Wesson Oil."

"What?" someone asked from the growing crowd as more crewmen slowly trickled in from the hanger deck below.

"Wesson Oil," Denoso repeated.

Many of the sailors looked at each other, bewildered. Others just shook their heads, tiring of the conversation.

"What's Wesson Oil got to do with it?" Santini asked.

Sitting next to him, Denoso placed an understanding hand on the young man's knee. Santini Immediately slapped it off. Denoso continued undeterred.

"Franklin, my good man, when you have enough Wesson Oil you'd be surprised how many women you can handle at one time."

Steeg had heard just about enough. "Gees, Bill, not only is that too crude to be believed, you can't tell me any of it is true."

Smugly, Denoso sat back in the couch with arms folded. "True as the sky is blue."

Steeg shook his head and turned back to the TV on the wall. "It's been gray and cloudy for the last two days, Bill."

"It is true," Denoso insisted. Steeg ignored him, as did most of the others in the room. "I mean it. Honest. I promise. Seriously. May God Himself strike me down in this very spot if every word isn't the truth. I mean that, Steeg. Absolutely."

Almost ducking in anticipation of the lightning bolt that might slam into the small room at any moment, Steeg said, "Me thinks thou protests too much."

"Do not." Denoso protested.

Sprinkles of laughter came from the gathering.

"What's the movie tonight?" Someone asked in an attempt to change the subject.

"'Fantastic Voyage' with Raquel Welch," someone else answered, and Steeg felt the return of a warm memory.

"Okay, do me one better," Denoso continued, directing his challenge to Steeg. "Give me a true story about you and some women you've been with."

Steeg looked across at the man on the couch, mildly amused. "Why?"

"Why not? You criticize me for my story, so let's hear what you've ever done. Assuming, of course, you've actually done something – with a woman that is."

Steeg's smiled coolly. "What would you like to hear?"

"Anything," Denoso shrugged. "Your choice."

Leaning back again in his chair, it took all of two or three seconds for Steeg to know he would accept the challenge if only to put Denoso in his place. "Well, I could tell you how I lost my virginity to a roof-top whore in Hong Kong in '67. That was before I was assigned to V3 Division, so maybe that's not good enough for this austere gathering."

"I wouldn't mind hearing it," Santini grinned.

Steeg shook his head. "No, I don't think so, Frank. It wasn't much fun back then. My so-called buddies in the Photo Lab took me to some bar in

Hong Kong, got me really drunk, practically had to carry me up to this hooker's place where the deed was done. Frankly, I was so plastered at the time, I don't remember too much about it."

"Well, tell us about something you do remember, then," Denoso demanded, pressing his challenge.

"Okay," Steeg thought for a moment. "A true story about something that didn't happen."

Denoso slumped back into his seat, disappointed. "How can it be true if it didn't happen?"

"Truth is, what didn't happen almost did," Steeg's voice lowered a touch as he began telling his story to the gathered group seated around him. "You guys know how important your girlfriend can be. Even you, Denoso, must appreciate the tremendous sense of self-worth – validation, even – another person's love and affection gives you, right down to your toes."

Across the cramped room, several heads nodded in agreement, all except Denoso, who had a blank, confused look of incomprehension on his face.

"Well, believe it or not, my girl was that kind of girl to me. I tell you guys in all truthfulness, she was my life. I had to be with her every possible moment. I needed her like you need air to breathe. Without her, I felt... Well, let's just say I couldn't even imagine being without her. And, when we were together, I couldn't keep my hands off of her. She was electric. Especially on that night..."

Steeg could see Grace across the small room at that very moment. It was September, 1966 again, and earlier that day the two of them almost fell into mourning over his '48 Buick DynaGlide as it was laboriously guided into his father's garage where the front end was jacked up onto blocks, never to be driven again. The car had broken down that afternoon on Highway 100 just north of the Excelsior Boulevard exit. Steeg explained in blissful detail how the old road boat had been their exclusive refuge, a hiding place for their most consuming moments of passion, each and every episode of which ended frustratingly unfulfilled for Steeg.

"You mean the two of you never actually got it on?" Santini gasped in disbelief.

"Nope, never did," Steeg admitted.

"How could he, you dumb jerk!" McIlhenny objected. "He just said he lost his cherry in Hong Kong on his first WestPac."

A couple of frustrated "sssh's" could be heard as Steeg returned to his story.

"Anyway, after my Dad and I finally got this huge, old, black sedan's front axel up on blocks – that tank had to weigh at least two tons, I swear – my girl and I kinda hung around for awhile, not really knowing what to do. For the first time in our two-year relationship, we were suddenly wheel-less! Thinking about it now, I think she was more upset than I was. It had been a warm, humid day, but the afternoon was turning cooler. Contrary to what most you guys probably think about Minnesota, there are days in September that are down right hot."

Bear's laugh was loud enough to be easily heard by everyone. "Yeah, and there are days in September in Minnesota when you have a foot of snow on the ground!"

Everyone laughed, and even Steeg chuckled at that one.

"Grace kept reaching for my hand, holding it in hers, then letting it go, then reaching for my hand again. We walked around the old car, looking for damage we couldn't see. My Dad thought I'd thrown a rod, but I didn't know for sure back then. Grace kept lightly touching my arm, then my shoulder, then holding my hand again. It was nice, really – kinda strange, but nice that she felt comfortable with me that way, like she was trying to comfort me in my moment of loss.

"The afternoon was slipping into evening, and the sun was getting low in the sky. We had dinner with my family that night. As I remember, it was a leisurely meal, a light, summery mix of deviled eggs, lean cold cuts, fresh vegetables, iced tea, and all the fixings for everyone to make their own sandwiches. Dad talked about the car and what might be done about it. My girl said almost nothing during the whole time, but she kept looking at me with those deep brown eyes of hers, making me imagine all kinds of things. After dinner, we went for a short walk around the neighborhood just to be alone.

"Later in the evening, Dad let me use his brand new Olds Delta 88 to take her home. Only, we didn't go to her house. It was long after dark when I backed the Olds down the driveway. My girl quickly slid across the long bench seat and held my right arm really close. It's funny. I can still feel the firmness of her gently swell against me with every breath she took. Gees, she was beautiful… "

He had taken the road that led to Grace's house, but when he came to the cross street where he normally would turn, Steeg kept driving straight ahead. Grace, nestled comfortably at his side, said nothing, silently agreeing to go somewhere else, anywhere else but to her house. He drove further west, soon crossing Xerxes Avenue and into Edina, where he continued to France Avenue. There, he turned north. It was a late Saturday night, and most every business establishment was already closed for the evening. He had to find some place for them to be alone together.

The entire afternoon and through the evening something had been building between them. For Steeg it had grown to a real sense of urgency. For Grace, he wasn't sure, but she seemed to hold him tighter than ever as she sat next to him. Steeg kept driving north, crossing the bridge that spanned the Crosstown Highway and heading toward the business district on 50th Street. Perhaps some place would still be open there.

When they made the turn on 50th Street, the Edina Theater was dark. Nothing on the opposite side was open. Steeg made an illegal U-turn at the corner to head back east. The old Pearson's Restaurant was open, with only a few cars in the parking lot.

"We could go there," Steeg offered. "Are you hungry for dessert?"

"Not for that kind of dessert." She said with a smile.

"Oh. I see. Obviously, I've been looking for the wrong place."

"Can't we just park somewhere?"

"Sure," Steeg nodded in agreement. "But where?"

"Anywhere," Grace held him closer.

It came to him in a flash of brilliance that surprised even him.

"I know just the place," he said quickly taking two right turns followed by a left onto France Avenue heading south.

"Where's that?" She snuggled into his arm.

"In plain sight."

"Where?" Grace asked, not fully understanding.

He drove with purpose now, and it seemed to take twice as long to get there than it took him to drive to where they had just come. But get there they did. From France Avenue, he turned back on 69th Street and immediately darted into the entry leading to the Southdale Mall parking lots. He turned onto the perimeter road that circled the entire shopping center area, looking for the entry to the overflow lot under the shopping center's large, blue water tower. He found it. The overflow lot, as with the rest of the parking lots surrounding the huge shopping center, was virtually empty of cars and bathed in darkness. All the overhead lot lamps were off. Slowing, he made his way down a lane of parking spots, each nose-to-nose pair of which separated by a six-foot long concrete barrier. He had his choice, so he picked a spot almost dead-center in the large expanse of nearly unoccupied asphalt. He doused the headlights, turned the engine off, moved Grace around and across his front to hold her close as his mouth pressed down on hers. She returned his kiss, then, trembling, pushed herself from him only a little.

"This isn't as private as it should be," she worried.

"It's perfect," he smiled confidently. "Who would ever think of looking for anyone in a parking lot after the stores are closed? No one is going to bother us here."

It was a still, humid night. They held onto each other, hands reaching, bodies hungering for each other more so than any other time they had been together. Precious minutes sped by faster than either of them realized. They clung to each other, almost desperate in their embraces, sheltered by the darkness surrounding them. Soon, breathing came in heavy, labored gasps for both of them.

"God, I need you so much," Steeg whispered.

"I need you, too," Grace reached up and pulled his mouth to hers.

It wasn't long before her skin glistened with a thin sheen of perspiration. He clumsily removed first one piece of clothing, then another, then another, until she lay under him completely exposed.

She reached for his belt to get it loose, but somehow the buckle was hung up on his shirt. He tried to slide the shirt over his head, but the belt held it tight. He pulled at it sharply until something finally gave. His shirt now off, together they worked his jeans down his hips. His head was spinning, and he could hardly breathe as he felt the rivulets of sweat trickle down his neck. He was completely inept, and more than a little embarrassed by his fumbling. At this moment, more than anything, he wanted to be cool, sexy, and in control. Instead, he felt gawky, totally out of control, and completely un-cool. But she was with him, and he wanted her so badly.

He wrapped both arms under and around her to hold her close and feel her body fully against his.

"I know it's not the cool thing to say," he gasped heavy breaths that came too fast. "But, I love you so much. I really do."

She reached up and caressed the side of his wet face, and almost said something in reply. Almost. Suddenly, her eyes opened wide in terror! She pushed him up from her and dove from the bench seat to the corner of the floor, curling up into a naked ball under the dash board.

The window glass, fogged over from their combined body heat and heavy breathing, ignited without warning and the interior of the Delta 88 was suddenly bathed in brilliant white light!

"What the heck is that?" Steeg complained, rising just enough above the dash to find a windshield now completely fogged over but for a thin sliver of clear glass where it met the dashboard. Through that clear tiny opening he could see part of an emblem on a car door that read *'Southdale Security Police'*!

The rent-a-cops had stopped just off the right front bumper, training their spot light onto the windshield. The moisture coating everything glass made the interior of the car light up brighter than a G.E. 100 watt light bulb.

Steeg swore as he urgently slid himself behind the wheel, his pants still gathered at his ankles.

"Oh, crap, Gracie, we're in trouble," he moaned, not knowing exactly what to do.

"Get us out of here!" She whispered in desperation loud enough the security cops could have heard her. She repeated, even with more urgency, "Get us out of here, now!"

His hand moved on its own, finding the key in the ignition. He turned it and the engine sprang to life. Slapping the shifter into gear, Steeg stomped the accelerator to the floor and his father's car launched itself ahead in a burst of power that pinned him to the back of the seat. A micro-second later, the car catapulted over the first concrete curb block, the front axle slamming back to the pavement followed immediately by another equally violent jolt as the rear axle vaulted over the same concrete divider. Grace cried out in pain as her head twice bounced off the dashboard undercarriage with both hits.

Steeg could see only that which the thin, clear line of glass at the base of the windshield could reveal, which wasn't much. There was the briefest moment of warning just before the front wheels smacked into and over another cement parking block. Grace yelped again. Then, the back axle bounced over the block! Then, another jarring hit on the front, followed immediately by another at the rear!

"Ooww! Stop hitting those things!" She pleaded, her bare body balled up under the dashboard.

"I'm sorry!" He yelled back. "I can't see!"

He reached across the instrument panel and punched the defroster controls over to maximum just as the front axle shot over another concrete barrier. He continued to squint through the fogged windshield, his foot still holding the accelerator right down to the floor. The side windows were fogged. The back window was useless. Off to the right, through the narrow slit of clear glass in the front, he thought he saw the exit that led to 69th

Street. He swung the steering wheel hard, the huge Oldsmobile banked, and Grace slammed hard up against the corner under the dashboard.

"Steeg!" She cried. "Please!"

"I'm sorry! I'm trying! I'm really trying!"

The short road led to 69th Street, but the 'Do Not Enter' sign he passed told him it was the entrance and not the exit through which he was trying to leave.

"I hope no one is coming in," he said to himself as the car roared onto the city street. Tires squealing, Steeg pulled the wheel hard to bring the nose of the Olds around to face France Avenue, almost plowing into the grassy median instead. With the car pointed in the proper direction and the glass beginning to clear, he again punched down on the accelerator, speeding through the red stop light at the corner to shoot down 69th Street and disappear deeper into the near residential bowels of Edina.

He took a zigzag pattern through the maze of streets, hoping to throw off any pursuers. He kept zigzagging until he found himself at the Highway 100 interchange at 66th Street. He took the highway and headed north. Driving calmly now, just below the posted speed limit, with the windows now almost completely fog-free, Steeg exited at the turnoff that led past the Edina Senior High School. In a quiet neighborhood a few more blocks to the north, he pulled to the curb, shifted into park, and turned off the car.

Only then did Grace crawl from under the dashboard. She complained as she searched the floor for her underwear. He said nothing, too embarrassed to speak as he pulled his jeans back up and retrieved his shirt from the back seat.

"We just can't do this any more," Grace was exasperated.

"I won't argue that," Steeg hurriedly pulled the shirt over his head, tucking it inside his pants. He wanted to apologize. She sat there in bra and panties holding her blouse in her hands as she shook her head.

"We just can't do this any more," she repeated.

"I know. Let's just get dressed and get out of here."

"I mean, I want to, but we can't keep doing this."

"I know, Gracie. Just get dressed and let's go."

She sat there holding her blouse across her bare thighs, shaking her head, but not dressing. She looked over at him, her chest heaved with each breath. She was trembling from real fear.

Why is she just sitting there? He wondered, her brown eyes more beautiful than ever. Grace did not attempt to dress, or hide herself from his view in anyway. *Good grief, I hope she's not in shock or something!*

He asked her again to get dressed, and as he looked at her, his gaze was met by the familiar, slight pout with the overbite he found so irresistibly attractive. That was when Steeg realized she wasn't in shock at all. *Oh, no. She still wants to do it!*

He leaned forward resting his head on the steering wheel. "We can't, Gracie," he said in desperation. "Please, just get dressed."

She didn't move. "I'm sorry, Steeg. I didn't mean for this to happen…"

"It's okay. Just get dressed so we can go now."

"It's not like I planned it, you know," she sat there in her underwear, lowering her arms to her side so he was sure to turn his head to see her.

And, he did. "Oh, gees. Please, let's go."

"Okay," she agreed, but she sat, her breasts swelling in her bra with each breath, looking at him.

He turned slowly toward her, feeling his resolve weaken by the second. Slowly, his hand seemed to move on its own as he ran his finger tips along her bare arm down to her hand resting high on her thigh. His eyes locked with hers.

A moment before their lips met, flashing red lights streaked across the interior of the car.

"Oh, no!" Steeg wanted to shrink away from the entire world.

"Oh, no!" Grace moaned, pulling her knees up to her chest.

The Edina Police patrol car pulled up behind them, headlights on high beam, red lights rhythmically flashing their steady beat. A moment later, the officer tapped on Steeg's side window.

It took more strength than he thought he had in him to hand crank the window to a fully down position. Steeg painfully greeted the patrolman. "Yes, officer?"

The police officer shined his flashlight into Steeg's face. He then beamed a quick circuit around the passenger compartment, coming to rest on Grace's amply filled bra.

"Oh, I see," the officer commented calmly. From where the beam of the flashlight remained, Steeg had no doubt the officer did, in fact, see. "Okay. Driver's license, please."

Steeg reached into his wallet, pulled the license from it and handed it to the policeman who instructed them not to move as he returned to the squad car.

Steeg looked over at Grace, who still sat there, knees to her chest, in her bra and panties.

"Will you please get dressed, now?" he pleaded.

With a slight shrug, she said, "He said not to move."

Steeg rolled his eyes in desperation. "I don't think he meant not to move so you don't get dressed. I think he meant not to move so we don't take off like we just did out of the Southdale parking lot!"

"I'm not sure," she offered weakly.

"I am!" He shot back. "He's probably on the radio right now linking this car with the plates the Southdale cops obviously took down! We are going to jail tonight and you're still sitting there in your stupid underwear!"

He was in trouble and he knew it. What irked him even more was that Grace didn't seem to appreciate the seriousness of the situation. But, she did take offense at his tone.

"Well, you obviously haven't minded my underwear in the past, seeing how you always want to take it off me!"

"That's not the point!" he spat back. "There is a time and place for everything, and this is neither!"

"Well, I didn't pick the time or the place – you did!"

He grimaced. "Pleeeaase! Get some clothes on before he comes back."

She lowered her voice as she tried to scrunch down in the seat. "Too late."

The officer was back at Steeg's window, handing him his driver's license.

"You from Richfield, eh?"

"Yes, officer," Steeg responded meekly.

The police officer directed his flashlight into Grace's face, down to her bra-clad breasts, then back to her face.

"And, who are you, young lady?"

"Grace Ofterdahl," she replied quietly.

"Are you from Richfield, too?"

"Yes," she acknowledged, hastily adding, "I'm really sorry about this. We didn't mean too..."

"Yes, yes, I know," he interrupted, shaking his head. "Look, you, Miss Ofterdahl, get dressed. Have a little pride in yourself. And you, stud, have more respect for your girlfriend, will you? If I ever see you two doing this again in my town, I'll throw both of you into the slammer. Or, worse, I'll call your mommies and daddies. Grow up! Now go home!"

And with that, the cop turned and went back to his car.

Steeg could hardly hide the irritation he felt for Grace at that moment. "Did you hear what he said?"

"Did you?!" she shot back at him as she flung her blouse on and then searched for her jeans.

"How could I not?!"

"So, why don't you have more respect for me?" she glared at him.

"What?!" he couldn't believe what she had just said. "That isn't what he said. He said 'GET DRESSED!'"

"Did not! He said you didn't respect me, and, you know what? He's right!"

"He is not!"

"Is too!" her voice cracked and a sob suddenly rose in her throat. "He's absolutely right about that! You don't!" She fought back the welling tears as she angrily retrieved her jeans from the car floor. Yanking them on, she pulled the zipper up roughly to make sure he knew she was really mad. "How could I possibly be so stupid to fall in love with someone who doesn't even respect me?"

Her voice trailed off into silence as she finished dressing, not easily slipping her still-tied canvas sneakers back onto her now sock-covered feet.

Steeg's forehead returned to the steering wheel with a thud. He was defeated, and he knew it. He started the car, put it in drive, and pulled away from the curb, dutifully signaling his intention for the benefit of the police officer still parked behind him. Down the street and around the corner, they were soon on Highway 100 looking for the 66th Street turn off to take them back into Richfield.

The V3 Division crew's quarters rocked with laughter. Guys were howling. From the wall of racks fronting that corner of the room, several men almost rolled from their bunks with belly laughs they could hardly contain. The black and white images flickering on the wall mounted TV screen were ignored by everyone having too much fun with Steeg's story to notice the top three open buttons on Raquel Welch's white lab blouse.

"I take it all back," Denoso gasped for breath trying to recover from his laughing seizure. "Your's is so much better than mine. You knew I was lying, you called me on it, and matched me one better. That's the funniest story I've ever heard."

Steeg smiled, nodding and accepting the compliment. Some of the other fellows in the room were wiping tears from their eyes. Others began to applaud. Steeg modestly held up his hands.

"Thank you," he acknowledged with a bow. "Thank you. You're a great audience. I'm here all week…"

More laughs. Jerry Terry came up behind him and patted Steeg on the shoulder. "Thanks, Steeg. We needed that."

"Me, too," Steeg accepted.

Terry pulled up a chair and sat off to the side. "So, what happened in the end?"

"The end?" Steeg raised an eyebrow. "Oh. Well, nothing really. I promised I'd call her if I heard the cops had contacted my folks about anything, or whatever. But, when I got home, everyone was in bed already. As far as I know, nothing ever came of it."

Terry shook his head. "Great story."

After awhile, attention turned to the movie, and everything quieted down. Steeg sat with his fellow shipmates only for a short while, finding the movie a little too uncomfortable to watch. He slipped back to the head pretty much unnoticed.

Near the center of the bank of six stainless steel basins, he toggled the cold-water tap to trigger a short stream of water into his left hand, and splashed it to his face. He did this two more times, wiping both hands down to pull the excess water away. He stared at the image in the mirror for a long time, wondering what he was looking at. There were times, and this was one of them, when Steeg hardly recognized the face in the mirror. At that moment, the one thing he knew he needed more than anything was to hold Grace close to him. But that wasn't possible. Not anymore.

"So what happened?" Bear was leaning against the open doorway.

Steeg looked over to his friend. "What do you mean?"

"To the girl. What happened with her?"

He stared at Bear for a long moment before he had an answer. "She's still in school back home."

"Oh, good. So, you two are still together, then?"

Steeg looked back at his reflection in the mirror, noting the circles under his eyes from lack of sleep. His head barely moved in a short back and forth motion.

"Not really."

Chapter 15

Battle Alert Condition #3

0430 HOURS
18 APRIL 1969
USS HORNET CVS-12
SEA OF JAPAN, NORTH OF THE 38TH PARALLEL

Two days earlier, North Korea had shot down one of the U.S. Navy's Super Connies, a C121 reconnaissance aircraft used to intercept radio transmissions and with its ultra-sensitive magnetic boom, detect submerged submarines. There had been no word on survivors. The North Korean government had claimed the aircraft had violated their nation's air space, forcing the Communist country to shoot the spy plane down. The C121, a large turbo-prop aircraft loaded with the latest communication and surveillance equipment, was bulky, slow, and typically unarmed. Its range to intercept and monitor radio transmissions and detect submarines was extraordinary. As such, the C121 had no need to fly anywhere near territorial waters of any nation under observation.

Before evening chow the day after the ship had pulled around and climbed to maximum speed, Captain Jackson A. Stockton, *Hornet's* commanding officer, informed the ship's company of what had happened, making it clear that the North Korean action was completely unprovoked.

"We are part of a massive military response to a criminal act committed by an enemy state against our country. We will arrive on station early tomorrow morning," the Captain announced over the ship's PA system. "Shortly after we arrive, we will go to General Quarters. Once we have gone to GQ, and after all battle stations are checked and made ready, we will go to Battle Alert Condition Three. While under this alert condition, all battle stations will be manned around the clock. Some designated water tight doors above the water line will remain open to permit passage between all decks to key areas like Sickbay, the mess halls, and sleeping quarters. Other water tight doors will be sealed and remain sealed. This may be inconvenient, but adjust to it. All sentinel posts and observer stations will be manned continually. There will be shift relief similar to regular shift cycles while at sea. When you are off duty, you will find your movements restricted. Adjust to it. All aircraft on the flight deck will be armed and ready for battle. Aircraft on the hanger deck will be fueled and ready to be moved to the flight deck as needed. Flight Operations will be 'round the clock, and we will have our own birds in the air, on patrol for defense and recon continually."

The Captain had explained the mission as two-fold: search and rescue, and, more importantly, a show of force. As such, the *Hornet* was now part of the largest single task force and convoy deployment since the Korean War.

The night before, when he had returned from the head after his brief conversation with Bear, Steeg lay fully clothed in his bunk, his flight deck boots loosened, but still on his feet. The rest of the crew relaxed in their racks, or lounged around the lone television watching the remainder of *"The Fantastic Voyage."* Having seen the film before, or, at least having seen parts of it before, he had little interest in seeing it again. Nor did he particularly appreciate the familiar sweet emptiness that grew in his gut, reminding him of the woman with whom he had first seen it. Sleep would not come easily.

Lying there, he felt the weight press against his side. Real fear was suddenly upon him. His pulse pounded in his head as the anxiety soared

156

within him. He could feel the perspiration beading up across his forehead. In near panic, his eyes darted across the darkened overhead, a terrible scream rising almost violently from somewhere deep in his soul only to silently catch in his throat. He was losing the one thing he valued most, his sanity, and he was helpless to stop it. The scream that wouldn't come choked him as Grace whispered in his ear.

"You told them about Southdale."

He could feel the hurt in her voice.

"How could you do that? That was between us. It was our secret. You told them our secret."

She lay next to him on the narrow rack, but he wouldn't turn to face her. He was too afraid of what he might see. The seconds moved by in slow motion as he felt her pull away from him. The weight next to him lessened, and then disappeared. Grace was gone.

Steeg's breath returned in short, desperate gasps. He lay there not moving for a long time, recovering from the rush of adrenalin that had overtaken him. Then, effortlessly, his eyes closed, and he was asleep.

Later, awakened by a deafening silence in the darkened room, the steady ship vibration of the last two days from full speed running was suddenly gone. *Hornet* had slowed to cruising speed, and the seas had calmed considerably.

He raised his wristwatch to his face. The illuminated dial showed half-past four. That meant more than five hours of sleep, and Steeg felt completely energized.

Unbelievable he thought to himself, quietly rolling from his bunk, retrieving his shaving gear from his locker and quickly making it to the center basin in the head without disturbing the rest of his shipmates. In less than ten minutes, fresh and cleanly shaven, he returned the shaving kit to the locker, pulled on his heavy jacket, laced up the boots that had not left his feet all night, and exited through the hatch that led to the aft port gun tub.

It was cold. The wind bit bitterly into his face and he shivered as he pulled the jacket collar up tighter around his neck. He looked out across gun-metal gray waves and a starless night sky faintly tinted by a small moon almost completely hidden by solid overcast. Everything was dark. No running lights or shipboard illumination of any kind was visible.

He walked through the forward hatch and down the ladder that led to Hanger Bay Three. On the Hanger Deck, just as cold but not as breezy as top side, everything was quiet, again washed in black-red night operations lamping. He cautiously worked his way around secured stacks of maintenance gear and a jet engine tester rack giving his eyes time to adjust to the dim lighting. As he reached mid-bay, he could more clearly see the aircraft parked there and the extended tie-down chains that firmly held them to the deck. As usual, Hanger Bay Two was packed with HS-2 and SH-3A helicopters, spooned into place in tight, neat rows running starboard to port, their long props folded back along the fuselages like wings on a dragon fly. No one was in Hanger Deck Control, so he took the hatch down to the second deck, and headed aft to the mess hall to grab the first cup of coffee of the day.

A warship operates on a 24-hour schedule. As such, the mess decks never really closed. There were designated meal hours for morning, afternoon, evening chow and "mid-rats" (midnight rations), but coffee and reconstituted milk were always available. Along the corridor that was the crew's mess serving line, the fully staffed galley crew was busy pulling together huge containers filled with the various elements that would be breakfast starting at 0530 hours. Wheeled racks of caramel rolls were being rolled from the bakery to the serving line. A large stainless steel kettle under an even larger Hobart mixer was filled with pancake batter rhythmically mixed by the rotating paddle. Three more cooks stood at a center stainless steel table. Bracketed by cardboard stacks standing waist high, holding three dozen eggs in each formed sheet, the cooks cracked whole eggs into lines of cereal bowls in preparation of moving the eggs to the grill to be cooked to order for each enlisted man coming down the line.

In the mess hall itself, Steeg grabbed a clean coffee cup from the racks stacked next to the twin coffee urns that waited for him. Toggling the near spout and filling the cup almost to the rim, Steeg found a lone table on the starboard side and sat down.

Just a few other sailors sat at individual tables. The port side was being set up by the mess crew. Steeg sipped his coffee and watched the action around him. Mess crewmen set up fresh fruit, small boxes of cold cereals, breakfast pastries, and donuts on the self-serve tables just inside the entrance to the room. Two tall rotary tracked toasters stood in the center of the serving tables. Another apron-wearing crewman made sure both toasters were on and operating before he pulled two large flat trays of sliced bread from another wheeled rack and positioned one each on either side of the machines.

The mess decks were near and dear to Steeg's heart. In the barely two years he had been on *Hornet* he had served KP duty on the Hornet no less than three separate times. The first time was shortly after he had reported on board. As the youngest recruit in CATCC, the division chief had no choice but to assign him to the mess decks to fulfill the division's KP obligations. It was standard practice in all divisions to assign the most junior "Boot" recruits to KP. Consequently, in early April of '67, Steeg found himself assigned to the scullery where he scraped uneaten food from thousands of metal trays, and then shove them into the massive washer for sanitation.

KP duty was typically a three-month temporary assignment and every division on the ship was obligated to send a representative to the mess decks. It was not the most rewarding work he had ever done, and it looked like a pretty bleak summer for him. However, things changed for Steeg when the ship made it to the Gulf of Tonkin just a week later.

To prevent radar equipment from overheating, CATCC's radar rooms were air conditioned. In the tropics, the benefit was obvious to anyone working in CATCC, or the other limited number of spaces aboard ship that were air-conditioned. The mess decks were not air-conditioned, and the heat and humidity was overwhelming. Most sailors could adjust to it.

Steeg did not adjust. From his head to his feet, his body erupted with bright red heat rash festers capped in white puss that seeped from every pore. Perspiration was literally salt rubbed into every wound, and there were thousands of 'wounds' on his body. The pain was beyond excruciating and, when he could take the torture no longer, he took himself to Sickbay.

In Sickbay, the ship's doctor told him it was the worse case of heat rash the he had ever seen. Prescribing calamine lotion baths, he promptly ordered Steeg from the mess decks and returned to CATCC. And, not only to return to CATCC, but actually live in CATCC's air conditioned spaces continuously until the infections subsided. That would take weeks.

CATCC's division chief was not pleased. Steeg's place on the mess decks had to be taken by another, more senior, more experienced CATCC airman. The Chief liked the other airman a whole lot more than he liked Steeg. Watching the rash-infested recruit unroll his mattress and make his bunk on the deck in the far corner of CATCC's main radar room, the Chief decided he didn't like Steeg at all. Within days after Steeg had returned to the division, the Chief's feelings on the subject became clear.

"You're gone." The Chief sat at the desk in the adjacent scheduling room as he raised his chin to peer down his thin nose at Steeg who stood just inside the hatch leading to the main radar room.

"What's that, Chief?" Steeg replied, not sure he heard what was said.

"I don't want you here," the E-7 petty officer stated flatly. "You're gone."

Steeg failed to resist scratching the calamine-covered flesh under his gabardine shirt as he sensed the onset of yet another situation over which he would have very little control. "I'm sorry, Chief. I don't know what to say."

"Don't say anything," the petty officer continued to stare him down. "Just leave."

"But, Chief, I don't know where to go. I just got back here."

"I don't care where you go. I don't want you here."

Confused more than anything, and a little hurt as well, Steeg was quickly learning the true meaning of exasperation.

"Chief, maybe there's something I could do to make this up to you."

"Don't think so, Patterson. You're gone."

He struggled to come up with some idea that would open up a way to stay in the air conditioned space just a little while longer. It was the only area on the ship where he was relatively perspiration, and pain, free. After several moments of non-productive panic, he resigned to his fate.

Defeated, Steeg dropped his hands to his sides. "I wouldn't even be here if I had just got my orders to 'Photographer's Mate A School.'"

Chief lowered his chin. "You say 'Photographer's Mate?'"

Steeg nodded, saying nothing.

"You a photographer or something?"

"Yes, Chief." Steeg acknowledged sadly. "High school yearbook. I loved it. The recruiter told me I'd be assigned to 'A' School. He said with my experience I had it made."

Chief nodded slowly. "Sounds like something a recruiter would say."

The E-7 drummed his boney fingers on the desk with his stare coldly locked on Steeg. After a long moment, he rose from his chair, walked around Steeg and said as he headed out the door leading to the 02 level passageway, "Get ready to move."

Whether out of fear, or the fact that his body was covered neck to ankles with crusty pink liquid, he didn't know, but Steeg stood there stock still, saying nothing as he watched the chief disappear down the passageway.

The second three-month tour on the mess decks came quickly after that.

The ship's Photo Lab was headed by Chief Robert L. Hillman, another E-7. Chief Hillman was a sixteen year veteran with a Master's Degree, absolute authority over his personal fiefdom that was the *U.S.S Hornet's* Photo Lab, and who poorly managed a 280 pound girth around his middle. He was a big man. Seated snuggly at his desk in the lab's finishing room, he conducted the interrogation.

"Yearbook photographer." Chief Hillman stated flatly.

"Yes, Chief," Steeg replied crisply from the steel legged, vinyl-seated chair that seemed to him to sit quite a bit lower than Hillman's chair on the opposite side of the desk.

"So, where's the yearbook?"

"Back home," answered the recruit eagerly. "I've got a lot of shots of all kinds of stuff in it."

Hillman was genuinely unimpressed. "How do I know that?"

There was a quick, uncertain dart of his eyes as Steeg asked, "I'm sorry, Chief. How do you know what?"

Hillman frowned. "How do I know you have 'all kinds of stuff' in a yearbook you say you have back home?"

In mid-statement, Steeg's confidence disappeared. "Because I ... Oh, yes. I guess you don't, do you?"

"No. I don't." His mouth tightened with concern, Chief Hillman placed his hands on the desk blotter, laced his fingers together, rhythmically tapping his thumbs against each other. "Okay. Let's see what we have here: photography; high school; tell me, Airman Patterson, what type of photography did you do in high school?"

"Mostly black and white."

"Mostly?"

"Well, all of it, actually. Black and white."

"Film?"

"Yes, Chief."

"I meant what type of film."

"Oh. Yeah. Sports shots with Tri-X 400, the rest almost all Plus-X 125."

Hillman nodded slightly. "That's good. Darkroom?"

"Beseller enlargers. Used the smaller lenses with 35 millimeter negatives. Different set ups with larger formats."

"Cameras?"

"I used the school's Speed Graphic quite often – that had four-by-five inch sheet film. All 35 millimeter was shot with my own camera, a Minolta single lens reflex."

"Through the lens metering?"

"Well, no. Standard release with separate view finder."

"Humph. Older camera," Hillman dismissed it. "You should check out their new 101 SLR's. Solid. Exceptional exposure metering and control."

"Thanks, Chief. I will."

His chair squeaked loudly as Hillman leaned back, taking the recruit in with a weary eye.

"Patterson, I'm doing this as a favor to a friend, and not because of anything you've said here." Pulling a form from the right side drawer of the desk, Hillman produced a ball point pen and proceeded to fill in the appropriate blanks. "Here's the way it is going to be. For the duration of the summer months, that means until September, Mister, you will be assigned to this space. You will sleep here on the counter in the file room. You will also be responsible for keeping the lab clean – and I mean 4.0 and squared away. Do you understand?"

"Yes, Chief," Steeg answered, not really knowing if he understood or not.

"During this time, you will do everything you can to learn everything you can about photography, this lab's production capabilities, and everything in it, from the chemicals, to the tanks. Do you understand?" he asked again.

"Yes, Chief," came the same reply, with the same uncertainty.

"Good. Now, here's the downside. You are the junior man in this division. Sometime in September, you will be assigned to S2 Division for three months KP duty on the mess decks. By then, or shortly thereafter, we will be relieved of duty in Viet Nam, and on our way back to Japan. By then, your medical condition should be cleared up. That makes you eligible for KP duty. Any questions?"

Steeg shook his head in resignation. "No, Chief. Thank you for the opportunity to be part of your team."

"Good man."

Hillman was good to his word. As soon as *Hornet* left the Gulf of Tonkin, Steeg was back on the mess decks. This time, assigned to the bakery, he learned to change flour and eggs into dough for breads, pie crusts and pastries, including the best sticky pecan caramel rolls available anywhere. Steeg remained on the mess decks until mid-December of that year, a full month and three weeks after *Hornet* had returned to her home port of Long Beach, California. Only small, shallow scars testified to the heat rash that had so painfully covered his body earlier that year.

The day after he had finished his three month KP duty tour, Steeg returned to the Photo Lab. That morning he sat down at the same desk with Chief Hillman for his annual performance review.

The Chief's written evaluation of Steeg's performance was not a good one. Sitting across from the E-7, Steeg read the sheet Hillman handed to him in silence. When he got to the bottom where he was supposed to acknowledge his acceptance of the review with his signature, Steeg looked up.

"What does 'intellectual plodder' mean?"

"Why do you ask?" Hillman calmly countered.

"In this report you describe me as an 'intellectual plodder.' I've never heard that term before. I don't know what you mean by that."

Hillman sighed heavily, looking off to his right at nothing in particular. "Well, it simply means you are the kind of person who talks a good game, but doesn't produce anything."

Steeg blinked several times, weighing Hillman's response carefully in his mind before he said anything. It took him a moment before he could continue.

"You say in this evaluation of my performance that," he looked back to quote the report. "'At best, Airman Patterson exhibits limited ability to master fundamental principles of photography, and does not have the essential skills or motivation to qualify for the third class petty officer exam.'" Steeg looked back up at the Chief. "I don't know where that comes from."

Hillman shrugged. "You haven't completed the required text work. You haven't even submitted a request to take the petty officer exam. Every other Airman 3rd since I've been here had that requirement nailed well within their first three months. I can't recommend you for taking the exam given your evident lack of drive or desire to be a Photographer's Mate."

The muscles around Steeg's mouth slacken. The reality confronting him at that moment was undeniable. There was nothing he could say. The Chief had obviously made up his mind about Steeg not continuing in the Photo Lab Division probably before he had agreed to take him on the previous summer. Gathering himself as best he could, Steeg handed the evaluation form back to Chief Hillman, who took it, but then quickly held it out for Steeg to take back.

"You didn't sign it, Patterson."

Steeg looked him straight in the eye. "I'm not signing it, Chief Hillman. I don't agree with it and I don't accept it."

"You have to sign it, sailor."

Steeg shook his head as he came to his feet. Hillman remained seated as Steeg stood up, leaned over the desk, and didn't blink. "You sign it. It's your report, not mine. I've been on mess deck duty for three months, and the day I get back here, you lay this on my permanent record? Fine. Go ahead. While you're at it, let's complete the paperwork on my request for a transfer. I have no doubt you already have most of it filled in."

Hillman stayed seated, but leaned back in his chair away from the airman. "Request granted," he said, picking up a pen and signing the evaluation form. "You're going to the hanger deck, my good man. You're not going to like it. In fact, you just might get killed out there. But, maybe you'll be able to do something more in their division besides just talk."

And, that was how Steeg Patterson ended up in V3 Division.

Sitting in the mess hall as the 0530 hours breakfast crowd began to trickle in, the humor of it all brought a smile to his face as he finished off his second cup of coffee. Hillman had been right, Steeg hadn't enjoyed being transferred from the relatively cushy air conditioned Photo Lab to the confines of the more rigorous '12-on, 12-off' 'round the clock schedule of the hanger deck crew. But, he had to laugh when, three days after reporting to his new division, V3 Chief Petty Officer Harland Cason called him into Hanger Deck Control where he was informed that, being the junior man in the division, he was being assigned to S2 Division for three months of KP duty effective immediately. He was assigned to the spud locker where he and Aronso Godfry, a thin, lanky black man about the same age as he, mostly peeled and washed huge kettles of potatoes for the duration of the three month stint.

Steeg grabbed a single-serving size box of Cheerios from the self-serve table, dumped them into a clean coffee cup, doused that with a good amount of reconstituted milk from the dispenser, and returned to his table to spoon down his breakfast. That was when Karl came up with his tray loaded with fried eggs, bacon, grits, toast, and two large pecan caramel rolls. Karl took the chair Steeg offered as he walked up.

"Hitting the line a bit early aren't you?" Steeg asked. "Shift's not over yet."

"I missed 'Mid-Rats' so Joe let me come down. Nothing's moving up there anyway," the tall blonde-haired sailor explained, diving into the mountain of food spilling over the edges of the tray. With his mouth full, he added, "Heard you really cut them up last night."

Steeg chuckled. "I guess so. It was pretty funny. Denoso was trying to BS his way through a story about naked hippies at a music festival with Wesson Oil, or something like that. He's okay, but he'd be better if he didn't have to always brag about stuff."

Karl nodded between bites. After he washed a mouthful down with some milk, he said, "Santini said it was about your girlfriend back home. He said you two got in trouble with the cops who caught you in a car at a shopping center?"

Steeg held up one hand to stop his friend. "Not exactly. I mean, yeah, sort of, but you would have had to have been there to get the whole flavor of the story – and I'm not going to repeat it here. Sorry you weren't there, but you're married now and I don't think Barb would appreciate knowing you were subjected to the sordid escapades of a wayward shipmate."

Karl almost choked as the laugh came up his throat. "Okay. Enough said."

The startling clanging of the General Quarters alarm filled the mess hall, immediately followed by the Boatswain's announcement.

"General Quarters! General Quarters! All hands man your battle stations!"

The alarm continued to sound as sailors scrambled from their tables.

"So much for breakfast!" Karl complained over the noise of the alarm, springing to his feet as he grabbed one of the caramel rolls and exited the mess hall with Steeg right behind him. Karl's nearly full mess tray remained on the table.

Chapter 16

Preparations for Recovery

**0800 HOURS
SATURDAY, 1 JUNE 1969
MORNING COLORS AND GENERAL MUSTER
ON THE HANGER DECK
USS HORNET CVS-12
PIER E, U.S. NAVY BASE
LONG BEACH, CALIFORNIA**

Whites were the uniform of the day, and nearly all of the ship's company of more than 1,800 men stood crisply at attention in neat divisional ranks across the three hanger bays. After the bugler blew morning colors over the PA system, the ranks stood at "Parade Rest" as each division took muster to account for all personnel. It was a formal procedure conducted every weekday morning while the ship was in port. But this was a Saturday, and it was unusual to have this many ship's company on board while *Hornet* was in her home port of Long Beach.

"What's up?" Steeg asked First Class Petty Officer Joe Bonia as the senior P.O. passed by taking count of the division one file at a time.

"Captain's got a big announcement," Joe replied in a low voice, checking off names from the division roster on the clipboard as he continued down to the end of the line.

On 23 May 1969, Captain Carl J. Seiberlich had replaced Captain Jackson A. Stockton in *Hornet's* normal one-year rotation of commanding officers. Due to the extended WestPac tour resulting from the Sea of Japan military action after North Korea's shoot-down of the C121 Super Connie reconnaissance plane, Stockton's tenure had exceeded the one year period by about three months. After being relieved on station by *Kearsage*, *Hornet* finally returned to Long Beach at 1700 hours on 12 May. Captain Seiberlich took command eleven days later.

Seiberlich was a World War II veteran who had come to the Navy through the U.S. Merchant Marine Academy. Graduated in 1943, he served on two merchant vessels before gaining his commission in the U.S. Navy, where he was first assigned as ship's navigator aboard the *U.S.S. Mayo*, DD-422 in 1944. In 1945, *Mayo* moved from the Atlantic to the Pacific for the duration of the war, taking part in the Japanese surrender in Tokyo Bay.

One thing the war had made clear to most career minded Naval officers, and Seiberlich was one of them, was the fact that aircraft carriers had replaced battleships as the dominate naval warship. Projecting air power had become, and would remain, the primary operational mission of the surface navy. To gain the flight qualifications necessary for advancement, Seiberlich earned his aviator wings in 'lighter-than-air' craft in 1952. That was the same year he received the Harmon International Trophy awarded by President Truman for his work in introducing the first operational variable depth towed sonar array. In the mid-1960's, Seiberlich qualified in helicopters and multi-engine fixed wing aircraft. This made him the only aviator in U.S. Naval history to land blimps, airplanes, and helicopters on an aircraft carrier.

He was less than two months short of his 42nd birthday when he took command of *Hornet*.

The PA speakers crackled as Captain Seiberlich's voice boomed across the Hanger Deck.

"This is your Captain speaking, and today is a day in which you can all take pride. *Hornet* has been selected for a great, singular mission destined to be remembered throughout all of human history. Each and every one of you will be there. Each and every one of you will have a piece of the most significant moment in all of human accomplishment. Gentlemen, I have the distinct honor to inform you that *Hornet* has been selected as the Primary Recovery Ship for Apollo 11 – the first manned landing on the moon. *Hornet* will pick up the three astronauts when they return. As your commanding officer, I have been designated Commander, Primary Landing Area Recovery Group, Task Force 130, for all Department of Defense forces supporting NASA in this operation.

"Every division, every department will have an essential roll to play in this mission. The eyes of the world will be upon us, gentlemen. What the world will see will be the finest moment in the long and honorable service of one of this country's greatest warships. I know I can depend on the finest aircraft carrier crew in the fleet to be nothing less than outstanding."

The Captain signed off on his address, and muster was dismissed to divisional spaces. All V3 members were ordered to the hanger deck crew's lounge. The full division, with the addition of a fresh batch of "Boots," now numbered almost 50 people, so it was a tight fit for everyone squeezed into a closed, non-air conditioned space.

Division Lieutenant Richard A. Blunt, the last to enter the lounge, was only able to go about six feet into the overcrowded room. It was unusual for Lieutenant Blunt to be in the lounge because he spent as much time as possible in "Officers' Country" and as little time as necessary in V3 Division spaces.

Bonia silenced the men. "Listen up! Lieutenant has something to say!"

The noisy chatter quieted down as Lieutenant Blunt cleared his throat.

"Well, men, this is going to be short and sweet," the officer began somewhat nervously.

"Thank you, lieutenant!" Someone yelled from the crowd. Laughter quickly rose and fell. Lieutenant Blunt smiled and relaxed, but only a little.

"Yes. Well, there're a couple of things you need to be aware of as a result of this new mission…"

"We just got back from a nine month WestPac, Lieutenant. Are we going to have leave time?" The question came from someone a few feet in front of where Steeg stood, but Steeg couldn't see who it was.

The lieutenant cleared his throat again and shook his head. "Maybe a few days, but nothing more than that. We're going to be shipping out in two weeks for 'at sea' recovery training. Until then, and probably continually up until the actual recovery, we're taking on a whole bunch of people and special equipment. We're going to have special air groups, different aircraft on board, C1-A Traders, E-1B Tracers, a whole squadron of SH-3D Sea King choppers specifically modified for this type of recovery. That doesn't count the TV people, their equipment and trucks."

"Is Walter Cronkite going to be on board, Sir?" This came from Santini in the far corner.

The lieutenant smiled and shook his head. "I don't think so. But, word has it the President will be here."

"Nixon?!" someone asked.

"He's the President," Lieutenant Blunt corrected, adding more firmly, "And he's your Commander-in-Chief, not 'Nixon' on board this ship."

The lieutenant turned back to the crew. "I just want you men to be prepared. Things are going to get more demanding because of all this. This is bigger than the World Series, men. Every person in authority will have an interest in making every subordinate's existence as miserable as possible if only to benefit their own career at your expense. All eyes will be on two places — the flight deck and the hanger deck. That puts pressure on me, and because stuff rolls downhill, that puts pressure on you. It won't be coming from me if I can help it, I promise. Just be prepared when people you'd normally never see, let alone hear from, are suddenly jumping down your throat about something you'd normally never have anything to do with."

Some of the guys looked at each other wondering what the lieutenant was getting at. Steeg caught Karl's eye from the opposite side of the lounge, and they both nodded at each other with reluctant understanding.

"That's about it for now," Lieutenant Blunt concluded. "With the new air group, we have a new Air Boss. He is Commander Ihram Michael Knauts. I have met him and he's a stickler for regulations and 4-0 appearance. You can expect him to pay you a visit this coming week. Until then, enjoy your weekend, and be ready for real work to start on Monday."

The lieutenant gave the group a relaxed salute, turned and left the room. The chatter volume quickly returned to maximum as Bonia tried and failed to take control of the group if only to dismiss them to resume duty, or go on liberty, as the case may be. The few men assigned to weekend duty remained in the lounge, allowing the remaining majority of the division to filter from the room back down to the Hanger Deck.

Letting other division members pass by, Steeg waited at the bottom of the ladder for Karl, one of the last men to exit the lounge.

"Did the lieutenant say the Air Boss was 'Commander Ihram Michael' and then say 'Nuts'?" Karl asked as he joined Steeg. "Or, is 'Nuts' the commander's last name?"

"Beats me," Steeg replied. "I think his last name is Nuts. You going into town?"

The blonde-haired sailor looked at his wristwatch and smiled. "If things go as planned, Barb is waiting for me on the pier right now."

"It must be great to be married," Steeg said as the two of them quickly walked across the hanger bay.

"It is. A lot better when we're back in Long Beach, though," Karl replied. "What are you doing?"

"Going into town," Steeg admitted. "You're probably not going to believe this, but I'm actually going to see a girl."

"Why wouldn't I believe that? You see a girl in almost every port we go to, so why not in Long Beach?"

"That's not what I mean," Steeg said as the two made the turn to the short passageway that led to the starboard side aft brow. The aft brow was where enlisted men entered and exited the ship while in port. "I mean a real girl."

Karl raised an eyebrow. "Not a 'professional' this time?"

"Nope, she's an honest to goodness real 'female of the normal.' I met her about a week and a half ago."

"Good," Karl judged as the two showed their weekend passes to the DOD[7], saluted the colors and made their way down the ramp. "You need someone to keep you in line."

"Yeah, I think you're right about that," Steeg agreed, following two steps behind his friend.

Marilyn Johnson was a born again Christian originally from Enid, Oklahoma. Slight in features, with long, brown hair and pale green eyes, she had moved to Long Beach three years earlier with her then five year-old daughter. She found the Lord while visiting a full gospel church, and tried to make ends meet working full time as a clerical worker for the city public works department. One night a week, she left her now eight year-old daughter with the church's youth group ministry while she handed out religious tracks on the mean streets of downtown Long Beach.

It was on one of those nights that Steeg first met Marilyn.

It was a typical comfortable late spring evening in Southern California. Steeg had left the Silver Dollar Bar on Long Beach Boulevard, feeling only slightly the effects of the too few drinks he could afford during his extended visit to the bar. The streets were busy with crowds of pedestrians and more than an annoying amount of vehicular traffic cruising down Long Beach and Ocean Boulevards. The noise and the congestion mildly irritated him as he made his way south to Ocean Boulevard. He crossed the intersection, and continued toward the Pussy Cat adult theater where he fully intended to spend the rest of the night. He would do so not for the entertainment, but because it was the one place he knew he could catch some sleep in reasonably comfortable padded seats and not be disturbed.

He was short of mid-block, and two doors away from the Pussy Cat, when he felt something hit his hand. Steeg didn't break stride as he held the religious track up to his face, quickly paging through it. It was like a miniature comic book, with drawings and dialog concerning the salvation available to all who seek and accept Jesus as their personal savior. Reaching the illumination of the Pussy Cat Theater marquee, Steeg turned the pages with his fingers, reading each panel. He was familiar with it all, having seen many like it during his enlistment in the service. Tracts similar to it were free for the taking at all sorts of places catering to the more conservative needs and interests of military servicemen. He had accepted Christ as his personal Savior more than two years earlier, and he agreed with everything the little pamphlet promoted. The fact someone had shoved it into his hand deserved at least a 'thank you' from him.

Looking over his shoulder back from where he had just come, he saw her near the corner, silhouetted against the pulsating blur of oncoming headlights at the busy intersection, handing out the pamphlets to people passing by. She seemed to be completely alone. That caused him some concern. This part of town, this time of night, was not the safest place for a lone woman to be. Nevertheless, he owed her a 'thank you,' and he was going to deliver.

When he reached her, she had her back turned to him.

"Excuse me," he said. She turned, only a little startled. "I just wanted to say 'thank you' for the tract. I really appreciate it."

She relaxed a bit and smiled. "You're welcome. That's very nice. The Lord be with you."

"I believe he is, every day."

She tilted her head slightly to one side. "Oh. Well, that's good. You know our Lord, then?"

"Oh, yes," he acknowledged. "I only accepted Him a couple of years ago, but I believe He has been with me my whole life... Tell me, are you a nun?"

She had a light and pleasantly modest laugh. "Oh, no. I'm just a normal woman."

He glanced around at the people passing by. "You know, you're not in the safest part of town to be doing this."

"That's all right. I'm protected."

He sighed as he looked around for anyone else who may have been with her. No one in the vicinity appeared to be helping her. "I understand, but, you should have someone with you just to be safe. Things happen out here from time to time."

She looked at him and smiled as she held up a thick stack of pamphlets. "Would you like to help?"

"Well, I don't actually do…" Steeg hesitated as his eyes met hers. The next moment, he took the offered pamphlets as he offered a slight apology. "I normally don't do this sort of thing."

"It's pretty easy," she said as she took a step toward an oncoming mass of pedestrians crossing the intersection, handed a stranger a pamphlet the person reflexively grabbed. She stepped back toward Steeg. "See?"

"Why, yes, I guess I do," Steeg smiled at the young woman, hesitantly stepping into the path of two people and handing a tract to each. Both of them took what he had offered, and without missing a step, walked on. He returned to where she stood watching him. "Two for the price of one. Not bad for a beginner."

"We're all beginners," she said.

Steeg stayed with her for the next forty-five minutes, handing out pamphlets until the small cardboard box she had perched against the wall was empty.

Satisfied, she picked up the empty box and tucked it under her arm. "Well, we did it. Thank you for your help."

"It was my pleasure," Steeg returned. "What do you do now? Go home?"

"I have to go back to church and get Linda Ann, she's my daughter, and then we go home."

"Oh, so your husband is picking you up, then?"

She cocked her head in his direction. "No, I'm not married," she stated as a matter of fact. "I'll be walking to church. It's only a few blocks away off Alamitos and 2nd Street."

Steeg knew the general lay of Long Beach. He looked at his wristwatch. It was past ten o'clock. "Alamitos and 2nd is more than a few blocks away. And, it is getting pretty late. Look, if you don't want me to, that's fine, but

I'd like to walk you to where you need to go. I promise it's on the level. I won't try anything."

She smiled warmly as together they turned to walk down Ocean. "I know that. Like I said, I'm protected."

Linda Ann was a cute, dark-haired little girl with a sweet, innocent smile who was perfectly comfortable with Steeg walking the two of them from the church.

Around the corner at Bonito Avenue, their two room apartment was in a small four unit building in the middle of the block. Marilyn led him up the outside stairwell to the open walkway of the second level. Her apartment was tucked in the corner facing the street. As she opened the door, she asked him to wait for her in the kitchen while she put Linda Ann to bed.

The apartment was very small, with a tight kitchenette and eating area squeezed into the rear, joining a single room with a small bed in the corner for Linda Ann, and a daybed at the adjacent wall. A small television sat on top of an equally small dresser on the opposite side of the room. The larger room was kept dark. It didn't take long for Marilyn to join Steeg at the table in the dimly lit kitchen.

"Thank you for seeing us home tonight," she said as she sat across from him.

"No sweat, anytime."

"So, do you go back to your ship tonight?"

"Not if I don't have to," he chuckled smiling, completely unaware of what he had just implied.

She looked at him, concerned she may have mistakenly suggested something she had not intended. "I'm sorry. That didn't come out right. I don't mean anything by that, you know."

As their eyes met, he replied as honestly as he knew how. "I don't expect anything. You're a good person. I'm happy to help out and be of service."

Marilyn smiled in appreciation as Steeg rose from the chair and stepped toward the door. With his hand on the door knob, he turned back to her.

"I would like to take you out for dinner, though. You and Linda Ann. I'll be back in town in two nights. If that's okay with you."

She hardly took the time for serious consideration as she reached for a pen and a small note pad resting on the table between the salt and pepper shakers. "It's a date," she said, scribbling both her work and apartment phone numbers down on the note pad. She easily peeled the slip of paper from the pad, folded it once, walked over and handed it to him. "Call me first, though, just to make sure. Okay?"

"Absolutely," Steeg took the note and shoved it into his pants pocket. He said "Good night," and with that, left the apartment letting her shut the door behind him.

Their dinner date was followed by three successive evenings when they either ate out or dined in with Marilyn preparing something on the kitchenette's tiny range top.

That Sunday, they spent the entire day together, starting with a rousing full gospel service at her church on 2nd Street, and a light picnic lunch on the beach with Linda Ann playing tag with the easy waves lapping the sand. At the end of the day, with Linda Ann already upstairs, Steeg said good night to Marilyn on the outside stoop. That was when she reached up and pulled him to her.

It was a warm kiss, pleasant for Steeg as he let it linger. As they parted, her eyes searched his. Several seconds passed and Steeg wondered if she could see anything worthwhile in him.

"I'm damaged goods, too, Steeg," she said, understanding more than he knew.

"What do you mean?" He asked with pause.

"Well, it's pretty obvious, isn't it?" She smiled as her head motioned toward the upstairs apartment. "Who was it that hurt you?"

He darkened as her words penetrated where he didn't want them to go. He looked away. "What makes you say that?"

Down the sidewalk he could see a familiar silhouette walking from around the corner and toward them. He pulled his eyes back to Marilyn, unable to hide the growing uneasiness he felt. He could hear the approaching footsteps.

"I can tell someone has, Steeg," she held his hand in hers. "It's okay. I won't do what she did. I promise."

He looked at her, only to turn toward the sound of steps growing louder to see the figure emerge from the shadows. He gripped Marilyn's hand tightly. Grace gave him a knowing look as she passed by the two of them and receded into the darkness. Steeg turned his head back to find Marilyn searching his face in an unasked question. His breathing returned. It was a long moment before he could say anything.

"I'm all right, Marilyn. Everything works, everything functions. I'm completely normal in all respects."

Marilyn knew Steeg was lying by the way he squeezed her hand so firmly. She eased her hand free from his and placed it over his heart. "Except here. There's something that's not quite right, here."

He mildly protested, but she had already accepted a fact about him that he could not. Despite that, or maybe because of it, they would grow closer over the succeeding days.

The two weeks after Captain Seiberlich's announcement were filled with busy and heavy work. Each day shipments of machines, equipment and men were loaded onto the ship. It didn't take long for the strain on the V3 Division to begin to show. Most, but not all of the equipment, had to be stored somewhere on the Hanger Deck.

Without the air groups on board, it should have been easy, but the squadrons would be the last to arrive, and, when they did, there had to be sufficient room for housing all the aircraft to be used in recovery operations. Material, trucks, vans and additional communication equipment arriving almost around the clock had to be positioned in limited designated spaces on the hanger deck in a way to assure adequate room for securing everything, and more importantly, moving all the yet to arrive aircraft.

Lieutenant Blunt would watch safely out of the way from the top of the Hanger Deck Control ladder as First and Second Class V3 petty officers used 100-foot measuring tapes bay-to-bay determining the best ways to divide the limited space. Roped off spaces indicated predetermined areas for aircraft, the twin mobile quarantine facilities (MQF's) to be loaded onboard at Pearl Harbor, as well as the replica command capsule and towing vehicles to be used in the recovery rehearsals. There was little space for everything else. Most of the larger items hugged the starboard side of all three bays, the largest of which was the gleaming white ABC Network broadcast control trailer and a support van shoved forward just inside the track for the 18 inch thick, deck-to-overhead steel paneled fire doors that separated Hanger Bay Two from Hanger Bay One.

Halfway through the second week things started to slow down. The exception was the arrival of a single, long flat bed trailer pulled by an International Harvester tractor. The flat bed carried a large white fiberglass dome to Pier E where *Hornet* was berthed. A second enclosed semi-tractor trailer followed the first. Together, the trucks pulled to a stop adjacent with the number three elevator. The dome was perhaps 15 feet in diameter and just as tall.

"That ain't going in here," Karl said, standing in the late afternoon sun between Steeg and First Class Bonia at the elevator's edge. "We didn't plan on holding that thing."

"Relax," Bonia said. "It's the NASA communication dome, holds all the satellite sending and receiving gear – real high tech stuff. It's going up on the Flight Deck."

"That's good." Steeg nodded. "What's next?"

The First Class Petty Officer looked behind him and into the hanger bay area. "I may be wrong, but I think we're just about done with as much as we can get done in Long Beach."

"We're not going on recovery training until the sixteenth," Steeg reminded him. "Sounds like we have a ready made opportunity for a four day pass!"

Karl liked the sound of that, but Bonia wasn't as supportive of the idea as the two men would have liked. He led them back into the hanger bay and to the hatch below Hanger Deck Control where Lieutenant Blunt was standing, papers in hand.

Bonia snapped a crisp salute, which the lieutenant returned with noticeably less enthusiasm.

"We're just about done for the day here, Lieutenant," First Class Petty Officer Bonia announced.

Blunt shook his head handing the papers over. "It doesn't look like it, Joe. These came down from the Air Boss."

Bonia looked at the papers, Steeg and Karl peering over his shoulder. They were neatly scaled drawings of Hanger Bay Two, the aft half of which had a dimensional layout of a large rectangular area surrounded by a wide frame around the perimeter. The large rectangle was designated 'White' with two smaller narrow rectangles, both labeled 'MQF.' The wide perimeter frame was designated 'Blue' and it extended from the starboard door leading to the flight deck escalator, around the white rectangle to the door leading to the aft brow. Together, the outlined shapes covered almost half of the total length and depth of Hanger Bay Two.

"What is this?" Bonia asked.

"The commander wants a white rectangle painted on the deck, surrounded by a blue walk path. It needs to be done before we get to Pearl. That's where the Mobile Quarantine Facilities will be loaded."

"Painted?" Steeg asked.

"You want us to paint on top of the non-skid?" asked Karl.

The lieutenant nodded.

Steeg shook his head. "That's not very safe, lieutenant. You paint the deck, and it gets wet, you're going to have a pretty slippery surface to work on."

"You're probably right, Steeg," the lieutenant agreed. "But the painted areas won't be walked on, at least not as much as the rest of the deck. It's going to be 'Show Time' gentlemen, and the Navy wants Hanger Bay Two to be center stage."

"When does the commander want us to complete this?" Bonia's eyes darted from the drawing to the hanger bay and back again.

"It needs to be completed before Pearl." The lieutenant repeated.

"That's going to be a little tough, isn't it?" Steeg queried. "We're going to have to block off Bay Two. Nothing can move across the area while it's being painted, and nothing will be able to move across the area after it's painted without damaging the paint job. Everything that moves on this ship moves through this bay."

"I know," Blunt agreed again.

"But, we have more supplies coming in, don't we?" Karl asked.

"Yes, we do," Blunt's reply carried a note of frustration.

"We'll get it done for you, Lieutenant," Bonia announced confidently, saluting the officer, turning and motioning the other two men to follow him up the ladder.

The three of them fit snuggly inside Hanger Deck Control.

"The last thing you guys want is the lieutenant to be involved with supervising this job," Bonia insisted.

"Yeah, but..." Steeg began.

"No 'buts' about it. Trust me on this one. We'll figure out a way," said Bonia. "In fact, Steeg, I want you to be in charge of the crew to get it done."

"Gee, thanks," Steeg didn't hide his displeasure. "When do I start?"

"Not until we pick up the air groups," Bonia ordered. "We will be at sea practicing capsule recoveries. We'll rope off only the section of the bay that will be painted. That's where your crew will work. We should be able to have enough free deck space on the port side of the bay for people to get through..."

"Not enough space for any aircraft, though. Nothing bigger than a tow tractor at best," Karl observed looking at the drawing again.

"Then that's what it will be," Bonia agreed. "The lieutenant says Hanger Bay Two is 'center stage' on this deal. I gotta feeling the paint job is only the beginning of a whole lot of things to come down. I need you, Steeg, to stay on top of the project once we get started."

"Okay, will do," Steeg accepted. "When is the actual recovery supposed to take place?"

"I don't know," the First Class admitted. "I think I heard they're scheduled to launch on July sixteenth. You can figure, what? Maybe six, eight days later we pick 'em up."

"That's more than a month from now," Karl complained. "How are we going to keep this paint job looking good for that length of time with all this activity going on? We got over a hundred civilians coming on board, television cameras, and cable running all over the place, this is not going to be easy."

"We'll do it," Joe said with certainty. "We're the only ones who can."

Steeg's free time was spent in Long Beach with Marilyn and Linda Ann. Mostly, with money being tight, they watched evening television in her apartment, all three on the daybed in the main room. Steeg often showed up with a small bag of groceries he would pick up at the Safeway farther up Long Beach Boulevard, north of the Post Office building by a couple of blocks. It added to his walking time, but he was often in town sooner than Marilyn was off from her job with the Public Works Department anyway. Marilyn seemed to appreciate his thoughtfulness, although each time he carried in a grocery bag, she would remind him that it wasn't necessary. Steeg always responded with "I know, but it's either that or I have to wash dishes. I've done enough KP duty."

Of course, he'd help clean up after dinner anyway.

The night of the 15th was another one of Steeg's special treats for dinner, this time at Arthur Treacher's Fish and Chips. The three of them sat together in a small booth against a front window, and they feasted on hot, greasy, batter-fried filets, fries, and vinegar.

"So, what's the big occasion?" Marilyn asked warmly.

Steeg shrugged. "Just to be together with two of my favorite people."

A small giggle escaped from Linda Ann between bites, and Marilyn smiled.

"Well, I will say one thing, since I ran into you I've been eating really good."

The way she said it tugged at his gut.

"What do you mean?" Steeg asked.

She responded with a short laugh. "You come into town, bring groceries, I eat. You come into town, take me out for dinner, I eat. Almost every night. Why do you do that?"

Steeg smiled as he shoved another fat slice of vinegar-drenched fried potato into his mouth. "Because I can't dance! Tried dancing once, Senior Prom – you know? I'm not very good. I'm much better at eating, so, that's what we'll do more often than not, if you don't mind."

Her eyes revealed her warm appreciation. "I can see I'll never have to worry about starving to death as long as you're around."

He could not help but remember Gracie's similar comments. As vivid memories filled his mind, he could feel the hollow reminder inside. His appetite quickly left him.

Sitting across from Marilyn and her daughter, an easy smile with nothing behind it hid the wave of emptiness that was suddenly upon him. Weakly, he replied, "It's the 'hunter-gatherer' in me. A male role thing, I think."

She reached across and placed her cool hand on top of his. "I think it's sweet."

They continued with the meal, Steeg saying little and eating less. As the sodas began to run dry, Marilyn offered to treat everyone to a movie.

"There's a show at the discount theatre down Long Beach Boulevard," she said.

Steeg knew the place. He had spent more liberties than he cared to admit sitting in the air conditioned splendor of the aged American Theater. At fifty cents a ticket, it was the cheapest entertainment in town.

"Sounds good to me," Steeg agreed. "What's showing?"

"'Fantastic Voyage,'" she said. Steeg became mildly light headed.

"Oh," he responded unenthusiastically. "Well, that's a pretty good film. Have either of you seen it before?"

Linda Ann shook her head as Marilyn responded, "I have, a while back."

"Yeah, me too. In fact, it was on the ship just awhile ago," he lied, but only a little. "If it's okay with you, maybe we could skip the movie and just take it easy tonight."

"Okay, sure, that's fine, too," Marilyn agreed, her green eyes holding Steeg's for only the brief moment he allowed.

"I'll tell you what. Let's get some refills on the sodas, and take a stroll through the Mall. How's that sound?"

Both girls agreed, and Steeg took all three drink cups up to the counter. He almost fell into shock when the girl behind the counter turned to serve him. It was Grace!

"They seem very nice, Steeg," she said with a smile as she took the drink cups and turned toward the dispenser on the back counter. "Let's see, that's two diets and an orange, right?"

Almost violently, Steeg leaned across the counter toward her. "You can't do this! It's not right. You're not being fair!"

Grace dutifully refilled the cups and brought them back to where Steeg stood. "Whatever do you mean? Here you go, three refills. Don't worry, they're on the house."

Steeg carefully grouped the cups between his two hands, and then glared back at the woman to vent his frustration and anger, but he stopped. The woman standing in front of him was not Grace at all. Cautiously, he glanced around the service counter. The only person there was the elderly woman who had just handed him the refills. Grace was gone.

The next hour offered Steeg a chance to regroup and gather himself. It was a relaxed window shopping tour of the mall down the street from "Treacher's" that went by too quickly. But it was getting late, so the trio began the substantial walk back to Marilyn's apartment, Linda Ann enjoying an oversized lollipop she couldn't possibly finish along the way. Marilyn's arm wrapped around Steeg's as they walked.

"I'll be shipping out early tomorrow morning," he said as they rounded the corner on her block.

"I know," Marilyn replied.

"I'm not really too sure how long this is going to take," he said. "This is kind of different, going out to practice picking up a space capsule, then picking up astronauts. All the press, all the dignitaries, and all the technology, it's all different from the normal stuff we do."

"It should be exciting, I would think."

Steeg nodded. "Yes, it will be, I suppose. I'll fill you in on the details when I get back."

They made it to the front step of the apartment building. Marilyn urged Linda Ann to go upstairs ahead of them. At the stoop, Steeg quickly took his leave.

"You could stay," Marilyn said. Her eyes avoided his and focused on his shirt pocket instead.

Steeg ran his fingers down the smooth softness of her cheek. Her eyes met his and he kissed her as tenderly as he knew how.

"You would be easy to be with," he said softly. "For the rest of my life, I'd be lucky to be with you."

He wished it were different. There was the familiar hollow feeling within him that had become his constant companion. And his hallucinations were more frequent, impossible for him to control. To say he carried excess baggage when it came to forming new relationships was an understatement of the highest order and he knew it. He also knew it wasn't fair to add any of that to the burdens Marilyn already carried.

"Besides, it wouldn't be fair to Linda Ann for me to stay the night." His excuse was convenient for both of them. "This mission will give us some time to figure some things out. When I get back, we'll catch up and we'll know what to do."

She nodded in agreement. "Good night, then," she said, her lips meeting his again. "Be careful."

Chapter 17

"T – Minus Three Weeks and Counting"

1000 HOURS
PEARL HARBOR, HAWAII
WEDNESDAY, 26 JUNE 1969
HANGER BAY TWO
USS HORNET CVS-12

It was called "Mobile Quarantine Facility" (MQF) and there were two of them. Both were modified Airstream trailers. Each trailer was shiny brushed aluminum on the outside, air conditioned and fully equipped. On the inside were sleeping quarters, a food preparation area, a conference table that performed double-duty dining purposes at meal times, and located near the rear door 18"x36" window that made the MQF look just a little bit more homey, a smaller worktable. Each trailer was hoisted from a four-axle, 16 wheel self-propelled gurney with a hydraulic-assisted lifting platform that elevated the enclosures from the pier up to a height even with the lowered number three elevator. Once on the elevator, the first MQF was towed into Hanger Bay Two, positioned mid-bay starboard side on the forward half of the large white painted rectangle that had been so carefully prepared only a week earlier. The second MQF soon followed, positioned directly behind the first unit, on the aft portion of the same white painted area. The second trailer was designated the Primary MQF, with the first unit to serve as backup if necessary.

In Pearl Harbor the Primary Mobile Quarantine Facility on the pier next to *Hornet's* number three elevator (note the television camera on the elevator platform between the two civilians wearing ties and white shirts).

The MQFs were the most obvious measure to deal with the primary concern of possible biological contamination the astronauts could bring back from the moon. Much of the training and preparation for the recovery operations focused on safeguards against the risk of contamination. In the water and on the ship itself, every conceivable measure was taken to protect against unknown "moon bugs." Even the UDT swim team members responsible for securing the command capsule's floatation collar would wear isolation suits as a precaution.

In addition to the MQFs, NASA loaded a new, full-scale mock up of the Apollo Command Module on board, replacing the earlier unit used in practice off the southern California coast. This new capsule would be used for enhanced recovery operations training enroute to the actual recovery area. Finally, more than 250 members of three specialized recovery teams joined *Hornet* in Pearl, bringing on board all of their necessary equipment as well. With the hoard of civilian personnel, television broadcast equipment, technicians, cameramen, combined with the C1-A Traders, E-1B Tracers and eight SH-3D Sea King helicopters, their pilots, support crews, and technicians embarked after *Hornet* had left Long Beach, it was cozy if not tight quarters for everyone concerned.

But it was the paint job on the deck of Hanger Bay Two with which Air Boss Commander Ihram Michael Knauts was most concerned.

"You wanted to see me, Sir?" Steeg saluted as he entered Hanger Bay Control. Lieutenant Blunt, seated at the status board, returned the salute. Aviation Boatswain Mate First Class Chas Farmer, sitting behind the lieutenant on the rear bench, nodded at the young sailor taking a seat next to him.

"You've done an outstanding job on the Hanger Deck, Patterson," the lieutenant said.

"Thank you, Sir. It wasn't me. It was my crew. They did the work, Sir."

Lt. Blunt handed Steeg a short handwritten note that had been scribbled on a small slip of blue-lined paper.

> *Lt. Blunt,*
> *Essential Hanger Bay Two is hospital clean. Under no circumstances is there to be any visible FOD, or dirt, or any other foreign material of any kind on that deck. All painted areas will be repainted once underway. This includes the padeyes.*
>
> *Cmdr I. M. Knauts*

"I see," Steeg said, looking at the note in his hand. *Cmdr. I.M. Knauts,* Steeg thought to himself. *He signs his name 'I.M. Knauts!' He certainly is NUTS! What kind of parent with the last name of Knauts would give their son a name with the initials 'I-M', anyway?*

Steeg looked up from the note.

"The padeyes, Sir?"

Padeyes are deck-embedded cups with welded steel crossbars enabling tie down hooks to anchor aircraft to the deck. From any direction, there was a padeye about every three feet. On *Hornet*, the total number of padeyes on the hanger and flights decks numbered in the thousands. Humorously, Steeg silently considered the idea that counting the number of padeyes on the hanger deck would make a fine disciplinary detail some day.

The lieutenant nodded. "Yes. It seems the padeyes collect dirt. Not enough to really be visible, but enough to need cleaning on a regular basis."

Steeg looked out the bay window to the painted deck below. The white area, surrounded on three sides by the four-foot wide pale blue painted path, showed the evidence of every foot print and tire track of the last two days. He couldn't see any dirt in the padeyes, but he knew there must be some. Otherwise, the Air Boss wouldn't have mentioned it in his note.

"Yes, Sir," Steeg acknowledged. "There's no doubt the areas need to be painted again."

Farmer spoke up. "Not just painted, Steeg. The padeyes need to be cleaned out. The Air Boss has ordered your crew to clean out each one of the padeyes every hour."

"Every hour?"

Farmer nodded and Lieutenant Blunt looked away.

"All the padeyes? Across the whole deck?"

Farmer nodded again. The lieutenant kept looking out the window.

Steeg collected himself. "Maybe we could rig up a high pressure air line, bring in some pneumatic hoses and blow the padeyes clean. That would be quick, efficient and get the job done with minimal disruption of all the other stuff going on down there."

"That's a good idea," Farmer agreed, but the lieutenant shook his head.

"I'm afraid that won't be possible," he said reluctantly. "I offered the same idea to the Air Boss, but he doesn't want any dust kicked up, coating everything, including the electronics of the NASA equipment and the ABC Network gear."

Steeg could feel the sourness begin to swell in his stomach. "That would mean we'd be using rags to swab out the padeyes."

The lieutenant nodded as he turned back to Steeg. "You should soak them in acetone. It cleans great, evaporates quickly and leaves minimal residue."

Steeg nodded. "Yes, Sir. That should do it." He paused to filter the latest development through his mind. He could see his small, six-man crew on their hands and knees crawling across the rows of padeyes that covered the hanger bay. Each man would have to drag a gallon can of acetone along as he swabbed each padeye one at a time with rags. The rags would quickly foul, and leave more dirt behind than what was picked up. He shook his head. "Acetone should do it."

Farmer could see Steeg's concern. "Denoso's gone to the base supply depot for increased stores of rags and bunting."

"Bunting?"

"Yes," Lieutenant Blunt fingered back and forth one of the small plastic planes on the status board. "The commander wants a fence around the white area. He's specifically ordered it to be made of red-white-and-blue bunting."

"A fence on the Hanger Deck? How's that going to work?"

"Denoso's come up with a plan to use wooden poles and empty five-gallon paint buckets," the lieutenant explained somewhat unenthusiastically. "The idea is to cut a hole in the lid, put the poles in the buckets, fill the buckets with sand to hold the poles in place, paint everything white and staple the bunting to the poles."

Steeg nodded, knowing the answer to his next question before he asked it. "And, the paint buckets are empty because…?"

"They'll be left over," Farmer answered. "Your crew gets to repaint the hanger deck as soon as we depart for rehearsals next week."

"Along with the hanger bay doors, and all the bulkheads in Hanger Bay Two," Lieutenant Blunt added. "The commander feels the walls need to be whiter, so we have new paint arriving in the next day or two – approximately 500 gallons of it."

GRACIE'S GHOST – THE HAUNTING 189

His mouth dropped open and Steeg had difficulty forming the words. "Five hundred gallons? That's – holy crap – that's, that's a whole lot of paint, even for the hanger bay. What's going on with all this?"

Lt. Blunt made little effort to hide his growing disgust. "Exactly what I warned you guys about when we were told of this mission. I told you there will be people who will use this thing as a springboard for career advancement, and everything else will roll down hill from that. It started before we left Long Beach. It's only picking up speed."

Steeg nodded, furrowing his brow as he scanned the hanger bay through the window. "I'm going to need some help on this. My little team of six guys isn't big enough."

"Maybe we can add a couple of men," Farmer offered. "But, everyone else has been assigned to recovery duties."

That snapped Steeg's head around. "I am on the recovery team. I am, aren't I?"

Farmer shook his head. "Sorry, Steeg. Karl has been assigned as lead Yellow Shirt for the recovery detail. We have to keep you on the paint crew."

Steeg slumped back on the bench, deflated. "You mean all I'm going to do is stand around sipping coffee watching a half dozen blue shirts clean padeyes and paint the hanger bay? While everyone else is in the middle of the biggest historical event since Columbus discovered America?"

Lt. Blunt left his chair and stepped to the door to leave Hanger Deck Control. "Your men respect you, and you've done an outstanding job with the hanger bay. Now, you need to stay on top of it as all these civilians screw it up without even knowing they're doing it."

At the door, the lieutenant added, "Besides, the commander thinks Karl looks better on camera."

The door quietly shut behind the officer. Steeg looked at Farmer without saying anything.

Farmer shook his head. "The lieutenant is right. Captain wants to make Admiral; Commander wants to make Captain. This is how it's done, Steeg."

Steeg's head slowly bobbed up and down as the full reality of his evolving situation became clearer in his mind. "And, Karl looks better on camera. I didn't even know there had been any auditions!"

"A Jeep? Where are we going?" Tom Kinsey asked, hurriedly following his fellow Yellow Shirts up the ladder that led to the aft port gun tub and then, into the crew's quarters.

"Denoso's got a jeep," Karl yelled back, leading the way.

"We're going on a tour of the island," Bear added from behind.

"A tour?" Kinsey echoed.

"Of Oahu," Steeg expanded, following close behind Karl. "Diamond Head, Waikiki, the whole island."

"How does Denoso get a Jeep? He's only a Blue Shirt?" Kinsey complained.

"He has his ways," said Bear as the group rounded the corner and entered the sleeping quarters. "Bring your civvies in a bag. We'll change on the road."

With lightning speed, the gang peeled off their working dungarees, slapped on crisp dress white uniforms, brilliant clean covers, and spit-shined black shoes. As they were dressing, Airman 3rd John Tyner came in and immediately asked if he could come along. They all agreed. In a matter of minutes they left the ship in mass, paper bagged civilian clothes in hand, down the aft brow to the pier.

Denoso was on the pier, dressed in a loose fitting green pull-over shirt, cut-offs, sandals and a big mustached grin, leaning against a white four-door Datsun sedan. Karl held out both hands as he led the group toward the small car.

"Where's the Jeep?" he asked.

"Didn't have any," Denoso responded. "Got this little baby instead. It's better, anyway. Not so 'military' in appearance, so we'll blend in better."

"It's kind of small, isn't it?" Bear came up to the car and ran a hand over the hood. "There're six of us."

"We'll fit," was all Denoso said.

"How is it you get away with wearing civilian clothes out here?" John Tyner griped.

"It's all in whom you know, young man," came the college educated Denoso's answer. "Let's get going!"

It was a bit of a challenge for the six grown men to find a way for all of them to fit inside the Japanese import, but, with Bear sitting on Steeg's left leg and John Tyner's right leg and Kinsey on the left side of the back seat, it worked, at least for a while.

"Where to first?" Denoso asked from behind the steering wheel.

"We'll go counterclockwise," Karl offered. "Honolulu first; Waikiki and nearly naked women next. After that, Diamond Head, then around the island."

"Sounds like a plan," Denoso turned the key and the little four cylinder engine sprang to life. "But first, you guys get into your civvies!" He shifted into gear and pivoted the overloaded Datsun in a hurried turn toward Astoria Street.

After the guys had changed from dress whites to pullover shirts and cut-offs at the base EM Club, Denoso skillfully zigzagged his way to Neches Avenue, turned right on Arizona Road and exited the base at the gate that opened to Kamehameha Highway.

Kamehameha Highway wrapped around the south side of Oahu, past the Honolulu International Airport, over the Keehi Lagoon bridge and into the Chinatown section of Honolulu. As fast as Denoso could drive, that was about all the time he was allowing for sightseeing. The mission was clear, as far as Denoso was concerned — get to Waikiki as quickly as possible. King Street was the more efficient route, a one-way street with less traffic than Kapiolani Boulevard.

"We're coming up on Hotel Street, guys," Denoso announced. "That's where all the hookers are, right?"

Laughter as Kinsey jokingly asked, "Wanna be dropped off, Steeg?"

Steeg shook his head, embarrassed by the barb. "That's okay. I've sworn off hookers."

"Good move," Karl said from the front seat, and Denoso sped along, taking a beach-ward turn on Kalakaua Avenue.

Parking was a challenge everywhere they looked. After cruising side streets and finding nowhere to store the Datsun, the parking gods smiled on them as they turned on Kaiolu Street. A car pulled away from the curb just in front of them. Denoso slid into the spot nose first and the men unfolded themselves from the tiny vehicle that had become smaller with every passing mile. A block later, they walked into a busy tourist trap area with shop after shop butted up against each other. As they passed an open-air eatery with a large, carved wooden Polynesian statue as a greeter, someone suggested it was time for lunch.

"Lunch, nothing!" Tyner declined impatiently. "The beach, man! The beach! Girls!"

The general consensus was in favor of the beach. Getting there was the challenge now. The sky was clear, the sun was everywhere and the humidity was perfectly matched with an unbelievably comfortable temperature. But this was new territory for everyone, and with all the tall buildings, you couldn't actually see the ocean from where they were, let alone the beach. At the next corner, the street sign read "Royal Hawaiian Avenue."

"That way," Steeg pointed to his right. "My Dad stayed at the Royal Hawaiian Hotel in World War II. He had pictures, and the place is right on the beach. This street will take us right to it."

And, so it did.

Waikiki Beach was a postcard come to life. They entered through the cabana area surrounding a small pool at the Royal Hawaiian Hotel. Bikini clad females of all types and sizes were everywhere a young man could look. Dispersing and pairing up so not to frighten the tourists, they strolled across the warm sand and enjoyed the sights.

"Any minute now you'd expect Connie Stevens and Troy Donahue to come up from the water carrying their surf boards," Steeg mused.

Tyner, walking about ten feet seaward from him, was too preoccupied to have heard Steeg's comment. "Ever notice," he smiled. "How so much more interesting women's butts are compared to guys' butts?"

Steeg arched an eyebrow toward his shipmate. "Yeah, I hope so."

A breaker wall ran up the beach to separate Waikiki Beach from Kuhio Beach Park. This was the stopping point for the men's walking tour. Kalakaua Avenue ran just beyond the palm trees that framed the beach.

They congregated at the low wall to consider their next move. Tyner and Kinsey suggested staying at the beach for a while longer. Who knew, maybe they would find some new friends of the female persuasion? On the other hand, Steeg, Karl, Bear and Denoso wanted to get to Diamond Head.

"It's a tour," Denoso explained emphatically. "Not a 'sleep-over.'"

"But the women – look at all the women here!" Tyner moaned.

"Some of us are married," Karl said firmly.

"Some of us aren't," countered Kinsey.

"All I'm saying is, it's hard enough dealing with the distractions," Karl continued. "Don't get me wrong. They're very nice distractions. I understand wanting to be distracted. But, it only complicates things by hanging around too long."

"Temptation too much for you?" Denoso chuckled.

Karl shook his head. "No. It's easier not dealing with it, that's all."

"Besides," Steeg chimed in. "Everyone sees Waikiki Beach when they come here. Not everyone ventures out to the rest of the island. We've seen the beach. Now, we have a limited window of opportunity to do the rest. I think we should stick to schedule."

Only a couple of mumbling complaints followed general agreement. Denoso looked at his wristwatch. "We need to make it to Diamond Head by 1400 hours…"

"Hey, not so loud," Kinsey shushed his friend. "Everyone will know we're not civilians."

"I think the secret's out," Steeg responded, tossing his hand across the sunbathing crowds that ignored the men completely. As far back as the Royal Hawaiian Hotel, every bikini-clad beach member one could see was looking elsewhere. A smattering of acknowledging low groans came from the other five.

"So, we walk all the way back to the car?" Bear asked.

"I don't think so," Steeg answered.

"What do you mean?" Denoso came back. "We need the car."

"That we do," Steeg agreed, smiling. "But we all don't need to go get it."

"What do you mean by that?" Denoso frowned.

"I think the driver should go get the car and pick us up right on that corner right over there," Steeg pointed to the street on the other side of the trees.

"Oh, no, that's not fair," Denoso protested.

"I think it's fair," Karl allowed. "And, as almost the junior man on this tour, and, as the guy who got the car to begin with, you should accept the responsibility for getting the car. Besides, you need to follow the orders of your superiors."

"Orders?! You're ordering me to get the car?!"

Karl nodded. "You are almost junior man, William. Only Tyner is lower in rank, and he doesn't have the keys, you do. You get the car."

"But...!" Denoso pleaded, searching the others for support that wasn't there. They all stood in silent agreement, smiling. After a long moment of pleading that got him nowhere, Denoso gave in. "Okay, I'll get the car. But, I still don't think this is very fair."

With that, he turned around and left the group, walking straight down the beach from where they had all just come.

When Denoso was out of earshot, Bear added, "Besides, he's the only reservist in the group. Eighteen months and out, my rear end!"

They all laughed as they headed toward the street to find a place to eat and wait for Denoso and the car.

A tunnel bored through the northeast rim was the entrance to Diamond Head, an inactive volcanic crater officially declared a Hawaii State Monument. The full carload required a more than reasonable fee at the walled summit. With the steady sea breezes keeping them cool, it was easily the most comfortable place to be.

As time passed, the guys were ready to leave. It wasn't the view they grew tired of, but thirst that compelled them back through the tunnels, and down the path to where the car was waiting. At the bottom of the crater once again, the stifling mid-afternoon heat washed the men in streams of sweat, gluing each man's shirt to his body. The car was hot to the touch, and all four doors hung open for several minutes in a vain effort to cool the interior. Still too hot to enter but unable to wait any longer, they climbed in, all windows opened, with the back seat arrangement made even more uncomfortable by Bear's sweaty body sitting on top of the thighs of the equally soaked Steeg Patterson and John Tyner.

"Let's get going," Kinsey urged from the rear left window seat. "Get some air moving through this thing."

Denoso didn't need another invitation. He rolled the car from the parking space with even the little bit of hot air moving through the open windows providing noticeable relief. They cleared the tunnel exiting the crater and followed the winding narrow street that took them back to Diamond Head Road. Once there, Denoso turned right and followed it down to Kaalawai, a small village where they stopped at a simple open market to buy food, water and a couple of six packs of Primo Beer, a local Hawaiian brew that came in dark glass bottles with a distinctive blue and silver gray label. Downing half the beer and all the food, each of them re-hydrated nicely as they recovered more fully right there in the parking area in front of the market. After a short while, they were ready to resume their trek heading north along the eastern side of the island on State Highway 72, a coastal route that would lead them to the north side of the island.

It was already past 5:00 p.m. by time they reached Puohala Village and the day was slipping away from them. After a quick stop at a gas station to relieve themselves and top off the tank, they were back on Highway 83 trying to put as much pavement behind them as possible before it got too late. It was a fast and slow route. Fast in the open along the shore; slow through the scattered small villages that dotted the north side of the island.

The poverty Steeg saw from the window surprised him. These villages were nothing like Honolulu. There were many small huts and framed houses, but almost all the houses and buildings were single story, and nothing else was above a story and a half tall. Businesses were few. It was not what he had expected. With the sun now lower in the sky, the temperatures were more pleasing, and having another man sitting on half his lap seemed to be just slightly less burdensome for Steeg.

Reaching the northern crown of the island where pineapple fields covered large swaths of land, they made the turn south on Highway 83 to continue toward Sunset Beach. Reaching the small town, they stopped at a tiny establishment to restock their food supplies and liquid refreshment, and then found a comfortable place to relax on the beach to watch the sun set.

The evening breezes felt great and the guys had the beach almost completely to themselves. The exception were a few groups farther down the open stretch of sand, a couple or two strolling along, and three bikini-clad young women of college age about 20 yards away laughing amongst themselves and, every now and then, looking over to the small group of six guys trying hard not to look like G.I.'s.

"I think they want to join us," Denoso announced as he opened the ice packed Styrofoam cooler they had purchased at the store just inside the town limits. He extracted a bottle of Primo and popped the cap off with the opener he kept on his key ring.

"Not if they know what's good for them," Karl said, glancing over to the three women as he retrieved a brown glass bottle for himself, plus two more. He grabbed the key ring from Denoso and removed all three caps, then walked over to where Bear and Steeg were lounging against a large boulder.

"It might be fun to ask them over," Kinsey offered. "Especially if we all go skinny dipping!"

"Skinny dipping?" Bear and Steeg both repeated simultaneously. Steeg reached up and accepted the bottle of Primo as Karl came up to him.

"I don't think that's a good idea," Steeg continued. "Nude sunbathing isn't legal in Hawaii."

"Is too," Kinsey countered.

"Is not," Steeg insisted.

"Is too!"

"Is not!" Steeg pointed a serious beer bottle in the direction of his red-haired friend. "Regardless of what you may have heard, nude sunbathing is prohibited in Hawaii. It's against the law. That's the way it is. It isn't going to change just because you happen to be in port this week. You've been reading Michener again, haven't you?"

"So?" Kinsey laughed. "Besides, the sun's going down, so it won't be 'sunbathing.' It'll be too dark to see anything in another twenty minutes anyway. Who's gonna know?"

The sun was going down, only a few degrees above the horizon. The few fluffy white clouds had started to turn shades of crimson, purple and gold. The sky was now becoming a rich, azure blue and the sun itself was growing larger as it lowered closer to a sea that stretched endlessly in front of them. There was an undeniable calming majesty about it.

What a beautiful spot You've created, Lord, Steeg prayed silently. *Thank you, Jesus, for the gift of this moment, and these friends. Be with each of them, and let them know You, too.*

Denoso interrupted the moment. "I think I'm going to go and invite them over."

"Please don't," Karl pleaded.

"Please do!" Kinsey countered enthusiastically. "I'll come with!"

The two sailors in cut-off jeans and short sleeve shirts turned down the beach to where the girls were.

"This could be trouble," Karl moaned.

"Could be," Steeg agreed. "And, I'm not going 'skinny dippin' no matter what."

Karl nodded, but from his other side, Bear disagreed. "I'll go if the others go. It's gotta be dark, though."

Karl cradled his head in his hands. "Please, don't encourage them, Paul."

"Come on," urged Bear. "You only go around once. Grab for what you can get."

"Yeah, as long as what you're grabbin' isn't any part of me," Steeg protested. "Count me out."

Paul 'Teddy Bear' Muggins smiled slyly at his friend from Minnesota. "That's okay with me. I'm the tie-breaking vote, if it comes to that."

"Don't count on that," Karl said. "Tyner isn't going to do it, either."

John heard that from where he was standing at the edge of the beach, looking at the sunset with shallow waves lapping at his feet. "Why can't I do it?" he asked over his shoulder.

"Because I order you not to," Karl replied.

"Oh."

Steeg chuckled. "When all else fails, pull rank."

"Absolutely," Karl bobbed his head in agreement as Denoso and Kinsey returned.

"Well, what's the verdict?" Bear asked and Kinsey waved his hand in disgust in the direction of the three females.

"They threatened to call the cops on us," Denoso spat. "I tell you, I don't know what's happening to red blooded American women these days."

"Liberation," Steeg answered sincerely.

"Nah, that ain't it," Denoso plopped himself down, cross-legged in the sand and took an impatient swig from his bottle.

"No, that is it," Steeg came back. "You're a college graduate and you haven't read Betty Freidan?"

Denoso looked at his shipmate and shook his head. "I was an Accounting Major."

Steeg shrugged as a couple of the others laughed.

The red-orange ball of sun was half-way into the sea, and the guys quieted to take in the beauty of it.

"I heard about your special detail for the recovery," Karl said sitting next to Steeg. "I'm sorry about that."

Steeg shrugged it off. "Orders are orders, Mister. You're ordered to paint, you paint. You're ordered to clean, you clean. My squad has been ordered to do both, every hour until the recovery. You did okay, though. You're lead Yellow Shirt, Karl. You're going to be on worldwide television." He punched Karl playfully in the shoulder. "A star is born!"

"Yeah, right," Karl smiled, kicking at the sand with the heel of his sandaled foot, somewhat shyly, but with pride, too. "We start full rehearsals next week. They're pulling out all the stops – dropping the new dummy capsule into the ocean miles from the ship; maneuvering for pick-up; swim teams jumping from helicopters, floatation collar drills; it's all pretty involved stuff. Then, bringing the pick-up helo into the hanger bay, positioning it in the right spot for the astronauts to get to the MQF; we're doing this over and over again, from splashdown to the MQF, until we'll be able to do it in our sleep."

Denoso, Bear, Klinger & Tyner on their Oahu tour in the rented Datsun. Those other two guys in the background must have been tourists. Steeg is behind the camera.

"How are my guys going to paint and clean if you guys are tracking up the hanger bay all the time?" Steeg griped.

Karl shook his head. "I don't know. Like I said, 'sorry about that.'"

The sun reduced to a sliver of color just above the horizon.

"God, it's beautiful here," Karl said.

"Praise the Lord," Steeg replied softly.

Karl nodded. "Amen, to that."

The sun had disappeared, and the remaining daylight hung in the late evening sky like a blue-gray mist. It was a good twenty minutes before darkness began to wrap around them.

"It's time!" Denoso whooped as he kicked off his sneakers, pulled his shirt over his head and dropped his cut-offs in the sand at his feet.

Kinsey let out a short yelp, close on Denoso's heels, stripping down as he ran. Bear sprang up and with a quick "What the hell!" he shed his clothes and joined Tyner who had done the same. In a fraction of a moment, they were butt naked and throwing themselves into the shallow surf.

Karl and Steeg looked at each other. Steeg shook his head, refusing to move from his spot, but Karl cursed himself as he gave in, peeled off his shirt, shorts and sandals before he ran into the water.

Steeg smiled as Karl's white butt cheeks quickly disappearing into silhouette. He looked over his shoulder to see who might have noticed what had just happened. Somewhat closer to the surf, the three women in bikinis stood giggling and pointing in mouth-opened amazement at the naked men splashing about in the water just off shore.

Chapter 18

4-0 and Squared Away

Wednesday, 02 July 1969
USS Hornet CVS-12
450 miles Southwest of Hawaii

Hornet and the rest of Task Force 130 had been at sea for three days. The weather had been perfect with easy seas, no rain, sunshine so bright, and humidity so perfect, the civilian technicians from NASA and the ABC Broadcasting Network considered the excursion less work and more a pleasure cruise. It was significantly less so for the ship's company. Duty stations operated on a 'round the clock' basis and 'round the clock' aptly described the Hanger Bay Two maintenance routine for Steeg and his six-man squad.

After arriving at the practice area, two recovery simulations were performed each morning, with each one taking nearly three hours to complete. Everyone was involved one way or another, including all backup crews for every critical part of the operation, and every part of the recovery operation was critical. Whatever the contingency that may arise, it had to be provided for, and 4-0 performance was demanded from everyone.

02 July 1969 was a Wednesday and rehearsal was scheduled to start early. Almost two hours before sunup, Commander Knauts and Lieutenant Blunt took their now regular morning inspection tour of Hanger Bay Two.

Only five foot, four inches tall with lifts in his shoes, Commander Knauts was more than a good head shorter than the lieutenant and as hard as rock. He started each day with a half hour calisthenics routine, concluding with a twenty-minute full out run – not jog – around the Hanger Deck. The commander received regular monthly shipments of an array of vitamins, minerals and protein food supplements, and he took pride in a body fat percentage of less than 10 percent. The result was a short, extraordinarily fit thirty-five year-old with a washboard stomach, who wore khakis with razor-sharp creases, spit-shined shoes so brilliant you could comb your hair in the reflection, and a person who practically exuded nervous energy all over anyone who came within arm's reach of him. However, the commander was still short, and if only for that reason, Lieutenant Blunt considered it wise to slouch as he walked next to the man.

"Better," Knauts said. He stopped at the forward edge of the blue painted path that bordered the large white painted rectangle containing the two MQF's. Hands on hips, the commander's sharp eyes perused the area with radar-like efficiency. "But still not good enough."

The lieutenant's shoulders slouched a little lower.

Carefully to protect the perfection of his trouser crease, the Air Boss squatted down over a padeye just outside the blue painted area. "Look here, Blunt," He pulled a ballpoint pen from his shirt pocket and poked it under the welded crossbar of the padeye. "There's this black crud still in there. That's gotta go."

"But Sir, that's Non-Skid from the original coating we gave the deck after Long Beach. It always looks like that," the lieutenant explained as respectfully as he could. Standing over the man stooped below him, Blunt felt uncomfortably under dressed, or, at least somehow out of uniform. Knaut's MacArthur-esque splendor was indeed magnificent! The lieutenant's mouth tightened to hide a stifled grin as a humorous thought invaded his mind: the only thing the commander lacked was a thin-stemmed corncob pipe, a pair of aviator sunglasses, and about a foot, maybe a foot and a half, of height.

The commander stood erect, tugging the gold braided brim of his hat closer to his eyebrows, and tried without success to level a stare straight into the eyes of the taller junior officer. "I know it's Non-Skid. It's not as clean as in the painted areas. I want every padeye clean. All of them."

Blunt looked down to his shoes, noticing his buffed shine was a poor match to the mirrored finish of the Air Boss's shoes. "Yes, Sir, they will be."

"Good." Knauts resumed his tour following the blue painted path at an excruciatingly exact pace. "Now, these walls still need paint. Things just don't look right down here. And, we still don't have the fence up, yet. What's going on with the fence?"

"It's pretty much done, Sir. We have the bunting and poles rolled up and waiting in the paint locker."

"Well, why isn't it up then?"

"The television people, Sir."

"Television people?"

"Yes, Sir," Blunt nodded in the direction of the ABC Broadcasting Network trailer on the forward starboard side of the bay. "They're still stringing lights in here. They put them up, then they take them down, move them around, adjust them, put them up again, then pull them down again, put them some place else. Mostly, they hang them from the overhead. Sometimes, they have lights on tripods. I guess they're trying all sorts of angles to get the best lighting they can, Sir."

Knauts bent his neck back to look at the overhead. "Well, crap! They've got ugly, thick black cables running across everything up there! That can't be. You tell those people we have to paint the overhead before recovery and they can't be putting black cables up there."

Blunt felt the morning's first hint of nausea. "Yes, Sir, but, Sir, I don't think we can actually paint the overhead."

"Why not?!" the commander glared, his left eye slightly tightening in a faint twitch Blunt couldn't help but notice.

"Overspray, Sir," the lieutenant replied quietly, trying his best not to irritate the Air Boss anymore than he already had. "If we paint the overhead, we'll have to drape the entire hanger bay in drop cloths, otherwise, paint will end up on everything: the equipment, the cameras, the lights, the MQF's."

Blunt's words registered. With a wide stance and hands on his hips, the commander looked about the hanger bay. After a long, silent moment, Knauts nodded in agreement.

"You're right. Okay, we don't paint the overhead. We just tell those TV people we will. Tell them to keep the cables off the overhead. I don't care if they have to string chandeliers up there, I don't want black cables on my overhead! You got that, Mister?"

"Yes, Sir," Lieutenant Blunt confirmed with dwindling enthusiasm as they continued their tour along the blue painted path.

"Look at these marks," Knauts complained pointing to the deck. "Tire tread marks on the paint. That's not acceptable, either. I thought this deck was repainted?"

"It was, Sir," Blunt replied. "But, they're still hauling equipment around with fork lifts, even during rehearsals. They have one TV camera mounted on a forklift they move around to shoot the recovery chopper as it's towed into position. They literally follow it from elevator two to the Primary MQF, Sir. That makes it real tough to keep them off the paint."

"Well, rope the area off for the love of Mike! Keep the forklifts from crossing on the paint. Do something, hang it all, to keep these areas spotless!"

'Keep these areas spotless' was the one order Blunt had heard more times than he cared to remember.

"This hanger bay is going to be center stage for the whole world to see, Lieutenant, and we all do ourselves proud when it is 4-0 and squared away, you got that?"

Blunt had heard that before, too. "Yes, Sir."

"Outstanding!" the commander barked, saluting the lieutenant briskly. "Gotta get topside to check out the new paint job on the Flight Deck."

The small man turned and hurried across the bay in the direction of the escalator, leaving Blunt standing alone next to the gleaming brushed aluminum shell of the Primary MQF, trying to will his growing nausea away.

Neither officer had noticed the silent observer of the inspection. John "Spanky" Gaffaney, a twelve year veteran and 2nd Class Aviation Boatswains Mate, had skillfully connived his temporary assignment to the Master at Arms Office into an extended billet that provided him the prestige of ship-wide policing authority while keeping him safely from the more rigorous duties of plane pushing on the Hanger Deck. From his perch at the top of the ladder that led to the MAA shack on the 01 level, Spanky had seen the entire exchange from the moment the two officers had walked into the bay. About five feet away from the bottom step of the ladder was the Primary MQF trailer where Lieutenant Blunt now stood. Watching from his perch, Spanky could see the lieutenant looked ill. He said nothing as the junior officer shoved his hands deep into his pants pockets, turned and slowly made his way to Hanger Deck Control.

The UDT (Underwater Demolition Team) guys had kept up their rhythmic leg kicks for more than half an hour. Lying on their backs in Hanger Bay Three just inboard from the number three elevator, the cooling sea breezes washed over them as they trained. The remarkably fit specialists hadn't missed a beat since Steeg had come down with his squad to begin the first padeye cleaning detail of the morning.

The petty officer stood watching the swimmers, sipping from his freshly filled coffee mug as behind him in Hanger Bay Two his squad made slower than usual progress. On their hands and knees cleaning the padeyes in the painted areas, it had taken them thirty-seven minutes to work half way across the white rectangle.

The Blue Shirts' pace was slower for at least two reasons. First, they were in no hurry, fully aware after the previous three days that this detail was made more sane if they stretched it out. Not directly connected to any specific operation for the recovery exercises themselves, each man intuitively knew that if the detail finished too quickly, someone higher up would simply find something else for them to do. Secondly, Steeg had passed along the lieutenant's instructions to hand clean with rags soaked with acetone the wayward tire tread marks that marred the deck. Whereas before they could rise and walk to the next padeye in line for cleaning, this new deck scrubbing instruction put the six enlisted men on their hands and knees continually.

The exception to the 'hands and knees' position was during the exchange of rags. A large sack loaded with clean rags rested against the port bulkhead next to the door leading to the paint locker. Steeg, keeping with his supervisory role in this detail, monitored the residue in evaporating acetone left behind as the crew cleaned. When the deck dried and a noticeable film appeared to leave a trail, he instructed the offending sailor to change his rag.

When five of the six men had reached the half way mark on the white rectangle, Steeg blew his whistle and motioned them together.

"This really blows, man," Santini spat.

Steeg looked at the man. "Why don't you tell us how you really feel?"

"I did," he replied with increased emphasis. "It blows!"

Steeg nodded, along with several others standing in a semi-circle in front of him. "Ours is not to reason why, gentlemen..."

"If we did, they'd find something else for us to do," interrupted Eddy Harrison, a thin 18 year-old with thick, horn-rimmed glasses strapped to his face.

"That's right," Steeg agreed. "So, listen up, we have a new request from the Air Boss."

A collective moan rose from the group.

Steeg continued undeterred. "The lieutenant has asked us to pay particular attention to the padeyes in the non-painted areas of the deck. We need to remove any evidence of Non-Skid build up from the padeyes."

More moans.

"And clean the insides of the padeyes to make sure all material that can be removed is removed."

More moans.

"In addition, there is concern that the bulkheads need more paint..."

Moans again, only louder.

"... So, we will work in teams of two to refresh the exposed white painted areas, AND one two-man team will spot paint the colored components including all painted signage, color-coded safety gear, fire hose spools, extinguisher racks, and water risers."

"Why that stuff?" Santini protested louder.

"Because, my good man," Steeg replied. "By enhancing the darker colors on the walls, we make the white walls look more white. That way, we will actually paint less of the large areas and more of the smaller details, making all this a little bit easier on all of us."

"Yeah, right," Santini griped.

"It'll be better than being on your hands and knees all the time," one of the other Blue Shirts blurted out.

"You got that right," agreed another.

"Besides," Steeg said. "We're in the middle of the Pacific Ocean, somewhere south of Hawaii. Where else you gonna go? What else you gonna do? Just some other crap detail the Air Boss wants you to do to make him look good. Keep doing this detail. At least you know what to expect."

"Not much, that's what," Santini grumbled.

"Maybe," Steeg agreed. "But, at least you know what the score is. The spot painting of the colored items was my idea, and the lieutenant liked it, so blame me. I just think that, in the long run, it makes things easier for you guys that's all."

A little less grumbling was heard as Steeg directed his squad to finish cleaning the padeyes in the painted areas. The men returned to their work.

Spanky Gaffaney, in dress whites and a black and gold MAA armband, came up behind him. With him was a civilian at least 40 years old, heavy set, and dressed in a plaid work shirt, gray trousers and a *Hornet* ball cap.

"Morning, 'Sheriff.' What's up?" Steeg asked as the two men came up to him.

"This here is Eugene Gunhofer," Spanky introduced. "He's with ABC."

Gunhofer extended a hand and Steeg took it.

"How can I help you, Mr. Gunhofer?"

Concern etched across the face of the on-location producer for ABC Broadcasting. "I don't know if you can, but I need some help understanding what's going on here."

"What's that?" Steeg responded.

"Well, I got word this morning that we've been ordered to remove our cabling for lighting the hanger bay, and frankly I just don't know what to do."

Gunhofer pulled a folded sheet of paper from his breast pocket and handed it to Steeg. The message was in Lieutenant Blunt's distinctive scribble. Steeg read it and then handed it back to the man.

"Yes, it seems you have been ordered to remove the cables," the petty officer agreed, glancing over to Spanky. The MAA shrugged his shoulders as he hid a slight roll of his eyes from the civilian. "I'm afraid I wasn't informed of this."

Gunhofer stammered with frustration. "Me n-n-neither. The note was stuck in the trailer door when I got there this morning." Exasperated, he added, "I can't do this. We have to have the cables to power lights and the cameras. Where am I going to put them?"

Steeg looked up to the overhead, noting the thick, black cables strung underneath the steel beams and along older existing cable runs that were all painted in white to match the overhead. Above, a long bank of aluminum hooded high-powered studio lamps ran almost the length of the bay, each lamp strategically pointing downward at its individual angle. It was clear to Steeg that Gunhofer was right – the cables had to be elevated and off the deck. In fact, as he looked closer, he was impressed with the way the TV crew had strapped the individual cable runs so close to the overhead. Except for the contrasting black color, the cables looked pretty nicely arrayed up there.

"Well, if we can't take them down," Steeg said, switching his gaze from the center support beam that ran port to starboard at mid-bay to the bank of lamps that crossed under it running fore and aft. "Maybe we can hide them."

Spanky and Gunhofer craned their necks to join in Steeg's examination of the overhead.

"Hide? How?" Gunhofer asked.

"In the existing structure up there, along with a bit of canvas," Steeg answered.

"What?" Spanky inquired.

"Look, do you have enough length in those cables so your guys can re-run all of them together? You know, have all the lines grouped in a bunch, strapped together with duct tape, or something?"

"Yeah, I guess so," the Producer nodded, but his concern remained.

"Good." Steeg pointing up at the port to starboard overhead I-beam. "Then, you can take that bundle of cables and reposition the entire run on the forward side of that I-beam up there. Split off the individual lines when the whole bundle reaches the string of lights you have mounted up there, and carefully tuck the individual cables above instead of below the lamp housings. Can you do that?"

Gunhofer nodded, understanding where Steeg was going. "Sure. We can do that."

"With the main bundle of cable tucked on the other side of the I-beam, we can cover a lot of the split offs at the lamp line in white canvas. It will be practically invisible against this overhead. That should make it so little of the actual cables are viewable on camera, and anyone on deck level looking up won't see half of anything that's up there now – only the cables leading to the lights you already have positioned, and maybe not much of that if we can tuck those leads behind stuff."

Gunhofer and Spanky both nodded in agreement. The Producer agreed to get his men on it right away and Spanky promised to ask the Ship's Chief Boatswain for help securing spare canvas.

"Sounds like a plan." Steeg said. A quick acknowledgement from the other two men preceded their individual departures.

With his squad still cleaning the deck and padeyes, Steeg made his way up to Hanger Deck Control. His coffee cup was too close to empty and it was time for a refill. Bonia was sitting in the command chair when Steeg walked in.

"I saw your little conference," Joe said pointing out the window. "What were you guys talking about down there?"

Steeg sat down on the rear bench, and downed the remains from his cup. "The ABC guy was told to remove their cabling from the overhead."

Joe glanced out at the long bank of aluminum-hooded lamps hanging over the bay. In Hanger Deck Control, the lamps were at eye level. "Who told him that?"

"The lieutenant."

Joe nodded. "The commander, then."

"Yup."

"So, how are they going to get any juice to all those lights if they don't have any cables running to them?"

Steeg smiled. "Hide in plain sight, Joe. Hide in plain sight."

The TV technicians, with the help of a painter's basket on a forklift, made fast work of the re-cabling job. Starting after the final recovery rehearsal of the day, they did it smart, disconnecting the cables not at the individual lamps, but at the huge junction panel near the ABC control truck. The cables were freed from the overhead, repositioned and grouped together for bundling with duct tape. The technicians worked along the overhead following the central I-beam that ran port-to-starboard as a guide to reposition the now combined cable grouping on top of the beam's bottom lip. They anchored the bundle with gaffer's cord, then draping canvas over the grouped cable running along the bank of lights as best they could. It was a clean job, and only the relatively short individual cable runs to the individual lights were visible. The cables weren't completely hidden from view, but the appearance of what could be seen from the hanger deck was so improved, no one in their right mind could complain about it.

Steeg had watched it all from Hanger Deck Control. As the television people worked, his six-man crew remained busy on deck spot painting the hanger bay.

When the re-cabling work was nearing completion, he carried his latest refilled coffee mug down to the hanger deck to take a look. The appearance of the overhead was a remarkable improvement. The whole bay, with the freshly painted colored elements and clean white bulkheads, looked better than he had seen it in the two years he had been with V3 Division.

Lord, I'm so good at this it's hard to be humble. He smiled to himself as he admired the quality of the work.

Chapter 19

Good, Better, Best

SATURDAY, 5 JULY 1969
HANGER BAY TWO
USS *HORNET* CVS-12

It was pre-dawn and the night sky was giving way to the gray-blue of morning. In the middle of the brightly lit hanger bay, Commander Knauts stood on the blue painted path, feet planted at shoulder's width, hands on hips, surveying the hanger bay. Lieutenant Blunt slouched behind him.

"Better," the Air Boss nodded with approval. The lieutenant waited for the other shoe to drop. It was a short wait. "But still not good enough."

The lieutenant's audible sigh was ignored as the commander quickly strode across the bay to the elevator opening. "We need definition."

The lieutenant stayed rooted to his spot. "'Definition,' Sir?"

"That's right, Lieutenant, definition," Knauts raised his voice to make sure the junior officer heard him as he made a sweeping gesture encompassing the entire hanger bay. "What we have here is a lack of depth, a lack of perspective. It's flat, lifeless. It needs something to make it stand out, something that is visible, easily identifiable, and an example of excellence; something that screams 'NAVY'!"

The lieutenant was lost. Not a praying man, nevertheless he could not help but wonder if praying would save him from the thinly veiled insanity that was Commander Knauts. The lieutenant didn't ask much. A Divine rescue, if only momentary, would be enough. He chewed on his lower lip as he watched his superior officer's head swerve first in one direction, then to the next, scanning the expanse that was Hanger Bay Two. This went on for several insufferable seconds.

"I've got it." The commander's head bobbed resolutely. "Garbage cans!"

The lieutenant blinked, not certain he had heard correctly.

"That will do it," Knauts reaffirmed. "Garbage cans, in each corner, lashed to the bulkheads with steel chain."

Blunt's mouth opened as if to say something, but was cut short as the commander corrected himself.

"NO!" he barked. "Not in the corners!"

Knauts ran to the opposite side of the elevator opening. "One right here!" he pointed to the deck just inboard from the elevator control panel. He ran back to the other side of the elevator opening, pointing to the deck again. "And, one right here!"

The commander then hurried down the blue path to the far corner where it turned toward the back door of the Primary MQF. Pointing to the port side bay fire door, he yelled back to the lieutenant still standing mid-bay. "Then, one right here!"

He hurried back to where Blunt still stood, searching the bay for one more spot.

"Where's the President going to be?" He asked himself. Blunt pointed toward the starboard door that led to the escalator. "Right! The escalator! He's coming down the escalator, down the walk path, around that far corner to the MQF. So, the best place for the garbage can is..." he strode directly to where the blue path met the starboard door to the escalator. "Right here! Every camera angle will have a garbage can in the shot. It's perfect!"

A stab of pain punished the lieutenant's stomach. He knew things were spiraling out of control. As the commander strode back to where he was standing, the lieutenant coughed out the words he regretted almost before they tumbled from his lips.

"We don't have garbage cans."

Knauts came to a rigid halt and glared at the junior officer. His reply was cold. "Get them."

Lt. Blunt mustered his courage as best he could. "Well, Sir, yes, but, we can't really have garbage cans on the hanger deck while at sea, Sir."

Knauts stepped in closer. "I said, get them."

The lieutenant swallowed nervously. "It's just that they'd be a hazard on deck, Sir. Aircraft and garbage cans, Sir? That's not a good combination."

"They won't have garbage in the garbage cans, you idiot! Don't you understand what I'm trying to do here?"

Without thinking, Blunt nodded his head.

"Well, if you do, then do as I say. Get the garbage cans, get the chain to anchor them to the bulkheads and put them where I tell you, you got that, Mister?"

The lieutenant nodded again. The Air Boss turned on a heel and left the hanger bay.

Lt. Blunt stood there feeling the numbness travel up his legs. He didn't see the Duty MAA walk up behind.

"He's kinda tough to deal with isn't he, Lieutenant?" Spanky asked. Blunt turned in the direction of the voice.

"That's true, Spank."

"What's he telling you to do now?"

"Garbage cans. Four of them chained to the walls."

Gaffaney looked up to the overhead and around the bay. "Your guys did a bang up job on the bay yesterday."

Blunt nodded again. "That they did."

"I may be out of line here, Lieutenant, but I think garbage cans, even garbage cans chained to bulkheads, don't make much sense on a hanger deck. Kinda dangerous, don't you think?"

"That I do, Spank, that I do."

"So, whadda ya gonna do, Sir?"

A long sigh signaled Blunt's resignation. "I'm going to find four garbage cans and some chain."

There was no doubt things were hopping. *Hornet* had been at it all morning, squeezing in three recovery reps before noon with a fourth starting at 1300 hours. All recovery contingent operations where humming at a higher level of efficiency and it was easy to see that everyone, from the UDT teams to flight deck operations, as well as the hanger deck recovery team and the television crews, had attained a comfortable proficiency in every aspect of their specified duties.

Steeg's crew also had successfully paced their cleaning activities with those of Karl and his hanger deck recovery crew. With each rehearsal, before Karl's team became involved, Steeg's crew would be on deck cleaning padeyes, spot cleaning marks and mars from the painted areas, and making sure everything was where it should be. When it was time for the recovery helicopter to be towed from number two elevator into place across from the Primary MQF, a two-man team from Steeg's crew would follow behind with acetone soaked towels to remove any marks or tracks. Then, McIlhenny and his tow tractor pulled the helicopter into bay three, onto the starboard elevator where it was raised back up to the flight deck to be prepared for another practice run. *Hornet* would then maneuver to pick up the dummy command module on the starboard side. Number three elevator was again lowered from the flight deck and the large starboard side crane would lift the capsule from the water, positioning it on a specially made dolly on the elevator platform. The dolly, in turn, would be attached by tow bar to McIlhenny's tow tractor and then carefully moved to the designated spot on the white rectangle very close to where the recovery chopper had been parked earlier. Steeg's towel team followed that procession as well, cleaning any tracks that the dolly may have left. It was all becoming very effective and efficient.

There was a short window of opportunity for afternoon chow before the start of the next rehearsal. Karl and Bear found Steeg standing in the mess line below decks.

"Coming fast enough for you guys?" Steeg joked as the line shuffled ahead at a steady pace. He grabbed three metal trays from the serving rack, handing two of them to Karl.

"Fast enough," Karl agreed, passing one of the trays to Bear. "How about you? You guys staying on top of things? The bay looks great."

"Yes, we are, and thank you very much."

The line moved quicker at the serving stations. Soup, burgers, fries, mashed potatoes and gravy, and some kind of steamed green vegetable medley were the main offerings. The guys loaded up. In the mess hall, they followed the self-serve table to scarf up their choices of fresh/canned fruits, bread, butter, and condiments. Steeg and Bear filled their coffee cups as Karl opted for a glass of milk and the three found a table.

"So, they dump the capsule just anywhere?" Steeg asked between bites.

Karl nodded. "Pretty much. They hook it to a harness and a chopper takes it out who knows how far? Today, they have to be dropping it pretty close to us, not more than a few miles, so we can get more recovery reps in quicker. There's some kind of transponder on the capsule the Captain locks onto to help find the thing. They plot a course to retrieve it."

"A lot of reps today."

"You can say that again," Bear griped. "I'm getting' tired of raising and lowering the elevator!"

"Oh, you poor guy," Steeg teased. "Wanna trade?"

Bear replied with a sincere shake of his head. "No thanks."

"Speaking of that, Steeg," Karl interjected. "I gotta tell ya, I don't know how you guys keep up with all the back and forth moving of everything up there. The deck looks like you could eat off of it."

"I wouldn't recommend it," Steeg chuckled. "There's so much acetone on the paint it'd probably kill you."

Karl and Bear both laughed, and then Karl added, "Your guys have a good attitude. It shows. With this garbage can stuff, you'd think they'd be pissed."

Steeg blinked. "What garbage can stuff?"

Bear's eyebrows arched up. "The garbage cans you're put in charge of. Haven't they told you?"

"Told me what?"

Bear looked to Karl, and Karl returned the look saying nothing.

"Told me what, guys?" Steeg repeated.

After a long silence, Karl spoke up. "There's going to be garbage cans on deck. They're supposed to add 'depth' and 'perspective' for the cameras."

Steeg's eyes went from Karl to Bear, and back to Karl again. "You're kiddin', right?"

Karl and Bear both shook their heads.

"We don't have garbage cans on a hanger deck. They're a hazard."

Karl shrugged.

"Whose bright idea is this, the TV people?"

Karl shook his head again.

"Then, who?" The answer came to him in an instant. "Knauts."

A quick, jerking nod from Karl who was now completely occupied with what remained on his mess tray.

Steeg slid back in his chair, exhaling in one, long breath. "This is not a good idea. It's stupid. In the worse case it's very dangerous. We do FOD patrols regularly. We collect and dump trash. We don't hoard it in containers on deck. Containers bump into aircraft, or aircraft bump into containers. Containers spill. Garbage cans are not a good idea."

Karl's mumbled response came as he took another healthy bite of his burger. "I agree."

"They're planning to put one right behind me at the elevator controls," Bear complained.

"How many are there?" Steeg asked.

"Four," Karl answered.

"Four!? That's ridiculous."

"They're supposed to be anchored somehow with chain," Bear explained.

"Chain? Four garbage cans tied to the deck with chain?"

"Or, to the bulkhead." Karl added. "It depends where the can is located, I guess."

Steeg came to his feet, taking his half-empty mess tray with him. "I've got to talk to the lieutenant."

He left the table, headed aft to dump his tray at the scullery, and exited through the aft passageway.

"It's the Air Boss's order," Lieutenant Blunt defended. Steeg stood in Hanger Deck Control, a single step down from the door, standing taller than the officer seated at the status board. "You want to bring this up to him?"

"No, Sir. But, it's not right, Sir."

"I agree."

"So we can't do it then, Sir?"

"We have to."

"But Sir, it isn't safe to have those things on a hanger deck. There's too little room to maneuver as it is."

"That's what I said to the commander when he came up with this idea. He didn't listen to me. You think you can do better? Be my guest."

Steeg backed down just a bit. "I don't mean that, Sir. I just…"

"Look, Steeg, we have an order, and we have to follow it. These things are going to be positioned as clear of the deck as possible, off to the edges as close to the bulkheads as they can be. They'll be chained to the bulkhead support beams or around tubes coming through the deck – except for the one by the aft bay doors, I haven't figured that one out yet."

"Aft bay doors? Between number two and three bays?"

"Yep," the lieutenant replied.

"That's where the chopper and the command module go through."

"Yep," the lieutenant replied again.

Steeg rubbed the bridge of his nose as he felt the beginnings of gathering pressure behind his eyes. He leaned toward the bay window and looked aft to where the bay door opening lined up with the port-side edge of the blue painted path. There was no winning this argument and he knew it.

Photo of Hanger Bay Two taken after the actual recovery showing the Primary MQF, the transfer tunnel, and the command capsule. Note the white rectangle area, the bunting fence with its paint bucket stanchions, and the painted walk path.

"Okay, Lieutenant," Steeg resigned. "We can anchor one garbage can to the deck with short chained tie-downs hooked to the handles and the chains hooked to opposite padeyes. Maybe even use two tie-downs on each handle, with their chains spread out to separate padeyes. Tightened up, the can should be pretty stable. Hopefully, no one will trip over the tie downs."

Blunt nodded. "Sounds like a plan, Steeg. The cans will be up here after the last run-through."

"Aye, Sir," His salute was returned by the officer. Steeg turned and left Hanger Deck Control, softly shutting the door behind him.

Chapter 20

"What Big Eyes You Have..."

WEDNESDAY, 9 JULY 1969
HANGER BAY TWO
USS *HORNET* CVS-12

Three days later Steeg and First Class AB Chas Farmer sat in Hanger Deck Control quietly observing the progress of Commander Knauts' inspection across Hanger Bay Two. *Hornet* and Task Force 130 was heading back to Pearl Harbor and the inspections continued. Lieutenant Blunt had assumed his regular slouch and followed closely behind the commander. The bay looked outstanding. The red, white and blue bunting fence was up, surrounding the perimeter of the white rectangle in perfect, crisp lines. The deck was spotless. The four galvanized garbage cans stood at attention in their predetermined locations, lid top handles oriented for and aft in perfect alignment with each container's side handles. There was nothing out of place, and everything was 4-0 in appearance. The interested observers in Hanger Deck Control knew inspection had to be going good.

That was when Commander Knauts stopped. Farmer and Patterson held their breaths as they watched the Air Boss pull a white handkerchief from his back pocket and stoop toward a padeye.

"What's he doing?" Steeg asked.

Farmer squinted, the disgust obvious in his voice. "He's checking the inside of a padeye. Oh, crap. He's showing Blunt his handkerchief."

The commander stood holding the white cloth inches from the lieutenant's face. They couldn't hear a word clearly, but they heard the reverberation of the commander's displeasure echoing across the hanger bay.

The Air Boss turned and left the lieutenant standing alone in the bay. The inspection was over.

"That didn't go good," Farmer said coldly, watching the lieutenant turn toward Hanger Deck Control.

"You think?" Steeg complained.

The two men waited for Division Lieutenant Blunt to arrive, his heavy footfalls coming up the ladder. The door opened, the officer came in and sat down heavily on the rear bench. Shoulders hunched over, he pushed his cover to the back of his head and rubbed both hands across his face. To Steeg the lieutenant looked hung over but he kept that opinion to himself.

None of them said a thing for a long moment. It was Lieutenant Blunt who finally spoke up.

"Well, men, it seems the padeyes collect dust."

Steeg and Farmer looked at each other. The lieutenant continued.

"What would either of you propose we do to keep dust from falling into the padeyes?"

Steeg shook his head, wishing he had a white flag to wave at someone. "Lieutenant, I don't know. I have no idea what else we can do."

"We could blow it out, Sir," Farmer offered.

"No go," Blunt answered. "The dust will kick up too much."

"There's no dust in those things," Steeg spat, his anger beginning to push through to the surface. "They're as clean as they can be."

"He showed me his hankie, Steeg."

"Bull. It was planted." Steeg was angry now. "Lieutenant, this isn't about dust. This isn't about anything but Commander Knauts and his ambition. The name of this game is to make sure we're all miserable so he can look good."

Blunt raised an eyebrow. "Maybe. You might be right about that, but if we don't do something, we all get it in the ass one way or another."

"It won't matter what we do, it will just get worse."

Farmer tapped a nervous finger on the status board. "The lieutenant's right, Steeg. We have to do something or we'll pay for it in the end."

Steeg turned to the window in disgust. "We've been paying for it since Long Beach, Chas. This isn't right."

They hadn't noticed Spanky Gaffaney come up the ladder. He stood in the still open doorway to Hanger Deck Control. "Why not give him the appearance of getting it done and let it go at that?"

They all looked at the MAA.

"Could you expand on that, Sheriff?" Farmer asked.

Spanky shrugged. "Go through the motions. Make it look like you're dealing with his complaint. Let it roll off your backs. It isn't worth driving yourselves crazy over. He's crazy enough already. Humor him."

In exasperation, Steeg said, "He's complaining about dust, Spank – dust in the padeyes."

"Yeah. Crazy, isn't it?" Spanky agreed. "Look, all I'm saying is, this guy will eat you alive if you let him. Roll with the punches and let him think he's getting what he wants. Maybe he'll let up."

"Maybe he won't," Blunt countered.

Spanky nodded in acknowledgement. "Maybe. The thing is it seems to me he can't afford to let you guys achieve the perfection he's hollerin' for. He has to keep resetting the bar higher every time, otherwise he doesn't look so good. That makes sense, doesn't it? I mean, ask yourself – what does he get out of all this? He doesn't give a rip about this hanger bay. He only wants the prestige and power that comes from making captain. That's what he wants. It doesn't matter how good a job you do, it only matters how good he looks making you do it."

The other three nodded in agreement.

Steeg chewed a bit on his lower lip as an idea took shape in his mind. "Okay, let's make sure everyone notices how good he looks by making us look absurd."

"How's that?" Farmer asked.

"Leave it to me," Steeg nodded as a squinted glint came to his eyes. "He wants the dust out of the padeyes, that's what he'll get."

They would be in Pearl for less than two days to load fresh provisions, necessary additional equipment for backup purposes, and to bring onboard about twenty other interesting people, many of whom dressed in dark suits, thin dark ties and sunglasses they wore all the time, even in the shade.

On 12 July, *Hornet* would leave for the Primary Abort Area ahead of the scheduled 16 July launch date of Apollo 11. For the two days in port, The V3 Division, and Steeg's hanger deck crew specifically, would maintain a 24-hour security watch over Hanger Bay Two.

The first watch would take effect the evening of the afternoon *Hornet* returned to Pearl. After the carrier tied up to the pier, Steeg and his six-man crew mustered at the base of the Hanger Deck Control ladder. Their flight ops colored shirts were gone, replaced with duty dungarees, flight deck boots and ball caps. They gathered around Steeg who had two large coils of ½-inch hemp rope at his feet and a stubby cardboard box in his left hand.

"You gonna hang us with those ropes, Steeg," the spectacled Eddie Harrison joked.

"Not unless you make me," Steeg jabbed back. "Now everyone listen up. You all have your watch assignments, right?"

General agreement came from the crew.

"Four-hour two-man watches, six watches every twenty four hours," Steeg repeated one more time. "That's two staggered watches per day per two-man team. You know which shift each of you has and you know who your partner is. Any questions?"

Santini raised his hands, and Steeg motioned for him to speak up.

"We gonna get liberty?"

"Limited." Steeg answered honestly. "You have a solid eight hour break between shifts. It's a legitimate break and you'll each have your pass to leave the ship. However, you must be back in plenty of time to relieve the shift before you. If you're not back, the shift before you cannot be relieved. That's not good for them, or for you. So, plan on short time on shore. Hang close. Try the EM Club on base. Is that understood?"

Heads nodded and some moans could be heard.

Steeg continued. "I know that leaves even less time for those of you who have to watch during the swing shift evening hours. Liberty after midnight is a drag, I know. Sorry about that. There will be no substitutions. You work your designated watch."

Steeg bent down and picked up a coil of rope. "Now, before the first watch, and before you other guys go wherever you intend to go, you will surround the painted area with these ropes. Tie it all off, stretching rope from bulkhead to bulkhead. I want it this high." He held his flat hand up to mid-chest level.

"That's going to get in the way of a lot of people," the fair-haired Airman 3rd Carruthers commented.

"That's the idea, Robert, " Steeg acknowledged. "Give enough room for people to duck under if they have to, but let's string this up to keep everyone off the paint."

"What's in the box?" Santini pointed.

Steeg smiled as he dropped the rope and opened the small box. He reached in to pull out a handful of paper wrapped drinking straws for the crew to see.

"This is part of your work uniform until further notice," he said as he handed a good amount to each man. "I want you to carry them in your shirt pocket while on watch. And, every morning until I say otherwise, you bring them with you to work."

"What for?" Harrison asked.

Steeg ignored the question. "Do not open them. Do not remove them from the wrapper. That will come later. For the time being, just make sure people see the straws in your pocket. If anyone asks any questions, tell them to see me."

The men took their offered drinking straws and put them into their shirt pockets as Steeg had instructed.

"Our mission, gentlemen, is simple," Steeg went on. "While in port, keep everyone off the paint, no exceptions. Stop every civilian from walking on the paint. Stop every officer from walking on the paint. If anyone questions your authority to do so, have them see me."

"So, where are you gonna be?" Santini asked with more than a hint of sarcastic accusation.

Steeg pointed up the ladder to Hanger Deck Control. "Right in there."

For the next two days, neither Steeg or his squad left the ship. It was easier and more recuperative for everyone to take their breaks on board. For the most part, Steeg was true to his word. Except for the occasional head break, and a quick shower and shave before morning muster, Steeg manned Hanger Deck Control continually, monitoring the cross-bay traffic during the day and duty watches during the night. During the night he was able to catch a few short naps sitting in the command chair while still appearing to be on duty.

Keeping people off the paint was not difficult, even during the more energetic loading of spare gear and equipment on the second day in port. Most of the equipment brought on board was loaded up to the Flight Deck, or stowed in the rear of Hanger Bay Three, avoiding Hanger Bay Two all together. The rope perimeter surrounding the painted area had to be modified somewhat at the hanger bay doors to allow passage of other dolly-loaded supplies and equipment. Nevertheless, nothing touched the paint at any time.

It was all a relief for Lieutenant Blunt. It was also reassuring for the lieutenant to see Steeg in Hanger Deck Control when he left the ship at night and then again when he came back on board in the morning. Each day the lieutenant took notice of the squared away hanger deck and the curious drinking straws in shirt pockets of Steeg and his squad. If it was easy for the lieutenant to compliment the maintenance crew, it was even easier to say nothing about the drinking straws.

It was also easy for the lieutenant to avoid the Air Boss. Commander Knauts spent most of his in-port time in meetings with NASA team members and *Hornet* senior command officers, including Captain Sieberlich. Every meeting they would repeatedly cover the details of the recovery operations plan point by point. This recovery would be executed more perfectly than any other before it. That made the commander's time in port too valuable for browbeating subordinates about paint and polish. There would be plenty of time for browbeating when *Hornet* put to sea again. Appreciating the short break from the early morning inspections, Blunt knew the harassment would resume as soon as the ship cleared Pearl Harbor's breakwater.

Chapter 21

"The Better to See Your Face, My Dear..."

SATURDAY, 12 JULY 1969
HANGER BAY TWO
USS HORNET CVS-12

Hornet cleared breakwater outside Pearl Harbor mid-morning on 12 July. Steeg was ready.

On the 07 level below Pri-Fly (Primary Flight Control), just forward of the S/N35 Radar Radome, Steeg's primary flight deck observer, Charlie Svensgard, triggered the mouthpiece of his sound powered phones. "Hanger Deck, Flight Deck."

Sitting on the rear bench in Hanger Deck Control Santini pressed his mouthpiece button. "Go ahead, Flight Deck."

"Hamster moving forward. Looks like he's headed for the starboard gun tub," Svensgard replied.

"Roger that, Flight Deck. Hamster on the move," Santini nodded toward Tom Kinsey sitting at the status board. "Do we have anyone near the forward starboard side?"

Kinsey shook his head, a shadow of concern crossing his face. "I don't think so, just Charlie up on the island for the best view. We got a man in Conflag One, but not on the flight deck itself."

There were three conflagration stations on the hanger deck, one in each bay, all of them above deck on the 01 level. The stations were equipped with the necessary fire sprinkler and bay door activation controls used in the event of a fire. Conflag One was located on the port side of elevator one. Although the view through the station's view slots was somewhat defused by almost four inches of heat resistance glass, Conflag One had a commanding view of the entire bay.

Santini toggled the mouthpiece again. "Conflag One, Hanger Deck."

"Conflag One. Go ahead, Hanger Deck."

"Heads up. Hamster may be coming your way."

"Roger that."

Kinsey got up to exit Hanger Deck Control. "I'm getting Patterson," he said as he left.

Steeg was in the crew's lounge. He followed Kinsey back into the snug space of Hanger Deck Control and took a seat on the rear bench next to Santini. Kinsey returned to the command chair at the status board.

"Where is he now?" Steeg asked.

Santini shook his head. The men sat pensively in silence for several more moments.

"Hanger Deck!" the voice barked over the squawk box, startling all three men. It was Spanky.

Steeg reached over and toggled the talk switch. "Go ahead, Spank."

"Just passed 'you know who' with the lieutenant. They came from officer's quarters on 02 Level, heading aft."

Steeg toggled back. "Roger. Thank you."

He darted from the small room, around the corner to the lounge. "'A-Team!' Commence Operation Blow Job! On deck! Now!" Five squad members left their seats and followed Steeg out the door. Before heading down the ladder, Steeg stuck his head into Hanger Deck Control, instructing Santini to stay on the sound powered phones.

234

On the Hanger Deck, the 'A-Team' met at the paint locker, each member grabbing a can of acetone and a fist full of clean rags, including Steeg.

"Everyone have your straws?" Steeg bellowed.

They all had straws.

"Good. Start at the Primary MQF. Remember, work in a line, go slow, and stay on your hands and knees until I tell you."

The five Blue Shirts ran to the rear of Hanger Bay Two, spaced themselves evenly starboard to port along the edge of the painted area, going to their knees as they wetted their rags with acetone from the gallon cans each man had.

"Hold up, men!" Steeg hollered, walking up to the middle of their line. "Take your boots off. Leave your socks on. Put your boots outside the paint." As he knelt down to unlace his boots, the men quickly followed his lead. Soon, they were all in their stocking feet.

"Okay, unwrap your first straw!" Steeg ordered. Walking down to the first man, he followed the line, taking each man's paper wrapper in turn. At the end of the line, he shoved the collected straw wrappers into his pants pocket, and took his place dead center in the blue painted path as the last man on the line.

Steeg held up a closed fist as a hold signal and looked to Hanger Deck Control. He didn't have to wait long. Kinsey made sure Steeg saw him as he spun his pointed finger in an overhead 'start engine' signal everyone recognized. In unison, the 'A-Team' went to their hands and knees to clean the padeyes. Steeg followed suit, pacing the line as he and each man, straws between lips, bent low to the deck and blew through the straws to de-dust the inside of their respective padeye. This was followed up with an acetone swab around the padeye and surrounding deck area.

Between straw-directed blows, Harrison, working next to Steeg, said, "You're the Petty Officer. You shouldn't be doing this, should you?"

"'The greatest amongst you is the least amongst you,'" Steeg smiled holding his straw in place between his teeth. Only John Dickenson knew Steeg considered his motives in accepting Christ suspect. Suspect or not, Steeg's evangelical responsibility to lead his squad accordingly was a good way for him to keep Jesus real in his life. "If it's good enough for Christ, it's good enough for me."

The line had progressed only two rows worth of padeyes when the commander and the lieutenant walked up to where Steeg was working. He looked up from his padeye feigning surprise, sprang to his feet and threw a sharp military salute that both officers returned.

"You call this supervision, Petty Officer Patterson?" the lieutenant asked, mildly irritated.

"We're a man short, Sir," Steeg explained. "Santini has to be in Hanger Deck Control."

The lieutenant turned to look up and find Santini and Kinsey looking down at him through the bay window. Commander Knauts observed the men continue along the deck, butts in the air, heads toward the deck, blowing through straws and swabbing with rags.

"Is this effective, Sailor?" he asked humorlessly.

"Yes, Sir," the Petty Officer answered resolutely. "It's the best way to make sure the inside areas are truly free of all dust and dirt without contaminating the surrounding area, Sir. It keeps things neat and clean all the way around, Sir."

The commander nodded, continuing to watch as the line of men slowly progressed across the deck. After a long moment, he said without conviction, "Very well."

The two officers passed Steeg, the lieutenant subtly nodding to the petty officer as the two officers continued aft on their inspection. Rejoining his team on his hands and knees, Steeg spied from under his arm the commander stopping briefly to look at the garbage can anchored to the deck near the bay doors. Several seconds went by and he wondered what the commander found so interesting about the garbage can.

He would find out later that night.

Late that evening, two cardboard boxes measuring approximately two-foot by one-foot by fourteen inches tall, arrived at Hanger Deck Control.

The sailor from Supply Division who had delivered them handed a letter envelope to the duty watch. It had "Lt. Blunt" handwritten on it.

It was 0300 when E2 Charlie Davis shook Steeg's shoulder and woke him up.

"What is it?" Steeg asked, the sleep hanging in his eyes.

"Sorry, Steeg, but they want you at Hanger Deck Control."

"What for?"

"Don't know, just told me to come and get you."

"Okay, give me a minute."

Steeg rolled from the top bunk, hit the deck with bare feet, and scratched his groin through his jockey shorts. He quickly donned the dungaree bell-bottoms and shirt hanging from the bunk's support chain, pulled his socks up, laced and tied his boots. When he pulled on his ball cap, he completed his ensemble in less than a minute.

"Let's go, Charlie."

Both boxes were open, stacked on the rear bench of Hanger Deck Control when Steeg arrived. Lieutenant Blunt, Chief Harland Cason, and First Class Petty Officer Joe Bonia were crowded into the small space waiting for him. Steeg barely made it inside the little room, standing on the top step just inside the door. Chief Cason reached into the top box, pulled out a small metallic container and handed it to Steeg.

"Brass polish?" Steeg asked taking the eight ounce container from the Chief. "What's this all about?"

"It's about what happens when you try to be a smart ass in this man's Navy," replied Chief Cason as he pointed to the boxes. "There are two gross worth of those things, and guess what they're supposed to be used on?"

Steeg did the math quickly in his head. "Two hundred and eighty-eight cans of brass polish – that's a lot of polish. Whatever it is that's supposed to be shiny must be pretty big."

Lieutenant Blunt said nothing as he sat at the status board, sucking on his upper lip and looking out the window across the hanger bay. Bonia and Cason stood facing the younger man, arms folded across their chests.

"Not big?" Steeg asked shaking his head.

"Not really," Cason said coldly, eyes boring right through the man. "They're pretty standard size, actually, and it shouldn't take too long, either. Personally, I think this amount of brass polish is overkill. You and your men should be able to get by easily with half the amount."

An uneasy feeling began to rise in Steeg's gut. "What exactly are we talking about polishing, Chief?"

Cason's lips barely moved as he answered through gritted teeth. "Garbage cans."

Without breaking eye contact with the Chief, out of the corner of his eye Steeg could see the lieutenant lower his head to his hands. Steeg felt light headed as he steadied himself against the doorframe.

"Oh, no." It was barely a whisper.

"Oh, yes," replied the Chief as he handed Steeg an unfolded piece of notebook paper. "It's straight from the Air Boss himself, and he mentions you specifically."

Steeg read the handwritten note.

> *Lt. Blunt,*
>
> *It would not be possible to describe a more vitally important or historically significant event to take place in the latter half of the twentieth century than the first man landing on the Moon. It is, however, entirely possible to describe the most embarrassing aspect of my Air Department's role in this most significant historical event. That embarrassment is you, Lieutenant.*
>
> *Judging from the antics I observed on the hanger deck this afternoon, it is evident to me that you lack the necessary skills or military bearing to effectively lead the V3 Division, or warrant serious consideration as a career naval officer. As such, I am informing you that measures are being taken to remove the burden of responsibility for V3 Division from you, effective at the earliest possible date.*
>
> *In advance of this, give Petty Officer Patterson both of these boxes and inform him I expect all four garbage cans to be polished so perfectly I'll be able to see my face in them during my next inspection at 0630 hours.*
>
> *Commander, USS HORNET Air Department*
> *I.M. Knauts*

Steeg looked from the note. The lieutenant still sat turned away.

"I'm sorry," he said. "I didn't think…"

"That's right," Chief Cason interrupted. "You didn't think. Neatly organized, but you didn't think it through at all, did you?"

Steeg shook his head. The Chief continued.

"You get your squad down here. You got almost three hours. If you hurry, you just might make it in time."

Squeezing past the young petty officer, Bonia followed the Chief out of Hanger Deck Control, leaving Steeg still holding the note and the lieutenant still seated at the status board.

"I'm so sorry, Lieutenant. I had no idea this would happen."

Lieutenant Blunt gave a slight shrug as he turned toward the enlisted man. "It's not your fault," he said, eyebrows raised in resigned acceptance. "It's mine. I should have made sure what you had in mind was the right thing. I should have overseen you better. I should have stopped you before you got started. I didn't. It's my fault."

Steeg looked down at the note in his hand. "It's handwritten. It's a personal reprimand, not official. Unless he made a copy, which I doubt, it won't even make it to your file."

Blunt reached over and took the note from Steeg. "It doesn't matter. What's done is done," he held the paper up to eye level. "This isn't a note, Steeg, it's a gauntlet. He's thrown it down as a personal challenge against me."

Steeg took a step toward the officer. "He can't prove anything here."

"He doesn't have to."

"We didn't actually do anything wrong, Lieutenant. This is just his ego. The most he can say is that we were trying too hard to follow his orders."

A dim glimmer of hope rose in the lieutenant's eyes, only to fade as quickly as it had appeared.

"You better go get your crew." Blunt sagged into the chair. "You haven't much time. Like it or not, Steeg, some of this is going to rub off on you now. You're in his crosshairs and for that I am truly sorry."

The garbage cans and lids were galvanized with a blue-gray zinc coating inside and out. This produced a fairly clean, albeit dull, finish that was medium gray in appearance and lacked luster. By 0400, the six-man 'A-Team' had finished their first application of brass polish on all four cans and all four lids, buffing earnestly to achieve the objective of a reflective surface in which you could see your face. But, try as they did, the effort had produced nothing approaching the desired improvement in the shininess and reflectivity of the original material.

"It's definitely cleaner," Santini said, Steeg leaning over his shoulder to inspect the work.

"It's not reflecting anything, though," Steeg observed.

The 'A-Team' had removed the cans from their chains and taken them into Hanger Bay Three to keep from soiling Hanger Bay Two. They worked bunched together near the number three elevator ramp, so it was easy for Steeg to see no one was achieving the primary objective for this project.

Steeg rubbed his chin. "It's a zinc coating on what kind of metal?"

"Steel, I guess," Harrison offered. "They're too heavy to be aluminum."

"Steel," Steeg repeated. "High carbon, or low carbon steel?"

"What's the diff?" Santini asked.

"High carbon is stronger, more rigid. It will also be darker in color, less luminous. Low carbon is softer, easier to bend. It will be lighter in color, more luminous. We can grind down a spot on the bottom of one of the cans to see what we have. If it's the right type, we can grind off the coating and polish the bare metal with air powered buffers."

"Whoa, Kimo Sabe!" Eric Hayes raised his hand. "That's a whole lot more work, even if we have shiny metal under this stuff."

The Blue Shirt was right. Grinding zinc coating off the cans would produce a whole lot of dust, and, if the grind and dust were caught up by sea breezes or the ship's ventilation system, they'd run the risk of contaminating the equipment in the next bay. There was only one thing to do.

"Okay, we're stuck with the polish," Steeg accepted. "Let's do it again on everything, this time, really put some elbow grease into it."

A scattering of moans as the guys took up their polish and rags for another try.

The try was in vain. There was no improvement and no reflection on the surface of the garbage cans. Dirty stained rags were piling up in the middle of their circle, as were empty cans of brass polish. Steeg looked at his watch. It was 0510 hours, and time was running out.

"Okay, look," he said. "We have six guys, seven counting me. There are four cans with lids. Santini, you and Harrison are relief. The rest of us grab our own can, polish and buff it out, then pass it to the next guy. The 'floater' polishes the lids. When you get a can from someone, you polish and buff it out again, then pass it to the next guy. Santini, you are first relief. When the first pass happens, you take the can from Hayes. Hayes, you take over as 'floater' on the lids, and the first floater is on relief. The second pass, Harrison you take the can from Carruthers. That puts Carruthers on lids as floater and Hayes goes on relief. On the third pass, Hayes, take the can from Simonson, and Simonson is on the lids, with Carruthers on relief. We keep going that way, taking turns on relief until 0630. If these cans can be polished the way Commander Knauts has ordered, they will be. If not, well, we'll just have to cross that bridge when we get to it. Any questions?"

There were no questions. Steeg grabbed a can of polish, a fresh rag from the bag, and took over Santini's position in the circle along with his garbage can. The 'A-Team' started with renewed effort.

Simonson brought it up first, only a few minutes and a quarter of the way into applying polish to his garbage can. "You know, Steeg, you're the Petty Officer on this detail. It doesn't look right, you sitting here getting dirty with the rest of us."

"Yeah," Carruthers agreed with a laugh. "You look better holding a coffee cup and watching!"

Steeg smiled. "Don't worry about it."

"I'm just sayin' this is no way for you to make 2nd Class," Simonson added. "Someone's gonna notice what you're doin'."

"Maybe," Steeg nodded.

It wasn't that he minded getting his hands dirty, because he didn't. With most of his adolescent free time spent digging ditches for his 'Old Man', Steeg was use to hard work. However, this polishing garbage cans was different. He was the squad leader and on the face of it, Simonson was right: he had a role to play and it may not be proper for him to be this close to the action. Nevertheless, Steeg felt he had an example to set for his men. He remembered enough of Scripture to recall the story of Christ's Last Supper. He could emulate that to set the example.

"I look at it as being of service to a greater cause."

"And your greater cause is garbage cans?" Carruthers chuckled.

Steeg chuckled, too. He imagined Christ in the upper room, wrapping a towel about his waist, taking a bowl of water, and kneeling down to wash the feet of His disciples. Christ knew what was shortly to happen to him and yet His instruction and teaching at that moment was the most important thing for Him to do.

Steeg tried to explained as best he could. "In a way, these garbage cans are more important than another chevron on my sleeve."

Some of the guys shook their heads. No one said anything.

Sensing their concern, Steeg wondered how he could directly apply his example to benefit his men. Perhaps there was a parallel with the protestations of Peter to whom Christ said if he would not let Him wash his feet, Peter could have no part of Him or his ministry[8].

"Don't be too put off, gentlemen." Steeg rubbed his polishing rag against the garbage can with renewed vigor. "It's the mission that counts, not my getting to the next pay grade. Always remember that the greatest among you is the least among you."

Santini chuckled. So did the others.

Steeg continued. "Serving others is what it's all about, men. If it's good enough for Jesus, it's good enough for me. I'm just trying to be of service that's all."

Santini let out a long, slow whistle. "Man, you are weird."

With a slightly embarrassed increase in his effort, Steeg buffed the polish from the metal can he straddled. A shallow smile hid a sudden fear: worse than being weird, at that moment he realized he was sorely spiritually ill-equipped. Worse yet, he was failing Christ by his poor Christian leadership of his men.

He sought the safety of the work at hand as he mumbled his reply: "You may be right, Frank."

"I don't see my reflection," The commander said flatly, leaning down close to the side of the garbage can. Steeg stood off to one side, Lieutenant Blunt slouched behind and to the right of the commander as usual. "When I give an order, I expect it to be followed to the letter, Petty Officer."

"Yes, Sir," Steeg felt the moisture in his mouth begin to coagulate into something resembling dry paste.

"So, why can't I see my face in this garbage can?" Knauts asked, peering into the clean, gleaming, yet unreflecting surface of the metal container.

Steeg knew the commander was not interested in any answer he had to offer. He knew the entire inspection of that morning was nothing more than an exercise in intimidation and humiliation. The objective was to put another person, especially an enlisted puke, in his place. For a long, pregnant moment, he didn't know what to say. So, he said nothing. The commander stood erect with a menacing stare that Steeg met and held. The long silence that followed soon became too heavy for Steeg not to respond.

"Well, Sir, we tried. We tried very hard, actually, to get these cans to the kind of effect; luster; finish, that is," Steeg began with words stumbling and his mind racing for something, anything, to say.

"That's not what I see, Sailor." Knauts didn't break the steel hard eye contact. Neither did Steeg.

"No, Sir. It's not. And I apologize, Sir."

"Apologize?"

"Yes, Sir," As their eyeballs continued locked in combat, Steeg felt himself begin to waiver, running out of things to say. "It's just that the finish of the metal isn't the type that, actually, polishes well. Sir. I'm sorry, Sir. Galvanized coatings on rough services just don't reflect very well."

"They don't?" the commander said, more as a statement than a question, just to make sure the petty officer knew he was unmoved by the young man's obviously sincere desire to get out from under the commander's grilling. He was also increasingly irritated by what he perceived to be Steeg's obvious lack of respect.

"Apparently not, Sir," Steeg searched for anything that would help this moment to quickly end. His own steely resolve gave way to real embarrassment as he blurted, "If I could, Sir, I would have done anything to get these cans to a mirror finish. Honestly, Sir, if I could have, I would have chrome-plated them for you."

It was then when Knauts blinked. His icy cold stare was broken. The commander's eyes glazed over as his ram-rod military bearing seemed to melt away.

"You would have what?" Knauts asked.

"I... I, ah, would have chrome-plated the cans for you, Sir." Steeg repeated more embarrassed. He noted curiously how the other man's entire body posture had suddenly changed.

Another pregnant moment of prolonged silence followed with Knauts looking more beyond Steeg than at him. The commander stood there, saying nothing. Steeg darted a quick glance to the lieutenant slouching behind and a little to the smaller man's right. In a moment their eyes met to share that neither one of them knew what had just happened. Steeg returned to the commander just in time to see the man's focus return to him.

"Patterson, I hope this has taught you something," Commander Knauts said, quickly regaining his composure and almost elevating himself inside his spit-shined dress shoes. He turned to the lieutenant. "Inspection over. You pass."

With that, Knauts turned about and took the blue painted path back toward the doorway that led to the escalator and the flight deck.

Chapter 22

The Great Shit Can Conspiracy

13:32 UT/9:32 A.M. EDT
WEDNESDAY, 16 JULY 1969
PAD 39A, KENNEDY SPACE CENTER

On the sand flats three and one-half miles away from Cape Kennedy's Pad 39A, the grandstands were jammed packed with spectators. Either standing or sitting were half the members of the United States Congress, more than 3,000 news people from some 56 countries, along with another estimated one million eyewitnesses. In addition, a worldwide television audience more than a billion strong watched as the launch count down ticked steadily toward its climax. The amply powered loudspeakers of the Kennedy Space Center pushed the last few seconds of the countdown across the sand flats. The assembled multitude, row upon row of cameras and photographers, and the million or so spectators crammed onto the barren strip of sand eagerly joined in the counting.

"Eleven... Ten – Ignition start– Nine... Eight..."

On top of the gigantic Saturn V SA-504 rocket, inside the command module called Columbia, the three astronauts sat firmly strapped into their seats. Commander Neil A. Armstrong was in the port-side seat, Lunar

Module Pilot Edwin E. "Buzz" Aldrin, Jr. was seated in the center, and Command Module Pilot Michael Collins was in the starboard position. The three men, each weighing 165 pounds, each within an inch of five-foot eleven inches tall, had been lying on their backs in the capsule for two and one-half hours.

Apollo 11 at lift off.

At the T-minus ten second mark, the Saturn V's first stage primary start engine ignited. On the sand flats, the masses of people saw the distant brilliance of the yellow-orange ball of flame erupting soundlessly at the base of the Pad 39A tower. A scattering of white gulls took flight across the shallow lagoon between the launch area and where the huge crowd watched in eerie silence.

"Six... Five... Four... Three..."

The other four first stage engines fired and the yellow-orange flame instantly grew to a huge yellow-white fireball bathing everything for as far as the eye could see in brilliant light. For the spectators gathered on the sand flats the only sound was the continuing amplified countdown.

"Two... One..."

At the base of the rocket, the massive hold clamps released and fell away.

"Lift off!"

Slowly, the enormous Saturn V began a steady rise from the pad. From the bottom of the monstrous rocket, hot colors billowed forth in growing plumes. From the sand flats, the spectators watched in stunning and eerie silence at the thrilling scene unfolding in the distance. When the rocket reached the top of the service tower, the great crackling roar of the rocket engines slammed into the gathered crowd and massively shook the ground under their feet.

The spectators covered their ears against the thunderous onslaught, and watched in awe as the powerful, steady climb of the towering Saturn V thrust the three astronauts free of Pad 39A, higher and higher still with ever-increasing speed. The gleaming shaft of silver and white climbed above the lazy, scattered wisps of clouds at 15,000 feet, continuing to claw its way mightily into the mid-morning sky.

Within 180 seconds of launch, the rocket reached an altitude of 37 miles and a speed of 6,340 miles per hour. Inside the command module, Mission Commander Neil Armstrong confirmed engine skirt and launch escape tower separations.

Back on the sand flats the echoing roar of the massive rocket engines faded, replaced with appreciative applause and a numbing absence of almost every other sound. The trailing remnants of thinning exhaust spiraled upward and across the sky, marking the path the rocket had taken into the heavens.

Half a world away, things were only a little quieter. *Hornet* was at the Primary Abort area located about 1,600 miles southwest of Hawaii. It was 0332 hours *Hornet* time[9] when Apollo 11 blasted off from the

Kennedy Space Center, and the ship was on full alert. It would stay that way until Apollo 11's trans-lunar injection burn scheduled for almost three hours later. After that, the space craft would be on its way to the moon, and *Hornet* would be able to secure from recovery operations and everyone would resume duties in preparation for 'splashdown' set for eight days later.

Unlike the dark crimson lamping of war zone duty, *Hornet's* hanger bays were brightly lit throughout the night hours for this mission. This afforded not only a greater degree of safety in the movement of machines, aircraft and personnel, it also provided expanded opportunity for spit and polish work in Hanger Bay Two. This meant that Steeg's 'A-Team' was fully involved with policing the bay, polishing all glossy metal surfaces on knobs and switch enclosures at, near and around the elevator control station, and, without fail, swabbing out padeyes with acetone soaked rags. Steeg, the crook of his finger holding steady his usual mug of fresh coffee, stood next to Bear at the Bay Two elevator control station, supervising his crew.

"What time does it launch?" He asked, taking another sip from his mug.

"Any time, now," Bear said, adjusting his sound powered phone headset to a more comfortable position.

They could hear helicopter engines on the flight deck above them begin to turn up. Three fixed wing aircraft, two C1-A Traders and one E-1B tracer, had launched earlier.

Behind Bear, Carruthers polished the brass handle of the elevator control switch. Steeg looked across the bay where Santini, Harrison and Simonson worked spot cleaning the padeyes on the painted area, while Hayes worked on padeyes of the open, non-painted deck. Everyone looked busy. Everyone was pretty much sick of the routine, too. No one was polishing any garbage cans, though, and that was an improvement.

Three days had passed since the commander had last inspected the garbage cans. Since arriving at the Primary Abort area, the Air Boss had continued his morning inspection of the hanger bays with Lieutenant Blunt slouching in tow, but, strangely, the garbage cans no longer seemed to be a keen issue with the man. After each inspection, the lieutenant returned to

Hanger Bay Control, let whomever was on duty know that they had either passed or, if something required additional attention, give instructions as to what it was and what had to be done about it. Then for the duration of the day, Lieutenant Blunt would disappear into "Officers' Country" to do whatever officers did in "Officers' Country".

The rhythmic 'thwap-thwap-thwap' of three SH-3D Sea King helicopter rotors gaining speed on the flight deck was more than loud enough to filter down to the Hanger Deck. *Hornet,* her speed steady, was still turned into the wind after the earlier launching of the fixed-winged birds.

"If the choppers actually launch, we've got problems," Bear said.

Steeg took another sip of coffee. "I don't think we're going to do much of anything here. Apollo 11 is going to go off like clockwork. You watch."

Steeg was right. Nothing happened. Apollo 11 went into Earth orbit as planned, and after nearly an hour of the helicopters spinning their blades on the Flight Deck, the engines slowly whined to a halt and finally shut down. The choppers would remain tied down to the deck, just in case. Flight operations would continue and not secure until after the space craft successfully completed its burn for trans-lunar insertion.

Some time later, in Hanger Deck Control, First Class Petty Officer Bonia asked for Steeg's help.

"They'll probably need to bring the C1-As down for a service check when they land, Steeg. Can you and your crew handle Bay One for me?"

Steeg nodded. "Sure. We'd appreciate the break from all this hard work we've been doing."

"Well, yeah," Bonia said. "It's just that the regular crew will be in Bay Three when the choppers come down, and I don't want the recovery crew involved if I don't have to."

"Why's that? Karl too tired or something?" Steeg joked.

"No, it's not that. Just need to keep the right gear in the right places, that's all. In fact, Karl and a couple of his guys can help you out."

"Sounds like a plan."

At 0610 hours that same morning, *Hornet* turned into the wind in preparation to receive the COD. It was called COD for Carrier On-board Delivery. With its twin 4,600 horsepower turbo prop engines, and over 50,000 pounds of gross weigh capacity, it was the largest aircraft to land on *Hornet*. The pilot brought the cargo plane in 'on-the-ball' fast, snagging the third wire with ease, propellers running full out just in case of a bolter[10]. The Green Shirt came from behind the starboard safety line to make sure the arresting wire was freed from the aircraft's arresting hook, then flashed the Yellow Shirt an 'up-hook' signal as he retreated with the cable being drawn back into place. The Director duplicated the 'up-hook' signal for the pilots, followed immediately with a signal for a half-pivot starboard turn, and then a cautiously directed forward roll. Keeping ahead and always in eye contact with the pilots, the Director made sure the turbo-prop cleared the number two elevator and reached slightly forward of the island's midpoint, before he crossed his hands in a 'brake' signal. This was quickly followed by a 'thumbs-in' and 'hands twirling' movement to order Blue Shirts to chock the wheels and apply the tie-downs. When everything was properly secured, the Director drew his hand across his throat to signal the pilots to shut down the engines.

Unloading the COD commenced immediately. There were two additional personnel from Pearl, many packages and bags of the daily mail delivery (the numbers of which were increasing as the date for the Apollo 11 moon landing came closer), and a special crate measuring almost five feet square and three feet deep. It was a container of keen interest for Commander Knauts. After the people and mail sacks were off loaded, and with a steady twenty knot wind still buffeting the deck, a Yellow Shirt and three Blue Shirts eased the crate down the rear ramp of the aircraft. They then placed it on a waiting four-wheeled dolly, and immediately rolled the whole thing onto elevator number two where it was secured with tie-downs. The flight deck crew left the elevator and returned to the COD. With the topside clear around the elevator platform, the alarm 'baw-oogawed' its alert. The wire cabled stanchions that was the flight deck elevator safety barricade rose from the recesses surrounding the inboard perimeter of the platform, and the elevator sank from the flight deck down to the hanger deck.

At the elevator ramp on the hanger bay, Commander Knauts stood with Karl, his recovery team, and waited as the elevator came to a halt, the safety barricade lowering into the ramp's recessed groove. As Steeg and Bonia watched from Hanger Deck Control, the Air Boss motioned to Karl and the Blue Shirts to roll the crate-carrying dolly off the elevator and into the bay. Once clear of the ramp, the crate was removed from the dolly, and the dolly was returned to the elevator and tied down. At the elevator controls, Teddy Bear spoke into his sound powered phones' mouth piece, sounded the alarm, and pushed the control switch to the 'UP' position. The elevator quickly returned to the Flight Deck.

"What's in the crate?" Steeg asked as he watched the Air Boss motioning instructions to Karl.

"Beats me," Joe replied. "But, I don't like it. Whatever is in it, it ain't good."

Steeg saw Karl turn and look up to him. Karl waved his arm, signaling Steeg to come on down.

"He's asking for you," Steeg nudged Joe, but Joe was having none of it.

"No such luck," Bonia said. "You better get down there, Steeg. Sorry about that."

"Thanks," Steeg resigned, coming to his feet and climbing the two steps to the door. "Bury me at sea, if it comes to that."

"You got it."

On the Hanger Deck, Steeg reluctantly joined Karl and the commander at the crate, offering a salute the commander didn't return.

"We gotta open this up," Karl started to explain.

"What's in it?" Steeg asked. The commander looked at the brown-haired Yellow Shirt, a slight smile on his lips and steel-like coldness in his eyes, not replying to Steeg's question. After a moment of looking first at Knauts, then at Karl, Steeg said, "Well, I'll get a pry bar then."

He turned around and double-timed it to the paint locker located on the port side of the bay at the base of the Hanger Deck Control ladder. Inside the locker, he grabbed a 14 inch pry bar hanging on the bulkhead, closed the door behind him and made it quickly back to the crate. Steeg attacked the near corner of the box and in short order had the top panel off and leaning against the side of the crate. Inside were four, brown paper-wrapped cylindrically shaped objects, each one about 30 inches tall. Commander Knauts reached in and pulled one of the paper-wrapped cylinders free of the box, placing it on the deck.

"Remove the paper," the Air Boss told Steeg. Steeg did so.

At first, he didn't believe what his eyes beheld. The most beautiful garbage can Steeg, or for that matter anyone else in the United States Navy, had ever seen. It was brilliant in its mirrored, chrome-plated glory, small slivers of silver-blue light bouncing across the faces of the men standing in the hanger bay. It was not unlike the way a mirrored ball would bathe reflected light across a ballroom dance floor.

"My God," was all Steeg could say in open-mouthed wonder. Everyone within eyeshot of the hanger bay turned their heads toward the source of the slivers of light bouncing across Hanger Bay Two.

"Yes, it is wonderful, isn't it?" Commander Knauts smiled as he stepped up to Steeg with characteristic menace. Through gritted teeth, he ordered, "Get the chain."

In the middle of the crate were four squat cardboard containers. In each container was a 10 foot length of 3/8 inch link chain made from polished chromium steel. Each length of chain easily weighed more than 40 pounds. With significant effort, Steeg pulled a length free from one of the cardboard boxes, holding it up in amazement.

Commander Knauts continued. "You will replace the galvanized cans with these. You will do so immediately. And you, with your so-called 'A-Team,' will polish these cans morning, noon and night, along with these chains. If I see so much as a finger print on any of them, I will personally see to it you are thrown into the brig. If I see so much as a spec of dirt in any padeye in this hanger bay, I'll have you thrown into the brig. If there is any smudge, mark or foot print on the paint in this bay, I'll have you thrown into the brig. Do you understand me, Mister?"

It was a cold, hard question. Steeg understood. "Yes, Sir."

"Recite to me what will get you thrown into the brig."

"Yes, Sir," Steeg replied, irritated on the inside, but coolly professional on the outside. "A finger print on a can or chain, Sir; a spec of dirt in any Hanger Bay Two padeye, Sir; a smudge, mark, or foot print on the painted areas, Sir."

Knauts nodded slowly. "Very good. There's no excuse, then. You have five minutes to get the new cans into place."

As the commander left the bay through the starboard door leading to the escalator, Steeg looked as his watch. It was 0622 hours.

Karl walked up behind him as he observed Knauts' exit. "I wonder what the astronauts are doing right now."

Steeg chuckled. "I don't know. But I'll tell you what: I bet whatever they're doin', it has nothing to do with garbage cans."

At that precise moment inside the command module Columbia, Neil Armstrong was busy coordinating things between his two pilots and Mission Control for the trans-lunar burn.

"Commencing burn on my mark," he said coolly. "Three... Two... One... Mark!"

The third stage engine jolted to life. The combined mass of the command module and the still-attached service module accelerated, punched out of orbit halfway through its second trip around the Earth. The spacecraft smoothly inserted itself onto lunar trajectory, steadily increasing speed to 24,000 miles per hour.

Before dawn three days later, Steeg was leaning on the rail of the port side catwalk outside the door forward of the bay two fueling station. Exposed to the rush of sea and wind, yet protected from the elements by the overhang of the flight deck above, the small jut-out just forward of the number two elevator was the most isolated and peaceful place on the ship. It was on this same catwalk in '68 where the guys played tag with the an approaching typhoon threatening Kowloon Bay and Hong Kong. To avoid being trapped, *Hornet*, along with her destroyers and DE's, plowed through wind, rain and twenty to thirty foot seas for two days. Waves were so massively tall they exploded over the hurricane bow and across the flight deck. Below on the catwalk, V3 crewmembers played 'Chicken' with the crashing wall of water just before it would reach the the jut-out. The rules of the game were simple. The last one to leave the catwalk before the wave hit was the winner.

But this early morning the sea was calm and the wind was a comfortable ten knots. With the ship too far at sea for any man-made urban illumination to interfere, the sky was a brilliant blanket of stars that covered the heavens to the horizon. It was the kind of night when Steeg appreciated his difficulty in sleeping.

What a beautiful creation You have made, Lord. You are truly great. The wonder of every thing, and still You care for me. How can that be? Looking at this, the majesty of Your creation, how do I measure up to anything worthwhile? Yet, You died for me. How does that make sense? I don't know. I don't really understand at all.

His head met his hands at the rail. The smooth blackness of the sea rushed below him as he continued his quiet prayer aloud.

"I feel, Lord, like a large part of me isn't there any more. I don't know how to get it back. It's my fault, I know. I don't know what to do to make it right. I need You to make it right for me. I've asked You, but I don't think that's what's happening. I feel like I'm slipping away and I don't know why You're not helping me get out of this mess. I want to believe. I need to believe. Help me believe. – Amen."

He raised his eyes back up to the starry heavens above him to marvel again at the stunning beauty of it all. Compared to what he saw all around him, he should have felt completely alone. But, he didn't. Strangely, he felt as if he belonged there.

The silver bright three-quarter moon hung low in the Western sky. He thought of the three astronauts hurtling through space at that very moment, and he wondered if the three men in the cramped capsule were busy tracking technical read outs on fuel consumption, oxygen and CO2 levels, or calculating long, complicated mathematical strings to prepare for tomorrow's scheduled landing on the moon. Steeg shook his head as he thought they might actually be so busy with what they were doing up there they might actually forget to look out the window at the wonder of all the stars he himself could see so clearly in the pre-dawn sky.

As Steeg looked up at the night sky in the South Pacific, Mission Control in Houston was concluding the morning update of news, weather and sports with the Apollo 11 Crew.

"So, you're the biggest thing in the news, gentlemen," said the Assistant Flight Director. "You're on every newscast, every front page of every newspaper. The whole world is tuned in on this. I hope you don't all get big heads from all this attention – Over."

Command Module pilot Michael Collins triggered his mic. "No need to worry about that," he said with a smile. Then, with honest reverence he added, "Houston, it's been a real change for us. Now we are able to see stars again. We're able to recognize constellations for the first time on this trip. The sky is full of stars, just like the nights on Earth. All the way here we have been able to see stars only occasionally, often only through monoculars. But we haven't been able to recognize any star pattern. Until now – Now we can."

"That sounds good to us down here," Mission Control replied.

Neil Armstrong then added, "The view of the Moon that we've been having recently is really spectacular. It's about three-quarters of the hatch window and, of course, we can see the entire circumference, even though part of it is in complete shadow and part of it's in earth-shine. It's a view worth the price of the trip."

"Roger that, Columbia."

Commander Knauts leaned in close to examine each chrome garbage can in Hanger Bay Two. Lieutenant Blunt followed close behind, slouched as usual. The inspection had taken too long, at least it seemed to be that way for Steeg who, along with Bear, observed the proceedings from Hanger Deck Control. For the better part of the hour, the Air Boss had progressed slowly across the hanger bay. He had paused at almost every padeye on the deck to make sure they were clean, checking the quality of the paint on the deck and the alignment of the red, white and blue bunting fence surrounding the MQF area. Judging from the tedium of it all, it was obvious the commander was looking for something to complain about. But the daily inspection had become standard procedure for Steeg and his "A-Team" and they had their duties well rehearsed and timed perfectly. Commander Knauts was nothing if not punctual. You could set your watch by his morning inspections. Because of this, his team had completed their latest round of deck swabbing, touch up painting and padeye cleaning just minutes before the commander's arrival. Steeg handled the polishing of the chrome-plated garbage cans personally.

The last can inspected was the one near the Bay Three fire doors. The commander's eyes scanned the container and the anchoring chains as if he had x-ray vision. After a long moment, he looked away disappointed.

"Get the MAA," he ordered the lieutenant.

"Sir?" Blunt questioned, confused.

"You heard me."

"Yes, Sir," the lieutenant nodded. He quickly headed toward the starboard ladder that led to the MAA shack on the 01 level.

From Hanger Deck Control, Bear asked, "Where's the lieutenant going?"

Steeg kept his eyes on the commander. As Blunt briskly walked away, Knauts stepped back to the chrome garbage can he had just inspected. His hand disappeared behind the curve of the metal container, then quickly returned.

The seconds passed slowly, too slowly for Steeg. He and Bear sat leaning over the status board, waiting for something to happen. The commander remained rooted to the deck next to the garbage can.

"I don't like it," Steeg offered.

"These inspections are just plain stupid," said Bear.

"Not to Knauts," Steeg replied. "This is something more to him. This is some kind of vendetta. What he gets out of it, I don't know. All I know is whatever is going on right now is not good for me."

After a moment more, Lieutenant Blunt, with Spanky Gaffaney in tow, joined Commander Knauts in the hanger bay. Neither Steeg nor Bear could make out what Knauts was saying as they watched him point a finger at Spanky's chest, gesturing first toward the garbage can, then to the lieutenant, back again to the garbage can, then back at Spanky. Spanky stepped toward the garbage can, bent down to look at something, then turned back to the commander, who immediately threw his hands in the air and continued his tirade. The Master at Arms held both hands out in a calming gesture, explaining something the two sailors in Hanger Deck Control couldn't hear. Whatever it was, the commander didn't buy it, raising his voice loud enough for both Steeg and Bear to make out through the closed control room door.

" ... It's willful disobedience of my orders, so take care of it!" Knauts roared.

In Hanger Deck Control, the two Navy men looked at each other as the commander turned and ardently strode away. Passing below Hanger Deck Control, the Air Boss directed a purposeful scowl at Steeg sitting in the bay window.

"That didn't go good," said Bear.

Steeg agreed. "I got a bad feeling about this."

Steeg's feeling was quickly verified. The lieutenant and Spanky entered Hanger Deck Control with Steeg and Bear still seated at the status board.

"I'm sorry, Steeg," Spanky's sincere regret echoed in his voice. "It's not legal, but there's not much I can do about it right now."

Steeg knew the answer before he asked the question. "Do about what?"

Spanky took a deep breath, exhaling slowly. "You're under arrest. By order of the Air Department Commander."

He was allowed his clothes, but he had to give up his belt and his bootlaces, along with everything thing else he carried on his person, except the dog tags around his neck. Spanky completed the ritual, and then led Steeg into the cell, the door to which clanged too loudly behind him. The small four foot by seven foot, white painted metal cage squeezed real claustrophobia from somewhere deep inside him and Steeg immediately wanted out. From the other side of the door, Spanky turned the key.

"I'm sorry," he said. "This isn't going to last too long. It isn't right. There're no grounds. The charges won't stick."

"What charges?" Steeg asked.

"Disobedience of a direct order, insubordination, and dereliction of duty."

Steeg shook his head as he lowered himself to the bare mattress on the single skinny bunk anchored to the bulkhead. Stretching his legs straight out before him, his toes almost reached the opposite side. "The charges may not stick, but they sure sound impressive. I might be here for a while."

Spanky rested his hands on the painted steel slats that served as bars for the door. "The lieutenant is working on getting you out. Hang loose."

Skeptically his eyes surveyed his surroundings. "What time is it? I haven't had morning chow yet."

The MAA looked at his wristwatch. "Five minutes to eight. I'll get a tray up for you. What would you like?"

As Steeg put in his breakfast order, Apollo 11 was wrapping up their Lunar Orbit Insertion (LOI) procedures. Most of the past half hour had been spent maneuvering the spacecraft. Using the main rocket as a 20,500 pound thrust-engine, the spacecraft sufficiently slowed for the moon's gravity to capture it into an oblong orbit that ranged in elevation from a minimum of 61.3 miles to a maximum 168.8 nautical miles.

Armstrong triggered his transmitter. "Mission Control."

"Go ahead, Neil," Flight Director Cliff Charlesworth replied.

"We're getting this first view of the landing approach," he continued. "This time we're going over the Taruntius crater. The pictures and maps brought back by Apollo 8 and 10 give us a very good preview of what to look at here. It looks very much like the pictures, but it's like the difference between watching a real football game and watching it on TV. No substitute for actually being here."

"We're all envious down here," Charlesworth came back. "Everything is solid green. We're going to need to stabilize the orbit, but that can come later. The surface scan is next up. Let's make sure cameras and all are ready for the telecast. It's scheduled for two hours from now."

"Roger that," acknowledged the astronaut.

Spanky had left the brig, leaving Steeg alone to eat a reasonably hot breakfast of bacon, eggs, fried potatoes, but cold toast with no butter, and a full Styrofoam cup of steaming black coffee that made it all worthwhile. He sat at the corner of the bunk where he could lean back against the bulkhead as he took bites of food from the metal mess tray resting next to him on the bunk. It was an understatement to say it was a quiet meal.

"I hope Spank is right and the lieutenant can get me out of here," he said to no one there, taking another careful sip of coffee.

"What did you do to get in here," Grace asked as she sat down at the far end of the narrow stitched mattress. He wasn't startle by her daytime visit. For some time now her unannounced drop-ins had been increasing, usually at night when he couldn't sleep, and always when he was alone. Each time, she was the same. She wore jeans and a wheat-colored pullover sweater. Her thick, wavy brown locks cropped close at the neck, framed her soft, clear face, and her beautiful brown eyes were so deep and inviting, he couldn't resist even if he had wanted.

"Fancy seeing you here," he smiled warmly. "It's nice to see you again. I was beginning to feel lonely."

"That's when you see me," she smiled. "When you're lonely, that's when I'm here."

He took another bite of cold toast, shaking his head in disagreement. "I was missing you earlier today, and I didn't see you. You weren't there. All I saw were stars."

"I was there," Grace calmly admitted, pulling her knees up close to her chest, wrapping her arms around her legs. "You were praying. I didn't want to disturb you."

Steeg looked at her for a long, silent moment. She gazed back at him, resting her head on her knees.

"I don't know what to do," he admitted, the hopelessness of so many things welling up inside of him. "I need you so badly and I don't know what to do about it."

"I need you, too. More than I can say."

Steeg emptied his lungs in one long sigh. "Is that you saying that, or are you saying what I want to hear?"

She smiled. "Yes, I'm saying it. And yes, I'm saying what you want to hear. I guess I'm more a part of you than I realized. I'm sorry. I didn't want to hurt you."

Another bite of toast and a quick swallow of coffee as Steeg willed himself free from an increasingly burdensome morass of self pity he had grown to despise.

"You didn't hurt me," he bluntly denied. "You went your own way. Good for you, bad for me. I'll get over it."

Her face saddened. "It's been more than two years, Steeg. I wish you would get over it. Find someone else and be happy. Someone like Marilyn Johnson. She likes you, you know."

"She's nice," he said looking away from Grace. "Maybe something could work out with her. If so, then maybe I'd be okay again. I don't know. We're going to talk things over when I get back to Long Beach…"

"Good. I hope things work out for the two of you," Grace said. "Just be honest with her."

Steeg glared back at the apparition. "Let's see if I got this straight. You want me to be honest with her? Like you were honest with me?"

Gracie raised her head in a sudden jerk, and his anger surged to the surface.

"That's rich! How honest were you when I came home for Christmas leave? Are you telling me you were completely true to what you promised? I don't believe it, not for a second! There's no way, not with the way you bolted within, what was it, four months? Not even that long. You had to be with that other guy long before then, seeing him behind my back, and leading me on at the same time."

The rage spilled out in a rush. "You weren't honest with me! You lied! LIED! For what?! So you could get laid without sinning?! What's wrong with you, anyway?! Why'd you do this? Why'd you handle this whole thing like you did? All you had to do was tell me, I would have understood. But you didn't tell me. You couldn't wait! You never had any intention of waiting! Not for me! Not for us! You just couldn't give it a chance, could you?! You're a coward! And, instead of doing what was right, you took the coward's way out!"

He could have continued, but she faded into nothingness, her brown eyes the last thing to disappear.

"It's just that we've got light bouncing all over the place every time the sun shines in."

Eugene Gunhofer, the on-location producer for the ABC Television crew, was upset. Sitting on the rear bench in Hanger Deck Control, an ABC-logo coffee cup in hand, Gunhofer was trying to explain the physics of optics and misdirected light sources to Joe Bonia and Bill Denoso, both listening patiently. "We've tried polarized lenses, different camera angles, extended glare shielding on the front of the cameras, but nothing helps. Every time the sun comes into the bay, we've got full spectrum refracted light bouncing all over the place."

Bonia nodded in understanding as Denoso peered through the window into the work of pure Navy art that was now Hanger Bay Two. Neither man offered a solution to Gunhofer's problem, so the civilian continued.

"Everything points to a beautiful, sunshiny day on the 24th. We don't know for sure which way the ship is going to be facing when the chopper comes down to the hanger bay, but if the boat is pointing West, the sun is going to be coming in from the left side. It'll bounce all over and we won't get jack on screen."

The First Class Aviation Boatswain's Mate nodded again. Denoso cupped his chin in his hand, and continued to examine the deck below without speaking.

Gunhofer struggled to drive home his point. "Look, guys, I'm not asking a lot here, just a little adjustment on the placement of things."

The two servicemen looked at each other, but said nothing.

"We can solve this, I know we can," Gunhofer pleaded. "Maybe we could drape the things in some of that red-white-and-blue fabric you made the fence out of?"

Bonia looked to Denoso for the answer.

Denoso shook his head. "No can do. We used all that we had for the fence."

Bonia turned back to Gunhofer and offered nothing.

Gunhofer pulled the 'you-owe-me' card. "I got you those porn movies."

Bonia smiled with an acknowledging nod. The skin flicks had made for a fun, yet annoyingly frustrating diversion in the hanger deck crew's lounge earlier that week.

"I got more of that sort of stuff, maybe a few other things you guys might enjoy."

Denoso turned toward the TV man. "I hope so. Those flicks weren't very high quality, you know."

"I didn't hear any complaints at the time," Gunhofer countered, miffed.

"True enough," Denoso agreed. "The thing is you gotta understand what you're really asking here. First, these garbage cans that you claim reflect light all over the place are Commander Knauts' babies. They're placed where they are by him, personally. We can't change that. They gotta stay where they are. Period."

Bonia cleared his throat. "Add to that the fact that if we try to drape anything on them to solve your problem, we have a real problem with the commander. For crying out loud, Gene, we've got one of our petty officers in the brig right now because the commander found a finger print on one of the cans!"

"The brig?" Gunhofer repeated.

"The brig – for a finger print," Bonia confirmed. "You want us to drape cloth over those cans, the whole division will be up on charges. That can't happen."

Gunhofer rubbed his brow in frustration. "If this isn't solved, we're all going to be fired. The Network won't allow this, believe me."

The three sat silent for several seconds. Then Bonia offered a 'by-the-book' out he was willing to try.

"Well, maybe we can come up with something," he said. "I'll talk with the lieutenant. Maybe a heart-to-heart with the commander might be the way to go. Maybe he'll go along with a change in the positioning of the cans. Maybe he'll let us remove them all together. Maybe he'll realize they really shouldn't be there at all, not while we're at sea."

Denoso let out a short whistle. "That's a lot of 'maybes'."

"Yeah, I know." The First Class Petty Officer acknowledged with faint hope.

"Sounds great," Gunhofer slapped his knee, drained his coffee cup in two gulps and stepped to the door. Turning, he added, "And, if you guys could do something about those windows, we'll be home free."

"Windows?" both servicemen repeated in unison.

"Yeah, light from the lamps bounce off these windows. Sure would be great to black those out somehow."

Denoso rubbed his eyes as Bonia shook his head.

"Or, some other way to keep light from reflecting off the glass."

"It's plastic, actually." Bonia corrected.

"Whatever," the TV man said. "Let me know how I can help on anything to get this done, okay?" With that, he exited Hanger Deck Control and headed down the ladder to the hanger deck.

Denoso left his chair and quickly followed after the television producer, telling Bonia he was going to work something out with the man on both issues. Bonia stayed seated as the college graduated reservist scurried down the ladder and caught up with Gunhofer half way to the ABC Network trailer.

Along with his belt and bootlaces, Spanky had also taken his wallet, pocket change and wristwatch. Steeg had lost track of time, and he had no idea how long he had been in the brig. It felt like it had been a very long time. It hadn't been as long as he thought, and that was confirmed when Spanky left his desk in the MAA office adjacent to the small two-cell block to ask if Steeg wanted noon chow or not. Steeg reclined at the head of the bunk, back against the bulkhead.

"What time is it?"

Spanky looked at his watch. "Just 12:30."

"Seems later than that for some reason."

"That's normal," Spanky nodded. "You don't have any reference points in here. No sun. No clocks. No PA system to hear ship-wide announcements. Nothing. That's done on purpose, you know."

"When's the next head break?"

"Whenever you want it."

"How about now?"

Spanky agreed, pulling the keys from his belt chain and unlocking the cell. For the second time that day, he led Steeg to the small toilet opposite from the two cells. It didn't take as long as Steeg had hoped. Too soon, he was done and returned to the cell.

"Any word from the lieutenant, yet?" he asked as Spanky turned the key and the bolt rattled into place.

"Not yet. You want something to eat?"

Steeg eased back into his former position on the rack. "Some coffee would be nice. Maybe an orange, or apple, or some kind of fruit. Not very hungry."

Spanky understood, telling the sailor he'd be out for a little longer this time, making his rounds before heading to the mess hall to pick up some coffee and fruit. With a friendly and sympathetic wave Spanky was gone and Steeg had the brig to himself once again.

"He seems nice," Grace commented from the end of the bunk.

"He's a good man," Steeg agreed, pulling both hands down his face wishing she hadn't returned. "At least he's not crazy like some of us in here."

"You're not crazy," she reached over and rested her hand on his knee. He could actually feel the warmth of her touch through the fabric of his bell-bottom trousers.

"You're not real," he groaned. "If that's not crazy, what is?"

"I love you," she sounded so convincing, as if she really meant it.

"I don't believe you."

"I know. I don't blame you, but it's true."

"Will you shut up, please?"

She pulled her hand away, saying nothing as she looked right through him. His eyes met hers as he wondered what Grace, the real Grace, was doing at that very moment.

Let's see, now. There's a five hour time difference between here and Minnesota. Spanky said it was 12:30. That makes it 5:30 p.m. Central time, right?

"That right," Grace agreed.

She irritated him with that. *It's not fair she can read my thoughts, too.*

"I can pretend not to, if you'd like."

He closed his eyes, willing her to disappear. Slowly, he opened his eyes to see her simply shrug her apology for still being there. *More than aggravating,* he thought. *All right, it's 5:30 in Minnesota, the middle of summer. She's probably at home with her husband having dinner... or, having sex.*

He saw Grace shake her head.

How do you know? He thought to himself angrily. *You're here with me! And, you're not real. You're a figment of my overactive imagination, nothing more.*

She nodded in agreement to that one, further exasperating him.

He spat, "All right, you can talk if you want!"

"Thank you," Grace bowed her head sarcastically.

"You're welcome," Steeg replied with equal sarcasm.

She motioned with an upturned hand to calm him. "Steeg, do you remember when you proposed to me?"

"I try not to."

"You told me you would love me always."

"Yeah, that always sounds good. Girls fall for it every time."

She leaned towards him. "It wasn't just some line with you. I believe you really meant it."

He restlessly rubbed his palms against his knees, not wanting to look at her or hear her any more. "Believe what you want. I use that line all the time now."

She leaned closer. "No, you don't. You haven't said it to anyone since. Not even to Marilyn."

He backed away as far as the bulkhead behind him would let him. "I don't want to talk about Marilyn. Leave her out of this."

"Do you love her?"

"She's great!" He countered a little too enthusiastically. "She's strong in her faith. I like her a lot. I like being with her. I need to be with her.... I need to be with somebody."

"That's good. But, do you love her?"

He didn't answer. Grace pulled back. They sat there like that for a long time.

"The thing is," Steeg began reluctantly. "It's becoming too comfortable having you as a companion. You're here because I want you here. You fill me up in ways I can't explain. It certainly isn't the sex thing. I can talk with you any time..."

"We don't always agree, though."

"Doesn't matter. Even our arguments are better than the loneliness. Without these talks, especially now that I'm in here, I don't know what would happen."

"You're not crazy," she reassured him again.

"If you say so."

"You're in pain."

"No, I'm coping as best as I can," Steeg chuckled at the irony of it all. "Constant and complete denial of reality will see me through this."

"You deny that I left you for another man?"

"No."

"Than what are you denying?"

"I'm denying," his jaw tightened as he felt the wetness gather in his eyes. "That you never loved me as much as I love you."

By sundown, the word about the skin flicks had sufficiently spread. This was verified by the line of sailors that ran from the hanger deck crew's lounge door, down the ladder to Bay Two, and then trailed aft toward Hanger Bay Three. The first show was scheduled for 2100 hours. Well past dark, Gunhofer and his lead technician completed their wiring of the lounge for full sound, erected a bed sheet as a projection screen, and somehow had found three large cardboard boxes filled with a variety of Hershey bars, peanuts and bagged candies free for the taking. With growing apprehension, First Class Petty Officers Farmer and Bonia stood inside the closed lounge door desperately discussing their mutual concerns.

"The line is almost into Bay Three, and it's growing!" Farmer exclaimed.

"Yeah, I know," Bonia said, worried. "This thing could get out of hand real easy. If the Captain finds out, we're all dead."

"Damn that Denoso!" Farmer cursed. "This was supposed to be just a division thing."

"Well, somebody talked," Bonia stated the obvious. "What do you want to do about it?"

Farmer looked around the lounge with the too-many rows of seating arranged facing the bed sheet projection screen hanging on the port bulkhead of the lounge. "This room is too small. We should have set this up in the ship's theater. Maybe we can move things to there."

The ship's theater was a make-shift conversion of a port side void in Hanger Bay Three. In a pinch, it could seat more than two hundred men at a time on right-angled tiers originally intended as supports for the void's slanted bulkhead.

Bonia disagreed. "No way, Chas. The theater means we'd need to involve Operations to set up in there. That blows it wide open, and if the Captain gets wind of this, you can kiss our careers 'good-bye'."

Farmer knew Joe was right. "Well, then, this is Denoso's deal, he should get this thing under control before it hits the fan. Where is he, anyway?"

Neither man knew.

At that moment, three men met secretly in the darkened Hanger Deck Control. With no overhead lamps, it was pitch black in the little room.

"How many tickets have we sold?" Asked the younger man.

"Over five hundred!" Replied a familiar voice.

"At two bucks a piece?!" Exclaimed the third man in an excited, yet controlled lower voice. "That's more than a thousand dollars!"

"You got that right," confirmed the familiar voice. "I love the free enterprise system!"

"How much to the TV guys?" The first man asked.

"Not a penny," the familiar voice answered. "They just want their little problem to go away."

"Frickin' A," the third man said.

"Just remember we still have to keep our end of the deal," said the familiar voice. "It's just the three of us. No one else can know. If anyone finds out who did it, we all go to jail, so keep your mouths shut."

"What time is it?" Steeg asked, scraping his fingers across a three-day growth badly in need of a razor.

"0630," Spanky answered, sliding the mess tray through the horizontal slot of the brig cell's door.

"Spank, it's like mid-day or night time, or something else." Steeg complained, taking the tray first, followed by the Styrofoam cup of coffee Spanky held for him. "How long am I going to stay in here?"

"I don't know. I'm sorry."

Steeg took his place at the far corner of the mattress, settling the tray next to him as usual. He brought the cup to his lips for a quick sip. The days had gone by too slowly. He was exhausted from too much restless napping and too little of everything else but going to the head. After three days, he smelled bad and he needed a shower. After three days, he doubted he had had more than a handful of hours of real sleep. His features were tired, and his eyes withdrew deeply into the hollows of their sockets. Over the rim of the coffee cup Steeg saw Spanky watching him. His friend's obvious concern bothered Steeg even more, so he changed the subject.

"How're the astronauts doing?" He asked, shoving half a slice of cold toast into his mouth.

"Headin' back. Left the moon yesterday, on their way back now. They should splashdown in a couple of days," with a noticeable tone of sadness the MAA added, "They had it all on close circuit TV. I'm sorry you missed it."

"Me, too." Steeg shrugged. "How are the guys? Any more trouble with the hanger deck inspections?"

Spanky shook his head. "Not that I've heard. Everyone is pretty pissed you're still in here, though."

"That's my problem, not their's."

"Blunt is really mad," Spanky continued. "The A-Team, too. They put Denoso in charge of that detail."

"Denoso?!"

"Yeah. For some reason Knauts recommended him. He's done okay, but the other Blue Shirts don't like it. They want you back."

Steeg laughed at that. "Well, they can't have me, dammit! I'm staying right here!"

"The lieutenant wants you back, too. I think he thinks he looks bad to the men, worried they might hold him responsible for all this in some way."

Steeg rejected that one, too. "Knauts put me in here, not Lieutenant Blunt. I did what Knauts wanted me to do, and he put me in here anyway. Okay, so I made fun of him with the padeye straw-blowing thing, big deal. It just isn't right that it blew up into this brig time, that's all."

The two men shared another prolonged silence before Spanky replied.

"The lieutenant's taken this all the way to the XO, you know. He doesn't want to press for Captain's Mast, because he wants to keep this off your permanent record. Actually, I don't think Knauts wants it to go to Captain's Mast, either. It might all backfire on him if it does. I guess the XO is going to have a private talk with the commander. Who knows? You might get out of here completely unscathed."

Steeg picked at the food on the tray, sliding a piece of cold but crisp bacon into his mouth, and leaving the rest, not really hungry enough to finish the meal.

"Who knows? I might end up in court martial and kicked out with a 'Dishonorable' before it's all done. That would be ironic, Divine poetic justice: joined in '66, out in disgrace in '69. No G.I. Bill for college after all." He finished the coffee and placed the empty cup on the tray, which he then carried to the door. Spanky took it through the horizontal slot.

"Just hang in there, Steeg." The MAA said as he turned to leave, mess tray in hand.

"Roger that, Spank. Will do."

Spanky left the brig and returned to the mess hall straight away, handing the metal tray and flatware to the scullery worker for cleaning. As he turned, John Dickenson called to him.

"Spank! Gotta second?"

"Sure, John," The MAA avoided three sailors moving past him to step toward the tall blonde-haired Yeoman. Together they moved to the side to allow others to pass by.

"What's this I hear about Steeg being arrested?"

Spanky nodded. "It's true. Commander Knauts ordered it."

Dickenson didn't understand. "Why?"

"Disobeying a direct order, dereliction of duty, etcetera, etcetera," Spanky didn't hide his feelings on the matter.

Dickenson shook his head. "I don't get it. Not Steeg – is there anything to these charges?"

"Not really," Spanky answered honestly.

After a moment, Dickenson asked, "May I talk to him? Is he allowed visitors?"

"I don't see why not," Spanky said. "Just between you and me, he needs to talk with someone besides himself."

"Besides himself?"

Spanky's face shaded with worry as he leaned in closer. "He's been talking to himself up there. He doesn't know I hear him, but it's like there's someone else in the cell with him. It's kinda spooky, John."

Before afternoon chow the next day, Spanky stuck his head through the door of his office. "You've got a visitor."

"Who is it?" Steeg shouted back. "Never mind. Tell who ever it is I don't want any!"

The foot steps were followed by the tall shadow of John Dickenson, Steeg's old Bible study partner. The Yeoman 2nd Class stopped in his tracks as he reached the cell door and saw Steeg sitting on the bunk. The sight sobered him.

"My God, Steeg," he barely whispered. "What's happened here?"

He waved a weary hand at his friend. "Ah, John, it's nice of you to drop in. 'I was a prisoner and you visited me…'"

John was somewhat relieved that Steeg still had his sense of humor. "Yes, and '... I was naked and you clothed me.'"

"Well, let's leave the sex thing out of this, okay?" Steeg chuckled, weakly falling back against the bulkhead. "Don't worry, John. It looks worse than it is. Give me razor and a bar of soap, and I'll be as good as new."

"Bar of soap is right," John agreed. "It stinks in here."

"Gee, thanks, John."

"Sorry, but it's true," John leaned against the slatted bars of the door. "How did this happen?"

Steeg offered a shallow shrug of his shoulders. "It's a long story."

"Bear told me Knauts had you arrested for a finger print on a trash can? That can't be right."

"Yeah, it does sound a little weird, doesn't it?"

John turned back in the direction of the office and shouted, "Can't he take a shower or shave, Spank? What's going on here?"

Spanky walked into the cell block, hands held open in resignation. "Orders, John, Commander Knauts' orders. There's nothing I can do about it."

"He can't shave? Clean himself? Brush his teeth?" John asked incredulously.

"Nothing," Spanky answered.

"Spank slips me some 'Double Mint' gum from time to time," Steeg said, pulling himself down the bunk and closer to the door. "Only one stick at a time, though."

John Dickenson looked at his brother in Christ with growing concern. "This isn't right."

Steeg shrugged. "It's what I get for being a smart-ass."

"This isn't right," John repeated. He turned back to the Master at Arms. "What's being done to get him out of here?"

"Well, the last I heard, the XO was going to talk to Commander Knauts about it. That was yesterday."

John nodded. "The XO. Does he know the whole story about this?"

Spanky wasn't sure if the XO was fully informed about everything or not, only that Lieutenant Blunt had spoken with him on Steeg's behalf.

"Okay. The XO's a good man – a fair man. That's something, I guess," John turned back to Steeg, his face etched with worry. In return, Steeg shrugged a shallow grin to lighten things up a bit. John shook his head again. "This isn't right. I can't promise anything, Steeg, but I'm going to try something on my own."

Now Steeg was concerned. "Be careful, John. I don't want any of this to get on you. What 'something on your own' are you going to try?"

"Something direct."

Primary Flight Control was on the 08 level near the top rear of the Island superstructure. The room had a too-low ceiling and a continuous bank of windows that wrapped around on three sides overlooking the entire Flight Deck. It was a small and cramped space. Two yellow-shirted officers both wore heavy military binoculars strapped around their necks; one of the men wore sound powered phones, as well.

John Dickenson found Commander Knauts sitting in his padded brown leather command chair sipping coffee. Knauts was a remarkable sight. His crisply creased khakis, a leather flight jacket with several sewn on service patches, silver leafs on the shoulders, aviator sunglasses riding high on the bridge of his nose, and his gold braided cover with the patent leather brim tightly screwed onto his head, made him primed for a Navy recruiting poster, or maybe a Hollywood movie. John was not afraid of the commander. John was rarely afraid of anything.

"How can I help you, Yeoman?" Knauts asked in a detached manner befitting his superior rank. John silently observed the smugness of the man as Knauts removed his sunglasses with one hand and lowered his coffee mug to the built-in cup holder of the command chair with the other.

"Yes, Sir. I'm following up on the conversation you had with the XO, Sir."

It was a bold move on John's part. He had not confirmed with anyone, least of all the XO, that any conversation had actually taken place.

"What conversation would that be?" the commander lied with a smile. "I don't recall having one – except for discussing his golf game back at Pearl. He's got a slice problem."

John wasn't fooled. Knauts' acknowledgement of any conversation at all with the XO was proof the conversation had taken place and had most certainly dealt with Steeg and his brig internment.

"No, Sir. Not the slice – about Petty Officer Patterson, Sir?"

"Oh, that." Knauts softly cleared his throat, then leaned forward in his chair as he lowered his voice so the two Yellow Shirts wouldn't hear. "I wasn't aware it was common knowledge. In fact, I was assured it wouldn't be a matter of record."

"Not officially, of course, Sir," John returned in a whisper matching the commander's. He pulled several sheets of paper from the folder he had brought with him. "But, there is the necessary paperwork."

Knauts looked at the sheets the Yeoman held, his eye catching the "UCMJ[11] Guidelines" title of the top sheet, and the "Court Ma..." partially covered title of the second sheet, which in turn covered at least a half dozen more sheets.

John continued. "Of course, Sir, which forms needing completion depend on the measures and decisions you make on the case."

"Case?" Knauts raised an eyebrow as he glanced up from the papers John held.

"Yes, Sir. After all, Sir, we can't keep a man in the brig indefinitely. We have to charge him with something, or return him to duty."

Knauts didn't flinch, his solid gaze locked onto the Yeoman like a cold vice.

Outwardly stoic, inwardly John's mind was racing. He was confident the commander didn't want any "case" made out of this. He was sure Knauts' motives against Steeg were driven by his ego (commonly known by most Operations' staffers as bordering on megalomania), and not legitimate charges supported by credible evidence. It was the lack of credible evidence John was counting on to make his bluff work.

Knauts on the other hand wanted people to know he couldn't be messed with, not by anyone, least of all an enlisted man. The XO had assured him that this would go no further, but he had also made it clear he expected Knauts to manage the situation for the greater interests of the U.S. Navy, the Air Department and *Hornet*. However, Patterson had embarrassed the commander on the Hanger Deck, and had deliberately undermined his authority in the Department. As far as Commander Knauts was concerned, putting the punk in the brig was the right thing for the Navy, Air Department and *Hornet*.

Knauts could not recall the XO mentioning anything about necessary paperwork at the meeting. Any official paperwork on this would find a file somewhere, and files in the Navy had extended lives far beyond that which was warranted or originally intended. Contemplatively fingering his lower lip, Knauts wondered if this little episode had sufficiently served its purpose.

"Well, I'm afraid it's a little embarrassing," Knauts began coolly with a shallow smile. "Actually, after my little chat with the XO, I realized I had forgotten poor Petty Officer Patterson was still in the brig. It's been so hectic you know, what with the round-the-clock operations with the recovery teams and all. I'm sure he's learned his lesson – probably learned it after the first night. It's unfortunate I was side-tracked, and I feel terrible about it. In fact, I was just about to issue the order to have him released when you came up."

"Oh, that's a very economical decision, Sir," John smiled, reaching into the stack of papers he still held, pulling out an already filled in release order and handing it to the commander. "Just need your signature at the bottom, and that should do it, Sir."

Knauts looked at the already filled in form, then back at the Yeoman with a wary eye. "Well, I guess you're right," he said, pulling a pen from inside his leather flight jacket. Signing on the line John pointed to, the commander added, "I trust you'll be able to see to it that this goes directly to the Master at Arms?"

"Yes, Sir."

The commander handed the signed release order to John, who tucked the paper back into his folder, threw the commander a snappy salute, did a crisp about face pivot and exited Primary Flight Control.

Not thirty seconds later the two Pri-Fly directors jerked alert, startled by the explosion of crashing glass. Commander Knauts sat in his command chair, his white knuckled fists clenched, the remains of his coffee mug scattered across the deck.

A *Hornet* shower was the equivalent of bathing in a tea cup. You stepped into the shower stall. You turned on the water. You quickly doused yourself in one turn under the spray. You turned off the water. You soaped yourself down using the loose water dripping from your body. You turned the water back on and rinsed the soap off as quickly as possible. You turned the water off and exited the stall. For the ship's evaporators to provide enough fresh water for all the crew and for all the food preparation in all three mess halls while at sea, *Hornet* showers were required from everyone concerned with personal hygiene. Unfortunately, there were those on board who were not so concerned. Steeg was not one of them, preferring a *Hornet* shower over no shower at all.

Free from the brig, his *Hornet* shower had never felt so luxurious, or so appreciated. Patting himself down until he was dry enough, he wrapped the white GI bath towel low around his hips and went to the head's center stainless steel sink to lather his four-day-old beard. The dark circles under his eyes were undeniable, but they were nothing a good night's sleep wouldn't help wipe away. Triggering a fresh blade on his Gillette band safety razor, Steeg's first swipe from his right sideburn to his jaw line effortlessly revealed perfectly smooth, whisker-free flesh.

AB 1st Class Petty Officer Chas Farmer walked through the doorway.

"Good to have you back," he said with a grin.

"Good to be had." Steeg joked for at least the third time since his release from the brig. He continued shaving.

"Yeah. I hear that. Look, Steeg, you've been through a lot, at least a lot more than you deserved," Farmer shoved his hands into the two back hip pockets of his dungarees. "So, it would probably be a good idea if you stayed off duty for a while."

"Why's that, Chas?" Steeg asked with half the lather scraped clean.

"Well, everything's pretty much taken care of anyway; no need for you to rush back in when there really isn't all that much to rush back in to do."

Steeg turned from the mirror. "What's that again?"

Farmer tried a rephrase. "It's just that, you know, Denoso's got the A-Team staying on top of things in Bay Two…"

"I'm sure the guys really like that," Steeg chuckled, returning to his shave. "They can't stand Denoso."

Farmer agreed. "Yeah, you're right about that. Just the same, it's probably a good idea to lay low for the next few days."

"Lay low?" Two more strokes with the razor and only a few more to go.

"Yeah, you know, there's no need to come back too soon after your ordeal."

A half-minute passed in silence as Steeg finished shaving. He triggered the faucet to rinse the razor and splash water across his now smoothly shaven face to remove remnants of the shaving foam. His eyes met Farmer's reflection in the mirror.

"My 'ordeal' as you call it was with Knauts. You're trying awfully hard not to tell me something, Chas."

Farmer sighed heavily. "Okay, here it is. Recovery is tomorrow morning sometime. After 0500, no one not wearing dress whites will be allowed on the flight deck or above."

Steeg shrugged. "Makes sense. The Navy wants to look good on worldwide television."

Farmer nodded. "Yeah, well, there's also going to be another hanger deck inspection. We figure somewhere around 0300, Knauts is coming down one last time to check things out. The Chief thinks it would be best if you weren't there when that happens."

Steeg turned, hands on hips, to face his senior petty officer.

"The Chief?"

Farmer nodded, then added, "Me, too."

"Why?"

"Do you think it's a good idea the Air Boss sees you so soon after you get out of the brig?"

"Why not?" Steeg answered. "He put me there."

"That's the point, Steeg. I don't know why, but whatever that man has against you, it ain't normal."

Steeg let out a clipped laugh. "'Normal' is a rare commodity for more than just Knauts right now."

"I don't know about that, but things are demanding enough with this recovery. The Division doesn't need any more pressure to muck things up around here, if you know what I mean."

That one struck a chord. He hadn't given much thought to how his predicament with Knauts had affected the rest of the Division, but Farmer had just told him that it had. It made sense in a Navy kind of way. Some of the crap Knauts had been laying on the lieutenant had fallen onto Steeg big time. Some of that crap had fallen onto the rest of the Division, in ways Steeg could only imagine. The lieutenant had been right. It really did roll down hill.

"I see," Steeg nodded. "So, you think if I keep out of sight for a while, things will go easier on the rest of the guys?"

"Something like that," Farmer agreed.

Steeg had just finished four days of excruciatingly boring inactivity sitting in a jail cell with only his delusions for company. The confinement in the brig and all that did - yet did not - happen there confirmed his suspicions. He may very well be losing his grip on reality. Strangely enough, what worried him most about that was the fact that he wasn't worried about it at all. Intellectually, he knew he should be scared about going insane. But in fact, he had developed an odd comfort in his hallucinations.

Nevertheless, the idea of doing nothing else while the rest of the ship made history plucking the first humans to walk on the Moon from the middle of the Pacific Ocean didn't sit quite right with him. It wasn't as if he was losing his chance for the folks back home to see him on TV, although that might have been something he could have arranged with the help of the ABC cameramen. It was simply a matter of not being a part of it all in some way, if only to clean out padeyes where the astronauts would be walking.

He rested his back side against the rim of the sink behind him. He knew Farmer was right, and that it would be best for the Division if he were to disappear for a while. He acquiesced, realizing it was time to place the Division ahead of himself.

"Okay, where do you want me?"

"Here, or below decks is fine," the senior petty officer said. "Try the ship's library, or the mess decks any time. That's okay. Just nowhere on the hanger deck, flight deck or above. If you see Knauts anywhere, head in the opposite direction. Avoid and evade."

Steeg digested that for a few seconds before he nodded and said, "Aye-aye."

The regulation overhead lamps, combined with the bank of powerful aluminum-hooded studio television floods, bathed the hanger bay so brilliantly it hurt the eyes to look. At 0300 sharp, Commander Knauts walked through the door from the escalator, onto the blue painted path, past the ABC Network trailers and into the hanger bay. Lieutenant Blunt greeted the senior officer with a salute he held until the Air Boss returned it. Except for himself and the commander, the bay was deserted.

"Good morning, Sir," Blunt offered courteously.

"Lieutenant," Knauts returned, his eyes quickly scanning the bay. "Big day, today."

"Yes, Sir."

The two officers turned in unison, following the blue painted path to make the circuit around the red, white and blue bunting that fenced the area for the Mobile Quarantine Facility trailers. The commander noted every padeye they passed and admired the brilliant luster of each chrome garbage can. He stopped at the center can positioned near the aft end of the number two elevator ramp, and took his time inspecting to make sure the surface was smudge-free. Satisfied, he glanced up toward the darkened Hanger Deck Control, the bay's overhead lights reflecting off the Plexiglas.

"No crew on duty?" he asked.

"Standard watch only, Sir," Blunt replied. "With flight ops secured, no one else is on deck."

Commander Knauts nodded as he asked, "Where's your – what do you call them, 'A-Team' – in case some details need extra attention down here?"

"I imagine they're asleep right now," the lieutenant answered frankly. "However, in a couple of hours they'll be giving the bay the once-over just to make sure."

Knauts led the junior officer back to the blue path. "The President is scheduled to arrive about an hour before splashdown. After recovery, the Captain and I will personally accompany the President when he comes down to address the astronauts. I'm depending on you to make sure everything is in proper order down here."

"Yes, Sir."

They continued the inspection, stopping once as Knauts knelt down to finger what he thought was a mar on the paint, disappointed to find it to be only a shadow cast by overlapping coverage of the overhead lamping. At the bay three fire doors, Knauts inspected the chrome trashcan for only a brief moment, and quickly turned to the lieutenant.

"It's an outstanding job your men have done down here, Blunt. You can be proud of their effort."

"Thank you, Sir. I am," the lieutenant responded, waiting for the little man to slap him with a back-handed put down of some sort or another.

It didn't take long to come.

"Although I'm somewhat disappointed the 'A-Team' isn't down here guarding the hanger bay," he pronounced, taking two long strides toward

Hanger Deck Control. "This is the day, lieutenant. We can't afford any more embarrassing incidents."

Blunt turned to follow the man, only for the commander to stop and again turn back to the junior officer.

"I want the 'A-Team' down here within the hour," he ordered. "It's too important to slack off on things now."

"As you wish, Sir." Blunt acceded with a sigh.

Then Knauts pointed up to Hanger Deck Control. "When I come back down here with the President, I want to see Patterson sitting in that bay window up there, sitting right in the center of that window."

The lieutenant's brow furrowed with concern. "Sir, Patterson isn't part of the hanger deck recovery crew…"

"So what?" Knauts spat back, not hiding his anger. "The recovery will be over by then. Make sure that punk is where I can see him. Do you have any more questions?"

"No, Sir." Blunt said, silently wishing all this was over.

"Good." Knauts tugged at his shirt to smooth away non-existent wrinkles. Certain his appearance was satisfactory, he threw a brisk salute to Blunt, turned and walked back from where he had come.

Some 250 miles from *Hornet's* position, Air Force One landed on the Johnston Island military airstrip just before 0500. Within minutes after coming to a stop on the tarmac, President Richard M. Nixon, Secretary of State Henry Kissinger and Apollo 8 astronaut Frank Borman exited down the ramp from the gleaming Boeing 707 with the Presidential Seals on either side of the nose and the familiar red, white and blue paint job. The three men were followed by two ram-rod straight Marines in dress blue uniforms and a two-star Navy admiral with an eagle-like squint from under heavy eyebrows. A short walk across the tarmac, the helicopter designated 'Marine One' waited. The entourage headed straight for it.

On *Hornet* in the dim gray-blue of pre-dawn, literally thousands of people caught up in the growing excitement were scurrying all over the ship, some with last minute preparatory tasks needing attention, but most just too antsy to stand still. Every Navy man from the flight deck to Pri-Fly was in dress whites and spit-shined shoes. Every other person carried a camera. Prematurely, many searched the remains of a fading star-studded, cloud-scattered night sky for a glimpse at the streaking fire trail of Columbia's re-entry, an event more than an hour away.

On the Hanger Deck, the activity was even more hectic with Hanger Bay Two the main intersection between the flight deck and below decks. Dressed in their standard blue shirts and dungarees, Denoso and the 'A-Team' repeatedly policed the hanger bay, directing foot traffic away from bunting fencing and painted deck areas as they made sure everything stayed 4-0 and squared away. The hanger deck recovery team gathered near the number two elevator control stanchion dressed in new color coded shirts freshly stenciled on the front and back with "USS HORNET CVS-12 Apollo 11 Recovery" in bold black ink. Each man's deck boots were spit-polished to a mirror finish, and their bell bottom dungarees were steam pressed to wrinkle-free perfection. The team looked as sharp as that type of apparel would permit. Division Chief Cason, First Class Petty Officers Farmer and Bonia, and Lieutenant Blunt stood below Hanger Deck Control dressed to the nines in their tropical whites, enjoying the moment. All around, crowds of civilian broadcast technicians, cameramen, NASA personnel, and ship's company, busily hurried about, getting to where they had to go, finishing final details of one sort or another, and double-checking procedures they had rehearsed endlessly for weeks. It was almost 'Show Time' on *Hornet*.

Eugene Gunhofer, the ABC Network on-location producer, found Denoso holding an acetone soaked rag wiping out a padeye inside the white paint area near the Primary Mobile Quarantine Facility. Gunhofer, standing on the unpainted track of the bay three fire doors, called to the sailor.

"Yes, Gene," Denoso responded with a smile as he stood and walked toward the man.

"Denoso, is everything taken care of?" Eugene's voice was raised above the pandemonium of all the surrounding activity as Denoso came up to him.

"Of course," Denoso reassured the man. "Do you see anything here that shouldn't be here?"

Gunhofer looked around, but the numbers of people moving through the hanger bay blocked most of his view.

"I can't really tell," he said. "There're too many people in here."

Denoso placed a hand on the man's shoulder and pointed up to Hanger Deck Control. "See any reflection off the glass up there?"

There wasn't any reflection at all. The windows were totally clear.

"No, I don't."

"Of course not," Denoso explained. "The panes have been removed."

Denoso walked the producer through the hustling pedestrian cross traffic and toward the port side fire door. "See a chrome-plated shit can here?"

The garbage can and chains were gone. Gunhofer shook his head.

"What did you do with it?"

"Beats me," Denoso grinned. "We showed up on deck as scheduled, and there wasn't a shit can anywhere in the entire hanger bay. Poof! They all disappeared. We have absolutely no idea what happened to them."

Gunhofer was incredulous. "You're kiddin' right?"

"No kiddin'," Denoso shrugged grinning.

"You guys are going to get your asses in a big wringer," the producer warned.

"Look, Gene, we came down here on time after an authorized break. The commander completed his inspection with the lieutenant, and everything was fine. The fact that the cans weren't here means it was okay with the Air Boss. If it's okay with the Air Boss, it's okay with us."

Gunhofer shook his head, repeating, "You guys are going to get your asses in a big wringer."

At 0612 hours, the Boatswain's whistle blasted across *Hornet's* PA system, followed by the announcement "Marine One Arriving!"

It was quite a large helicopter, very much like a 'stretch-limo' version of the SH-3D Sea King. It had a deep blue paint job, sparkling white trim, large American flag decals on both forward sides of the twin-engine cowling, "UNITED STATES OF AMERICA" in white and gold emblazoned against the deep blue of both sides of the rear fuselage, and the Presidential Seal on the starboard and port side cockpit doors. There was no mistaking the heavy 'whoop-whoop' drone of Marine One's long rotor blades beating the moist morning air loud enough to be heard all the way down to the hanger deck. The helicopter landed perfectly just aft of the number two elevator. Blue Shirts rushed to the craft, slapping tie down chains onto the landing struts and chocks around the forward wheels. A red carpet was rolled from the Island structure to the starboard side sliding door of Marine One. The Honor Guard of eight sailors in full dress white uniforms quickly formed along both edges of the carpet, four on a side, standing at attention. Marine One's door slid open, an integrated stair lowered from the aircraft, and a Marine in Dress Blues exited to await the rest of the contingent. The Navy Admiral was first, immediately followed by President Nixon. As the President's foot touched the flight deck, the Chief Boatswain blew another four-toned whistle, and all eight Honor Guard members' right hands snapped to rigid salutes. Eight bells sounded, followed by "Commander-in-Chief arriving" over the PA system, and the President and his entourage strode passed the Honor Guard to shake hands with Captain Sieberlich, the Executive Officer, and several senior staff officers waiting at the end of the red carpet.

"Welcome aboard, Mr. President!" the Captain smiled as he shook hands with his Commander-in-Chief.

"Thank you, Captain," the President was beaming. "It's an exciting day, isn't it?"

"That it is, Sir. That it is." Sieberlich agreed, turning to introduce his Executive Officer and staff. In turn, the President introduced Secretary of State Henry Kissinger, and Apollo 8 astronaut Frank Borman.

"Of course, you know Admiral Zumwald," President Nixon acknowledged.

"Of course," Captain Sieberlich smiled broadly as he threw a crisp salute that CINC PAC-SE Asia returned in kind. He turned back. "It's a great honor to have you here, Mr. President."

"The honor is all mine, Captain," the President insisted. "I have to tell you, we saw your ship from the air coming in – magnificent sight! You should be very proud."

"Thank you, Mr. President. I am," Captain Sieberlich gestured toward the near door leading into the Island, suggesting they head up to the bridge for some refreshments and a short tour. In mass, the entourage turned and followed the Captain's lead through the door.

Dressed in steam-pressed, heavily starched dungarees and his blue *Hornet* baseball cap with the gold 3rd Class Petty Officer insignia on the crown, Steeg was half-way through Hanger Bay Three when Marine One landed. Before the President had exited the helicopter, Steeg had double-timed it into Hanger Bay Two, taken the ladder two steps at a time and into Hanger Deck Control. Farmer greeted him at the door and pointed to the vinyl padded stool next to the command chair at the status board.

"Good of you to make it," Farmer chided. "Sit there."

Steeg took the seat offered. On the bench behind him, Denoso and Santini sat, still in their blue shirts. Santini wore sound powered phones as usual.

As Farmer slid into the 'Command' chair next to him, Steeg leaned toward the First Class Petty Officer. "So much for 'Avoid and Evade'."

"It wasn't my choice," Farmer responded softly. "Knauts ordered that you be here."

"Good to have you back," Denoso offered sincerely from the rear bench.

"Good to be had," Steeg had begun to grow tired of the old saw, but he used it again anyway.

"What's going on up there?" Farmer asked over his shoulder.

"Their just outside of the Island, talking," Santini responded. "Okay, wait a second... They're going into the Island now."

"They'll head for the Bridge," Farmer said. "Nixon's gonna get the full treatment, starting with a bird's eye view of the re-entry."

Steeg turned back to the bay windows to give Hanger Bay Two a quick once-over visual inspection. "Wow, Denoso, you guys did a good job out there. These windows are perfectly cle..."

He caught himself before he finished the statement as he noticed the window Plexiglas was gone. Steeg reached out with his hand and pushed it through the opening where the plastic panes should have been, but weren't.

"What did you do with the plexy?"

"It's in the lounge," Denoso answered, adding, "That's not the only thing gone."

Steeg looked back at Denoso. Denoso said nothing, nodding him back toward the hanger bay. Steeg looked out the window, not knowing what he was supposed to see, or, in this case, not see. After scanning the bay forward and aft a couple of times, he realized what was missing. A slight dizziness strong enough for him to steady himself against the status board came over him.

"The cans are gone," Steeg barely whispered. "Chas, the cans are gone."

Farmer nodded. "Yep, they're gone."

"How?"

"The commander had them removed," Farmer shrugged. "After all the crap he put you and your team through, heck, put us all through, he took them out. What is that, crazy or what?"

Steeg turned back to Denoso, who returned his unspoken query with a raised eyebrow and a bewildered shake of his head. The two men held each other's eyes for several long seconds before Steeg returned to Farmer.

"That doesn't make sense," Steeg said. "Not even a little bit."

"Well, I'm sorry, Steeg. I didn't know you were so emotionally attached to the garbage cans. The fact is, after this morning's inspection, he obviously had the things taken out. No one else could have done that, only the commander."

Steeg glanced back at Denoso again. Denoso returned the look but said nothing. After another few moments of silence, Steeg picked up where he had left off.

"Chas, something about this doesn't seem right to me," he said. "I got a feeling I shouldn't be here."

"You gotta be here," Farmer affirmed. "The lieutenant said the Air Boss ordered him to make sure you're sitting right where you are right now."

"Yeah, so I was told. But, just think about this for a second. What if Knauts wasn't the one to take out the garbage cans? What if it was someone else?"

"What are you talking about? Steeg, the lieutenant was with the commander for the inspection at 0300 this morning. Everything checked out. Crap! The lieutenant said Knauts even complimented the 'A-Team' specifically on the great job they had done, the 'A-Team' Steeg — your 'A-Team.' You can take some pride in that, don't you think?"

Steeg agreed, but added, "I'm just concerned that the cans were removed by someone else, that's all."

Farmer shook his head and told the younger man not to worry. "There wasn't anyone else down here, Steeg. No one else was in this bay until I got here at 0430, and when I got here, the cans were gone. The commander took them out, probably because he heard about the TV guys' complaints."

What complaints were those? Steeg wondered.

It was 0635 hours *Hornet* time when, somewhere over the Mariana Islands, speeding at 22,300 miles per hour, the Apollo 11 Command Module Columbia re-entered Earth's atmosphere. At sea level the high cumulous clouds revealed only scattered blots of blue morning sky. There was no flaming trail visible from *Hornet*, but everyone above decks craned necks just the same in the hope of seeing something. The President, his dignitaries and Captain Sieberlich were on the port side of the Bridge, outside trying to see what couldn't be seen. Over the ship's PA system for all to hear, an exciting eves dropping on the clipped conversation between Mission Control and the astronauts had been taking place. This was replaced with the static hissing of dead air caused when radio contact was broken by the friction created with Columbia's re-entry. The loss of signal spanned about 4 minutes, and seemed much longer than that to everyone listening. The entire ship waited in complete silence until the PA system crackled back to life.

"Apollo 11, Apollo 11. This is *Hornet, Hornet,* over."

Several seconds of hissing was replaced with a thrilling response.

"Hello *Hornet,*" it was Neil Armstrong's voice. "This is Apollo 11 – reading you loud and clear!"

The resulting cheer roared across the ship so loudly it would have surprised no one on board if it was heard all the way back at Pearl Harbor.

Several more minutes passed before the PA announcement came. "Port side – nine o'clock, chutes spotted!"

Thirteen miles from the ship, a 'bull's eye' in NASA terms, Columbia floated down from the cloud line. At 0651 hours, there came another PA announcement.

"*Hornet*, Swim 1 – Splashdown. Apollo 11 has splashdown."

Columbia had hit the water so hard that it tipped upside down. The Command Module stayed in the inverted position until three large balloons in the top cone inflated, forcing the capsule back upright. It took nearly ten minutes. Three UDT swimmers clad in special bio-isolation suits plunged twenty feet from one of the three hovering SH-3D Sea King helicopters launched just prior to re-entry. Two of the swimmers tried to make quick work of attaching a floatation collar around the Command Module, but it took almost twenty minutes to complete the job. Finally, nearly a half-hour after splashdown, the third swimmer climbed onto the collar, opened the hatch, tossed in three biological suits for the astronauts to put on, and quickly closed the hatch to minimize exposure to any 'moon germ' contamination.

Eight minutes later, the three astronauts in hooded gray isolation suits and full-face respirator masks emerged from the Command Module, climbed down to the floatation collar and into the waiting inflated orange raft. The UDT man who had delivered the suits sprayed each man down with a disinfectant as an added decontamination measure. The procedure completed, SH-3D Sea King helicopter number 66 moved to hover overhead, positioned to hoist each of the astronauts one at a time from the raft into the helicopter.

UDT swimmer securing Columbia hatch; Collins, Aldrin and Armstrong in the raft dressed in their bio-isolation suits, floatation vest prepared for hoisting.

On board *Hornet*, Spanky Gaffaney stood at the number two elevator ramp on the hanger deck, watching the choppers near the horizon circle above the sea, doing that which their crews had trained for weeks to do. Karl, Tom Kinsey and the rest of the hanger deck recovery team gathered at the tow tractor behind him, and Bear was at the elevator controls as usual. Spanky didn't see the ABC cameraman off to his left standing on top of another tow tractor, aiming his mounted television camera at the Master at Arms, beaming his profile and the picturesque scene to a worldwide television audience.

With the three astronauts still sealed inside, Chopper 66 rode the number two elevator to the hanger deck. Karl and his team sprang into action, moving onto the elevator platform to execute perfectly the steps they had practiced more times than any of them could count. Efficiently, the tow bar was attached to the tail wheel. McIlhenny skillfully maneuvered the tow tractor into place, driving the tractor's tow hook into the bar's tow loop perfectly. Checking to make sure all was ready, Karl blew his whistle and signaled the blue shirts to remove tie downs and chocks, then directed McIlhenny who towed the bird tail first off the elevator and into the hanger bay.

The bay, awash in extraordinarily bright overhead TV lamping, had been cleared of non-essential personnel. However, crammed at the open fire doors to both Hanger Bays One and Three, hundreds of sailors and visitors, along with the entire civilized world through the wonder of television, witnessed the helicopter being moved into Hanger Bay Two. As the hanger deck recovery team led the SH-3D deeper into the bay, scores of cameras flashed and clicked away from the lines at the fire doors. Television cameramen followed each inch of progress as the team carefully moved the helicopter into position abreast of the Primary Mobile Quarantine Facility. Karl let out another blast from his whistle and signaled for chocks and tie-downs. The large metal chocks hit the deck loudly, blue shirts sliding them around the wheels, immediately followed by steel tie-downs dragged across the paint, and then hooked into padeyes and tightened.

Steeg watched from his perch in Hanger Deck Control. *So much for that paint job,* he thought as the chocks and chains scrape across the deck near the MQF.

From around the far end of the Primary MQF, Steeg grimaced as two suited civilians pulled a white painted wooden staircase across the painted deck toward the starboard side of the 66 bird. *More paint scraped up!*

After only a moment, Steeg heard the applause and cheers rise up as the three astronauts in isolation suits stepped from the helicopter, waved to the gathering in Bay Three and quickly walked to the MQF, entering through the windowed rear door held open by a NASA technician in a powder blue short sleeve shirt. The applause continued long after the technician had closed and sealed the door behind the astronauts. A simple stenciled sign above the MQF door read "HORNET + 3."

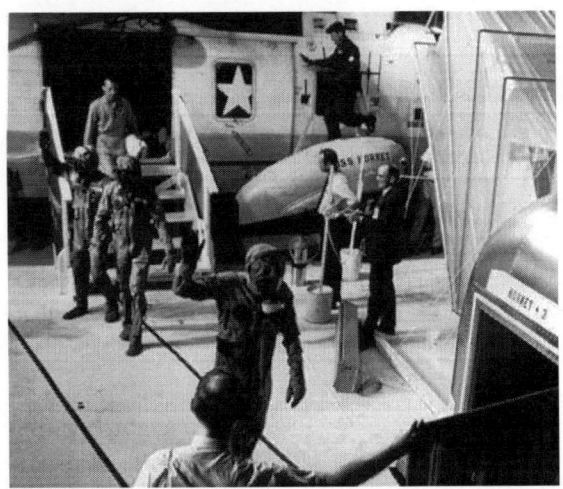

Collins, Aldrin and Armstrong de-plane and head toward the MQF. The plastic shroud in the upper right corner is the transfer tunnel to be attached to the recovered command module.

Karl and his team prepared to move the helicopter back up to the flight deck. Steeg turned to Farmer. "When does the President come down?"

Farmer turned to Santini. "Find out when the President is supposed to get down here, will ya?"

Santini triggered the sound powered phones. "Flight Deck, Hanger Deck."

"Go ahead Hanger Deck," the reply was instantaneous.

"You got a handle on the President's schedule? We need to know when to expect him."

"Wait one, Hanger Deck." This was followed by several seconds of dead air.

"What's the difference?" Farmer asked. "We gotta stay here anyway. We're 'On Duty' you know."

"Yeah, I know," Steeg agreed. "But if there's time, I'd like to take a head break. I just want to make sure I'm where I'm supposed to be when I'm supposed to be where I'm supposed to be... If you know what I mean..."

"Good point," Farmer nodded.

"Almost an hour," Santini informed them. "They say the President will be down by 0900."

"Thanks," Steeg rose from his stool. To Denoso he said, "After they get the helicopter out of the way, get some guys back down there with rags and touch up paint."

Denoso nodded, and Steeg exited Hanger Deck Control for the nearest head located on 2nd Deck aft of the gedunk.

As the petty officer made his way down the ladder and through the port side hatch, Farmer turned his attention to Denoso. "You're sure Commander Knauts took those cans out of here?"

"Of course," the Division Yeoman answered with a slight shake of his head. "Who else?"

As a commissioned officer in the United States Navy, Commander Knauts' most significant shortcoming was that he was, in fact, short. He was lean, physically tough, and at all times pristinely flawless in any Navy uniform he happened to be wearing. He suffered from obsessive-compulsive tendencies, held an understandable, albeit intense, dislike of anyone possessing "tall genes," overcompensated constantly for profoundly deep feelings of inadequacy, and felt justified in destroying any subordinate who did not pay proper homage to his hard won rank and authority. But, it would be height deprivation that would prove to be his undoing right in front of the President of the United States and the entire civilized world.

With the three astronaut heroes finally ensconced within the sterile environment of the Primary Mobile Quarantine Facility, in meticulous fashion Karl's recovery team moved SH-3D Sea King helicopter number 66 from its position along side the MQF, out of Hanger Bay Two into Hanger Bay Three, and onto the starboard number three elevator. After anchoring the aircraft smartly to the platform, Karl's team retreated to the bay and the helo was returned to the Flight Deck.

Within minutes Hanger Bay Two filled with hundreds of 'authorized' personnel. There were more than forty civilians representing various government contractors that had supplied key components for the Lunar Module, the Command Module, and the Mobile Quarantine Facilities. Seventy-eight people from NASA were in attendance. Nearly two-dozen staff officers along with CINCPACFLEET, and CINCPAC SE Asia, well over one hundred people from the ABC Television Network, and a dozen government dignitaries, seven of which, including Secretary of State Henry Kissinger, occupied two rows of five chairs each opposite the Primary Mobile Quarantine Facility where President Nixon would soon address the astronauts.

There were scores of Marines in dress khakis, scores more *Hornet* officers and enlisted men, and at least a dozen known Secret Service agents dressed in dark suits and ties, along with an unknown number of other Secret Service agents mingling in the crowds across all three hanger bays. The fire doors separating the first and third hanger bays from Bay Two were open half-way and roped off, restricting access by the even larger 'unauthorized' throngs congregating in those areas.

From Steeg's seat in Hanger Deck Control, every inch of deck not painted had a person on it. A sea of people jockeyed for space with TV trailers and cameras mounted on aircraft tow tractors. The red, white and blue bunting fence, now curled back onto itself to allow room for the positioning of the yet to be recovered command capsule, helped control the positioning of the throng below as well. The large white rectangular area holding the two MQFs was remarkably free of anyone on two feet.

At 0858 hours, four ship's company Marines escorted the President of the United States through the door leading from the Island escalator, and into the gathered crowd surrounding the blue painted path of Hanger Bay Two. Following the President in the procession was Captain Sieberlich, then the Executive Officer and, finally, the significantly shorter figure of Commander Knauts.

Someone, probably the Marine Sergeant leading the procession, yelled "ATTENTION ON DECK!" as loud as he could, clearly heard as the hundreds of people filling the bay fell silent as soon as the President had stepped into the bay. The procession neared the first turn in the path just below Hanger Deck Control. There was no band, so there was no "Hail to the Chief" to herald the President's coming. This gave the trek from the escalator across and around the path to the end of the Primary Mobile Quarantine Facility a funeral-like somberness that struck Steeg as oddly depressing.

Bringing up the rear, Commander Knauts was a good fifteen feet beyond the door, only two or three steps behind the XO, when his head jerked back around to look behind at where the path started, searching the spot where one of the four chrome garbage cans should have been, but wasn't. He tripped over his own feet, but recovered efficiently with well conditioned reflexes saving him from sprawling across the deck. Quickening his pace to maintain distance with the XO ahead of him, Knauts looked back again to confirm the garbage can was not where it was supposed to be. He was right – it wasn't there. As he rounded the first turn, he looked for the two cans at either end of the elevator ramp, but the crowd was too massive and too thick to see anything beyond the first row of people. Desperately, he jumped up to try to elevate himself high enough to see over the people, but to no avail. He tried again, harder, and jumped higher. He could see nothing but people and the distant blue horizon of the ocean outside.

Everyone lining the blue painted path's perimeter in that immediate area noticed his odd hopping. Some chuckled as the commander tried two more jumps while he continued down the path to keep up with a procession oblivious to what he was doing.

Out of sight, standing in a 01 level storage cage overlooking the bay from the starboard side not far from the Master at Arms shack, the ear piece of the agent-in-charge crackled to life.

"We've got some kind of jumper out here."

The agent-in-charge triggered his radio. "Say again?"

"An officer in the parade is jumping up and down for some reason."

The lead agent's reply was cold and crisp as it crackled over the radio. "Keep an eye on him."

An emotion with which Commander Knauts was all too familiar began to overtake him. It was a massive feeling of something terrible coupled with an all-consuming rage. The pounding pressure grew between his temples with each step he took.

Ahead, the President had arrived at the end of the path. The Marine escort peeled away as the President turned the corner to walk toward the modified Air Stream trailer that was the Primary Mobile Quarantine Facility. The Captain, Executive Officer and Commander Knauts were to walk straight ahead to the rear row of chairs and take their seats behind Secretary of State Kissinger and the other dignitaries in the front row. When Knauts reached his seat at the last chair in the second row, he had a clear view of the fire doors. The spot where the chrome garbage can should have been was occupied by two civilians, one in a suit and tie, the other in slacks and a white, short sleeved dress shirt. The chrome garbage can wasn't there.

From Hanger Deck Control, Farmer, Denoso, Santini and Steeg had witnessed the commander hopping down the path. They followed his progress every inch of the way. Denoso and Santini leaned over Steeg and Farmer's shoulders watching as each officer in the procession, except

Knauts, took their seats in the second row of chairs. Knauts simply stood at the last chair looking toward the fire doors.

"He's not sitting down," Santini stated the obvious.

"What's he doing?" Farmer asked, confused.

"It looks like he's..." Denoso paused to make sure. "...Shaking."

Through the window at the rear of the Primary MQF, Neil Armstrong, Buzz Aldrin, and Michael Collins returned the "A-OK" sign President Nixon made with his thumb and forefinger, indicating "Job well done." Separated by the MQF's large stainless steel door, the window was barely adequate to frame all three astronauts, but it would have to do. President Nixon stepped to the pedestal microphone that would allow the men inside the facility to hear him. Their responses were linked to an external speaker so the President could, in turn, hear them.

"Well, gentlemen," the President began. "I just wanted to be here to welcome you men back, and to thank you on behalf of America for your remarkable achievement. But, actually, I know I'm going to get myself in trouble with Pat if I don't invite each of you to a special dinner we're planning at the White House in your honor."

Chuckles all around.

As the President resumed speaking, he paused abruptly. From the corner of his eye he caught the sight of a naval officer frantically elbowing his way through the standing spectators, quickly followed by two of his own Secret Service agents apparently in pursuit. The President blinked, and then quickly turned back to the men in the window of the MQF.

"I must say in all seriousness," he began again, barely missing a beat. "This is the greatest week in the history of the World since the Creation..."

Denoso leaned all the way out the window of Hanger Deck Control watching Knauts shove through the throng blocking the ladder below.

"Get out of here," he told Steeg. "Now!"

Steeg was watching, too, and didn't need any further encouragement. Darting out the door, he froze at the landing as Knauts reached the base of the ladder, both men's eyes locked onto the other.

"... As a result of what you have done..." the President could be heard over the loudspeakers in the bay. "... The World has never been closer together..."

The ladder held spectators on every step, but Knauts ignored them all, elbowing his way up two steps at a time. Steeg turned to retreat, scrambling behind Hanger Deck Control and into the crew's lounge. He wasn't fast enough. Knauts crashed through the lounge door before Steeg could close and lock it, thrusting him backwards, stumbling as he tried to avoid the officer's tackle. Struggling to retreat deeper into the room, Steeg was jolted from his feet as his pursuer grabbed him from behind, wrapping his arms violently around his neck, sending both men crashing over chairs, across a card table and onto the deck. Steeg tried to right himself, but the side of his face took a direct hit from Knauts' steel-knuckled fist, sending the sailor reeling with the punch. The two men fell backward together, rolling through several more chairs noisily tumbling in every direction. A sharp pain exploded from his left side as Knauts landed another punishing blow just under his ribs. The officer, on top of the enlisted man now, hat gone, uniform smudged with dirt, the left sleeve torn at the shoulder, threw a hard knee into the petty officer's groin that hit the intended mark. Steeg almost blacked out from the pain as he felt his throat being squeezed ever tighter by the smaller man's vice-like grip. Outside the still open lounge door, the President's voice could be heard.

"... We can reach for the stars just as you have reached so far for the stars..."

Steeg tried to breathe but couldn't. In his blinding rage, Knauts vehemently cursed him through clenched teeth as he bounced Steeg's head violently off the deck several times. Steeg struggled through the pain, clamping his hands onto the fingers gripped so savagely around his throat. The tremendous power of the smaller man surprised him, and it took everything Steeg had to pry Knauts' fingers away enough so he could at last take a breath. He knew he didn't have enough strength to break the grip completely, and when that reality hit home, Steeg said a quick, silent prayer.

Help me, Jesus!

It was then the commander was pulled off of him by two dark suited men with short crew cuts.

"Let me go!" yelled the commander as Farmer, Denoso and Santini ran into the lounge to see the Secret Service agents not gently wrap the commander's arms behind his back and cuff him. "You can't do this to me! Do you know who I am?! Takes those off of me!!"

The tirade would have probably continued but for the balled up yellow skull cap one of the agents retrieved from the floor and shoved tightly into the commander's mouth.

Steeg slowly, painfully rolled to his knees, then tried to pull himself up onto a sofa while rubbing circulation back into his neck. Farmer came over to help him, stepping over the commander who, still on the floor, whimpered unintelligibly with the skull cap gag stuck halfway down his throat. No one could understand what he was trying to say.

"Gees, Steeg, I'm sorry," Farmer said as he helped the man to the sofa.

"Me, too," Denoso added, righting a fallen chair and sitting across from him. "I can't believe he reacted like that."

Steeg nodded, massaging his neck, trying to find his voice. The side of his face was slightly swollen and bruised, and his jaw hurt to move. "You sure," he began painfully. "You sure it was the commander who took those cans out of here?"

Denoso looked toward Knauts laying on the floor, then back to Steeg. "Well, yeah. But, after this, maybe not."

Steeg shook his head. "Yeah. Maybe not."

One of the Secret Service agents called his immediate superior on his secure radio, requesting the Master at Arms be summoned to the lounge. It took awhile. The President had finished his speech and exited the hanger bay before Spanky and a Boatswain Chief arrived. The agents explained they had pursued the commander from the ceremony on deck, stopped the assault in the lounge in the appropriate manner and radioed for assistance.

When the Chief asked Steeg why the commander had attacked him, Steeg simply shrugged and said he didn't know why.

When Knauts was un-gagged, he hollered from his disheveled position on the floor, kicking his feet out violently in Steeg's direction. "It's that punk's fault, all of it! That man caused it all – destruction of government property – undermining my authority as Air Boss – he's been plotting against me since I reported on board, trying to embarrass me in front of the Captain, damage my career, ruin me! He's a disgrace to the uniform, the service, the flag, and to everything American! I demand you arrest him! Arrest him, that's an order! – Do you hear me? That's an order!"

As the commander continued his ravings, the Chief looked over to Spanky. "Put the gag back in."

Spanky did so.

The passageway outside the lounge door led to a port side egress ladder to the 02 level. This was the way the Chief and Spanky, with assistance from the Secret Service agents, took Commander Knauts. Once through the hatch to the 02 level, they made their way across to the starboard side, and then down to the brig.

Like the lengths of chromium steel chain and the four chrome-plated garbage cans, no one in V3 Division, or anyone else in the entire air group, ever saw Commander Knauts on *Hornet* again.

The day before *Hornet* pulled into Pearl Harbor to off-load the Mobile Quarantine Facilities, the Columbia Command Module, NASA personnel and the three astronaut-heroes, Steeg was back on the hanger deck supervising the 'A-Team' as they conducted their morning policing duties. Later, from inside their quarantine trailer window, the astronauts would take part in several official ceremonies. Among the planned events would be the re-enlistment of several *Hornet* crewmen, an act of devotion to duty Steeg considered admirable, but, in light of his own experiences, completely idiotic.

Checked out the day before in Sickbay, Doc determined Steeg was fit enough to return to duty, albeit on a limited basis. The obvious signs of abuse, suffered as a result of falling down one of the ship's ladders, demanded more than a modicum of precaution.

The bruising and swelling was noticeable, particularly around the neck and jaw areas, but nothing was broken and there was no obvious bleeding. Steeg had voluntarily acknowledged his own clumsiness to the Doc, and it was confirmed by First Class Petty Officer Farmer who had accompanied him to Sickbay.

Placing a cold pack against the side of Steeg's face, the Doc said, "Keep ice on it for the next few hours to control the swelling. You should look almost normal by tomorrow."

Steeg said he would do so.

"Here's some aspirin for the pain," Doc said, handing the sailor a bottle of fifty tablets worth. "Keep them handy the next time a ladder slugs you in the jaw."

Steeg looked at Farmer and then to Doc. All three men knew that all three men knew. "Thanks. I'll do that."

The Doc turned to Farmer. "Light duty. Two days. Any problems with that?"

Farmer shook his head. "No, Doc. I'll make sure it's followed."

"You take care, Petty Officer Patterson," the Doc patted his patient on the back as Farmer helped lead him to the passageway. "And be careful of those ladders."

Steeg, holding the cold pack against his face, waved with his free hand as he let Farmer lead the way. "Will do, Doc."

Now, with the ship steaming back towards Pearl Harbor, the hanger deck again was almost serene. With 'A-Team' members polishing what needed polishing and picking up what needed picking up, Steeg walked around the Command Module now connected to the Primary MQF by a sealed plastic transfer tunnel. Since the tunnel had been connected to Columbia, NASA personnel and the astronauts themselves had traversed the distance between the two confines several times to transfer Moon rocks and other materials while safeguarding the rest of the ship from any risk of "moon germ" contamination.

Rounding the aft side of the MQF, he passed the rear window where the President had stood the day before. Compared to the huge crowds of the day before, the hanger bay was practically empty. It was all quiet, and that was good enough for Steeg.

Steeg caught sight of movement in the MQF rear window. Working on some papers at the small table on the other side of the glass sat Neil Armstrong. The latest American hero looked up from his work and saw Steeg. He smiled at him and Steeg smiled back with a nod. Then, with the greatest sense of respect he had felt since he first put on the uniform, Steeg came to attention and snapped a salute to the first man to walk on the Moon.

Armstrong returned the salute.

Chapter 23
A Kick in the Head

1530 HOURS
30 JULY 1969
USS *HORNET* CVS-12
250 MILES SOUTHEAST OF HAWAII

They were called "CARQUALS" and they were an annual requirement for all Navy pilots. Carrier qualifications were refresher training exercises for take-offs and landings on an aircraft carrier. Four days earlier, *Hornet* had off-loaded the astronauts at Pearl Harbor, along with the Command Module, Mobile Quarantine Facilities, all civilians and crews for the ABC Broadcasting Network and NASA. Before her scheduled return to her home port of Long Beach, *Hornet* would serve as the CARQUAL platform for Hawaii based Navy Reserve pilots to fulfill their annual quota of take-offs and landings. For the most part, all of the pilots would be flying the small, but quick and powerful A-4 Skyhawk, a fighter bomber light enough for *Hornet's* lighter weight deck configuration and standard (non-steam) powered catapults.

CARQUALS presented demanding challenges for the carrier's Air Department. Because the Apollo Recovery squadrons were no longer on board, *Hornet* was almost "plane-less." With the exception of a single E1-B Tracer and one SH-3A helicopter for emergency SAR (Search and Rescue) operations, no other aircraft were onboard after the warship left Pearl. A half-day of steaming and the "Grey Ghost" was on station, ready to begin CARQUAL flight operations for the reservist flying in from their Navy Air Reserves Stations.

A Navy pilot lands his A4 Skyhawk on *Hornet* to complete CARQUAL requirements. Note the crewman (a Green Shirt) near the rear of the aircraft making sure the arresting cable is clear. The man in the lower right corner is the Yellow Shirt plane director preparing to direct the pilot to the catapults for another take-off.

And so, it began. A steady sequence of one A-4 after another zeroed in on the glide path, catching the "Meatball" on the Fresnel Lens array of the Optical Landing System and, more often than not, snagging one of the four arresting cables across the angle deck to come to an efficient, albeit sudden, stop on the flight deck. Quickly releasing the arresting cable, the pilot would raise his arresting hook, power his aircraft forward, clear the angle deck for the next pilot in cue to land, and be directed by a flight deck

Yellow Shirt to line up with one of the two catapults forward of the Island superstructure. In position within seconds of landing, the A-4 was then hooked up to the shuttle tongue, catapulted off the bow and back into the air.

This flying parade repeated endlessly for hours, each pilot making his required number of carrier take-offs and landings. Word had it that a full two and one-half days were scheduled for CARQUALS before *Hornet* would steam eastward for California. It would prove to be somewhat shorter than that for Steeg Patterson.

In Hanger Bay One near the number one elevator pit, the entire roster of division Blue and Yellow Shirts congregated around V3 Division First Class Petty Officer Joe Bonia.

"About half-way through this afternoon's festivities," the 1st Class PO began. "The planes are going to need to refuel. As most of you know, that is where we come in."

Making sure he had everyone's attention, he pointed toward the Hanger Bay Two fuel station near the number two elevator control stanchion.

"That fuel station is our objective," Joe then swung his pointed hand forward. "The plane comes down elevator number one nose forward. Blue Shirts line across the front of the wings and, upon direction of your Yellow Shirt, you push the plane backwards off the elevator."

Joe led the crewmen toward the center of the bay, and stopped. "You will back the plane to roughly this spot."

He signaled for Steeg to hold up an eight foot long, heavy gauge aluminum tube with a looped handle on one end and an eight inch long by one inch-diameter right angled rod at the other. The whole thing was painted yellow.

"The tiller bar is inserted in the axel of the A-4's nose wheel, and then turned to port. This will cause the nose of the aircraft to turn toward starboard. This turn is held until the aircraft is spun 180 degrees and faces toward the stern. Any questions so far?"

No one raised a hand, or said anything, so Joe continued.

"This is where you Blue Shirts have to be nimble. As the aircraft comes around, you'll need to switch from the wings' leading edges to the trailing edges and continue pushing. The A-4 is a light aircraft, and with a full crew pushing it, the bird will move fairly easily. But, be careful. We're going to have to move these aircraft to the fueling station quickly, but we don't want to rush so much that we damage the aircraft or make it roll out of control. Pay attention to your Director. Any questions?"

A hand shot up, and Bonia nodded toward the sailor who asked about the actual fueling.

"Don't worry about that. It's not your job. The fuel station will be manned by V4 Division Purple Shirts. They'll handle hoses, hook ups, topping off tanks and all that. All you guys do at the fuel station is chock and tie down the aircraft so it doesn't go anywhere during the refueling. Then, stand away. Do nothing to run the risk of starting a spark. Don't rub your hands on your clothing. Don't comb your hair. Stay away from the aircraft during fueling, and don't touch it! You won't be grounded, and you could blow us all up. Anyone have questions about that?"

Some of the recruits looked warily at one another suddenly more concern. Steeg and Karl looked away hiding their grins. No one raised a hand to offer a question, so Joe continued.

"With refueling completed, you then pull chocks and tie-downs, get behind the wings and struts and push the aircraft to the number three elevator. You then spin the aircraft nose to Port, back it onto the elevator, chock it and tie it down. It then goes back up to the flight deck where it'll be directed to the Cats and launched. You got that?"

Everyone nodded. Another hand shot up.

"How long do we go tonight before a break?" Hugh Bauer, the strapping young Airman 3rd from Montana, asked.

"It's difficult to say," Joe admitted. "You can count on at least a couple hours after sunset because of night landing quotas, but how late into the night, I don't know. It won't go all night, though. They'll break off and return home, then more of the same for the next two days."

Joe looked at his watch. "Okay, we've got time before the first refueling cycle starts. Let's split the crews. Half go to chow, the other half stay in Bay One on stand-by just in case something has to come down ahead of schedule."

As the two crews split off, Joe waved Karl and Steeg over. "I want you two to take the first plane, okay?"

The two Yellow Shirts nodded.

"Karl, you'll be the Director. Steeg, you're on the tiller bar."

"No problem," Karl said. "Anything special you want from us on this?"

Joe shook his head. "Nah, it's just that half the crew has never done this before. Let's use all the Blue Shirts from both crews on the first few planes just so they can all get the feel of things. After the first couple of planes, they'll be coming down here fast enough to break into two even teams. By then, everyone should be comfortable with the routine."

"If that's the case," Steeg said, steadying the tiller bar on the loop handle end. "We'll need an extra one of these."

"They're going to drop another bar down with the first plane from the flight deck," explained Joe. "That should be enough, and I don't see us needing more than that. Our speed is going to be controlled by how fast the fuel is pumped into the tanks anyway. We'll need to be smooth and efficient, but if we go too fast, we'll have a traffic jam waiting for fuel at the pump."

"So, we're not refueling each plane as it lands?" Steeg asked.

"No. They'll 'Daisy-Chain' 'em, probably every third one, until all of them are topped off," Joe elaborated.

Overhead you could hear A-4s being launched off the catapults. It was mid-afternoon. It was going to be a long day.

Two hours later, the combined hanger deck crew was gathered at the number one elevator as the first A-4 was being readied on the flight deck for its hanger bay tour to the fuel pumping station. Steeg stood, tiller bar in hand, next to Teddy Bear at the elevator control panel.

"I guess you're anxious to get back to Long Beach," Bear said.

"I guess I am," Steeg acknowledged with a smile. "I've got some catching up to do."

Bear nodded. "That girl – what's her name – Marlene?"

"Marilyn," Steeg corrected.

"Yeah, Marilyn. So, how's that going?"

"Not bad," he said as he remembered their departure in Long Beach. "There's some reason to be hopeful there, I think."

"She write to you a lot?"

The question was somewhat of a rude awakening and only mildly uncomfortable for Steeg. He hid it well. No, Marilyn hadn't written him, ever. What surprised Steeg was that it didn't bother him. In fact, until that very moment, he hadn't even given it a thought. He had dropped her a couple of letters after departing *Hornet's* home port, but the last letter he had written was before the ship left Pearl for the Primary Abort Area well before launch day for Apollo 11. It should have disturbed him that Marilyn had never answered even one of his letters.

"Oh, sure," he lied in response to Bear's question. "She's pretty busy, you know, single Mom and all. But, she still manages to fill me in on the 'Straight Skinny' back home."

"That's good," Bear replied. "It's important to stay in touch, especially when you're at sea for any stretch."

"That's true," agreed Steeg. "It should be a nice homecoming."

Bear triggered his sound powered phone's mouthpiece, acknowledging the alert from the flight deck. "Elevator One ready."

To the gathered assemblage in the hanger bay, he yelled, "Stand clear!" as he threw the switch for the warning alarm, then pushed the control lever to start the center bay elevator in a downward dissent. The large platform eased down the enclosed center deck shaft, sunlight spilling into the hanger bay from the flight deck. The platform with the anchored A-4 descended all the way down until it came to a smooth stop flush with the hanger deck.

"Walk, don't run!" Steeg yelled out as the mass of plane pushers eagerly moved onto the platform to take their positions along the front edge of the wings. In both hands Steeg carried the bulky yet deceptively light tiller bar around the aircraft to the nose wheel. After a bit of a clumsy effort, he succeeded in getting the bar's rod all the way into the wheel's axle. He hand signaled his readiness to Karl. The blonde Kentuckian had just retrieved the spare tiller bar from the platform and handed it to Bear for safe keeping.

"Remove chocks and tie-downs!" yelled Karl as he trotted to his place near center bay. Blue Shirts at the port and starboard wheels did so. The rest of the crew braced themselves against the aircraft ready to push. "Off brakes!"

Steeg looked up to the pilot in the cockpit. With one hand on the tiller bar, he flashed his free hand open three quick times and made sure the pilot understood. The pilot released the brakes with a thumbs-up signal back to Steeg. En masse, the crewmen leaned into the plane, which seemed a great deal heavier than Joe Bonia had led them to believe. Some grunts and groans could be heard as the A-4 slowly backed down the platform.

"Come on, girls!" Steeg admonished as he walked, tiller bar in hand, keeping the aircraft on a straight path toward where the platform met the Hanger Deck. "Put your backs into it. We don't have all day!"

More grunts and groans.

"Hey! Be glad it's not a Phantom!" Steeg scolded, referring to the much larger MacDonnell Douglas F-4 Phantom, the premiere fighter-bomber of the Viet Nam conflict. "Get this thing off the elevator!"

The plane moved just slightly faster, the wheels easily rolling off the platform and onto the deck. The nose wheel and Steeg soon cleared the elevator. He looked to the rear of the aircraft for Karl's indication when he should move the tiller bar to port. It didn't take long. Karl gave a short whistle, the pre-arranged signal for Steeg to make his move. His view around to the rear of the aircraft was sufficient for him to see Karl's arm pointing in the direction of the turn, so Steeg easily levered the tiller bar to port.

The problem was, the rest of the crew heard the whistle, too, and, true to form, a critical number of the crew assumed it was a "Stop" signal from the Director. As too many of the Blue Shirts stopped pushing the aircraft, the A-4 slowed to a stop two-thirds of the way through the 180-degree turn.

"No! Push-push-push-push!" Karl yelled at the men. The crew of Blue Shirts hesitated just enough to make their tardy effort useless. With the momentum lost and the nose wheel turned at a 90-degree angle, the A-4 was too massive for even their large numbers to prevent the aircraft from coming to a complete stop in the middle of the hanger bay, nose pointed starboard at a four o'clock position.

"Ah, come on, guys!" Steeg complained, draping his arms over the looped handle of the tiller bar. "You never stop pushing in the middle of a turn!"

"Okay, pay attention!" Karl said as he came around from the rear, waving both arms up to the pilot to make sure he saw the "Brakes on" signal of his crossed arms. "We gotta straighten the nose wheel, back the plane up just a bit to move the nose around to complete the turn, and then push the plane to the fuel station. Do not, I repeat, DO NOT stop pushing until and unless you hear a long – not short – whistle. Any questions?"

As the crew shook their heads indicating their complete understanding, no Yellow Shirt could have prepared them for what was about to happen.

Some hours earlier, and almost two hundred miles away, two massive plates of the Earth's crust met at a submerged mid-Pacific fault line. It was at this point where a relatively minor slippage occurred. The eastern plate fell below the western plate just enough to displace several million tons of sea water within a fraction of a second. A barely noticeable swell in the ocean's surface traveled quickly in a southeasterly direction. The speed of the miles-wide hump steadily increased as it traveled. By the time the wave approached *Hornet* the swell was barely more than five feet high, with an easily sloping hump more than three miles wide, nearly 500 miles long and moving faster than anyone could have anticipated. In the middle of the Pacific, the wave was practically invisible, nothing more than an indistinguishable rise on the horizon. It was nothing the warship couldn't handle.

Steeg held the loop handle of the tiller bar close against his stomach, preparing to pull the nose wheel from its right angle turn. Karl gave the pilot the "Release Brakes" signal. The Blue Shirts were in position, but just as they started to push, the deceptively powerful rogue wave met the ship at a 45-degree angle and wedged under the bow. The deck swiftly rose upward, and *Hornet* was lifted into a starboard to port roll as the immense power of the swell ran along the beam toward the stern.

With the brakes released, the A-4 rolled backwards. The tiller bar Steeg held slammed violently into his gut, picked him up off the deck, and whipped him around the nose, over the tip of the aircraft's starboard wing and across the hanger bay.

Thirty-seven feet later, Steeg landed on the left side of his head, nearly snapping his neck as he tumbled to a stop against the port side steel roller curtains. He lay unconscious in a disheveled pile, his left leg twitching in spasm the only sign of life.

The light was blinding as the ship's doctor flashed it first in one eye, then the next.

"That looks better," he said. "How you feelin'?"

"Fine, I guess," Steeg's mouth was dry and his voice sounded strangely hollow to him. He didn't recognize the doctor examining him.

"Do you know where you're at?"

Laying flat on his back, Steeg looked around as best he could without moving his head. The overhead was close, filtered fluorescent lights softly lit the surrounding area. He could feel the mattress under him, thicker and softer than a normal rack. An antiseptic odor filled the air.

"Sickbay," he answered.

"That's good," Doc said. "Do you know what date it is?"

He hesitated, not certain. Then, he knew. "Sure. It's April 17th."

A slight frown crossed the doctor's face. "What year is it?"

"1967," he answered without confidence. He corrected himself. "No. Wait. It's 1968."

A sigh was followed by another question. "Okay. Who's President of the United States?"

"Johnson, of course."

Doc patted Steeg's arm. "That's good. I want you to get some rest, okay? Just take it easy for a while. I'll be back."

The doctor left the ward. Steeg tried to raise his left hand to see the time on his wristwatch. His left arm wouldn't move. He could raise his right hand though, and he did so to feel thick bandages covering his head. That was when he realized he had been injured in some way. He should have felt more concern, but sleep suddenly returned too quickly for him to be bothered.

Doc was back, this time with two enlisted men Steeg also didn't recognize.

"How you feelin' today?" Doc asked again.

"I'm a little thirsty," Steeg said through lips coated with dried spittle.

"Get him some water," Doc asked one of the other men. He turned back to Steeg. "Do you know what the date is?"

He tried to recall it, but couldn't. "I'm not sure."

"That's okay. Do you know who the President of the United States is?"

He could feel the first pricks of fear as he struggled to remember but couldn't. He tried to shake his head in answer, but the bandages wouldn't let him move. "I'm not sure about that, either."

The other man returned with a paper cup filled with water. The doctor took it from him and helped Steeg take three short, quick sips.

"Thank you," Steeg said, relaxing back into the pillow.

Doc continued. "Do you know where you are?"

"I'm in Sickbay," he responded, a little irritated.

"Do you know where this Sickbay is located?"

"Deck two."

"Do you know what ship you're on?"

"*Hornet*."

"Do you know what division you're in?"

"V3 Division."

"That's good. Do you know what happened to you?"

Steeg did not know. He just couldn't remember.

"I'm a little hungry," he said, becoming more than aggravated by the questioning. "Could I get something to eat?"

"Sure," Doc answered. "Do you know how long you've been in Sickbay?"

"No," Steeg impatiently admitted. "Educate me."

The doctor chuckled. "Okay. Three days."

"Three days?" Steeg was stunned. "What the heck happened?"

"You were thrown," the doctor answered. "By an airplane, so they tell me. You have a skull fracture and a concussion."

Doc rose to his feet allowing Steeg a moment to digest what he had just shared with him.

"You also have some memory loss," he added. "That's not unusual with some head injuries. Let's give it another day, maybe two, and see how things are."

Doc told the second enlisted man to get Steeg some food, but nothing solid, and then returned to Steeg, saying he'd be back the next morning for another visit.

Later that night, with the Sickbay ward lights low and no one else around as far as he could tell, Steeg pulled himself to a sitting position with difficulty, noticing for the first time the catheter tube running to a plastic collection bag.

"Well, this complicates things a bit," he said to himself.

His left shoulder and arm were extremely sore and it hurt to move. Steeg took small comfort noticing he was able to move the fingers of his left hand easily, but his left arm and shoulder was too painful. Covered barely by a too-small cotton gown, he knew long excursions were out of the question unless he found the courage to remove the catheter. Even if he had his uniform, he certainly wasn't going too far with his head wrapped in a turban of bandages and a long, plastic tube dragging a half-filled pee bag behind him.

There was a telephone on the ward desk next to the door leading to the hallway. Steeg, carry his collection bag with as he gingerly walked to the desk, picked up the phone and dialed a three-digit number.

"Hanger Deck Control," Farmer answered.

"Chas!" Steeg almost yelped.

"Hey, Steeg, how you doin' fella?"

"I guess I'm fine, but, Chas, I need your help."

"Sure, what do you need?"

"I need to know what happened to me."

Farmer recapped the events as he understood them from the debriefing Karl had given. It wasn't a pretty picture. He had lain in a pile on the port side deck of Hanger Bay One for a long time. No one was sure what, if anything was broken. There had been some blood and no one dared move him even to a stretcher to take him to Sickbay for fear of worsening his obvious injuries. In fact, he had lost so much color some of the crew thought he was dead.

"Gees, I could've been killed!"

"That's what I mean. We thought you were. The way you hit that deck, you looked dead. How you feelin' now?"

"I'm fine," he said. Fully aware he was lying he repeated himself. "I'm fine. No problems. But, I need a little re-orientation."

"How's that?"

"Can you tell me what the date is?"

A brief hesitation, then, "It is August 2nd."

"What year?"

There was a long hesitation before Farmer came across with a flat response. "It's 1969, Steeg. Remember, we picked up Apollo 11? We had President Nixon on board? Worldwide television coverage, the whole bit, remember?"

Steeg was incredulous at the news of Nixon as President. *I thought the guy was extinct after the California governor's thing!*

"Sure, Chas, I remember all that. A few things are just a little mixed up, that's all."

In fact, Steeg remembered none of it. He would keep that to himself.

The next morning in Sickbay, another game of twenty questions ensued with Doc joined by four medical department corpsmen. Steeg sat on the edge of his bunk as the doctor led him through the latest round of questioning.

"Do you know what day it is?" asked the doctor.

"August 3rd," Steeg answered calmly.

"That's good," replied the doctor. He looked up to the four corpsmen standing in a semi-circle facing the patient, and then returned to Steeg. "Can you tell me what year it is?"

Steeg didn't bat an eye. "1969."

The doctor nodded. "That's good. Tell me who's the President of the United States?"

"Nixon," Steeg answered quickly.

"Are you sure?"

"Yes," Steeg replied. "He was just on the ship when we picked up the astronauts. Don't you remember?"

The doctor smiled and laughed lightly with a satisfying sense of real relief. "Oh, that's very good. You show remarkable improvement since yesterday."

"Thank you, Doc. I try."

Steeg didn't feel as if he was lying about any of this. In fact, he was telling the truth. He was doing exactly what he should do – answering the questions put to him by the doctor. The fact that he had prepped himself for this little quiz didn't really bother him. The phone conversation with Farmer the night before was simply judicious study. It wasn't that he didn't value medical treatment. Steeg valued more getting out of Sickbay and back to work on the Hanger Deck.

The doctor turned to the Chief corpsman, asking him to take Steeg's pulse and blood pressure. As the corpsman wrapped the pressure band around Steeg's upper arm, Doc continued with Steeg.

"It's interesting. I hope this isn't becoming a habit with you."

"What do you mean?" Steeg asked.

"Well, it's just a little strange, don't you think? A week and a half ago, you come down here for a little visit to get treated for a lot of bruises and a sore jaw, telling me you fell down a ladder. Now, here you are again, carted down on a stretcher unconscious with a concussion. I've treated you before, Patterson, so when I looked up your file, guess what I found?"

"What?" Steeg's eyes stayed steady on the Doc, but he could feel his insides tightening.

"Last year you came here for treatment. Your hands were all cut up and bleeding, you had a big knot on your head, and you had a mild concussion, as well. Don't you think all that is kind of curious?"

Steeg remembered none of it, so it wasn't hard for him to hide the nervousness caused by Doc's questioning. "I can see where it looks a little strange, Doc, but it's just a string of bad luck, that's all."

"Bad luck?" Doc's easy smile turned down with obvious concern. "I hope this isn't becoming a trend with you. You know, it would be unfortunate if these events were related in some way, maybe part of an effort to get out of the service, or some other silly idea. It wouldn't go too good for you if that was what really was going on here."

The blood pressure band around Steeg's upper arm tightened as the corpsman pumped up the pressure beyond the necessary threshold, and then turned the little knob on the hose to bleed the pressure as he took his readings.

Except for the excruciating heat rash that had racked his body on his first WestPac, the crawling constant pain of which was still vivid in his memory, Steeg could not recall falling down a ladder, or being treated at Sickbay for anything. He looked down at his palms. There were shallow traces of pale scaring across both of them. He had no idea how they got there.

"Nothing could be further from the truth," Steeg lied, hoping his uncertainty over the events the doctor had just outlined didn't show on his face. "The Navy is my life. Why would I want to leave it?"

"Pulse is steady," the corpsman said. "BP 125 over 70."

"Solid numbers," Doc looked at his patient, once again flashing a pen light in his eyes, all the while not believing a word Steeg had just said. "The Navy is your life, is it? That's unusual to hear, especially from someone with your obvious talent for BS."

"I don't know what you mean, sir."

"Yeah, I bet you don't," Doc put the pen light back in the breast pocket of his white coat. "How do you feel generally?"

Steeg shrugged. "I guess I feel fine. But, I wish I didn't have this bandage wrapped around my head. It's a little uncomfortable. How about this tube coming out of my dick? Do I need that anymore, or can it be removed?"

The doctor understood well enough. "The bandages are precautionary. It wasn't a bad fracture. You're lucky you have such a hard head. First ladders work you over, and now a whole hanger deck. It's amazing you're not dead. We'll probably take the bandages off tomorrow. As for the catheter, I guess you can get around good enough to use the head when you need to, so we'll remove it today. I want you to stay one more day here for observation, however. It's just to make sure. Okay?"

Steeg nodded in agreement. He could handle one more day in Sickbay without too much difficulty. The doctor and the four corpsmen turned and left the ward, exiting down the passageway that led toward Doc's private office. Steeg remained seated on the bunk.

He was aware of being in Sickbay only about half the time he had actually been in Sickbay. It wasn't his fault he had been knocked unconscious for three days. Sitting there now, he wondered how bad it could have been. If it had been serious, certainly they would have airlifted him off the boat for treatment instead of keeping him on board. The fact was, he was still on the ship. If that was the case, and it was, he couldn't be hurt as bad as all that. Still, he had been out of it for three days. That was curious.

Now, with the help of Chas Farmer, his grasp on the essential details of what was going on around him was good enough for him to feel reasonably comfortable to do what he had to do to free himself from *Hornet's* medical facility. Nevertheless, he would follow the doctor's orders and stay in Sickbay the additional twenty four hours.

After about ten minutes, the chief corpsman came back into the ward.

"You ready to have the catheter taken out?"

The question generated a mixed response.

"You bet," he answered enthusiastically, but then Steeg took pause. "Say, it's not going to hurt is it?"

The corpsman chuckled under his breath as he pushed Steeg back down to a laying position on the bunk. During the next few excruciating moments, Steeg had his answer.

After the uncomfortable procedure, the corpsman showed Steeg the locker where his dungarees, flight deck boots and baseball cap had been stowed.

"After you get cleaned up," the corpsman said. "If you're still up to it, get dressed. We have a few things for you to do for the remainder of your stay."

Do? Steeg thought to himself. *Do what?*

In the Sickbay head, he didn't take a shower because he didn't want the bandages to get wet. His skull was uncomfortable enough without drenching the strips of cloth bound around his head. Instead, he stripped down, more clumsily than he liked, and stood at the sink with a washcloth and a bar of soap, painfully reaching the smellier spots with arms and shoulders that didn't want to move as freely as normal. Most of this exercise in personal hygiene was performed using his right hand, which was fine. After all, he was right handed. For the first time, he could see in the mirror the extent of the deep blue and purple bruising that ran from under the bandage, down the back and left side of his neck, across the collarbone to his left shoulder. The bruising was massive. It not only looked sore, it was. No wonder he could hardly move his left arm. Removing the soap from his body was even more challenging than ragging it on, using his left hand only to steady the work his right hand had to do. The whole process took at least three times longer than it would have under healthier circumstances, but it was refreshing just the same. With no shaving gear, he had to let the stubble stay as it was. But, there was a fresh, boxed tooth brush and a tube of toothpaste, so that helped a lot.

A towel wrapped around his waist, Steeg returned to the locker where his dungarees were kept and, with effort, pulled on his uniform as best he could. Anticipating a difficult time with his yellow shirt, he was disappointed when he found it had a long, seven-inch tear at the neck and down the front. The rending helped make the shirt easier to get on over the bandages, but it looked like crap. He may be able to get one of the corpsmen to help him get a dungaree shirt to replace it.

As he stiffly laced up his final boot, a corpsman returned to the ward carrying a standard Navy mop and a bucket containing a spray bottle of '409' cleaner, two rags, a plastic bottle of pale orange liquid soap of some kind, and a scrub brush.

The corpsman placed the bucket and mop at Steeg's feet. "Here you go, clean the head."

The corpsman turned around and left. Steeg looked first at the bucket filled with its contents, then at the corpsman's back retreating down the hall, and then toward the head.

Aaah, the Navy! He thought to himself. *I'm a cripple, and they want me to clean the head. It's not a job — it's an adventure!*

What Steeg didn't realize was the doctor had ordered the cleaning detail to make sure he was capable of returning to duty. Doc figured if Steeg could handle the job, it would be helpful physical therapy for the injures he had sustained in the accident. On the other hand, if the job proved too much, it would be sufficient reason to keep him in Sickbay for a few more days.

Steeg knew none of this as he grabbed the mop and bucket with his good hand, and shuffled painfully into the head to begin a monotony-busting round of Sickbay sanitation patrol duty.

Doc was good to his word. The next day he removed the bandages, flashed a pen light in Steeg's eyes a couple more times just to make sure everything was registering just fine, took another pulse and blood pressure check, followed with a pat on the back.

"You're free to go, sailor," said the Doc as he wrote out the details for Steeg's conditional release on a small note pad.

Steeg was released, restricted to light duty for at least one week, whereupon he was ordered to return for another check up. Steeg agreed, taking the hand scribbled slip of paper Doc gave him and shoving it into his pants pocket.

His head still hurt as did the rest of his upper body, and although he couldn't raise his left arm above his shoulder, what movement he did have on his left side was an improvement over the no movement he had only two days earlier. The treatment he had received was adequate given the examination results from which Doc and the corpsmen had to draw their assessments. However, the facilities onboard were limited. The x-rays had shown some stretching and, in some case, rupturing of tendons and connecting tissue between the skull, his upper spine, and the skeletal structure of his left shoulder. But, they had failed to reveal the wayward bone chip lodged between the sixth and seventh cervical vertebrae at the base of his neck. The jagged little piece of bone had already punctured the protective outer layer of the spinal disk, compromising the liquid cushioning it was supposed to provide.

Over the coming years, the collapse of the disk would lead to more pain. The vertebrae itself would continue to push the chip relentlessly into the main nerves leading from the spine. It would directly impact the functionality of his left arm and hand. It would never be a completely debilitating condition, just a condition painful enough to be a constant life-long reminder of an accident he would never remember.

He left Sickbay by the starboard passageway, hesitantly climbed the ladder with more effort than it should have required, and ascended into

Hanger Bay Three. Dressed in his old dungarees and torn yellow shirt, Steeg's first destination was to the V3 Division Crews Quarters for a quick shower, shave and a change of clothes. He strode across Bay Three to the ladder that led up to the aft port gun tub, where he entered the short passageway that led to the division's barracks room.

The space was deserted. The absence of everyone seemed a little odd to him. He knew the ship was at sea, but he didn't know the status of air operations for the Air Department. He had heard no aircraft engines, props or turbo-jets, running up on the Flight Deck. From the quiet, he assumed Air Ops had been secured. In fact, standing now at his locker, it occurred to him he hadn't actually seen any aircraft in the bay he had walked through.

At sea, but no aircraft on board? He thought, effortlessly spinning the combination lock to open the locker. *And, how is it I remember this combination, but I don't remember the last 16 months?!*

The answers to both questions were not forthcoming. It was August, 1969, but for Steeg, it was April, 1968, and for some reason he couldn't understand, *Hornet* was not in dry dock undergoing repairs in Long Beach, but somewhere at sea! Somehow, he had lost more than a year of his life. It made him uneasy. His reflexes where still a little wobbly as he stripped down, wrapped a bath towel around his middle, grabbed his shaving kit from the locker, closed and locked the locker door and walked to the head. As with the day before, the shower and shave took him longer than he preferred, and only just a bit easier for him. After he finished in the head, he returned to the locker, retrieved fresh skivvies, trousers and stopped as he pulled his dungaree shirt from the locker shelf. He wasn't sure if he should wear the blue dungaree shirt, or put on his Director's Yellow Shirt. He struggled for a moment as his mind worked out the details.

Light duty. I'm on 'Light Duty' for a week. No plane pushing, therefore, no Yellow Shirt.

Satisfied in the soundness of his logic, he buttoned the stiffly starched dungaree shirt over his white T-shirt, tucked the tails in and secured the shiny brass buckle of his navy blue web belt. Carefully, so as to not aggravate his still sore head, he eased on his *Hornet* ball cap. A sense of normalcy began to return to him.

Nevertheless, his mind was still clouded with a foggy confusion that just wouldn't let up. He braced himself against the sides of the locker with both hands trying to piece it all together, wondering how he could regain the memories he had lost.

This is so weird, Lord, he prayed silently as he opened the small drawer at the bottom corner of the locker. *I need to remember what I don't remember, but if I don't remember things, how can I remember what I need to remember?! This one's a little beyond me. You're going to have to help me out.*

The drawer was crammed with odds and ends accumulated over the years, some more familiar than others. A note pad; three pocket-size paperback books - Shakespeare's "Hamlet"; Nietzsche's "Thus Spoke Zarathustra"; an English translation of "Summa Theologica" by Thomas Aquinas; an overused sewing kit; pens empty of ink; a few photographs of him with Karl, him with Kinsey, him with John Dickenson. There were a few other photos of sailors he did not recognize. His fingers pushed deeper toward the bottom of the drawer. He pulled out a familiar, tattered envelope. At the torn corner was the return address.

Grace Ofterdahl
302A Gage Hall
Mankato State College
Mankato, MN

Carefully, Steeg opened the envelope, removed the single folded sheet of handwritten stationary, opened it and began to read.

April 17, 1967
Dear Steeg,

I'm sorry I haven't written you for so long. I've tried to write this letter at least a dozen times, but I haven't been able to. But now I have to and I still don't know how. So I'm just going to say it and hope you'll understand.

I'm marrying Stewart Smalley in June. We met at school. I fell in love with him. He asked me to marry him, and I've said yes.

I know I'm not doing a good job writing this, and I really can't explain it all. I don't want to hurt you, even though I know that's what I am doing. I'm sorry. You're really a great guy. You'll always be very special to me. I'm sorry.

Thank you for loving me. It's meant more to me than you know. Stay safe.

Grace

The dog-eared corners and the wrinkles from repeated folding told him he had read the letter literally more times than he could remember. He closed the letter once more, returned it to the envelope, and slid it back to the bottom of the lower locker drawer, taking care to cover it with the books, pictures and clutter.

The Lord knew he wasn't remembering much of anything, but Steeg remembered the first time he had read the letter. He remembered CATCC Division. He remembered standing behind the scheduling board where he wrote aircraft status notes backwards on the Plexiglas with a grease pencil. He remembered the afternoon mail call when he anxiously opened the envelope, so excited to get a letter from her. He remembered her written words slicing into him, the overwhelming sense of utter defeat, the bottomless pit of despair, and the crushing loss that pushed in on him as his knees began to buckle. Except for the eighteen inches of clearance between the bulkhead and the scheduling board behind which he stood, Steeg would have dropped all the way to the floor. His legs wedged tight against the board frame as the shock hit him and his whole body sagged.

A simple, one page, handwritten note was all he had left of the one person who still meant more to him than anyone else ever could. He wished his memory would fail him now. Once again his insides were ripped from him, hollowing him out as if for the first time. It was as if God Himself was removing his very soul.

Steeg struggled to regain control. A wave of rage, all consuming, surged up from some dark place inside him. The permeating heat of his fury swept away in an instant everything that mattered to him. He slammed his right fist into the locker frame with such force the metal bent inward. After a few moments, his anger cooled to a low boil as he looked at his scuffed and bloodied knuckles. He should have broken his hand but he hadn't. There was no pain. Black emotions still flowed through him so strongly he felt an oddly satisfying sense of joy in the self-inflicted wounding.

That was a good thing.

Chapter 24

Short-Timer

1300 HOURS
01 SEPTEMBER 1969
NIMITZ ROAD ATHLETIC FIELD
US NAVY BASE
LONG BEACH, CALIFORNIA

Boxes of fresh hamburger and hot dog buns, trays of fresh fruits, raw veggies, bags of chips and Sterno-heated pans of brats, beef patties, rich, dark brown baked beans and sauerkraut covered one long tabletop. On the concrete slab, a large steel water trough filled with water and ice kept cold the innumerable cans of beer and soda. The tiled roof of the large outdoor cabana-like structure shaded everything from the heat of a bright afternoon sun, including additional tables free for the sitting.

It was a special *Hornet* Air Department congratulatory picnic for a job 'well-done' on behalf of the Apollo 11 recovery. Less than forty feet away, the well-stocked base concession stand was doing plenty of business with a larger than normal crowd of military personnel enjoying themselves on this hot Labor Day. On the field, a loosely organized game of touch football was being played between increasingly sweaty and dirt-streaked members of *Hornet's* hanger deck's V3 Division and the flight deck's V1 Division.

The game was approaching the mid-point beer break, which struck Steeg as a little funny seeing how so many of the players on the field were actually carrying their own cans of refreshment with them as they played the game! Everyone had a beer or soda either in their hand or somewhere within easy reach, and no one was really keeping score.

Sitting on a shaded table top under the protective roof of the gazebo, his feet resting on the attached bench seat, Steeg watched the progress of the obvious fun but, equally obvious, poorly played game. He had satisfactorily completed his 'light duty' stint on schedule the previous month, passing the follow up medical check by assuring the Doc that he was fine, experiencing no difficulties in doing just about anything he could think of, or was asked about by the doctor.

He had not been entirely truthful. Although the bruising on his neck, back and shoulders had almost disappeared, and he had regained almost all physical motion once so limited on his left side, he didn't mention the continual pain at the base of his neck, the constant nerve spiking down his left forearm, thumb and forefinger, or frequent headaches that were truly incapacitating. Often the headaches were preceded by small sparkling patches in the corner of his vision. Within minutes everything he could see would disintegrate into millions of indistinguishable flashing slivers of light. The vivid light show and the resulting loss of sight would last upwards to thirty minutes, sometimes longer, and then his sight would return to normal. That was when the pain would come. In a rush, crushing pressure would throb behind his eyes. Nausea would often follow, then a sprint to the head for cold water in the face, and closer proximity to a toilet should the gathering nausea mutate into something more projectile in nature. The only advance warning Steeg would have of a pending headache was the onset of the vision problems. He quickly learned to use the sparkling patches to alert him of things to come, making a timely retreat from wherever he was at the moment. This helped him manage the situation a little more effectively and less noticeably to those around him. Or, so he hoped.

The hallucinations of his "imaginary friend" continued. He would see Gracie almost anywhere, suddenly appearing without warning. When he was in town, he would see her walking on the opposite side of the street, or sitting in a café, or riding on the bus going back to the base. To Steeg, it seemed she was everywhere. However, the Grace he saw was different. She no longer spoke to him and she ignored him as if he wasn't there. She was as real as could be, but silent with no voice, no sound. Gone, too, was the young girl with the neat brown curls, the roll collared sweater and jeans. Instead, Grace now wore her hair long, almost halfway down her back, and often braided. Her clothing differed almost every time she appeared in his mind. He would see her seated in a room somewhere he didn't recognize, or walking down a sidewalk talking with other people or, most disturbing, making love to a man he could see but didn't know.

The visions were silent and more than terrifying. Her lips moved soundlessly when she looked as if she was talking with someone he may or may not see, but she did not speak with him, and he was still sane enough to know not to speak to her. That morning he was startled awake by another vision. It was short and jarring: Grace's head snapped around from the blow of a closed fist and blood spurted from her split upper lip. Steeg jerked up in his bunk to a sitting position, his forehead slamming into the overhead vent pipe. He slumped back to the mattress as pain shot down to the base of his neck, across his shoulder and down his left arm to his finger tips. It had not been a pleasant way to start the day.

Sitting on the table in the shade at the Air Department picnic, Steeg knew a truth he would never reveal. He had not fully recovered from the accident he could not remember. The thought came to him that he might never fully recover. He preferred not to think about it. He would get through this. With God's help, he would get through this.

For the few weeks leading up to the Labor Day weekend, CARQUALS that had ended off of Hawaii had resumed off the west coast for California based reserve pilots. The ship's company had been expanded to include a contingent of enlisted Navy reservists. Onboard *Hornet* during their annual two-week long "training cruise," the reservists had the opportunity to actually train not at a land-locked Navy base, but aboard a real warship. That was pretty exciting for the reservists, but it had delayed the ship's return to her home port of Long Beach. Many of the "regular Navy" crew were upset, anxious to return home to loved ones left behind in June when the ship had departed for the Apollo 11 pick up.

The new round of CARQUALS hadn't bothered Steeg that much. He had no one in Long Beach, and he didn't remember anything about the Apollo 11 recovery mission. As far as he was concerned, it was as if *Hornet* had just left dry dock.

He stayed in the shade of the gazebo debating the merits of a planned leave to return to Minnesota over Christmas. It was almost too many months away to worry about, and besides, after what would most certainly be an uncomfortably prolonged visit with his parents and siblings, there were only so many pool games he could play at Wedge's before he would find himself screaming, fleeing to the airport, desperate to get away. It seemed so pointless. Steeg knew the only worthwhile reason to go home was to see the one person he couldn't see. So why bother?

Leave was a funny thing. It was a welcomed break from the routine of military life, but for a single guy with few personal obligations, it also held the easy potential of turning into a black abyss of desperate loneliness and isolation. He briefly wondered if his sister, Mary might be able to fix him up. The prospect sent a shiver of real fear down his spine and he immediately knew he preferred almost anything to that possibility. It might be better for him to stay on the ship. Surely there was something, or someone, in Long Beach who held more satisfying potential.

"Hey, Steeg!" Teddy Bear yelled from the playing field. "We need a blocker! Get in here, will ya?"

"I'm not very good at that sort of thing," Steeg yelled back.

Some of the other guys waved him on as Bear shouted, "You're a 'body' and that's good enough!"

His chuckle brought a characteristic easy smile as he shrugged and resigned himself to help out his division in the titanic struggle taking place on the scraggily playing field before him. Two steps from the table, Bear yelled at him to remember his beer. Steeg turned to the water trough, retrieved something in a chilled aluminum can, turned and jogged easily toward the sweaty gathering on the athletic field.

"Ya gotta keep your hydration up out here, ya know," Bear slapped him on the shoulder, slopping the beer from Steeg's freshly opened can onto his sneakers.

"Okay, listen up," Karl motioned to the gang as Steeg and Bear joined the loose huddle. "John, deep post; Bobby, left flat; Jim, I don't care where you go, just get open – on two – break!" Karl, the only one without a beverage in his hand, clapped once to break the loose huddle and everyone took their places on the line of scrimmage.

John Hugelen, an extraordinary twelve-string guitar player with freakishly large hands and long fingers, lined up outside Steeg's position.

"How you going to catch a football with a beer can in your hand?" Steeg asked.

"How are you going to block that guy in front of you without spilling yours?" John shot back.

"Good point," Steeg agreed. He quickly darted to the rear, placed the can upright in the grass, and returned to the line.

Karl set the team, held his hands out to receive the snap from Augie, and yelled "Hut – Hut!" Nothing happened. Along the line, men looked at each other, then at Augie who still held the ball on the ground, completely unaware he had screwed up.

"Augie!" Karl yelled. "Snap the frickin' ball!"

That Augie understood. The football whipped squarely into Karl's waiting hands.

The man Steeg was to block tried a faint to his left, but Steeg met it easily and, with his fists at his chest, he stopped the man cold in his tracks. It wasn't much of a hit, only the slightest of glancing blows as their heads slid past each other.

The next thing Steeg knew, he was on his hands and knees looking at the grass spinning wildly below him. As he raised his head to see the others running past and around him, the entire Earth seemed to tilt to one side. Then, nothing but blue sky as the nausea swept over him.

"You okay?" Karl asked leaning over Steeg laying on his back in the grass.

"I don't know," Steeg reached up. "Help me get to my feet, will you?"

Karl did so, taking the man's hand as Steeg pulled himself up to a sitting position.

"I don't feel so good," Steeg admitted. "I think I'll get back into the shade."

Karl helped his friend all the way up, and walked him to the gazebo area where he handed Steeg another beer from the trough. "Take it easy, okay."

"Sure thing," Steeg took the offered can, opened the pop top with a noticeable amount of difficulty and brought it to his lips.

He didn't drink. His stomach was doing flip-flops. As Karl walked back onto the field, Steeg lowered the beer, staggered from the table and made his way haltingly to the restroom facilities behind the concession stand. After a prolonged wait in the smelly confines, during which nothing happened, Steeg exited the restroom and walked out onto Nimitz Road, his back to the park area he had only minutes before left.

Across the bay, he could see *Hornet* moored at Pier E. Strangely, although he knew he was on the peninsula that fronted the base harbor on one side and the breakwater on the other, he couldn't remember how or why he was there. Nevertheless, he could see where the ship was, so, despite the long trek he knew he had in front of him, he started walking down Nimitz Road to traverse the several miles that would lead him to Pier E. He was completely unaware of the empty gray Navy base shuttle bus parked at the curb in front of him. It waited to return the Air Department personnel to *Hornet*.

Saturday night, September 6, 1969 was like most Saturday nights while the ship was in Long Beach. There were plenty of *Hornet* sailors hanging out at The Silver Dollar Bar about a half block up from East Ocean on Long Beach Boulevard. It was a small, dimly lit dive with a long bar on one side of the room, two pool tables on the other side, a few tables and chairs scattered across a well worn carpet of undeterminable color badly in need of cleaning. As one of the larger ships ported at the Terminal Island U.S. Navy Base, when *Hornet* was in port, the Silver Dollar was at its busiest. But then, the same could be said for just about every business in town between Pine Street and Atlantic Avenue. An aircraft carrier had a lot of sailors.

The clientele at the Silver Dollar wasn't exclusively V3 Division personnel. Other sailors from other ships and the Navy base itself were also in regular attendance. That notwithstanding, on this night the Minnesota contingent was especially well represented with Teddy Bear, Tom Kinsey, and Steeg Patterson sharing a dimly lit table in the corner. At the nearest of two pool tables playing a 3-man game of elimination were John Hugelen, the guitar man, Jimmy Dettwiler, the lanky blonde peace-loving hippy with a too-long short haircut, and Joe Massinni, another AB Third Class Petty Officer who, with his chiseled movie star features, was unusually and inexplicitly dateless. There wasn't a uniform to be seen in the busy, smoke-filled tavern and the guys from V3 Division were no exception. They were all in civilian clothes, most loudly Jimmy Dettwiler, who wore sandals, flared tattered jeans, a multi-colored paisley shirt, a metal peace emblem hanging from a linked chain around his neck, and a shamelessly ridiculous pair of circular translucent blue spectacles resting half way down his nose. Almost every time the young man leaned over the pool table to take a shot, his peace medallion would swing over and usually hit a ball out of position, just as it did at that moment.

"I'm going to take that chain and strangle you with it," John could be heard grumbling from the other side of the pool table.

"Peace, brother," Jim said peering over his wire framed blue lenses, holding up two fingers. The meaning of the Churchillian style V-split had profoundly changed from that of "Victory" to the placidly pacifistic "Peace" over the embarrassingly short span of just a few years. It was another example of how the world was so well-practiced in abandoning honorable things for easy answers to suit every change in the wind.

Joe Massinni reached across the table and grabbed the cue ball. "My shot," he said firmly, placing the white orb behind the pool table's second diamond.

"Hey! That's not fair," Jim protested.

"It is now," Joe sighted the line up for his planned shot carefully. "From now on you move a ball with anything but a cue stick, it's a scratch."

Watching from his chair across the way, Teddy Bear laughed.

"Put that thing in your pocket, Jimmy!" he yelled. Jim waved him off; leaving the medallion hanging from around his neck as Joe calmly stroked the seven ball into the corner pocket.

The collection of beer bottles had grown on the table around which Bear, Tom Kinsey and Steeg sat. Before sun down, the three of them had bussed in together from the base, hoofing it from the "E-Club" locker facility about two miles away to the Silver Dollar just as the evening sky started to turn a cool, dark blue with the fleeting remains of day light. No one had had anything to eat since noon chow aboard ship, making the effect of the beers on each man more substantial more quickly.

Taking turns paying for the rounds, each man had drunk three; each man was feeling it more than any of them fully realized; no one really cared. It was Steeg's turn to pick up the forth round. He looked about the crowded establishment for the lone, overworked waitresses making the circuit around the tables. Even in the dim lighting of the bar, it wasn't hard to find her. She was the shortest person in the place, had long wavy light brown hair streaked with gold, dressed in a tight fitting plaid shirt with a button down collar, the top two buttons unbuttoned, and she wore black jeans she had poured herself into that left nothing to the imagination. She was on his 'eight o'clock' when she turned from her latest delivery to see Steeg with his hand raised high. The waitress smiled and waved an acknowledging hand back at him. Steeg marveled at her efficiency as she slalomed between the tables and effortlessly arrived empty tray in hand.

"Another round, fellas?" Her voice was so feminine it almost made Kinsey weep. Kinsey, youngest of the three, bit down on his lower lip in a completely hopeless effort to control his rushing hormones.

Steeg placed a five dollar bill on the tray. "Another round, please, my good lady."

The waitress took the money, smiled as she folded it twice, and making sure the guys were watching, seductively slid the money into her blouse.

"I'm so lonely," Kinsey moaned audibly as the waitress left to fill the order.

Bear wagged his head in amazement. "It sure is nice to see someone so young really enjoy what they do for a living. I like her attitude."

"I like everything else she's showing," Kinsey moaned again.

"Down, boy," Steeg cautioned. "She can chew you up and spit you out without even batting an eye. Under all that firm, soft roundness is a too young woman as hard as nails. Not the type to bring home to mother."

She returned in near record time with three more bottles. She smiled as she took her time bending over to place a bottle carefully in front of each man. With each placement, her fingers lightly traced their way up the moisture-coated neck of each bottle.

Kinsey actually whimpered as she turned to leave for the next customer. With a slight trembling of his hand, he brought the fresh bottle to his lips. "This might be my last round."

"Whadda ya mean?" Steeg complained. "I just paid for the second time. You both owe me."

Bear chimed in. "Well, true enough. But who wants to sit around here just getting drunk? There's a John Wayne double feature at the Grand. That's more fun than sitting here peeing your money away."

"Literally," Kinsey added.

Steeg waved them both off in true plane director style. "I like John Wayne as much as the next guy, but I've got two more rounds coming, and I'm going to collect."

Kinsey looked at his wristwatch. "I think the next feature starts at nine o'clock."

"Yeah? What's playing?"

"Classics," Bear said. "'The War Wagon' with Kirk Douglas. 'The Alamo' with Richard Widmark."

"Gees," Steeg groaned. "'The Alamo' is like six hours long all by itself. We won't get out of there until dawn for cripes sake!"

"You got something better to do?" Kinsey asked.

Steeg shook his head. "Not really. I just don't want to stay out that late. I like the 'War Wagon' though. That's classic 'Duke' if you ask me. I could stay for the 'War Wagon' then come back here and wait for you guys. The 'War Wagon' is the next feature, isn't it? If it isn't, I'll have to do the Pussy Cat Theater thing. Those shows, they're like only forty-five minutes long. That's better for me. I need my beauty sleep, you know."

Kinsey shook his head. "Sorry, the next feature is 'The Alamo.'"

"Skin flicks just frustrate me, anyway" said Bear. "The 'Duke' is better. You gotta come with us, Steeg. The bar closes before 'The Alamo' is over. We can't have you sitting on the sidewalk outside. In your condition, you'll be arrested. Besides, we stay here, buy two more rounds to keep things fair, and we've each drank a six-pack worth, for the love of Mike! A frickin' six-pack, each!"

Kinsey fell into his best Scanda-hovian accent. "Yawh, das vright. That's vhy ve're Minnah-soo-tans, don-cha-no!"

"Yawh, you betcha!" Steeg returned, and all three of the more than slightly inebriated men laughed.

"Okay – okay, one more round!" Bear dug into his pocket as Kinsey waved the waitress over.

"My kind of Navy man," Steeg slapped the table top. The waitress, anticipating the order, came to the table with a fully equipped tray holding three more fresh bottles.

Once again, she was very deliberate in her bottle placement. Each man carefully observed her every movement. As her fingers took the five dollar bill Bear held up for her, she asked with the friendliest smile, "You want me to remove the empties, or are you building a shelter for the winter?"

"Leave 'em!" Steeg commanded with a majestic wave of his hand, the words clumsily sliding from his lips. "Life is short. Before we shrug off this mortal coil, we must leave a monument as testimony to the fact that we were here."

The girl rolled her eyes as she turned back toward the bar.

"I don't think she likes you," Kinsey's eyes locked onto the shapely Levi's-encased hips retreating into the shadows. The stares of his tablemates joined his.

"Understandable," Steeg replied. "It's an aura, I think. There's something about me that activates the female 'Ignore Him' gene. I'm used to it. It's an effect I have on all women."

"Well, not all women," Bear offered. "What about 'What's her name'?"

"What 'What's her name'?" Steeg slurred from under a questioning eyebrow, tilting his bottle up for another swig.

"You know, that girl you were seeing," explained Bear. "I thought you and her had something going?"

"Who?!" Steeg was more confused.

"It was 'M' something," his friend replied. "Maxine? Madeline? Marlene? Melinda? I don't know – 'M' something…"

"I don't know what you're talking about," Steeg denied, tipping the bottle into his mouth and downing two more large swallows. He returned the bottle neatly to its ringed place on the table, looked up, and saw Gracie dressed in, of all things, a flannel bathrobe, sitting in the chair across from him! On either side of her sat Bear and Kinsey. He blinked as he said, "One more time, eh? What are you doing here?"

"What do you mean what am I doing here?" Kinsey bounced back. "I'm drinking beer and wasting time until the John Wayne movie starts."

Confused by an alcohol-induced fog, Steeg's eyes darted from Kinsey, to Bear, to Grace, and back again to Kinsey. He stumbled with his explanation. "Yeah, well, I know. But, it's odd to see," he paused, looking at the apparition of Gracie as she pulled her bathrobe closer to her chest. "To see, uh, each of us here when it's so, uh, crowded."

"Crowded? Odd? Yeah, right," Tom replied, taking another short sip from his beer bottle.

"So, who is she?" Bear asked.

Instantly, real panic surge through Steeg. "You mean you see her?"

"See who?" Bear was confused now. "Her, who? No, not me. I mean who is the girl you were seeing?"

Gracie looked through Steeg with a hollow sadness he had never before seen. Through his intoxicated haze, he tried to comprehend what was happening to him. It was difficult. He couldn't understand how he could be this crazy when he felt so completely normal in every other way. Across the table, a drawn and tired Gracie soundlessly mouthed something as she pulled her fingers tightly through hair that fell well below her shoulders. She was talking to someone Steeg could not see and as usual, he could hear nothing.

"Steeg?" Bear asked, waving a hand in front of his face. "Helloooo. Anyone home?"

He turned. "I'm sorry. I guess I kinda tuned out there for a minute."

"Who is she?" Bear repeated.

"My old girlfriend," Steeg replied flatly. He looked back to Gracie just as she faded into nothingness.

"I thought she was your new girlfriend?" Bear continued.

Steeg shook his head, more to clear the fogginess, less to respond to Bear. "I'm sorry. I guess I'm a little confused."

"You can say that again," Kinsey opined. "That's it. No more beer for you, my friend!"

"So, you've been out with her since we've been back?" Bear continued.

"Out with who?" Steeg asked.

"The 'M' something girl!" Bear repeated, his frustration showing. "Whatever her name is!"

Fingers of both hands met at the bridge of his nose, and Steeg pulled them down across his face. "I'm sorry. I don't know what to say... No, wait. Yes, I do. No, I haven't been out with her since we've been back. That much I do know."

Kinsey threw a pointed finger at him. "You've changed," he said with more than a little irritation in his voice. "You know what I think? I think that knock on the head changed you."

Steeg nodded, a crimped downward turn on his lips. "No argument there, Tom. Things do tend to get mixed up a little bit more than usual. I'm sorry for that. Hopefully, it'll improve before too much longer."

"I hope so," Kinsey said, lifting his bottle one last time. "Although you're not half as boring as you used to be."

"Gee, thanks." Steeg used a chuckle and a smile to cover his search of the vacated space between his two friends to make sure Gracie was no longer there.

Watching Steeg stare aimlessly at nothing at all, Bear leaned back in his chair feeling more than a little sadness as he realized his friend had no memory at all of the 'M something' girl.

The next Monday, after morning quarters, and as the entire V3 Division crammed into the hanger deck crew's lounge waiting their work assignments for the day, Denoso walked in and announced everyone should get their leaves scheduled right away.

"What's the rush?" Jerry Terry asked. "Holidays are three months away."

"Won't be here for The Holidays," Denoso answered.

"Why not?" Augie barked.

"Because, we'll be busy," Denoso responded.

He would have expanded on the point had it not been for Lieutenant Blunt entering the lounge at that moment. First Class Petty Officers Farmer and Bonia, and Chief Cason closely followed the lieutenant. Bonia called the room to order.

"Listen up! The lieutenant has an announcement!"

Lieutenant Blunt thanked the petty officer, and took two steps forward into the gathering. "As some of you may, or may not know, we have a new mission. The Captain has informed us that *Hornet* has been designated Primary Recovery ship for Apollo 12."

Rumblings, grumblings and miscellaneous chatter surged through the room.

"This is a huge honor in recognition of your outstanding job done for Apollo 11," Blunt continued. "We are receiving medals, Presidential Unit Citations, for our role in the recovery. You should all be proud.

"That's the up side. The down side is, with a mid-November launch for Apollo 12, we don't have much time to get caught up on leaves most of you have accumulated to excess since before the last West Pac. That's over a year ago. So, you will put in your leave requests today without fail. Everyone see Denoso and he'll take your requests down. Those of you with seniority and the most days on the books will have priority should too many ask for the same days off. We need to get all leaves taken before the last week of October. Any questions?"

There were bunches of questions. Hands shot up all across the room, and the resulting discussion continued for well over an hour.

Later, Karl and Steeg shared the same mess table at afternoon chow. Karl, beginning to tackle a mess tray easily twice as full as his friend's, asked if Steeg was going home during his leave.

"Well, I was playing around with the idea of maybe going back for Thanksgiving," Steeg admitted. "But, Apollo 12 puts an end to that. Denoso has me scheduled for 30 days starting September 15th. I don't know if I'll get that much," He took a sip of flat tasting coffee – the same flat taste everything seemed to have lately. "I don't even know what I'm going to do back home except lay around and eat."

"Home cooking ain't a bad thing, Steeg," Karl said. "I'm staying here, but I'm still taking the time."

"Well, sure. You and Barb together makes all the sense in the world."

Karl shoved a fork full of mash potatoes into his mouth. "This time around, it should be pretty boring, though, don't you think?"

"What, leave or Apollo 12?"

"No, the pick up. Let's face it Apollo 11 was fantastic, the first men on the moon, all the excitement, the President, and all that stuff. No way Apollo 12 can match it."

Steeg shrugged. He had no memory of the Apollo 11 recovery operation. He still had issues over the fact that it wasn't 1968, amazed he wasn't on the barracks ship tied to Pier D with *Hornet* resting on blocks in dry dock while he chipped paint, or chipped non-skid, or chipped something, anything. Almost everything from 1968 to when he woke up in Sickbay the previous month was completely gone.

"I don't know," Steeg's nonchalant shrug masked the uneasiness caused by his abbreviated scope of recall. "Apollo 12 might be pretty exciting."

"Maybe," Karl said, then added with a hardy laugh, "Hopefully you won't get thrown in the brig again!"

Steeg nodded with a smile across the table at his friend from Kentucky, successfully concealing the fact that he didn't have a clue as to what Karl was referring.

"Anyway, I guess it's getting close to that time," Karl added, continuing with his lunch. "You goin' to 're-up'?"

"Re-enlist? You kiddin'? I've got a year to go on my hitch yet."

Karl nodded. "That makes you like me – a 'Short-Timer.' This is when they start to lean on you to sign up for it. They'll offer you the next pay grade, extra leave time, shore duty somewhere."

"Yeah, like Kodiak, Alaska," Steeg grumbled. "They'll put Italy posters on the wall as they're talkin' to ya, but they'll ship you off to some barren rock north of the Arctic Circle after you sign on the dotted line."

"Well, I don't know about that, but being a 'Short-Timer' is something that makes your last year kind of special, I think."

"I like the sound of that – 'Short-Timer'." Steeg smiled. "What I really like about it is the idea that I'm within countdown range of getting out and getting back to the sanity of civilian life."

"I'm thinkin' I'm gonna sign on for another hitch."

"Why?"

"Why not?" Karl asked back. "It's the most important work I've every done, probably for you, too. You should consider it. You're a good Non-Com. You could have a good future in the Navy."

Steeg shook his head. "No, Karl, I don't think so. Read any newspaper, or watch Walter Cronkite. This war – a war that's a real war with real death, real destruction, but a war that's not a war because the politicians haven't declared it yet – has gone on for how long already? Since '63 or '64, killing how many of us so far – I don't even know how many – there's no end in sight as far as I can tell. On-again, off-again peace talks going nowhere, we bomb, we stop bombing, and then we start bombing again. It isn't going so great, Karl, and I don't think it's going to be too great for the guys who fought it, either. I might be wrong, but I am not banking on parades, trumpets and flowers when I get home. It ain't gonna to be like that. I joined up for two reasons and two reasons only. First, to get the G.I. Bill so I could be the first person in my family to go to college. That's pretty important to me."

Karl understood. "There's nothing wrong with that. College grads earn a heck of a lot more money than drop outs."

"Yeah, so I hear," Steeg agreed, picking up his tray to leave. Karl still had half his lunch to finish, and Steeg didn't want to wait. "I'll tell you what, though. The last thing I'd ever consider is making the Navy a career choice. The way things are now, I like the idea of being a 'Short-Timer.' I think I'll keep it that way."

Karl stopped Steeg as he turned to leave. "So, what was the second reason?"

"Second reason?"

"Yeah, you said you joined the Navy for two reasons. The G.I. Bill was one, what was the other?"

An embarrassed flush came to Steeg's face. "Oh, yeah, the other reason. Well, it's a little silly, so you gotta promise to keep it to yourself."

Karl nodded as he slid another fork full into his mouth.

Steeg screwed up the necessary courage. "Okay, the second reason was that my girlfriend told me she was turned on by the uniform."

Karl nodded with understanding. "Good reason."

Chapter 25
Home again

Steeg vaguely remembered his last trip home. It had been in April of 1968 when *Hornet* was two months away from finishing a prolonged period in dry dock that had begun almost immediately upon return from WestPac in October of 1967. Dry dock was not a pleasant place for a warship, or its sailors, to be. There was a lot of noise, a lot of dust, and a lot of disagreeable odors no one could avoid. Almost every square inch of the ship's hull was scraped and chipped to bare metal, covered in red iron oxide (a.k.a. 'red lead') primer in preparation for the finishing coats of battleship gray above the waterline, and pitch black sealant coating below. The same noise, dust and odor problems held true for the interior spaces as well. Both the flight deck and hanger deck went through complete refinishing work. Catapults and arresting gear systems were completely overhauled, as were the boilers and engines below decks, along with the evaporators so vital to the fresh water supply while at sea. Operational spaces were repainted on the 02 level, communication equipment for the Combat Information Center (CIC) was upgraded or, in several cases, replaced entirely. Radar equipment for the Carrier Air Traffic Control Center (CATCC) was enhanced as well.

Even with a small army of civilian workers helping out on the major tasks, dry dock in Long Beach was hot, dirty work. Spread across two 12 hour shifts for 'round the clock' duty carried by the bulk of enlisted personnel, the type of work done hurt a man all over. There was little chance for any kind of real physical recovery. The work shifts were scheduled in such a way to make for a very long day, every day of the week. Hundreds of air hammers thundered everywhere all hours of the day and night. The racket was constant and inescapable. Ship's crew berthing was in multi-level barracks boats moored at nearby Pier D. Overcrowded and offering few amenities, the barracks boats provided a brief respite from the round-the-clock clatter. Creature comforts were limited to thin stitched mattresses on aluminum alloy framed racks stacked four high and a central head located on each level. The smell was both remarkable and unmistakable at the same time.

That being 1968, Steeg had counted himself fortunate to fall in with a couple of new friends he had made while fulfilling his KP duties on the mess decks the last few months of the previous year. Together, the three of them went in on a two bedroom rental house in Long Beach shortly after *Hornet* had pulled into port. For a short time, they had a very comfortable off-base housing arrangement where they could live almost like normal people. Unfortunately, within a few months the arrangement had soured for Steeg. Too many shipmates learned of the little house on the near west side, and understandably, many of these mates appreciated a place other than barracks boats to crash. Soon, it was too many. Literally hundreds of them sacked out at the small two-bedroom house. The peace and quite he once valued so highly simply disappeared. Steeg found himself back on the barracks boat soon after New Years.

At that time, due to his relatively recent reassignment to the V3 Hanger Deck Division, Steeg had virtually no seniority. Consequently, his turn for leave came not during the more in-demand holiday period between Thanksgiving and New Years, but in April of '68 instead. Despite this, or perhaps because of it, when his turn for leave came up, Steeg welcomed it.

As best as he could recall, Steeg had appreciated the short, two-week early spring break in Minnesota. It gave him a chance to catch up with old friends and recover some of the hearing loss he had suffered after long months of continual punishment from the air-hammer cacophony common to the dry dock facilities of the Long Beach Naval Base.

It had been a typical early Twin Cities' spring with only scattered, receding mounds of snow cowering under evergreens and in the shadows of house overhangs. Brown-green lawns were revealed, softening for the spring rains to soak in. The air in Minnesota smelled sweet to him, and it definitely was cleaner than L.A. He remembered being startled by how much he had missed it.

Oddly enough, he could not remember much of anything specific he had done while home, nor could he remember returning to the ship after the leave had expired. Everything from that point in April of 1968 until he had opened his eyes in Sickbay the previous August was lost in an impenetrable fog emptied of all memory.

He wondered if he shouldn't be frightened by it all, losing such a big chunk of his life as he had. Perhaps strangely, it made sense to Steeg that if he could not remember what he had lost, the reason for him to panic over what he had lost was, itself, lost. He found it difficult to be afraid of something he couldn't remember, so he wasn't.

Now, it was 15 September 1969. He was flying home on a Republic Airlines flight out of Los Angeles International. Steeg peered from his window as the plane descended on final approach for landing at the Minneapolis/St. Paul International Airport. The trees below were puffy balls turning a thousand shades of green: some a rich, forest green; others tinted various pale, dry greens, in preparation of the coming deeper browns, reds, and yellows of fall. These balloons of seasonal change rested against a backdrop of still more green pastures, lawns, and other green open spaces. All of this was knit together by gray-black ribbons of pavement that formed a loose patchwork quilt stretched wider as the plane eased lower and closer to the approaching runway. From the position of the sun in the west, he figured it would be just before sunset when he'd make it to the baggage claim area. He would be right.

Steeg was anxious to get home. Even with these full thirty days worth of leave, he still had another two weeks of unused leave on the books, but it would have to stay there. V3 Division wanted everyone back a full two weeks before scheduled departure to prepare for the Apollo 12 recovery. That was fine. In his entire enlistment, Steeg had never before taken a full thirty days off at one time. This would be a first for him. He was almost concerned he wouldn't have enough to keep him busy over the next four weeks – almost.

He watched from the window as the airliner made smooth contact with the runway, the seat belt pulling at his middle as the jet engines reversed to slow the plane. Steeg prayed silently to give thanks.

Thank You, Lord, for protecting me and keeping me safe. Thank You for my home; for a family that loves me, and for this time to be with them. Help me remember what I should, and not remember what I shouldn't. And, Lord, please keep Grace close. I pray for her happiness. Please provide it for her. Bless her union. Bless her work. Keep her safe. You are the only one who loves her more than I do. Look after her always. I pray this in your name, Jesus. Amen.

His mother brought the hot cast iron pan to the table and lifted the fried eggs from it onto his plate. "There you go two eggs over easy, just the way you like 'em."

"Thanks, Mom." Steeg reached for the salt and pepper shakers to complete the preparation.

His father was half-way finished with his breakfast. "So, it's your first morning home. What do you have planned?"

To Steeg, his father looked tired. His hair had taken on more gray, and the dark circles around his eyes concerned him. "Well, it's Tuesday, so I was thinking I'd give Wedge a call and see what the guys are doing, maybe drive around town a bit, check out some old places I haven't seen for a while. That sort of thing, you know."

His mother smiled as she brought a plate with four slices of buttered toast to the kitchen table. "That sounds like a nice idea. Take it easy. Relax."

Dad grabbed two of the slices of toast from the plate and returned to his breakfast. "I hope you can find enough to do so you don't get too bored."

Steeg dug into his eggs, suddenly hungrier than he had first realized. "Yeah, well, I know. Still, it's just nice to be back."

His dad nodded. "Still, if you get bored, I might be able to get you on the job site working. It's a good way to keep busy and earn some easy cash at the same time."

Steeg looked up from his plate, his face not hiding the stunned surprise. "Gee, Dad, that sounds like fun. I finally get some time off, and you want to put me to work."

Dad hid his grin with a sip of coffee. "Can always use a good worker, son. So, if you get tired of hanging around, doin' nothing, let me know. I'm just looking out for you."

Steeg shook his head. "The more things change…"

Both men shared a comfortable chuckle.

"Vikings' got a game on Sunday," his father continued. "They're gonna win again, I can feel it. Capp has a way of getting it done, and this year, Grant has the whole team firin' on all cylinders. Mark my words; it's gonna be Super Bowl this year for the Vikes."

"You got tickets?" Steeg cast an interested smile in his father's direction.

"You kiddin'? Every game is sold out. No way you walk up and buy a ticket at the window anymore, not with this team. Scalpers are selling, though."

"If their sold out, that means it's on TV, no black out, right?"

His dad nodded again as the last bite of toast went into his mouth.

"Well, then, that takes care of Sunday afternoon," Steeg smiled. "Perfect. On Sunday morning, we can go to church!"

His father stopped in mid-chew. "Church?"

His mother smiled warmly at her son. "That sounds like a good idea."

"We don't go to church all that much."

Steeg cleared his throat. "Well, we never were all that much on church-goin' anyway. But, St. Mark's still is there. We're still members. It'll be Sunday. I thought I'd go. You don't have to come if you don't want to."

His father 'harrumphed' something unintelligible.

"Dad, you okay with me borrowing the Olds this morning? I could drop you off?"

His father shot a disgruntled look back at his son. "Drop me off? No, You're not dropping me off. You can take the Olds. I got another set of wheels, anyway."

"Another car?!" Steeg raised himself halfway from the kitchen chair to look out the window and across the driveway toward the garage.

"Nope," his father replied with a satisfied smile. "A truck. Got me a Ford F-150 pickup. It's unbelievable!"

"This I gotta see!" Steeg wolfed down what remained of his breakfast and hurried out the back door. His father, pressing the remote button above the light switch on the wall, followed closely behind.

They met at the garage as the double door slowly rose. Inside, parked where his old Buick once sat resting on blocks, was a brand new white pickup truck with twin latched metal tool containers mounted on either side of the rear box and a tubular steel overhead carriage that straddled the whole back side of the truck. Steeg let out a long, low whistle of appreciation as he walked the length of the near side. The front door of the cab had freshly painted signage with a phone number.

Patterson Plumbing and Heating

"Dad, you did it. You went out on your own!"

His father looked confused. "Yeah, well, you remember. I told you all about it the last time you were home."

The sudden rush of fear surprised him. Steeg remember nothing about his father going into business for himself. The one thing he did know was he did not want to be a concern for his parents and that included not concerning them with the accident or anything that had happened to him as a result.

"Oh, yeah, that's right. I didn't mean... that is, I was talking about the new truck. The new truck really makes it official for you. It's good you did it."

"Had to. I was beating up the Olds too much. Just like I said about startin' the business – I'm just getting' too old not to do it. Runnin' out of time, so I figured it had to happen before time ran out."

"What are you talking about? You're not old!" Steeg ran his hand across the stenciled signage on the door.

"Maybe not, but I'm not getting any younger, either."

"This is great, Dad. So, how you doing at it?"

His father shrugged. "Not too bad. Actually, I'm subbing for Midwest, of all people, my old employer! It's real different this way – I get paid more, but that's because I do it all on bid. I gotta cover all the costs. There's no 'safety net' anymore, but that's okay. I have more say in how things get done. Midwest gets the job done without hassling with suppliers, or deliveries, or employees. I get to do that stuff for them."

Steeg now knew why his father looked so tired. "What about the hours? How you handling getting everything done on time?"

A slight nod of acknowledgement came from the older man. "Yeah, well, that can be a little rough some times. That, and the union giving me grief if I hire help that isn't a card-carrying member. I'm small potatoes, but they've tried to shut me down more than once."

Steeg could imagine how his father handled those situations. His father was not a man who let others push him around, and although a union member himself, he remembered more than one occasion when his father had complained about the strong-arm tactics the union had used on a job site where non-union laborers worked. As far as the unions were concerned, the Twin Cities were their exclusive territory.

"Well, just the same, Dad, this is really great. You have to feel good about this."

His father smiled and nodded in agreement.

"Say! I have an idea! Why not let me borrow the truck. I'll park it in parking lots every where I go and make sure everyone sees it. It would be like free advertising!"

The disapproving glare from his father was all the answer Steeg was going to get.

"On the other hand, I guess the Olds will do just fine."

The older man's frown turned briefly into an affirming smile, which quickly dissolved away as he turned and left the garage.

"I gotta get going," his dad said as Steeg followed him back toward the house. "I'm going to be late for work if I hang around here any longer. It's good to have you home, Steeg. Relax and enjoy it."

"Thanks, Dad."

"And, if you do get bored, remember, I have a spare shovel."

Steeg responded with a little less appreciation. "Thanks, Dad. I'll try and keep that in mind."

His phone call to Wedge was answered by Wedge's mother. After he introduced himself, she offered how nice it was for him to call, and then added how quiet their house had been since Wedge had been drafted into the Army.

"The Army!" Steeg was caught off guard.

Her surprise matched his. "Why, yes. You were here weren't you, Steeg, for the party? Oh, I'm sure I remember seeing you here. Everyone was here to send Butch off with a bang. Wait a minute, of course, you were here! I remember you brought that pretty red-haired girl to the party…"

Steeg had no idea what the woman was talking about. "Mrs. Widger, you'll have to forgive me, I'm a little confused about something. When was the party for Wed…, I mean, Butch?"

There was a hesitant pause on the other end of the line. "Oh, my. Let me think… Oh, yes, now I remember. It was the last Saturday in April…"

Steeg finished her sentence for her. "1968."

"Yes, that's right. Last year. Oh, my, now a year and a half ago already. He should be getting out pretty soon."

That bit of news irritated Steeg more than the fact that Wedge had been drafted. "Where is he stationed?"

"Europe, Germany of all places. It's odd. My husband fought the Germans in World War Two, and my son is stationed there now, more than twenty years later. Isn't that curious?"

Steeg shook his head. Wedge had lucked out. Instead of getting black foot rot from wading through rice paddies in Viet Nam, Wedge was at some beer garden in Germany quenching his thirst. How appropriate.

"Yes, Mrs. Widger, it certainly is curious."

He thanked her, said good-bye and hung up the phone. Standing alone in his mother's kitchen, he strained to remember anything about a party and a red-haired girl. He remembered none of it. He remembered coming home on leave that April, but everything else after the flight from California was an indistinct shadowy blur. And, who was the red-haired girl Mrs. Widger had mentioned?

His mother walked up from the basement laundry room, placing a wicker basket full of freshly folded towels and wash cloths on the kitchen table.

"Who did you call?" She asked, fingering the stack of wash cloths as she caught her breath.

"Wedge's Mom." His hand remained on the receiver resting in the phone's cradle.

"Oh, how's she doing?"

"Fine, I guess." He wasn't certain of Matt's phone number. "Mom, do you remember me dating anyone the last time I was home?"

His mother paused, looking over to him with concern. "That's a funny question to ask. Don't you remember?"

Reluctant to answer, he was nevertheless tardy in controlling the subconscious shake of his head.

"Really?"

"No, Mom, of course I remember," he recovered poorly. "I know I went out with someone, but it was just a casual date and I can't remember her name. She had red hair…"

"Red hair? That doesn't sound like anyone you brought home for me to meet. In fact, Steeg, you haven't actually brought home anyone, not since Gracie."

He released an audible sigh as he removed his hand from the telephone receiver. "Where's the phone book, anyway?"

She turned to the twin drawer cabinet next to the refrigerator, pulled the thick volume from the lower shelf, and flopped it down on the table in front of him.

"Thanks," he mumbled, slightly embarrassed as he flipped through the pages to find Matt's home phone number.

She watched him as his finger dragged down a page of names. There was something different about him, she could feel it. She didn't know what it was, or what might be bothering him, but it concerned her.

"Got it!" he grabbed the receiver from the wall mounted phone and quickly fingered the rotary dial to call Matt's house. It rang several times. There was no answer, so he let it ring several more times. He hung up the receiver.

"Who were you calling?"

"Matt."

"No answer?"

"No."

She pulled a chair out and sat down at the table. "Well, you know, it is mid-morning, a week day, kids are in school, and most people are at their jobs working. You're not going to find too many home right now. Maybe later."

He remained standing, looking out the kitchen window at nothing in particular. "I need a reference point of some kind. I need to do something to back-fill some details for me."

"What do you mean?"

Steeg shook his head. "Nothing, Mom."

She gave a slight shrug of her shoulders. "Well, you could visit your sister, Mary. She'd probably appreciate that, and it would give you something to do."

Mary had married at the ripe old age of nineteen. It had been a June wedding in 1968. Steeg had forgotten that, too.

"Yeah, I could do that, I guess. Where's she living now?"

His mother retrieved a piece of paper and a pen, wrote Mary's address and phone number down, and handed it to Steeg. He shoved the paper into his shirt pocket.

She left her chair and took up the laundry basket. "Your friends will be around later this evening. Take the car and go for a drive around town. It'll do you some good."

His mother walked from the kitchen and disappeared down the rear hallway. He wondered if any of his friends would be around at all on this trip. As far as he knew, those who hadn't enlisted may have all been drafted by now, Matt included. As for a drive around town, where would he go? Old high school haunts? The Southdale Mall? The lakes? The parks? He knew of nowhere he could go where he would not be reminded of Grace.

Mary and her husband, Bernard – he preferred Bernie – had set up housekeeping in a small, two bedroom apartment in central Richfield. Bernie was at work. He was an Army-trained diesel mechanic and a Viet Nam War veteran. Steeg could not remember meeting him, which was fine for the moment.

"We watched the Apollo 11 recovery on TV," Mary placed a hot cup of freshly brewed black coffee in front of him and sat across from her brother at the small round dining table. "I looked but I didn't see you at all."

Steeg averted his eyes, looking out the sliding glass patio doors to a swimming pool area that was closed for the season.

"That's probably a good thing, Mare. I'm not all that photogenic."

"Oh, yes you are," she took a sip from her too-hot brew. "We were very excited about you being part of it all. What did you do?"

He mildly scalded the tip of his tongue and quickly put his cup back on the coaster to let it cool. "Nothing much. There were a lot of things going on. It's all kind of a blur."

Her face scrunched, confused. "Really? Wow. The biggest thing since the Great Flood, you're there and you don't want to talk about it? That's a little strange, don't you think?"

Steeg was beginning to feel uncomfortable, wondering if he had made a mistake coming there. But, he needed someone to help him if not remember, at least re-orient him with people, places and things. His sister was his only readily available resource.

"You're right, Mare. We're preparing for the Apollo 12 pick up, so I guess I'm a little preoccupied with that. Apollo 11 was historic, no doubt. I didn't have that much to do with it, but that's going to change with Apollo 12."

"Maybe we'll see you on TV next time."

"Maybe," He sampled his coffee again. It was still too hot. "Mare, you remember my last trip home – do you remember me dating a girl with red hair while I was here?"

Her face scrunched again, wrinkling her nose. "You don't?"

Embarrassed, he shook his head. "I don't remember her name. I'd like to look her up again while I'm home, but I can't remember who she was. I thought you might know."

"This is too weird, don't you think?"

He couldn't look at his sister. She was right. It was too weird.

Mary sighed, picking up the conversation point somewhat reluctantly. "Well, other than what you told me with your brief introduction at Wedge's party, I don't know anything about her. I think her name was Daphne something. She had red hair, wore too much make up and she was a little taller than you. She wasn't your type. Where'd you find her, anyway?"

He searched for an answer, any answer. "I'm not sure, probably from some alcoholic haze."

Her concern for her brother suddenly escalated. "You really don't remember, do you?"

Steeg leaned back in the chair, his eyes meeting hers. Several long moments of silence followed.

"You don't remember." Mary stated flatly. "Why don't you remember?"

He couldn't answer her. He took a deep breath and let it out in a rush. "I guess some things aren't worth remembering, Mare."

"A non-answer answer. Interesting."

His sister leaned forward, cupping her coffee mug with both hands. Something wasn't right with her brother. She was going to find out what it was.

"Okay, what's going on with you?"

He offered a quick chuckle to evade the question. "Nothing much, Mare. I'm on leave and I'm sitting here with you drinking coffee instead of carousing with the guys and drinking beer. I'll agree that sounds a little odd, but what can I do?"

She didn't take the bait. "It's Grace again, isn't it?"

Again? What did she mean by that? His denial came too quickly. "No, it isn't Grace again."

Mary shook him off. "Yes, I believe it is. I hoped you were done with all that. I thought you were finally over her with what happened the last time you were home."

Steeg brought his coffee to his lips. It was still hot, but he took a healthy gulp from the mug anyway. It scalded, radiating all the way down to his stomach. A quick gasp for a cooling breath preceded his "What do you mean?"

Mary was growing irritated with his dodging. She charged ahead. "When you were home last time, you sat around the house, hardly went any where except to Wedge's to play pool. Bernie and me, we were getting closer to the wedding, preoccupied with all the stuff that goes along with that, so maybe I didn't pay that much attention to you then. But I do know you didn't date anyone. Then, Wedge's big 'Going into the Army' party, and you show up with Daphne 'what's her name.' Out of nowhere, you have a date. It didn't make sense."

"I'm capable of getting a date, Mare."

"I'm not saying you're not. But it didn't fit at the time. Not after your little visit with Grace."

Her words stopped him cold. His eyes locked onto hers and the sudden silence between them spoke volumes. Mary saw a truth she didn't like.

"You don't remember that, either, do you?"

The subtle shake of his head was barely there.

"My goodness, you were drunk weren't you? Really drunk."

After leaving his sister's apartment, Steeg drove for several hours, going nowhere in particular, yet everywhere in general, well into a sunny mid-September afternoon. He drove through the old neighborhood, passing the high school – it hadn't changed much at all, except it looked as if a second gymnasium had been added behind the original. The whole rear of the school had been expanded closer to the old football field. He had spent a lot of time on that field, not as a player, but as a high school yearbook photographer taking pictures at every game, and, whenever possible, photographing every cheerleader in sight.

Steeg couldn't help but pull into the crowded parking lot and drive down to the crossroad where the field gates still stood. Classes would be letting out soon, so he stayed in the car, knowing he didn't have time to dawdle. Students in the last Phys-Ed class of the day dressed in their gym clothes were running laps around the track. As he sat in the idling car, the memories of days long ago filled with Grace rushed over him. This felt something like torture to him, and he couldn't deny it. He also couldn't deny an almost insatiable hunger for it.

He heard a far off whistle blow and the students on the track stopped what they were doing, turned and jogged toward an instructor dressed in khakis and a golf shirt of bright Richfield red. The instructor motioned toward the main building complex and the kids galloped from the field, passing no more than twenty feet from his car. Steeg slipped the gear shifter into drive, turned down the road that lead to 73rd Street, turned again west toward Lyndale Avenue, then south toward the pizza joint he and Grace had frequented not frequently enough. They used to have really good pizza at that place.

Reaching 76th Street, Steeg turned west, drove to Penn Avenue to turn north. At 69th he turned west again, heading toward the Southdale Mall. He didn't go directly to the mall, however. He managed to circle around, doubling back more than once to drive by her parent's house several times. All the windows had shades tightly drawn. There appeared to be no one about. He was tempted to park the car and walk up to 'meet the folks' – the parents who had tolerated him so politely, except for Grace's mother, of course, who hated him outright and never very much cared if he knew it or not. Steeg laughed to himself at the idea of just dropping in for a visit. Maybe her mother would give him her new phone number. He laughed again, knowing how well that would go over – "Hi, Mrs. Ofterdahl, I just dropped in to let you know I was home on leave. Would you be able to see your way clear to give me Grace's phone number? I'd really like to talk with her on this visit. You know, just like the last time I was home?" Although he knew how well that would go over – not very well at all – he missed Grace so much the thought of renewing acquaintances with her parents was almost too delicious to pass up. The final time past the house he slowed, the sidewalls of the car tires rubbing up against the concrete facing of the curb. The car rolled to a quiet stop, but keeping the gearshift in drive, he decided against the idea of the surprise visit. After a brief pause, Steeg checked over his shoulder for oncoming traffic and pulled back into the street.

He drove to Southdale, visiting the overflow parking lot where the tall, blue water tower still stood. He found what he believed to be the very spot they had parked the night Grace and he were almost exposed, literally, by the Southdale Security Police. He remembered, too, the mad scramble from the parking lot in the very car he was sitting in now. Steeg could see her, balled up under the dash board, every stitch of clothing somewhere else other than on her. He stayed in the parking lot, vivid memories replaying in his head, for almost an hour, until he couldn't stand it any longer.

Wherever he drove, Grace was there. Everything he saw held a memory of her. The drive down Minnehaha Parkway was excruciatingly pleasurable for him. As he drove he could feel her with him again in the car.

He finally parked the Olds against a curb on the east side of Lake Nokomis, directly across from the very spot where he had first proposed to her. The lake was deserted. The beaches had all been closed after Labor Day. The day was warm and breezy, so a few scattered walkers and bicyclists were out and about. Steeg rolled down the windows to let the gentle early fall breezes in. He stayed in the car and watched the passers-by from the cooling shade of a boulevard elm tree with leaves beginning to turn from green to gold.

Somehow, during the entire visit with his sister, Mary, he had succeeded in not telling her anything that had actually happened to him. That was easy if only because he was unaware of most of what had happened! He had been told about his accident and how the airplane tow bar had thrown him across Hanger Bay One, but he remembered none of it. In fact, judging from what Karl had said to him about being in the brig, Steeg wondered if he shouldn't consider his loss of memory something of a blessing! Blessing or curse, he was sure he had done the right thing not telling Mary about any of it. She knew he had some difficulty in remembering certain things from his last trip home, but his sister had chalked that up to too much alcohol on his part, and Steeg was comfortable in letting her think what she wanted in that regard.

At the same time, he was able to get quite a few details out of Mary about his previous trip home, and, in particular, his meeting with Gracie. Apparently, Steeg sought Mary out after he and Gracie had met.

From what Mary told him he had told her, Steeg had kept some of Gracie's belongings – several photos, a simple gift she had once given him, a couple of keepsake bobbles of some sort that he felt might have had some sentimental value for her – and he had stored all of it away in a small cardboard box. On his previous visit home, Steeg had found the box and decided to return the items to Gracie. Either he hd no qualms about his real reason – to see Gracie again – or Mary had deduced on her own the real reason for his returning the small collection of things. Whatever the case, he returned them. Of course, he wasn't too excited about trying to find the new Mrs. Stewart Smalley in Mankato, or wherever the young couple called home. So, the only convenient way to return those things was to take them to Gracie's parents which, according to Mary's account, he had done. Somehow, after he had given the box with its contents to her mother, he and Gracie connected via telephone, and together they arranged for a short meeting on campus in Mankato. He drove down and they met.

Mary wasn't able to tell Steeg what had transpired during the meeting, but she did say the meeting disturbed him enough for him to seek her out, take her to Bridgman's Ice Cream Parlor and actually pay for her towering hot fudge sundae out of his own pocket, just so he could tell her all about the meeting with Gracie. Mary related how Steeg had commented how thin Grace looked, and how he was concerned about her health. She smoked cigarettes during the entire meeting in Mankato. That was new. Grace had never smoked before, at least not when they were together. Mary recalled how he had asked her if that sounded as strange to her as he found it, and that was when his sister realized, even after all that had happened, Steeg was still completely in love with Grace. He told Mary how Grace seemed genuinely happy about seeing him again despite the obvious signs being extremely bothered by the meeting. Steeg had related to his sister how comfortable he and Grace were sitting together in the student lounge on campus recalling shared experiences, updating each other on their individual life circumstances, how so many things had changed, how it had been no one's fault, and how each of them hoped the other would be okay. Mary remembered her brother hadn't said anything about meeting Gracie's husband. In fact, Mary recalled him saying Gracie hadn't said much of anything at all about her new husband. Nor did she remember him say that Gracie said she was happy – maybe he hadn't asked that question.

What Mary shared with him that morning in her apartment had told him a lot. He had discovered that last year he met Grace in Mankato. It was a meeting that upset him. She was indeed married, thinner, looking less healthy, and of all things, a smoker! None of that sounded all that pleasant to him. No wonder he had been upset by the meeting!

The last thought elicited a light chuckle that momentarily lifted his spirits. Sitting in the car, he looked across Lake Nokomis and saw only Gracie. A series of very interesting questions came to his mind.

Why had the meeting taken place? Oh, sure, he knew he obviously had wanted to see her again. But how had that actually happened? Even though he kidded himself about it, he couldn't imagine Grace's mother actually giving him her phone number when he returned the small collection of items he had kept, so he was certain he hadn't been the one to call her. Grace would have had to call him, wouldn't she? Could that be possible? Even if he had called her to set up the meeting, why had she agreed to meet with him? What did she get out of it? After all, she was married. What could she possibly gain by meeting with him almost a year after she had dumped him and married the other guy? That didn't make sense to Steeg at all.

The more he thought about Grace and all that had happened, the more the darkness swelled deep within him. He struggled against something worse than anger rising fast and bursting forth as his closed fist slammed hard onto the rim of the steering wheel.

"I don't get this!" His voice took on an uncharacteristic foreboding that echoed beyond the car. For Steeg there was only one person to blame for all of the pain. "I trusted You. Why? My life is crap! It turned to crap as soon as I put myself on Your side! You remember San Diego? You remember the bus bench downtown? Well, I do! I thought You were supposed to protect me, provide what I needed. Well, remember CATCC and what happened there?! How about the Photo Lab? Wow, God, thanks for the help on that one! Good job! Then, I'm in V3 Division, where I barely walk away from something that almost kills me, and I can't remember anything that's happened over the last year! If this is you helping, Lord, do me a big favor and don't help any more, okay?"

The heel of his hand punched down on the steering wheel rim one more time and it sprang back at him. He cursed as he directed a balled up fist at no one he could see. "But that's not the worst of it.

You out did Yourself with Grace. You really dropped the ball with her, and that really pisses me off! We had something and You took it! We were to be together, but that wasn't what You wanted, was it?! She leaves, and You just let it happen! Why?! What's left for me but to beg You to 'unplug' me from what I feel for her – beg You! And, what do I get as an answer? I'm hallucinating! I see things that aren't there! You give me a ghost that haunts me around the clock, and I can't stop it! Why?! Why is that happening? Why are You letting it happen? If You're God, prove it! Go ahead, prove it! Do something about this! Patch it up! Make it go away! Strike me down! I dare ya! I've got nothing left thanks to You! Do something about it, or stop wasting my time!"

His palms slammed down hard and he gripped the rim of the steering wheel until his knuckles turned white. The echo of his protestations returned to him from across the grassy knoll lining the near shore. About a hundred yards away he saw a gray-haired elderly man turned toward his direction.

He remembered Grace appearing to him in the Silver Dollar Bar in Long Beach. Her worn, flannel bathrobe, her tired look, and the pain he saw in her face. He remembered her longer hair, a good look for her, full and flowing. Now, sitting behind the steering wheel of his father's Oldsmobile, he wanted to reach out and touch that hair, to comfort her, to remove the pain he had seen. But, he couldn't. She wasn't there.

He couldn't control the apparitions of Grace, he never could. He couldn't will her to appear, and he had little ability to make her disappear whenever she haunted him. It didn't matter. He suspected he was ill, probably with some kind of schizophrenia. His depression quickly outgrew his anger. He sagged in the car seat, his breathing slowing to something more normal. He knew he should probably seek help, but he didn't want it. Apparitions of Gracie were preferable to no Gracie at all.

Parked on the east side of Lake Nokomis, Steeg Patterson resigned himself to an interpersonal relationship with nothing more substantial than mist. He had been cursed with it, so he would accept it. Until, and unless, he could find some way to free himself of the curse, or find enough diversion to keep him from going completely insane, Steeg would continue as best he could on his own. At least this way he would know who to blame.

Today, tomorrow, or for as long as it would be, Gracie's ghost would appear when she would. Until someone else good enough came along, that would have to do.

End of Volume One

Notes and Comments

[1] http://www.history.navy.mil/photos/usnshtp/cv/scb125cl.htm
The designation 'CV' for U.S. Navy aircraft carriers stood for "Carrier (C) Attack (V)" or, Attack Carrier, in civilian parlance. This type of labeling extended to the carriers' embarked squadrons as well, with 'VS' commonly used as designation for Attack Squadron 305 (or whatever number applied). With the expansion of the roles the carrier assumed after World War II and the Korean conflict, the carrier 'CV' designation expanded as well. CVA described a conventionally powered (i.e., diesel) attack carrier. CVN noted a nuclear powered attack carrier. CVS, with 'S' representing 'submarine', was the designation for the Essex class carrier modernized in the mid- to late 1950's and converted to handle anti-submarine warfare duties.

[2] Ibid. Between 1954 and 1959, fourteen modernized *Essex* and *Ticonderoga* class aircraft carriers of the SCB-27 type were further updated under the SCB-125 modernization program. New features not known or accepted when the earlier scheme originated in the 1940's included:

- The British-developed "angled flight deck"
- Moving the after aircraft elevator from the centerline to the starboard deck edge, greatly facilitating aircraft handling
- Joining the flight deck into the forward end of the upper hull to create the so-called "hurricane" bow. This provided a covered location for the carriers' secondary conning station, the portholes for which are visible across the upper bow plating.

The SCB-125 program significantly changed the ships' appearance, effectively extending the life of these World War II era ships at a significant cost savings during a time of rigorous defense spending cutbacks.

[3] Ibid. Fleet Rehabilitation and Modernization (FRAM) was a program initiated to extend the useful life of World War II era U.S. Navy ships of all types.

[4] The Minneapolis-St. Paul Metropolitan Airport first came into being when several local groups came together to take control of the former bankrupt Twin City Speedway race track, giving the airport its original name, Speedway Field. Soon after, in 1921, the airport was renamed Wold-Chamberlain Field for the World War I pilots Ernest Groves Wold and Cyrus Foss Chamberlain. In 1944, the site was renamed to Minneapolis-St. Paul Metropolitan Airport/Wold-Chamberlain Field, with "International" replacing "Metropolitan" four years later.

[5] Maximum speed capabilities of U.S. Navy ships are confidential and never published. The Essex class carriers in World War II had an estimated top speed of 27 knots. After several upgrades and constant overhauling, during the Viet Nam era *Hornet* was believed capable of a top speed near 33 knots.

[6] FOD stands for "Foreign Object Damage." A FOD patrol was a daily routine on both the flight deck and hanger deck where teams of enlistment personnel would police the area picking up debris to protect aircraft from damage.

[7] DOD: Duty Officer of the Deck (or 'Day').

[8] John 13:8.

[9] There's some general confusion about the actual timing of the Apollo 11 events and the local shipboard time in the abort and recovery areas in the Pacific. With *Hornet* on Hawaii local time, and using a simple time zone chart on a global map, there would normally be a five-hour difference between Cape Kennedy and *Hornet*. However, Florida was on daylight savings time in the summer, and Hawaii, similar to Arizona, Puerto Rico, Virgin Island, Guam, and American Samoa, did not follow daylight savings time. This had the effect of adding an extra hour to the time difference between *Hornet* and Cape Kennedy, making *Hornet's* time

six hours behind Florida, even though there are but five time zones between the two locations.

[10] A bolter describes what happens when a pilot misses hooking the arresting wire on a carrier landing. Every fixed wing aircraft landing on an aircraft carrier is done assuming a bolter. This is why the pilot goes to full power immediately on touchdown. This way, if the pilot misses the wire, the aircraft, already at full power, simply lifts off the angled deck and flies around for another landing attempt.

[11] UCMJ stands for Uniform Code of Military Justice.

Discussion Questions

1. Why did Steeg Patterson questioned his motivations for accepting Christ? How did this impact his own relationship with God and with those with whom he lived and worked?

2. Steeg complained to God about things that happened to him, holding God responsible for the consequences of his poor decisions and actions. When is it fair to blame God and what is gained by doing so?

3. Steeg proposed marriage to Gracie just months after they graduated from high school. What would have happened had they married before Steeg joined the Navy?

4. When Steeg returned home from basic training for his Christmas leave, Gracie asked him to accompany her to Mass. Why did Gracie do that, and what were the motivations for Steeg agreeing to go?

5. Early in the story we learn of Steeg's lack of personal confidence but his complete confidence in Gracie. How central a role did God have in Steeg's life at that time and how was Steeg's relationship with Christ reflected in his relationship with Gracie?

6. Loyalty is generally considered an admirable trait. When would loyalty be dangerous? In what ways was Steeg loyal to Gracie? Given is his frequent complaining to Him, how loyal was Steeg to Christ?

7. Given the story up to this point, what was Steeg's biggest mistake, was he aware of making this mistake, and what should he have done to resolve it?

Afterward

The Origin of "The Grey Ghost"

In the early months of World War II, the United States and Great Britain suffered a series of devastating military defeats across Indochina, the Philippines, and a large swath of South Pacific islands at the hands of superior Japanese military forces. Needing to stem the tide of these losses, the United States prepared a dramatic retaliatory strike against Japan itself. Less than five months after the December 7, 1941 Japanese sneak attack on the U.S. Pacific Fleet at Pearl Harbor, the USS *Hornet* CV-8 would become a primary target for destruction by Japanese naval forces.

On 18 April 1942, under the command of Army Lieutenant Colonel James H. "Jimmy" Doolittle, 80 U.S. Army Air Corps volunteer officers and enlisted men in 16 converted B-25 bombers flew off *Hornet's* flight deck and into history. Although the Doolittle Raiders inflicted relatively minor damage to their military targets in and around the Japanese capital, the propaganda value of the Doolittle raid was huge for an America just beginning to recover from the shock of Pearl Harbor.

The months following the Doolittle raid on Tokyo saw America increasingly enmeshed in the long, drawn out island hopping campaign that would characterize the entire war in the Pacific. At the Battle of Midway in June 1942, America finally gained a permanent advantage. *Hornet* and her Squadron 8 warplanes provided critical contributions to the United States' victory. However, by late summer, more than two months of bloody battle in the seas around Guadalcanal in the Eastern Solomon Islands cost the United States' Pacific Fleet dearly. Of the initial four fleet carriers *Hornet* CV-8, *Enterprise* CV-6, *Wasp* CV-7, and *Saratoga* CV-3, only *Hornet* remained operational. In late August, *Enterprise* and *Saratoga,* severely damaged by Japanese bombs and torpedoes, had to return to Pearl Harbor for extensive repairs. Then in mid-September, *Wasp* took three direct enemy torpedo hits. To keep her from falling into enemy hands, one of her own escorting destroyers deliberately sunk the carrier. This left *Hornet* CV-8 the lone fleet carrier on station.

To keep their garrison on Guadalcanal supplied and fighting, the Japanese regrouped with 4 carriers, 4 battleships, 10 cruisers and 30 destroyers. Fully re-supplied, the fleet steamed toward Guadalcanal in late October with the intent of destroying what remained of the U.S. Pacific Fleet.

Anticipating the Japanese action, CINCPACFLEET (Commander in Chief, Pacific Fleet) Admiral Chester Nimitz, ordered the expedited repair of *Enterprise* at Pearl Harbor. With a Herculean effort, Navy and civilian personnel restored the warship to battle-ready condition, and the carrier rejoined *Hornet* off the Santa Cruz Islands in early October. A depleted and badly outnumbered task force met the Japanese threat: one battleship, six cruisers and fourteen destroyers.

The First Battle of Santa Cruz Islands took place early on the rainy morning of 26 October 1942. When U.S. reconnaissance first spotted Japanese ships steaming toward their position, *Hornet* and *Enterprise* launched aircraft to blunt the enemy attack as the Japanese did the same.

When the battle began, the Japanese quickly found their anticipated target and directed their full attack against *Hornet.* With *Enterprise* partially hidden from view in a fortuitous squall, Japanese bombers and torpedo planes set *Hornet* ablaze from bow to stern within seven minutes, inflicting punishing blows from two suicide planes, seven bombs and two torpedoes. For the duration of the initial onslaught, *Hornet's* crew fought fires and the enemy at the same time.

For *Hornet's* officers and crew it was a most desperate hour. With power knocked out, *Hornet* was dead in the water, a sitting duck for the Japanese. Then, *Enterprise* emerged from the quall like a savior. The Japanese shifted their attention, hitting *Enterprise* with two bombs.

Severely damaged, and with *Hornet* wounded and burning, *Enterprise* kept fighting. The battle continued until late morning.

The U.S.S. Hornet CV-8 under attack off Santa Cruz Islands. Note the listing to starboard and the flight deck damage aft of the island superstructure.

After the long attack ended, *Hornet,* severely damaged, transferred over 850 wounded and non-essential crewmembers to escorting destroyers. The cruiser *U.S.S. Northampton* took the heavily damaged and smoldering *Hornet* in tow. Late that afternoon, as *Hornet* engineers and "snipes" struggled to fire up the undamaged boilers to breathe new life into the carrier, the crippled ship came under attack again.

Six enemy torpedo planes dove from the cloud cover. To evade the attack, *Northampton* cut the towlines to *Hornet,* leaving the carrier once again adrift and nearly defenseless. The skies filled with anti-aircraft fire from *Hornet* and surrounding escort ships to shield the carrier. Five of the six attacking torpedo planes were shot down, but one plane succeeded in launching a torpedo into the starboard side of the valiantly struggling *Hornet*. Taking on water quickly, the carrier soon approached a list of more than 18 degrees to port. When it looked as if *Hornet* would capsize, the order was given to abandon ship.

After the remaining crew and officers disembarked, the concern shifted to keeping *Hornet* from falling into Japanese hands. The ship was dead but afloat, still too highly valued a prize for the U.S. to give up. Thus, the decision was made to sink her. Two U.S. destroyers moved into position and fired 9 torpedoes and 300 5-inch shells into *Hornet*, but the ship refused to go down. Hours went by and day turned to night. When Japanese surface forces were detected closing on their position, the two American destroyers left the area, leaving *Hornet* alone and still smoldering.

Two Japanese destroyers found the abandoned warship and put four more torpedoes into her. At 0135 hours, 27 October 1942, USS *Hornet*, CV-8 sank into the 16,000-foot deep waters off the Santa Cruz Islands of the South Pacific.

Two and one-half months after being sunk, the USS *Hornet* CV-8 was officially stricken from the Navy's "List of Active Ships."

The carrier that launched the Doolittle bombing raid on Tokyo was dead. Cheers would resound from every Japanese ship and island stronghold in the Pacific theater.

Almost three months before the Battle of Santa Cruz, a keel for a new Essex class carrier was laid on Slipway Number 8 of the Newport News Shipbuilding and Dry Dock Company in Newport News, Virginia, given the hull number 395 and designated USS *Kearsarge* CV-12. A year and 27 days later, due to a shortage of ship building facilities, the ship would be launched with only 75 percent of it actually built. Work would continue on hull number 395, now renamed USS *Hornet* CV-12, for another three months. On 29 November 1943, *Hornet* CV-12 was officially commissioned as a United States Navy warship.

A month of sea trials followed. More finishing work was done. A fresh paint job was applied – the new "dazzle" pattern camouflage designed to hide the ship from enemy submarines and surface vessels, although some thought it did the opposite and made the ship easier to see. Visible or invisible, *Hornet* still looked good.

By early 1944, *Hornet* CV-12 was on station in the Pacific, back in the war, and, with its new camouflage paint job, the "Grey Ghost" was born.

***

Photo # 80-G-K-14466   USS Hornet operating near Okinawa, 27 March 1945

U.S.S. *Hornet* CV-12 – the 'Grey Ghost' – in theatre with her 'Dazzle' camouflage.

U.S.S. *Hornet* CV-12 circa 1954, before SCB-125 modernization and FRAM II conversion work: vintage WWII Essex class configuration with a straight flight deck, mid-port side number two elevator, and the twin gun tubs in the open bow.

U.S.S. *Hornet* CV-12 circa 1967: note the angled flight deck, the starboard side elevator platform aft of the island superstructure, and the enclosed 'hurricane' bow configuration.

A Sneak Peek

THE PATTERSON CHRONICLES

VOLUME 2

GRACIE'S GHOST
THE RETURN

Frederick Loeb

Available now at amazon.com
and at better book stores everywhere.

10:35 a.m.
April 19, 1971
Student Commons
Normandale Community Junior College
Bloomington, Minnesota

Because of his predilection for conserving gasoline and his natural curiosity to learn just what "Whappituie" really was, Steeg held Ace Johansson's previous summer recommendation responsible for his enrollment at Normandale Community Junior College for the fall semester. After officially registering at the small, suburban college, Steeg's first official act was to join the college's Vet's Club, the requirements for which involved only verification of his military service and a modest fee to cover the cost of the club's sweat shirt.

The Vet's Club was made up of eighteen recently discharged Vietnam veterans. Most of the men were either ex-Army or Navy, although there was one Marine, Charlie Edwards, and two Air Force veterans, Tom Hasselmen, and Arnie Meisch. Of all the club members, three had been wounded in combat, with the de facto club leader, Phil Denzer, the most severe. In 1968, along a nondescript trail among many that snaked between small villages and major cities of South Vietnam, Phil had successfully avoided the intended consequences of a "Bouncing Betty" land mine. He only lost both legs at the knee and not his life. He was a strong man who wore his personal resilience proudly every day, making his way around the small campus in his wheelchair with admirable ease. The Vets' Club was an elect conclave providing both context and content to this higher education experience for Phil and every other veteran at the school. The context was the mature comradery the club provided men bound together by their common military experience. The content was the frequent club parties. The parties were known for two things: "Whappituie" and a healthy number of "Vets' Club" girls. "Whappituie" was a truly potent mixture of all things alcoholic contributed by each club member to a large rubber trash can. The "Vet's Club" girls were young women students who attended the parties without male escorts.

Normandale Community Junior College had first opened its doors at 9700 France Avenue South in Bloomington in the late summer of 1968, around the time when *Hornet* was making preparations in Long Beach for its final West Pac cruise to Vietnam. With an initial enrollment of a little more than 2,000 students, many part-time, it was a small college by every definition. By 1970, the enrollment had grown by only a few hundred. It was an intimate educational environment, a somewhat uncomfortable fit for any student who wasn't a teenager, and especially so for a military service veteran. The age and maturity disconnect from most of the younger students was a major contributing factor to the strength of the Normandale Community Junior College Vets' Club.

By April of 1971, Steeg was in his third term as a college student. On the north end of the Student Commons closest to the vending machines area two long tables constituted the unmarked, yet universally recognized, Vets' Club territory. Only Vets' Club members, and certain young women welcomed as kindred spirits, were permitted to sit at these tables. Anyone else would quickly pick up on the non-verbal coolness from veterans sitting there, and they would soon relocate without the need of further encouragement.

With his hair longer so it met his collar, and wearing his *Hornet* CVS-12 navy blue windbreaker, Steeg arrived early the spring morning of April 19th to beat the onslaught of heavy weather. By 7:30 dark gray rain clouds were low in the sky. By 7:40 the skies opened up. Rain pounded the campus in swirling, wind-driven sheets, painting the normally open and bright Student Commons in a dark green as if it were twilight. He was the first to arrive at the corner tables that morning, so he slapped some coins into the vending machine for his morning cup of bad coffee, grabbed a chair, sat down and opened his chemistry text to study the chapter he had failed to get to the night before. Chemistry wasn't his strong suit, but it was a pre-requisite for his Engineering degree. Studying in general wasn't his strong suit, either. The refresher class on algebra had been too easy. He sailed through it with straight 'A's' while barely cracking a book the entire first term. Things had become a little tougher with advanced algebra, and trigonometry proved to be significantly more demanding. He pulled a low 'C' in that one. Steeg most enjoyed the English Composition, Literature and U.S. History classes, and this was reflected in the superior grades for those subjects. That should have told him something about his true interests and areas of highest academic potential, but he ignored it. Steeg's goal was set on becoming a Mechanical Engineer and to work with his dad to build the family business. The struggles with Trig caused him only small shadows of doubt.

Without looking up from his text book, he felt more than saw the slender wisp of Gracie Ondracek pass by on her way to the vending machine room.

Gracie Ondracek was a truly friendly, outgoing young woman. With her clear, clean features and brilliant white golden blond hair, she was the opposite of Gracie Ofterdahl. Richfield High School's Class of '66 Homecoming Queen, Steeg had known her since their sophomore year, when he was a novice student photographer for the yearbook, and she was a first-year cheerleader on the junior varsity squad. She was so cute in her short-skirted, red and white cheerleader uniform he had to take her picture at every opportunity. But, then, as a hormone-infused fifteen year old, he had to take pictures of all the cheerleaders at every opportunity. He enjoyed just being around cheerleaders and his camera was a ready excuse. He liked her from the start, although he never had any feelings other than 'like' simply because

Gracie Ondracek was the kind of pretty, easy-going personality who made friends effortlessly. Everyone liked her, ergo 'Homecoming Queen' Class of '66. After high school, Gracie delaying entering college to do some traveling. Returning home to Richfield, she worked full time at her father's law office in Minneapolis. Not entirely convinced a four-year college was the right thing for her to do, she decided to give the new two-year institution in Bloomington a try the winter before Steeg and Ace returned from the Navy. For both Steeg and Gracie, it was a pleasant surprise to meet again.

She placed her coffee cup onto the table across from where Steeg sat.

"You didn't show on Saturday." The disappointment in her voice coolly hung between the two of them. She slid her rain-soaked jacket from her shoulders, gave it a quick shake, draped it over the back of her chair, and then, sat down.

Steeg looked up from his chemistry book. "Show? What show?"

"You know d a r n well what I mean, Steeg Patterson."

Steeg feigned ignorance.

"You missed a good time," She continued. "And, there were a lot of people there!"

"I bet," he sniffed.

She supported her claim by quickly listing more than a dozen names, almost none of whom Steeg remembered.

"That's nice, Gracie," he dismissed.

"It was nice," she said, taking a sip from her cup. "It would have been nicer if you had been there."

"Ace was there, wasn't he?"

"You mean Horace?" She confirmed. "Yes, he was."

"I know he was," he said. "I live with the guy, remember?"

"Then, why'd you ask?"

"Just trying to make conversation, that's all," he explained. "I'm sorry, Gracie, but the idea of going to a five-year high school reunion to see a bunch of people I hardly knew then and certainly don't know now, just didn't make sense to me. Why go when the only two people I really care about from high school I see almost every day anyway?"

"Who are they?" she asked coolly.

"Ace and you, of course," he answered truthfully.

She smiled warmly at that. "You're sweet."

"Yes, I am," Steeg returned to the too-slippery chapter of his chemistry textbook.

The student traffic began to pick up as Phil Denzer wheeled his chair into his normal corner spot across from Steeg and next to Gracie. A brisk "Good Morning!" followed a thudding of books from his lap onto the table top. "How's the coffee?"

"About the same," Steeg offered.

"It's okay," Gracie added.

Soon, other club members began to show up. The short of stature Arnie Meisch with his thinning crew cut walked in, followed by the pudgy Clay Panek. Right behind came the too-tall Dennis Palmer, Charlie Edwards, the Marine who always seemed to be in uniform even when he wasn't, then Doug Loew, the dark haired under-fed long distance runner on the college's cross-country squad. They took turns in the vending machine room to secure their beverages of choice, and took their seats around the main table.

"You were missed," Ace Johannson said, his rain-drenched jacket lightly sprinkling some of the outside weather onto Steeg as he plopped down on the chair next to him.

"Yeah, so I heard," Steeg acknowledged, brushing the droplets from his sleeve. "Gracie told me all about it."

"So, you've already talked with her, then?" Ace seemed surprised.

Steeg returned a suspicious look as he pointed to Gracie. "Ace, she's sitting right across from us."

Gracie Ondracek was conversing with Phil Denzer. Ace gave her a quick "Hi, Gracie, how you doing?" and then turned closer to Steeg's good ear.

"Not Ondracek," he paused to make sure he had Steeg's attention. "The other 'Gracie' – Ofterdahl."

The students rushing into the commons area from the cascading torrents outside brought an increasing clamor that filled the air. Despite that, Steeg had heard Ace as if they were in a totally quiet room. He cautiously looked Ace in the eye.

"You saw Grace at the reunion?"

Ace nodded slowly.

"Interesting," Steeg said. "Was her husband there, too?"

Ace shook his head equally slowly.

"Interesting," Steeg repeated. "So, did she ask about me?"

Ace nodded in response.

"And?"

"She wanted to know where you were." Ace replied.

"What did you say?"

"I told her the truth. I told her you decided not to come, that you were visiting your folks for the weekend."

"And, that was the truth. Although you could have told me this last night when I got back to the apartment."

"Oh, sure, like I knew when you got back," Ace protested. "When did you get back, anyway?"

Steeg shrugged. "Pretty late, I guess it must have been around two o'clock or so."

"And, when did you leave this morning? Because when I got up you weren't there!"

"Oh, well, gee-whiz, Mom, I'm sorry I didn't check in with you!" Steeg sarcastically complained.

"Are you boy's having a lover's spat over there," Gracie asked with a laugh from across the table.

Steeg diverted Gracie's concern with a hooked thumb in Ace's direction. "Ace's just raggin' on me about my nocturnal proclivities."

"Proclivities, my ass!" His friend bellowed. "This guy never sleeps. When he does sleep, he snores so loud he keeps you up. He's awake every morning before four o'clock, and he expects me to wake up when he does just to keep him informed on the happenings of the day!"

Steeg held up a calming hand, "No, no I don't. I just said you could have let me know sooner some how. You could have left me a note taped on my mirror, or something like that."

"Oh! A note!" Ace remembered, fishing his wallet from his back pocket. "That's right! She gave me this to give to you."

Steeg took the twice-folded small piece of paper and opened it.

> *Steeg,*
> *I'm sorry you couldn't make it. When you have time,*
> *call me.*
> *Grace*

Below her signature, she had scribbled a phone number with a 332 exchange, indicating somewhere close to downtown Minneapolis. He looked at her message for a long moment, committing the phone number to memory before closing the note and sliding it into his breast pocket.

"Interesting," Steeg said again.

"Very interesting," Ace echoed.

"I don't get it, though," he frowned. "Why would she give you this to give to me? Where was her husband?"

Ace leaned in closer and in a lowered voice said, "There is no husband. She's not married."

VIII SNEAK PEEK